ALLEN COUNTY PUBLIC LIBRARY
ACPL ITEM
3 1833 05167 2837
DISCARDED

D0594227

In the Last Blue

Carme Riera

Translated from the Catalan by
JONATHAN DUNNE

THE OVERLOOK PRESS
Woodstock & New York

This edition first published in the United States in 2007 by
The Overlook Press, Peter Mayer Publishers, Inc.
Woodstock & New York

WOODSTOCK:
One Overlook Drive
Woodstock, NY 12498
www.overlookpress.com
[for individual orders, bulk and special sales, contact our Woodstock office]

NEW YORK:
141 Wooster Street
New York, NY 10012

This work has been published with a subsidy from the General Director of Books, Archives, and Libraries of the Cultural Ministry of Spain

Library of Congress Cataloging-in-Publication Data

Riera, Carme.
[Dins el darrer blau. English]
In the last blue / Carme Riera ; translated from the Catalan by Jonathan Dunne.
p. cm.
I. Dunne, Jonathan. II. Title.
PC3942.28.I37D5513 2007 849'.9354—dc22 2006051525

Book design and type formatting by Bernard Schleifer
Manufactured in the United States of America
ISBN-13 978-1-58567-853-2
10 9 8 7 6 5 4 3 2 1

To my father

Dramatis Personae

AGUILÓ, PERE ONOFRE, merchant. Based in Livorno. Organizes the escape.

AMENGUAL, Father VICENT, Jesuit. Father FERRANDO's rival. Wrote the *Life of the Venerable Eleonor Canals, Who Died in Odor of Sanctity*, followed by *The Triumph of the Faith in Three Cantos*.

ANGELAT, BARTOMEU, city chronicler. Author of a *History of Majorca* among other works.

BELLPUIG, ONOFRINA, Marquise of Llubí, the VICEROY's wife.

BONNÍN, CATERINA, mother of MARIA AGUILÓ, the wife of GABRIEL VALLS. Mentally disturbed. With her shouting, involuntarily contributes to the arrest of the false converts.

BONNÍN, MIQUEL, mattress maker. Experiments with flying machines. He is SARA DE LES OLORS' father.

CABEZÓN Y CÉSPEDES, Inquisitor, who was replaced by the Reverend NICOLÁS RODRÍGUEZ FERMOSINO.

CORTÈS, AINA, CAP DE TRONS' daughter, lover of Juli Ramis, with whom she has a son.

CORTÈS, RAFEL, COSTURA, informer.

CORTÈS, RAFEL, CAP DE TRONS, visionary, faithful observer of the Old Law, JOSEP JOAQUIM and BALTASAR's father.

FERRANDO, Father SALVADOR, Jesuit, COSTURA's confessor.

FUSTER, AINA, also known as ISABEL FUSTERA, wife of the count's administrator GABRIEL FORTESA.

HARTS, ANDREW, corsair captain.

HUGUETA, MADÒ, mistress of the brothel.

LLABRÉS, JAUME, Canon of the Cathedral and Judge of Goods Confiscated by the Holy Office.

MARTÍ, PERE ONOFRE, known as MOIXINA, married to QUITÈRIA POMAR, with whom he has two children, one of whom involuntarily betrays the stowaways.

MAS, BEATRIU, known as LIMP, prostitute in the city brothel, friendly with the former Bishop BENET, accused as a result of helping RAFEL ONOFRE VALLS.

MIRÓ, POLÒNIA, COSTURA's maid.

MOASHÉ, JACOB, rabbi in Livorno.

MONTIS, NICOLAU, Marquis of the Bastida, President of the Great and General Council.

PERES, JOÃO, sailor, who settles in Livorno in the Widow SAMPOL's service.

PIRES, BLANCA MARIA, the merchant SAMPOL's widow. Lived in the city and then in Livorno, helping the fugitives.

POMAR, MARIA, the gardeners PEP POMAR and MIQUELA FUSTER's daughter.

POMAR, QUITÈRIA, PERE ONOFRE MARTÍ's wife.

PUIGDORFILA, GASPAR, Head Bailiff.

RODRÍGUEZ FERMOSINO, NICOLÁS, Inquisitor of Majorca. Incorruptible and upright unlike the Warder and other jailers and familiars.

SAMPOL, widow by the name of BLANCA MARIA PIRES.

SARA DE LES OLORS, visionary, daughter of MIQUEL BONNÍN, mattress maker.

SEGURA, AINA, MADÒ GROSSA's sister, lives with her grandchildren, who are also imprisoned.

SEGURA, PRÀXEDES, known as MADÒ GROSSA, healer.

SEN BOIET, former bandit, professional troublemaker.

SOTOMAYOR Y AMPUERO, ANTONIO NEPOMUCENO, Marquis of Boradilla del Monte, VICEROY of Majorca until a couple of months before the flames. Manages his wife LADY ONOFRINA's maritime business.

TARONGÍ, ISABEL, married to JOAQUIM MARTÍ, a Christian who makes his confession to Father FERRANDO. They have two small children. He accuses his wife of being a Jew.

TARONGÍ, JOSEP, CONSUL for the English.

TARONGÍ, RAFEL, ISABEL's brother, who dies under torture.

VALLERIOLA, JOSEP, friend of GABRIEL VALLS.

VALLERIOLA, XIM, tailor, married to RAFELA MIRÓ. They are COSTURA's neighbors.

VALLS DE VALLS MAJOR, GABRIEL, known as RABBI, the crypto-Jews' patriarch, married to MARIA AGUILÓ, father of MIQUEL VALLS, who emigrated to Alicante, and of RAFEL ONOFRE, MARIA POMAR's fiancé.

WILLIS, Captain. Agreed with PERE ONOFRE AGUILÓ and the Widow SAMPOL the charter of *The Aeolus* to save the Majorcan Jews.

Part One

I

AT TIMES HE WOULD STOP AND WATCH, OTHERS, TREADING as softly as he was able, he would pass in front of the wall that enclosed the garden, without losing sight of the gate that had to open soon. With meticulous insistence he would recall the motive that had brought him there and in the dead of night kept him awake and alert, waiting only for the expected signal. He tried to pay minute attention to each of the countersigns Captain Andrew Harts had given him almost a year previously, the imprint of which since then he had borne on the first page of his memory so that, when the moment came, everything would be accomplished to perfection. Sure as he was that what had happened to Harts necessarily had to be repeated in his person, he was convinced that soon he would be called and his merits appreciated in exact proportion to his courage. But this time the boy didn't want just to feel like a strong and powerful man, or even to disparage Captain Harts, who nearing his forties was going downhill, however much he liked to boast to his friends of the parties and fuss made over him by three hundred wives in a hundred different ports. No, what made João Peres embark on the first ship heading for Majorca and what kept him there, in an alley of the city, close to the city wall, at the risk that the Bailiff's men would lay hands on him, was much stronger than the desire to possess or the need to boast, since he believed that the rest of his life depended on the expected signal, as he had witnessed it in dreams. And this occurred long before the night that Captain Harts casually told this story, no doubt intending to intensify his heroic aura and to test his ability to relate exploits in front of a crowd used to hearing from sailors of adventures that happen only far away to those daring enough to go in search of them.

João Peres believed, without having doubts or finding objections, though he did later press him for details, all that befell *The Swan*'s captain over two heady spring nights the last time he put in at Majorca. He believed him, not because he thought that the ring Harts showed was proof enough, as the latter affirmed, but because the facts, calmly pared in front of two rows of pitchers, which slowly emptied as the words filled with meaning, coincided, with chilling precision, with his recurring dream, contributing a plethora of details that among the images he had captured while asleep he had been unable to take down and that now were proving vital in guiding him to the scene where, while he was awake, everything would be repeated. Because this enclosed garden in dreams had not occupied a particular place in a particular city until Captain Harts finished recounting his story:

If you don't mind listening, Harts began in his husky voice, *I'll tell you a good one. One that'll amaze you as much as me, who still can't quite believe my luck. Many strange things had happened to me up till then, and I had heard about many others, but none like this. From now on I swear I'll be much more careful before I brand someone a liar, because if such unusual events have befallen me, they can have befallen others. And the next time I put in at an island, I'll be prepared for anything . . . What I'm about to explain to you occurred just three years ago, one night in June. A sou'wester had been blowing for days, easing the journey of my xebec, which from Algiers had set sail for Majorca. This was the fourth time* The Swan *had dropped anchor in Port*

Pi. Allied with the Majorcan corsairs for the past twenty months, I was going to settle accounts with my partners who owed me money and, after loading oil, we would weigh anchor for Livorno. The knowledge of Catalan I had picked up some time previously helped me in my dealings, since the Majorcans also speak this language, softening the words and modulating the tone, so that it sounds much sweeter. I had arrived two days before, I remember it very well, and it was Thursday. In the evening I went to see the count's administrator, who I usually dealt with, since the count and I, though we had known each other for a long time, never talked money. Gabriel Fortesa and I, on the other hand, rarely talked about anything else. It was dark when I left the count's offices with the solemn promise that the following day Fortesa himself would pay me the ounces I was owed. This had satisfied me. Since it was late, I decided to stay inside the city wall, in a bed where I knew I would be made welcome, instead of going to sleep on board. It was a little colder on account of the sou'wester and the night, which in those parts tends to be humid and sultry, did not weigh at all heavily. For this reason, because it was cold, I wrapped myself in my cloak, not because I was afraid of anybody or because I would avoid a fight if someone troubled me at that time. I confess I had only one fear: that the Bailiff's men would find me and force me to sleep in the prison for not doing so on board the ship. I was hurrying towards the soft bed I told you about, and the open legs awaiting me, when on passing in front of the wall of the garden adjoining the inn called S'Estornell, I heard a sound of footsteps. But when I turned round, I didn't see anybody. Thinking that I was mistaken, I continued along by the wall, with my hand on my pistol just in case. I forgot to say that the Majorcans are a very bellicose people and the fights between bandits, among whom were renowned brigands who still wander freely, lasted until a few years ago. It wouldn't be strange if, having seen me leave Descós' house, they had stuck on my tail in order to relieve me of any money I might be carrying. Without letting go of my pistol I advanced as silently as I could, to be better able to hear any repeat of the disturbance. I was about to turn the corner when again I heard the sound of footsteps. Now I was certain that someone was walking very closely. I turned round abruptly, waving my weapon, but the street was deserted and not a shadow was in sight. The owl's call, which in another place would have struck me as sinister, accompanied me for a few seconds. With no other option but to press on, I tried to advance more quickly, but the person following me likewise quickened their pace. I stopped suddenly and they also stopped. Don't think that this mysterious duplication, which was beginning to get on my nerves, was due to the echo. On other occasions I had been in that area and nothing similar had happened. I was about to turn and go after that scarecrow and find out, once and for all, why he was following me. But dread, I confess, held me back. I strode forward and my taunter's steps also lengthened. I don't have much time for belief in ghosts, witches and evil spirits, but what was happening to me went against my principles. Fearful now more of the supernatural than of anything, I commended myself to God and crossed myself. On making the sign of the cross I turned to face the wall and it was then that I became certain that in effect somebody was following on the other side, perhaps because he had confused me or because he enjoyed putting me on my mettle. Suddenly freed from so many vain terrors, I prepared to comfort a wife in distress and made up my mind to take no notice of the walking shadow still pursuing me. I was already crossing the street and heading in the opposite direction when they called me. First it was a barely perceptible whistle, as if the whistler did not wish to arouse anyone else's suspicion and only my ear, used to the sound of his footsteps, could pay attention. Weary, but curious, I stopped. The wall was too high for me to see what was on the other side and also, at least this is what I thought, for him to see me. The voice became much more audible:

"Hey, you, don't run. Listen. You won't regret it."

"Would you mind telling me what's going on," I replied, "since we've never seen each other before? Are you sure that you're not mistaken, my friend?"

"Not at all, sir. Forgive my following you, Captain Harts," answered the kind and pleasant voice of a young man. "Come closer to the wall and I'll explain what this is all about."

I immediately obeyed, intrigued to know what would be the outcome of my fright.

"Follow the wall another fifty paces and we'll meet. I have to discuss a matter that will interest you."

An iron gate creaked open on its hinges. In the light of a candle that he himself was holding I set eyes on my pursuer. He was almost a boy. Although he was dressed as a servant, he possessed good manners and a face that struck me as well-proportioned and not at all rustic.

"Captain Harts," he said, "would you mind stepping inside, because what I have to tell you is not something that should be discussed in the street?"

Trusting that he wanted to offer me a more advantageous deal than the one I had closed with Fortesa on behalf of the count, I passed through the gate. A few steps behind the servant was a maid, no more than a girl. She was not wearing country clothes as maids in Majorca normally do, nor was she wearing a scarf. She had on a white dress made of silk and taffeta, and a veil covered part of her face in the Moorish tradition. In one hand she held an oil lamp, while with the other she protected the flame against the breeze.

"Good evening, Captain Harts. My mistress has sent me to request the pleasure of your company."

"I'm in a bit of a hurry right now, and besides I'm not sure

it's a good time to be paying formal visits. If you want to know the truth, I have another appointment, an engagement . . ."

"Postpone it, sir," she said with a conspiratorial smile as she took my hand. "My mistress would never forgive me for letting you go. I am to lead you to her now. You won't regret it, I assure you."

I allowed myself to be led, proud, if I am to be honest, that my merits had reached such a well-placed lady. As we headed through a grove of oranges, I noticed the combined odors of jasmine and myrtle with such sweet intensity as if a curtain of perfume had fallen on the other senses, especially that of sight, now that the fruit trees were growing thicker and the sky had become overcast. However much I inquired of my guide where we were going, she did not answer me. I supposed that she wished to confuse me so that entering by a secret place I wouldn't know where the house was to which they were leading me. Having walked a while longer, we took a path that led to a cave that turned into a passageway.

"Do not be afraid, Captain Harts. I have no option but to take you through this inhospitable place, but, as I said, I'm following my mistress' orders."

We advanced another hundred paces and the girl abruptly halted in front of a door. She clapped her hands and the door was opened from inside. We passed into an enclosure that was less cold, but just as gloomy. The scent of basil was overwhelming, which made me think I may have been in a reception room.

"It has been a pleasure to be your guide, Captain Harts," my companion told me, releasing the hand she had so gently taken. "But now I must leave you. Another servant will direct you to my mistress' chamber."

I remained for a few moments all alone. Shortly a lad appeared, or so I deduced from the voice, who had to lead me in the dark. Together we passed through a succession of rooms. Finally, having informed me that his mistress was waiting for me behind the last door, he withdrew. As soon as I crossed the threshold, in the shade of the room, I saw an unmade bed with the curtains drawn. The hangings of red damask swayed, illuminated by a lamp that stood on a sideboard laden with viands and fruit. From behind the bed-curtains a voice like rustling leaves welcomed me.

"Do not be afraid, Captain Harts. I have sent for you because your fame has stolen my heart and given me the necessary daring. Eat and drink as much as you want. The journey has been a little long and you must be hungry."

I picked at some fruit and sampled a glass of wine, much more eager to look and to listen than to dine. But when I lay down on the bed to discover how to the voice must surely correspond a beautiful physiognomy, the lamp went out. I would have said by magic if a gust of wind had not also moved the damask just as I drew back the curtain.

"Madam, I hope to serve you as you deserve, but I would like to know your name and to see with my own eyes all the perfections I imagine," I said.

"Captain Harts," she answered, laughing, as with expert hands she made me welcome. "I'm very grateful for your words, with which you display a courtesy I appreciate, but on no account may I tell you my name, much less allow you to know my person. That is why my servants have brought you to my chamber through places unseen by other visitors. I am, as you may suppose, an important lady in this city and only the affection I have for you, owing to your merits, has given me the daring with which you are now familiar. But let us dispense with compliments, Captain Harts, and may the dawn be later this night than any other."

The bed was much softer than I had expected and the body of that unknown beauty, who soon ceased to be so, infinitely warmer and more tender. The night was the shortest I have ever lived and also the most intense. The act of love was followed by words and again by the act. My lady, inquisitive like all women, wanted me to explain in minute detail what my life was like, which she already knew something about, how long I had been a captain, how many men were under my command, what the ship was like, if it accepted passengers, how many people it took and where it was heading. I responded to all her questions and yet was unable to convince her to tell me her name and to show me her face, limbs and body I had covered in delirious kisses and caressed with exciting unease.

The distant lark's song preceded our farewell. Before leaving I made her promise that the following night she would again send her servant to open the gate in the wall, when it was dark. And she made me swear that I would never discuss our meeting with anyone, at least while I was in Majorca, since she thought that to make me swear eternal silence was to condemn me to perjury, for from what she had been able to discern of my person, I was of the kind that relish words almost as much as the deeds themselves. With identical ceremony, without allowing me to see the places I passed through, she had me leave that palace through the same secret door that led into the garden, accompanied by the same attendants. On reaching the street the servant who had followed close on my heels handed me a bag full of money as a gift from his mistress, which it seemed ill-mannered to refuse.

Aroused by so many emotions, as soon as they opened the gates of the city wall, I made my way to The Swan. *I recovered my strength by sleeping for a couple of hours, but the day became tedious for me as I waited for evening. While watching to see that my men stowed the cargo safely I thought about nothing other than the coming night. I was constantly reminded of my lady. The virgin oil in the jars had the same color of syrup as her imagined hair, long and heavy to the touch, which at times*

I supposed was blond, at others I likened to a dark varnish.

When the hour arrived, I walked with unrestrained desire to the wall enclosing the garden, intending to examine where exactly the secret gate opened and what houses were on the other side. Although I had promised not to tell anyone in Majorca about our meeting, and I am a man of my word, I wanted to know who the garden belonged to and to find out, from whatever source was available, what was at the end of the passage I had been led along. But I hardly had time to take anything in or to make the chance acquaintance of a neighbor, because as soon as I arrived the gate was opened.

"Welcome, Captain Harts," said the servant. "Our mistress is expecting you."

Without addressing me, only with a smile, the girl who had accompanied me the day before took my hand and again we crossed the garden and the orange grove until we reached the secret entrance that led to the passageway, which this time seemed longer and chillier than on the previous occasion. On emerging at the other end I deduced that we were not in the same place because the scent of the sea, a little offensive, mixed with seaweed and shells, which, as you can imagine, I do not confuse with any other, entered all my pores, and through my ears I recognized its dark and opaque murmur against the rocks, which I supposed were very close.

"We have to climb a fairly steep staircase, Captain Harts," my guide informed me. "Take care."

I counted sixty steps separated by four landings, where the maid waited so that we could catch our breath. At the end of the last landing the girl pushed open a door.

"Captain Harts, please forgive me, but my mistress orders me to blindfold you. Here there is a little more light and you know that you mustn't see her."

I had no choice but to acquiesce. She tied a bandage round me, which must have been made of silk, because it was soft to the touch, and left me alone. I could hear the tuneful sound of a lute being played in that same room. Suddenly my beloved greeted me:

"Good evening, Captain Harts. I hope this place is as acceptable to you as the one last night. Please come close . . ."

I took a couple of paces towards the voice with my arms outstretched, not so much because I wanted to embrace my lady as to avoid bumping into anything. To tell the truth I felt absolutely ridiculous. I wanted to tear off the bandage and, leaving aside courtesies, to possess her at that very moment with my eyes as well. Her hand guided me by the arm and made me change my mind.

"Sit down, captain," she said, helping me to do so. "I shall play for you if you wish. Do you enjoy music?"

I lied. Used to the sea's endless murmurs, I conceive of no other music than that of the waves. Besides, to be honest, I didn't much feel like listening to music. To delay the work I had been called for struck me frankly as a fraud. But, as one has to on such occasions, I dissembled and answered as follows:

"Very much, madam. Music raises the spirits and soothes the afflictions."

"That depends," she replied. "Sometimes it deepens the sorrows."

And as she said this she sighed wistfully.

"Are you hungry, captain, or perhaps you're thirsty?"

"No, madam, I am full of desire and I only want you."

"Have patience, it's still early and I so like to hear you talk of the sea!"

I had to fill a long period with my adventures. She listened carefully. Sometimes, her curiosity aroused, she would ask for details of distant ports that she had heard of, since she seemed very interested in travels and sea voyages.

"Madam," I said, when I was tired of giving explanations,

"do not draw out my torment. Let words cease and allow the tumult of my blood to speak."

And as on the previous night we fought a bloodless battle on the same stage we were seated on. It must have been just before daybreak when she fell asleep with her head lightly resting on my chest and it was then that I finally decided that the time had come to remove the bandage. Concentrating as hard as I could, stirring as little as possible, I loosened the knot and pushed the bandage on to my forehead.

The vision lasted only a few moments, but it was enough for life. I shall never be able to forget what I saw, because it seemed like something out of Paradise. Her face in the light of the moon, which was already setting, displayed harmonious features. Her brow was lofty and white like the rest of her countenance, which seemed almost transparent, like the foam of the waves. Her long and abundant hair resembled saffron more than syrup. Her eyebrows looked like two small bows about to shoot arrows from her eyes, the color of which, because they were closed, I could not ascertain. Her fleshy lips were pink and tender. Her limbs and the other parts of her body appeared to have been embroidered in a tapestry such as I have contemplated in a Venetian palace, owing to their perfection. I have left aside her feet because the wonder of those two drops of curdled milk deserves special mention. Like turtledoves asleep on the taffeta cushions that were on the stage, sweet and warm, I could not resist the temptation to kiss them in adoration almost like someone who kisses a sacred relic. No, the vision did not disappoint me. On the contrary it heightened my desire that this exalted body should once more be mine, although to achieve this I had to deprive myself of the pleasure of looking.

I tightened the knot again and, caressing her as I had almost not ceased to do during those two prodigious nights, I soon scattered sleep from her eyes and we again embraced until the punc-

tual and impertinent lark announced the arrival of the cursed dawn. Not without cries and promises we bid each other farewell until the following night, which would be our last, at least for some time, since my ship was leaving Port Pi for Livorno the very next day.

On board The Swan *the crew was waiting for me in an excited state, since there had been a fire on board during the night. Fortunately the sailors had been able to put it out, but this accident would delay our departure for a few hours until the damage was repaired. The news, which on another occasion would have made me furious, almost did not trouble me, immersed as I was in concerns about my lady. I was trying to think of a way I could discover her name and lineage without compromising her honor. It seemed to me that from the presents her servant had handed me, as on the previous night, I could draw some information, since on a diamond ring he had given me, together with another bag of Majorcan ounces, were engraved the initials SP. Wanting my lady to see how it sparkled on my little finger, I put it on and before attending my sweet appointment I decided to visit the workshop of a silversmith I knew in Segell Street to try to find out where the ring could originate from. The silversmith received me warmly, but did not settle my doubts. He directed me to a colleague, who did not clarify anything either. In his opinion the initials could refer as much to a name as to the words Still Present, especially if, as it seemed, it was a lovesick lady who had given it to me.*

I was hurrying along by the wall in the direction of the gate when I heard footsteps. Laughing at my fears of the first night, I supposed that they were the footsteps of the servant walking on the other side. Suddenly, however, I realized that it was not the sound of a single person, but of a group, and I turned round.

There were in effect four armed men who fell on me without giving me time to defend myself with my pistol. They hit me and beat me until leaving me stretched out and half dead in the middle of the street and, however much I asked them the motive for their attack, they did not answer. They fled when they heard the sound of the patrol. And thanks to that I am alive and still have the ring, which they pulled off my finger, but fortunately must have dropped in their hurry to escape. I dragged myself to the gate in the wall and there called for help, but nobody opened, though they must have heard me, because when I arrived they threw over a note that the darkness did not permit me to read. As best I could, I sought refuge in Descós' offices, where Fortesa took me in. But nor did he want to tell me, if he knew, who that lady was. The garden belonged to a bachelor merchant and adjoined a convent. The count's administrator did not know of the existence of any secret passages. While they saw to my wounds, I read the letter: "Captain Harts," it said, "with the greatest sorrow and regret I realize that you are not the person I expected, since twice you have broken your oath. Do not enter my property again under pain of death, which you would be nearer than you are now. I wish that the wind had never directed the sails of your ship towards our island, filling me with hopes that in such a short time have vanished. A curse on you and a curse on me for having been unfaithful to him who has yet to arrive by sea and give me what you have not been able to."

He walked up and down in front of the wall that enclosed the garden, going over the story that Captain Harts at times had read from some sheets where he claimed to have recorded his life and at others had improvised and that coincided in so many details with his dream. Except that now he and not Harts was the messenger Cupid and his mother Venus were sending to that lady, who on bright days would scan the distant sea, signaling to the ships that headed towards the island, in case one of them carried the beloved who would never betray her.

He walked up and down, imagining weary, voluptuous delights, the heady aroma of the rose bushes, the murmur of captive water and finally the gentlest touch of the unknown beauty, whom he would embrace being blind if that was what she wanted. But the bell of St Clare's ringing for vespers and then for compline made him understand that the wait, that night at least, had been in vain. He was already turning to leave when suddenly he heard a sound of footsteps. His pulse racing, he stopped short to see if they would also stop as had happened to the captain. But this time the sound was not linked to him. It came from further away and grew more audible as someone approached from the other end of the street. In the pale light of the dawn, which was just breaking, he made out an indistinct shape trying to run, but which stumbled and suddenly fell to the ground. Curious rather than fearful, and wondering if that bulky shadow might be bringing the expected signal, he went up to it and in the early morning light saw that it was a woman. Without daring to lift her up he stood and observed her for a few moments, trying to find a place for that figure in the memory of his past dreams, which he could not do. As always when he searched among the old, dreamed images for a space in which to fit a new one, the origin of which he was unable to identify with those he had witnessed with his eyes closed, he paused for a moment to catch the scent of that person. But the mixture of dust and ashes, in which he later discerned a hint of musk perfume, did not help him at all. What he smelled inside, so inside that outside not a drop was spilled, was the fragrance of the rose bushes gently pressed by the breeze, the heady aroma of the jasmines and the snow-white flowers of the oranges. These smells that coincided with those Harts described to him at his request were, however, as nothing compared to the smell that for so many years had filled his room at night and that emanated from the long, hanging hair of his beloved. To breathe it in, to lower his head and bury his face in the warm nest of that hair, was one of the motives for his journey and the reward for all the possible services that the mysterious lady could demand of him. The smell, the memory of that smell he had dreamed of, entreated him and sometimes distracted him from his adventures in the brothel because a faint smell could excite him much more than the deftest or boldest of caresses.

Leaning towards the ashen figure, he bends more to smell than to look at her. He smells thick, black locks that emerge from the loose scarf, emitting a vinegary odor, which closer up is confused with the odor of reheated oil, which he does not like at all. He stands up again and asks her if she is wounded, if he can be of service.

But she does not answer, she looks at him in consternation and squeezes her chest, where João Peres observes a bloodstain.

"Are you wounded? Tell me where I can take you so that they can help you . . ."

She sighs deeply and suddenly closes her eyes with their long, dark lashes, her features soften and Peres finds her face more acceptable. Her bodice is not properly buttoned up, as if she had dressed in a hurry, and her striped skirt of coarse material is smattered with mud. However much he goes over Harts' story, he is sure that this girl does not appear in it. She has nothing to do with the Moorish slave girl and bears absolutely no resemblance to the unknown beauty with the angel skin. The captain may have forgotten to mention her, perhaps he left her lying on the ground like a beaten dog without helping her and for this reason he disregarded her in his story. But no, such suppositions lead nowhere. The girl shouldn't be there, she is not part of the action, she does not belong to the adventure. She has abruptly emerged, expelled from the belly of darkness into the early morning light, without having been called, without being needed. But her presence upsets him and moves him with a tender feeling that goes beyond pity for a wounded girl. He decides not to forage again in the memory of his old dreams for some detail that might clarify the situation he must now confront without antecedents or assistance.

"Where can I take you, madam, so that they can help you?" he repeats.

She does not answer him because she has lost consciousness. Peres does not know what to do with her. He is unfamiliar with the city. Judging by her appearance, the girl could be a maid or the daughter of artisans. *Where could she be going at this hour? Was she fleeing from someone or perhaps chasing them? Was she leaving or coming home?*

In the district there are noble houses, two convents, a couple of orchards. Further on, just a hundred yards away, St Eulalia's Church. Peres doesn't know which way to turn. Perhaps the most sensible thing would be to leave. Someone else will come by who can help her. What he has to do is go. Head for the quay gate and, as soon as they open, cover the short distance to Port Pi, where *The Minerva* is at anchor. What is this poor woman to him? He needs to return soon, for nobody to notice that he has not slept in his place, not to arouse suspicions that could lead to a punishment, the worst of all possible punishments: a ban on leaving the ship. Anything but that, he thinks, as he moves away from the girl. His only concern is to be back here tomorrow at nightfall to try his luck again. What's more, if the Bailiff were to come and catch him with the wounded girl, he has no hope. Who will be considered guilty if it's not the foreigner, someone passing through, who's just committed a crime? He walks quickly, afraid that he might be clapped in prison with nobody to demand even a scrap of justice for his cause. The captain doesn't care about this sailor without a fortune, whom nobody recommended. Who is going to care? The priests of the seminary he escaped from two years before? His father, who never helped him out despite being a powerful merchant? Peres is not exactly his favorite bastard . . . His friend Do Barros, the only one to whom he confided the real reason for his journey, thought he was mad. "Who knows what truth there is in Harts' story?" he told him. "Besides, the beauty may already have found someone from far away to comfort her. Four years is a long time to wait for you without knowing that you're coming . . ." he added mockingly when Peres insisted on the steadfastness of his faith, derived from a dream.

He flees without running in order not to arouse suspicions, because after daybreak the streets begin to be busy with morning people: clergy on their way to say Mass, stonemasons hired to fortify the bulwark, party-goers who, like him, are on their way home, wrapped in their cloaks to avoid being recognized. He's about to turn right, but he cannot avoid the temptation of looking to see if the girl is still there, lying on the ground. He sees the indistinct shape dropped like a heap of dirty clothes and imagines he hears a groan. And suddenly he runs back and swoops up the girl in his arms and decides to take her where she can receive treatment. Carrying her body, he heads in the opposite direction to that in which he had fled. He goes towards St Eulalia's Square. On the dusty street he now steps along there is a trail of blood. *At least I'll know where she was coming from,* Peres says to himself, *though it might be better not to go there.* As he walks, he asks God for an open door from which a good Samaritan might emerge to help him. But all the doors are closed. Recalling Harts' story, he searches among the houses on the left for the offices where Fortesa administers the count's business. The house has a wide gable, Harts told him, and a coat of arms on the porch: a lion on a silver field. He'll knock at the door and say he's a friend of the captain. The blows resound. A woman leans out of a window.

"I'm a friend of Captain Harts, madam. I found this wounded girl in the street."

"We don't have happy memories of Harts, sir," the woman answers, "and I don't know how I could help you. But I know the girl, her name's Aina Cap de Trons. She lives in Segell Street. It's fifty paces away, just behind the church. Her house is on the corner of Argenteria, on the right, the last house."

She doesn't wait for a reply. She slams the window and the wood creaks. A flock of sheep led by a dog fills the young day with bells and forces Peres back against the wall. The shepherd does not even notice the load he carries in his arms. The cloud of dust makes him cough and erases the trail of blood. The bell-tower of St Eulalia's is visible in a whitish sky as if the lazy light had taken longer than expected this morning. As he turns into Segell Street, dark spots reappear on the ground. The shops are not open yet. There is no smoke coming out of the chimneys. The poor light does not encourage you to rise early, thinks Peres, who always wakes up later when the day is overcast like today. He's tired. He reaches the right door almost out of breath. He pushes it and it gives way. Inside everything is dark. A musty smell accosts him.

"Is there anyone at home?" he asks.

Nobody answers. The room is windowless. A streak of light filters down the stairwell, just enough to be able to make out piles of old clothes strewn around. It stinks of poverty, urine and dirt. No, he can't leave her here. Drained of his strength, he climbs the stairs to the second floor. The light enters through the loose shutters and the slanting rays hit upon the objects, retrieving them from the shade. Last night's embers seem until recently to have smoldered on the extinct hearth. The humble earthenware is stacked on the shelf, but there is still an embroidered linen cloth on the table as if there had been a party. On top, inside a jug, an oil lamp burns alone, next to some covered dishes. Peres sets the girl down on a bench as gently as he can, though she doesn't regain consciousness. He doesn't dare loosen her clothes or feel her body to examine her wounds. He dries his bloodstained hands with a cloth and to hide the blood that's left he rubs them in ash. He hears a panting coming from further away, from further inside. He goes in search of somebody to tell how he found Aina. He sees a room with a low bed and a man lying on it, draped in a sheet. His nightshirt is bloodied. But he isn't moaning. The groans come from further back. In another room a young man is sprawled on the ground, his hands on his genitals.

"What happened to you?" asks Peres in a nervous voice.

"Leave right now, get out of here," the invalid tells him. "Leave!" he repeats.

Peres obeys. He heads for the door. But he has to stop first. His mouth is too small to contain the bile pushing up from his stomach. When he steps into the street, the clouds spread out and the sun pours through like an egg yolk. But the neighbors haven't realized that the day has begun, since the shops and workshops are still shut, their windows closed. From the chimneys there is no smoke. Peres stands still for a moment in the middle of the street and then suddenly shouts out:

"Help here, help here!"

His voice reverberates. It is a bellow that lands on each door, that filters through the cracks and penetrates to the houses' most recondite corners. It beats like a clenched fist against the walls and bounces off the clay. But nobody seems to hear it. Nobody appears at the windows or emerges from the porch. Standing right in the middle of the street Peres waits for any sign, however small it may be, that the angel of death has not beheaded everybody with his flaming sword.

II

"THINK ABOUT IT CAREFULLY, MY SON, AND WHEN YOU'RE clear in your mind, write it down and, with the testimony, come and see me and we'll sit down and talk about it. *Ego te absolvo a peccatis tuis in nomine* . . ." The confessor's thin wax fingers crossed the air full of incense just as the organ attacked the first notes of the *Te Deum* and the packed church filled with the choir's voices. *Te Dominum confitemur* . . .

With lowered head Rafel Cortès, Costura, returned to his place, kneeled down and in his most intimate voice accompanied the singers: *Te aeternum patrem omnis terra veneratur* . . . Although it was an evening celebration, the sun poured through the stained-glass windows, illuminating them with its thick rays. The colors of the glass glowed and the figures of Christ, the Father Almighty, the Virgin Mary and other saints in the divine retinue, who occupied the rose windows, shone in all their splendor as if truly the aura of sanctity surrounded their heads and ran down their bodies, which were no longer of this world. *Tibi Cherubim et Seraphim incessabili voce proclamant.* Although he was attracted by the contemplation of the windows, Costura could not keep looking at those blinding figures for more than a few seconds and, dazzled, he lowered his eyes towards the tabernacle where the Host had been exposed in the gold and silver monstrance, which also glowed, though not as much as the windows. *Sanctus, Sanctus, Sanctus, Dominus Deus Sabaoth.* He gazed for a few moments at the receptacle around which the jeweler who had made the monstrance had placed seven radiating points and then lowered his head and covered his face with his hands as a sign of recollection. He had just been absolved, he felt comforted, not only because his confession had been entirely genuine and he had not omitted a single fault, but also because everybody had seen him approach the confessional and stay there the requisite time, neither too much nor too little, with devotion painted on his face. Now in his pew, his ears ringing with the *Te Deum—te Prophetarum laudabilis*—he tried to focus on his penance, which was to say a rosary, because the written testimony the confessor had asked him for when he referred in passing to the acts carried out by his cousin Rafel Cortès, Cap de Trons, troubled him. But he was determined that nobody, least of all Father Ferrando, should question his Catholic faith.

With his head lowered and his eyes closed Costura did not move a single muscle. Only his swollen fingers nervously manipulated the beads of the rosary. Concentrating as hard as he could, he mentally recited the Hail Marys. At times he became distracted, assuring himself that he was on the right path to salvation, not like his relatives in the Street who secretly persevered in the law of Moses, proud to belong to the Jewish people, although they had no choice but to act like Christians and also to take part in the religious ceremonies. In his case, however, it was the opposite: he had willingly renounced the old religion and however much Cap de Trons upbraided him, he did not intend to practice their rites again or to refrain from eating pork or fish without scales. He was sure that he would feel no guilt when his relative again held up the example of his mother, a committed Jew, who in her agony held the consecrated Host in her mouth only to spit it out before dying, offering her life to Jehovah, her sovereign Lord, nor would he waver when Cap de

Trons insisted on informing him that Jews who had arrived from the other side of the ocean bore certain and reliable news of the imminent coming of the Messiah. What's more, now, surrounded by people who did not reject him, cradled by the music, *Tu rex Gloriae, Christe, Tu Patris sempiternus es Filius*, and the sweet aroma of incense, he felt he was taking part in ceremonies that struck him as much more beautiful than his own people's ceremonies, practiced on the quiet in the secret of their homes. Not for nothing did attending these solemnities make him feel much more than a spectator, a protagonist, a co-participant with all the other faithful in the magnificence there on display. *Tu ad dexteram Dei sedes in Gloria Patris.* It was as if the treasures preserved in the church, the precious stones so delicately mounted around the base of the monstrance, the gold leaf on the reredos behind the high altar and the embossed silver on the doors of the shrine were also partly his, as the light of day or the dark of night was his, everyone's or nobody's.

As a child he would have liked to be a priest, to dress up like those who had just celebrated the Forty Hours in a white chasuble, embroidered with gold thread, probably by consecrated hands as well, and to receive the clouds of incense that the acolyte had thrown at them, swinging the censer in front of them, but his mother made him change his mind. *Te ergo quaesumus.* The fact of being able to say Mass, the miraculous fact that God should descend to his hands just because he uttered some holy words, struck him as the best thing in the world. Rabbis did not enjoy so many privileges. What's more, even in places where they could practice their cult openly, the ceremonies they performed were much less beautiful. The way they beat their chest or banged their head against the Wailing Wall did not seem to him worthy of joyful contemplation. On the other hand the movements of the priests during Mass, who now were kneeling, now standing, now sitting, were harmonious and measured like the gestures of their hands. *Salvum fac populum tuum, Domine.* Not only that, being a priest meant being able to lavish pardons and blessings, and also to impose punishments, to know everybody's weaknesses and their innermost desires. Perhaps this was why he found it natural that Father Ferrando should probe his conscience so carefully and not only express interest in his spiritual life, but also in that of his relations, who did not visit his confessional as much as he would have liked. Convinced that he would do the same as his confessor in such a situation, he was unable to conceive any reason for not having to write the testimony and it didn't occur to him that writing down his accusations would require much more effort than simply repeating them aloud. He didn't even dare to find some excuse to put off the appointment so that he could gain a little time. *Fiat misericordia tua, Domine, super nos.*

The day's solemnity was already over when he decided to leave the church, which had slowly emptied as the priests withdrew to the sacristy. He was careful, however, that those who were still there should notice his presence. Before leaving, therefore, he made sure he visited St Savior's Chapel, where some ladies he knew in the congregation were praying. The sacristan, accompanied by two acolytes, was going round putting out the candles that had burned during the celebration, and the church, which no longer received the sun's full light, was almost dark. Although the lack of light did not favor the building and he tried to avoid being there when this happened, he waited to be one of the last to leave in case Father Ferrando should finish confessing and, before going to the sacristy to remove his stole, bump into him, since he was sure that he would give him a nod and a broad smile. This deference on the part of the confessor pleased him. It was also good for him that the others should see it, since it confirmed his position as a fervent Christian under suspicious eyes.

He headed slowly towards the main entrance. He dipped his fingers in the holy water, carefully crossed himself after the manner of priests and left. He walked across the square and took the street that led to the inn called S'Estornell to see if in Descós' offices he might find the wife of the count's administrator, Fortesa. He wanted to hear from her own mouth everything he had heard from others: that it was she who had recognized Aina Cortès, wounded and unconscious, in a sailor's arms and given him directions so that he could take her to her house. He wanted to know why she had been unable to help her right there, given that they were related, and above all what the sailor had said to her. If it was true that he had come across Aina by chance in the street, as the Bailiff's men who questioned him had reported: that while he was walking up and down between the inn S'Estornell and Maroto garden, waiting for a tryst with a lady whose name he refused to divulge, a girl appeared either fleeing from someone or chasing them. When he approached, he saw that she was wounded. *Had she, Isabel Fustera, witnessed someone pass by before Aina, and did this person happen to be Canon Amorós' servant, who, bleeding, sought help as far away as possible from the Street?* But Isabel, who did not trust the meddlesome Rafel Cortès, Costura, and hated his constant dealings with priests, received him coldly and was only willing to repeat what everybody knew: she only said where Aina Cortès lived because she thought that the forty or fifty paces separating her from her father's home would in no way worsen her condition and she did not want her husband, let alone her lord, to rebuke her for having taken in a stranger who was also a foreigner and, as she suspected and later verified, a sailor from a corsair ship, whose crew her husband wanted nothing to do with. The problems with his former ally, Captain Harts, had taught him a cruel lesson.

Rafel Cortès, Costura, returned home happy to have started by questioning—*I behaved like a priest,* he said to himself, *but I didn't forgive her*—finding out the information about his cousin the confessor wanted from him, but happier still because of the disquiet his visit had caused Isabel, considered among the people of the Street to be a Jew with the strength of her convictions.

He spent long hours awake that night. To see if sleep would come if he walked a little, he even climbed up on to the terrace of his house, which was slightly bigger than the others and had a good view of the surroundings. As so often before, he saw the dark silhouette of Pere Onofre Martí standing with his body turned to the East, contemplating the warm, starry night. "Pray!" Costura exclaimed in a loud voice. "You need it. Adonai does not like cuckolds." This was the explanation Costura gave for Martí's misfortunes. Everything started to go badly for him the day someone twisted his ear with the story that his second wife, Quitèria Pomar, ten years younger, was having an affair with a man of her own age.

Between the clotheslines he thought he made out the bald head of Miquel Bonnín, in the same position as Martí, and it occurred to him that Father Ferrando might like to accompany him one evening, when it was dark, to witness the spectacle afforded by his terrace, after he had invited him to dine on lobster, the shell of which he would sprinkle in front of the porch as a provocation. Perhaps this way his cousin, Rafel Cortès, Cap de Trons, would finally get the message and stop pestering him with his arguments to return to the authentic road.

Hoping to catch any movement his neighbors made, on the lookout for anything that might happen, Costura took up his normal sentinel's position on a stone bench. His wife had died almost five years previously and he didn't need to worry what hours he kept. Hence he could stay up for as long as he liked. The only maid who lived in the house slept downstairs, right next to the workshop, and was going deaf. Upstairs he could make as much noise as he wanted and know that she would not notice. She slept soundly and he had never woken her. There were even times he had been given a job and the deadline was approaching when he had taken his tools and worked through the night, saving himself last-minute efforts so that he could keep his word. For this reason he almost hadn't slept the night of the disturbance Father Ferrando was so keen for him to describe, setting some very valuable rubies in an ornament a gentleman from Alaró had ordered for his marriageable daughter. In the weak morning light, because the day had started cloudy, as he was going to fetch his tools, he heard a sound in the street and from the window thought he saw a man in disguise trying to flee, staggering along, holding on to the walls as best as he could. Then, a few minutes later, when the figure had managed to turn towards the square and been lost from sight, he noticed how Aina Cortès, Cap de Trons' daughter, left her home and in a mess, as if she had dressed in a hurry, struggled in the direction the man in disguise had taken. Without respect for her honor or that of her family, without paying any attention or caring that she might set tongues wagging, she fled in pursuit of a man, that everybody might confirm what they already suspected: that the good-for-nothing Juli Ramis, ex-seminarian and ex-bandit, as well as serving Canon Amorós, officer of the Inquisition, visited her at night in her own room. He saw, but he heard nothing, only footsteps. No shout, no threat, no brawl. He stayed at the window, however, because he thought he might soon see his cousin chasing after the fugitives or at least cursing his daughter for showing him up and causing him such public disgrace. But the street remained deserted and, although the day had begun, overcast on account of the clouds, there was still no smoke coming from the chimneys. *Not much wood will burn today,* observed Rafel, *it's Saturday.* And he smiled again, thinking about the observance of his relatives, who had reached an agreement: those who could would celebrate the Sabbath without working or even lighting a fire, but taking it in turns. Some families were excused from this obligation in order to safeguard the rest. He was about to leave the window and go down with his tools to the workshop when he caught sight of a young man entering Segell Street with a woman in his arms. He was making difficult and painful progress, with his eyes on each of the closed doors as if waiting for a sign. On passing in front of Costura's house he looked up, perhaps aware that somebody was watching him. A few paces further on he recognized Aina's house and kicked the door open. Could this stranger be the man in disguise he had seen earlier? Or was it a good Samaritan who on finding a woman in need was taking her where she could receive help? *I won't move from here until I know the outcome of this farce,* Costura decided, excited by such developments.

He didn't have to wait long because the young man quickly emerged from Cap de Trons' house and in the middle of the street shouted for help, disturbing the whole district.

Accompanied by the old maid Polònia Miró, who had been frightened by the foreigner's shouts and come up to be with her master, Costura continued watching for a time. Then, seeing the young man make off and fearing the arrival of the patrol, he decided not to go out in search of more facts, but to climb to the terrace, since he had the intuition that from there he could find out things that downstairs might escape him. Besides, he had plenty of morning to listen to the neighbors' gossip. From his private watch-tower he looked towards the house of his relative, who, just as he had imagined, was contemplating the new day and praying as was his custom on Saturdays: *In thee, O Lord, have I put my trust, let me never be put to confusion. Deliver me in thy righteousness, incline thine ear unto me and save me. Be thou my stronghold, whereunto I may always resort. Deliver me, O my God, out of the hand of the ungodly, out of the hand of the unrighteous and cruel man. Thou art my hope, even from my youth. Through thee have I been holden up, thou art he that took me out of my mother's womb . . .*

Cap de Trons' prayer, intoned with far greater strength than on other Saturdays, was perfectly audible. His cousin had no reason to be ashamed of his songs of praise. Christians also used psalms to pray to God the Father Almighty. Even he had confided to his confessor that when saying his prayers he sometimes preferred psalms to Our Fathers, not because he hoped to satisfy both Adonai and Christ, as some of his relatives did, but because they seemed to him more varied and this must make them more pleasing to divine ears. Rafel Cortès, Costura, left Cap de Trons there, communicating with God, with the suspicion that the ardor of his song was a more persistent way of seeking divine help before confronting his family's problems, and returned downstairs not to delay his appetite any longer. Before the bowl of soup the maid had just served him, he found out from her, who had been told by the woman next door, that the previous night Rafel Cortès had endeavored to wipe out his whole family. "He's praying on the terrace as always," Costura observed without taking what Polònia said too seriously, supposing that she was exaggerating as usual. "You can believe it," she insisted. "I saw Madò Grossa go by with a pile of bandages to bind up the wounds of at least half a dozen persons."

Rafel Cortès did not comment. He imagined that the bandages being carried by Madò Grossa, the healer, midwife and also quack, who had the power to cure many ills, were not so many as Polònia claimed. Rafel Cortès lived with his daughter, Aina, his two sons, Josep Joaquim and Baltasar, and his brother-in-law, a little dim-witted and old by now, whom he took charge of when his wife died. Even if they were all wounded—Cap de Trons' wrath could have unpredictable consequences—they couldn't be seriously wounded, whether it was their father or not, they were young and able if not to attack him, at least to defend themselves or to keep out of his way by dodging his blows. For this reason what he could know from what his maid had told him were just suppositions that Costura idly shuffled while finishing his bowl of soup in front of the gaping Polònia, who did fast, because she always had done and always would do until the day she died.

Rafel Cortès opened the workshop and stood in the porch, disposed to converse with whoever should come by first, as he used to every day about whatever triviality. But this Saturday, intrigued as he was to know everything that had taken place at his cousin's, he was only interested in details that one or another could give him of the affair.

"It was pretty serious," remarked Xim Valleriola, the tailor, who seemed more weighed down than ever this morning, as if the excitement he felt had added to his hunchback.

"What do you mean?" asked Cortès, who was as skillful as a weasel at getting to the bottom of something, pretending not to know what it was about.

"Haven't you heard? Haven't you heard anything about what happened? Well, it concerns you. It's your cousin . . . It concerns you a great deal," the tailor smiled, wrinkling up his hooked nose in a sarcastic grimace.

"Would you mind telling me? I don't know what you're referring to."

"Well, it was serious. Your niece, Aina, your cousin Rafel's daughter, returned home wounded in the arms of a foreigner . . ."

"I feel sorry for her father," he said, hoping the tailor would tell him something he didn't know.

But Valleriola fell silent, unconvinced that his neighbor hadn't heard about it. They had known each other since childhood and the tailor considered Costura the most inquisitive person in the world. Also, Polònia had told him sometimes that her master almost didn't sleep, that he frequently worked at night and wandered about upstairs on the lookout for anything that might happen in the Street. It was the tailor's wife who emerged from the porch and asked Cortès if the young man's cries had woken him up as well or if he had been up for some time when he heard them.

Costura did his best not to answer and suggested that the affair couldn't be that serious if, as every Saturday, Cap de Trons was giving thanks to God from the terrace.

"We'll find out when Madò Grossa comes if she's willing to tell us," concluded the tailor's wife in her piping voice. "It's not so important to us as it is to you, since you're closely related."

With careful precision Costura recalls even the gestures that accompanied the words of Valleriola and of his wife, Rafela Miró, whom his mother would have liked him to marry when they were both young and she seemed a sensible girl . . . He was the one who refused, since he didn't find her at all attractive. If there was one thing that satisfied him, it was not having fulfilled his mother's desire even if, by going against her, he had been left without descendants. But although when he married he would have liked to have children, now he was pleased that God had not sent them. His wife did not give him any and perhaps this is how God avoided them being branded half-castes by the people of the Street. "If you marry Joana," his cousin warned him, "you'll be making a serious mistake. Adonai will call you to account. Have you thought that in front of her you'll never be able to keep the law of Moses?"

But Costura did not heed him, similarly ignoring the wishes of his mother, who, aside from being upset that her future daughter-in-law was not of their lineage, considered her beneath him. Joana was a slip of a girl when the baker's wife took her from the orphanage to help attend to the customers and to relieve her of the more onerous housework. Sprightly, with eyes like olive leaves, she grew up almost on her knees, scrubbing floors with a backache that lasted until her death. Thinking about the times she could spend sitting down, like a lady, more than anything else, she agreed to marry Costura, who was already in his forties on the day she turned seventeen. Their courtship was brief. Rafel Cortès did not need to imagine what the girl's life had been like before he asked her to marry him, because he had seen her grow hour by hour, since she left the orphanage at the age of twelve to work in the bakery. Many summer evenings, as he walked up and down the terrace in the twilight, he had watched the girl, who, being so tired, lay on her folding bed in the baker's attic. And often, also, Costura had felt disturbed as he imagined that young, bruised body at the mercy of sleep and of the elements. His decision to marry Joana was influenced not only by the desire to have a woman between the sheets; there was something stranger, a kind of tenderness for that child who had never known her parents, whom he saw grow, confusing in a dense muddle the feelings of protection and possession. If one thing worked out for Costura, it was his marriage, despite the difficulties it caused him, because Joana served him in and for everything with affection and, what's more, devout as she was, her presence at early morning Masses and novenas of every kind brought more customers to his workshop, who preferred him to other silversmiths who did not seem so well converted. Costura accompanied Joana to church as often as he could and little by little, either because her kindness and faith brooded inside him, or because he felt distant from his own people, who rejected him, he gave up observing the Old Law. The death of his wife, only seven years after their wedding, left him disconsolate and much more orphaned than if he had lost his mother, who, although she had stopped looking cross at her daughter-in-law as in the beginning, breathed a sigh of relief on the day she was buried. In front of Joana, old Aina Bonnín had been forced to conceal her beliefs, afraid that the pious girl might denounce her. From now on she would no longer have to put up with the stench of bacon, nor would she have to grumble her way through the rosary. For Costura, on the other hand, the death of his wife was like a divine punishment that, to start with, he didn't know whether to attribute to Adonai or to God the Father, since both of them had reasons to unleash the strength of their arm on his sinful body. During the years of his marriage, like a good Christian he kept the commandments, but from time to time he continued practicing certain rites, spurred on by his mother and his bothersome cousin, who, as often as he could, in their chance meetings and, even more, in the visits he paid to his aunt Aina, did not stop telling him to keep the Old Law, which he was doubly required to do, as a Jew and as a pure descendant of the tribe of Levi, from which the Cortès of Majorca originated.

A few months after Joana's death, in search of a little comfort, he visited the confessional of Father Ferrando, who had confessed his wife, and asked for help. He explained how her example had led him to abandon his former beliefs. During his long conversations with the priest, Costura grew used to speaking unreservedly about life in the Street and did so not to betray anybody, but to empty his acute pain in a friendly ear, which none of his own people provided. Some quickly expressed their condolences without hiding the fact that deep down they were happy about his misfortune; others didn't even do that. But as always it was his cousin, Cap de Trons, who offended him most of all, affirming that Joana's death was proof of Adonai's vengeance and no doubt, irritated as he was in divine wrath, he would soon plague him with greater sufferings.

For the first time in his life, Costura turned on his cousin and told him that it was possible that God the Father had punished him with his wife's death for not having persevered in the faith he had been baptized into and, at his and his mother's bidding, for having played a double game that annoyed the Most

High, who took away what he most loved in the world, the only person he cared about and with whom he wished to share eternity in a single heaven.

In the empty hours following Joana's death, many nights her pale green, slightly anxious eyes kept him company until he finally managed to fall asleep, imagining that he was doing so in her young, accepting arms. Then, as the years went by, her presence seemed to diminish, although quite often the memories, like a flock of unpredictable birds, would cross his mind and suddenly stop, as if seeking to spend the night in the shelter of the old, fond images that paraded there at the slow pace of processions. No, at no point did he wish to remarry. A second wife would have been a hindrance in his decision not to abandon the Catholic faith if, as his mother demanded, she had to be from the Street. But even after his mother's death he didn't seriously consider it, although he could have married a Christian, as Father Ferrando proposed. He had enough with Polònia for the housework and for some time had not been in need of other services that, prior to being married, he had obtained fairly cheaply at the brothel near St Antony's Gate. Not even the memory of past pleasures with Joana, which from time to time still came to his mind with precision and luxurious details, excited him enough to go and deposit his seed in another body. He preferred the action of his own hand on his penis before reaching the liberating spasm. But though he censured his lack of chastity, Father Ferrando was less interested in this matter than that he continue in his observance, without which he could not be saved.

Costura carefully went over the facts as the confessor had asked, trying not to be distracted by the past, by Cap de Trons' former misdeeds, which Father Ferrando already knew about, and not to get entangled in the memory of Joana, whom he always ended up calling on when examining his conscience so that she could help him and encourage him to persevere. He was afraid of omitting some detail that might be important for his confessor and yet seem minor to him and for this reason he took the decision to give as thorough an account as he could, which included the exact reproduction of his conversation with Valleriola as well as his maid's suppositions, even though what Father Ferrando was looking for was not a minute description of what had taken place in the Street, Aina Cortès' comings and goings or the presence of that foreigner, but what had happened inside Rafel Cortès' home and, except for Cap de Trons himself, nobody had spoken to him about that, perhaps because his own people did not trust him. Everybody shunned him. Madò Grossa did not want to chat with him after dispensing her cures, claiming that she urgently had to assist at a birth. Polònia suddenly became dumb, fearful that he might talk about it, that he might go and tell someone who really shouldn't know about it, and did not want to share with him what everybody was murmuring in secret and keeping quiet in front of him. But soon Costura, without needing to question anybody or use captious arguments, obtained the information he so desired, reliable and first hand: his cousin, Rafel Cortès, Cap de Trons, sent for him to explain to him all that had taken place.

A resplendent angel, with feathers whiter than a dove's, bearing a flaming sword in his hand, appeared to him in dreams and by his presence succeeded in waking him. "So it wasn't in my sleep that he gave me orders. Archangel Raphael, our patron," he continued, lowering his voice in a more confidential tone, "came in the name of Adonai to accompany me, as he accompanied Tobias, and to remind me of what our name means: God's help, God's healing. I also was stunned when I woke up and saw the divine apparition and, trembling like a poplar leaf, I fell to the ground in a daze. But he said:

"'Do not be afraid, Rafel, peace be with you. Bless the Lord for ever and ever and may his name be blessed by yours. I have come down from heaven, where I serve in the Lord's secret chamber with the other six angels. There are seven of us, as the Bible says, and there's no doubt it says the truth. I have been sent by the Most High, who also gave me the task me of guiding Tobias on the road to Rages to his uncle Raguel's house and of saving him from the large fish and demons who would have killed him as they killed the seven husbands of Sarah, whom I then gave him to wife, as the Lord instructed me . . .'

"'I know who you are,' I replied without lifting my face so that his splendor did not wound my eyes. 'You did not eat or drink on the journey, but were given an invisible food and a mysterious drink that no one saw either. This miracle was a gift of the Most High.'

"'By order of Adonai I have come down from heaven,' continued the angel, 'and I've come to you. Sent by Almighty God. *Go and talk to my servant Rafel, who has the same name, and tell him I give him my blessing because his righteous life has met with mercy in my eyes and because he has never renounced my law and has tried to persevere and make his family persevere in times of shame and adversity.* To those who believe in him the hand of the Lord will be kind, but on those who shame and mock him, those who have abandoned Jehovah's ways, like your relative Rafel, unworthy to bear this name, the Lord's fist will come down heavily, because his people will be punished for their sins. But although you are a just man and have found favor in the Lord's sight, the Almighty has one complaint about you that incurs all his wrath.'

"'I've done all I can to make my cousin return to the faith of Israel,' I dared to interrupt him.

"'It's not enough. You're not to let up until you bring him back to the right road. But this is not the only cause of God's complaint. You've forgotten the pact sealed by Abraham the

Patriarch in his name and in that of his descendants and obeyed by all your ancestors in freedom or captivity at the hands of heathens. Without obeying the pact no son of Judea can enter Paradise.'

"'I haven't forgotten it, patron,' I told him. 'I've been circumcised since I was twelve . . .'

"'But your sons and your relatives haven't,' replied the angel, 'and this sin will fall on you, on you and your children, whom you are depriving of the glory of the Most High.'

"'Patron,' I said with my head touching the ground, 'none of my relatives would accept it, since this is the unmistakable sign that they belong to the Old Law and is taken by Christians to be absolute proof. Our missing foreskin leads straight to the flames.'

"'The Lord will curse you and your children for ever and ever. He said that the sign of his pact was circumcision, without which nobody can enter Paradise. You'll be worse than your cousin Rafel, who has abandoned Adonai, if you do not fulfill the pact with your God.'

"'But how am I to do it?' I asked him.

"'Add poppy juice to the wine they'll drink at supper on Friday. This will deepen your sons' sleep and during the night consecrated to the Lord, while they are asleep, execute God's commandment. First lay your hands on their heads and say the prayers that will make your sacrifice pleasing in the sight of the Lord, who sees everything in his infinite wisdom.'

"A cold shiver ran down my spine and I couldn't get the words out. When I was able to speak, the angel had disappeared, but the room was still shining . . . All my fear of performing the Lord's commandment vanished like smoke off warm bread. I immediately searched for the necessary implements to carry out the task the angel of the Lord had set me and between prayers I waited for evening. My sons' sleep was sound and with care I managed to escape their notice until the knife was already probing their private parts as the Lord had instructed me. Then, thinking they were waking from a very bad dream, they got up in pain, but without shouting out. Knowing that God was with me and his hand was guiding me, I went into my brother-in-law's bedroom to accomplish the Almighty's commandment on him as well. I was about to do so when I heard a sound I didn't like at all coming from my daughter's bedroom. *First I shall finish what God has commanded me,* I said to myself, *and then I'll see to my honor.* Onofre was asleep and had relieved himself. Either because the stink of his body made me retch, or because I was in a hurry to commit the act, I cut in the wrong place and missed twice more. Awake, trembling with pain, he turned on me, but I pushed him back on to the straw mattress and, while he kicked and groaned, I was finally able to circumcise him. When I went into Aina's room, I was blinded with anger. Juli Ramis had just put his pants on, but not buttoned them up, and Aina, horrified to see me, did not know which way to look. Without discussing it, or letting the scoundrel promise to marry her, a promise he would surely go back on, just so that I would let him go, I attacked his private parts with the knife, not intending to seal any pact with Adonai, but to castrate him for good. And because Aina intervened, cackling like a hen about to burst its craw, she also got a couple of cuts in the chest. You already know the rest. I sent for you because I think my days are numbered and I'm glad. Almighty God will have pity on me and won't make me witness the shame brought about by my daughter's dishonor. But I don't want to die without you knowing how much I desire your salvation and how the angel of the Lord spoke of it during his visit."

"Stop threatening me," Costura interrupted him, "because if you harp on about it, I'll tell Father Ferrando everything and then they'll stick you in a sanbenito."

Cap de Trons appeared not to hear him, because he paid no attention to Costura, who was incensed and shouting out, "I swear I'll tell him, as my name is Rafel." This outburst of anger was the result of the terrible suffering Cap de Trons had caused him while he listened to his story, since more than once he had been afraid that his cousin would fall on him with circumcising passion as he had done to the rest of his family and, although he was stronger and younger, he had no weapon with which to defend himself should his cousin attack with his sacrificial knife, the hilt of which he could see sticking out of his pocket. But nothing of the sort happened. Rafel Cortès simply informed him and then, ignoring Costura's promise to report him, thanked him with unusual kindness for having listened and assured him that he was the only person who knew the miracle of the angel's apparition and warnings and that he had confided in him inasmuch as it concerned him, because he hadn't wanted to explain to his sons that it was by divine intervention that he had finally dared to impose on them something they would never have received willingly.

Taking refuge in his insomnia, Costura now pared all the facts his confessor only half knew about, unsure how he had to put them down on paper and whether he should record it all, just as his cousin had described it, or could offer a summary very similar to the one he gave aloud that afternoon, in which he had included only the essential details directly affecting Cap de Trons and his daughter Aina and omitted the fact that the wounds to his sons and brother-in-law were with the intention of keeping Jehovah's pact, which he doubted his cousin had achieved despite what he said. If Father Ferrando obtained a document in his handwriting that proved such a thing, there was no doubt that he would institute proceedings, which the whole district would blame Costura for. He had not threatened his relative in vain. Meanwhile Juli Ramis must have reported the affair by now. Everyone from the Inquisitor to the Viceroy must already know about it. *It won't be because of my testimony . . . And besides the sailor's testified as well.* Perhaps Cap de Trons—it was no coincidence his nickname, Thunderhead, made reference to his insanity, which was widely known—had gone too far in his position as an affronted father and extended his anger to his whole family. But if that was the case, why was everyone in the Street hiding it from him? If Cap de Trons had acted justly, defending his honor, why conceal the consequences of his conduct? No, no doubt his cousin's intentions were those he confessed, even though Costura did not believe in the angel's apparition. Jehovah's angels had better things to do than to come down to earth to talk to a scatterbrain like Cap de Trons. As for him it was clear that the angel's threats were the same he had heard from his cousin so often before, except that this time, while discussing religious matters, Cap de Trons did not refer to the deferment of the debt, as he normally did since being unable to pay him back the fifty Majorcan ounces plus interest. With the money Costura had lent him, he had wanted to buy a consignment of linen for his sons to weave, teaching them the profession he had as a young man before he married and inherited the second-hand clothes business from his father-in-law. But the loan served another, secret, more profitable purpose: to flee from Majorca and for this reason Cap de Trons sent his eldest son to Ferrara, who, under the pretext of buying linen, looked into the possibility of settling there and, seeing it was possible, stayed there for good, forgetting to give his father the money back.

Later, however, they ended up arguing again about the terms of the debt's payment and Costura, more vehemently, encouraged by his cousin's meek attitude, had threatened beyond the shadow of a doubt to take the case before Gabriel Valls, who with impartiality resolved differences and executed justice among the inhabitants of the Street. They hardly ever had recourse to the courts, since these did not recognize their laws. Costura was sure that Gabriel Valls would say he was right, which he clearly was. Cap de Trons had agreed to repay the loan in a period of five years, and that was six years ago and he still had to pay more than a third. Was it his fault that Onofre had not come back? Was he by any chance responsible for his cousin's misfortunes? For his daughter Aina's dishonor or his brother-in-law's dim-wittedness? But it was better not to mention any of this in his testimony, in case Father Ferrando should suspect that his accusations against his cousin were motivated by a desire for revenge, which was not true, or at least was only true in part. As a result of the trouble the Inquisition would cause Cap de Trons, he only stood to lose: in the confiscation of goods, debts were not taken into account.

For this reason Costura, who no longer felt cradled by the unctuous fragrance of incense, but by the rancid smell of frying that filled his house, and no longer considered that he was taking part in any solemn ceremony, wondered whether he shouldn't go and see Gabriel Valls before talking to the Jesuit, because if the Holy Office opened proceedings against his cousin, there was absolutely no doubt that he wouldn't get his money back. But it was also clear, and he knew this because Father Ferrando had directly insinuated it, that the chances of the Viceroy entrusting him with the monstrance for the Clares were directly proportional to the firmness of his Christian convictions, which naturally involved denouncing his cousin. And to carry out this work was his life's burning ambition. Joana would have been so pleased that her husband's hands were the ones entrusted with working the gold and silver inside which our Lord would be exposed to the faithful. What's more, it seemed to him that by kneeling in front of his monstrance, priests and friars and inquisitors and familiars and nobles and citizens and pious ladies and all God's people would not only be making obeisance to the Body of Christ, but also to the intricate receptacle protecting it, which he, a poor silversmith from the Street, had crafted with pride so that the Host might shine in all its splendor. He had prepared the drawing in which he hoped to show the perfect filigree of his future work. The sun's lushest rays converged on a single point like golden arrowheads, as on the Cathedral monstrance, the model all silversmiths had to draw inspiration from. But on his monstrance the arrowhead rays intersected two stars of gold and silver. The Stars of David and of the Three Kings came down from heaven to light up the monstrance as a sign of absolute deference to Christ. On the base he wanted to set some pure diamonds he had bought from a merchant from Antwerp and kept as his greatest treasure, resolved not to use them except on such an occasion. The diamonds, on receiving a thin stream of light, magnified it and sparkled. The monstrance could be his life's work, the work that enabled him to survive after death on earth, since he had no children to turn to in his old age. His obsession with the monstrance made him continually weigh up the chances he had that the Viceroy should choose him for the job and not some other silversmith in the city, and he always reached the conclusion that, with Pere Valls dead, who had crafted the monstrance of St Michael's, only Nicolau Bonnín could rival the quality of his work. But Bonnín had less chances. Although he fulfilled his obligations, he was not considered to be a good Christian as Father Ferrando believed Costura was, especially if the testimony he had to give him the following day convinced him fully.

III

RAFEL CORTÈS, COSTURA, SIGNED HIS TESTIMONY JUST AS the dark of night gave way to the livid gray of morning. Tired out, he did not want to read it and flopped on to the bed in his clothes. He simply loosened his pants and unbuttoned his doublet to rest for a while before the light and, above all, the racket of Polònia in the kitchen prevented him. But he could only close his eyes, because the tiredness and tension accumulated over so many hours disturbed him, rousing him instead of helping him to doze. Not even summoning his most admissible memories could he have sweet dreams and, since it was useless to go in search of them because he wouldn't find them anywhere, he got up, prepared to tackle the day with the rising sun. He washed in the bowl the maid had left for him, shaved his beard, which was beginning to turn white, combed his thinning hair and put on clean clothes. The twice folded sheets of paper caused a bulge in his trouser-pocket and he decided that, although they were protected by his cloak, they were safer against his chest, covered in a new doublet the color of a friar's frock, which Joana had sewn for him. With his cloak over his shoulders and his hat in one hand he took his leave of Polònia, telling her that he was going to Mass and then for a stroll because the day was conducive and, should he happen to bump into someone, he might go down to the shore.

The city streets were empty, though on weekdays at that

hour they were full of people, since with the arrival of the good weather saddlers, hatters, tailors, rope-makers and other artisans came out of their gloomy workshops to work in front of the porch. Not even the beggars who slept out in the open had gotten up early to wait for the faithful on their way to church, with their singsong prayers and wretched responses. Costura hated them and was pleased they weren't there. The distant rattle of a carriage, which must have been passing close to the city wall, abruptly broke the silence of this Sunday morning and some startled pigeons took wing behind the wall of the garden towards which the silversmith was heading. Their small silhouettes were precisely outlined in the sky, under which spread the canopy of a conventual palm. Costura, whenever he passed that way, could not help being reminded of the market's extremely high roof. He envied the building's artifice and aspired, if not to emulate it with the monstrance, at least to be remembered, as he remembered Sagrera, for the merits of his work. Father Ferrando would tell him off if he knew how much he desired to achieve a fame that outlasted him. He had previously warned him that the good Christian should not be swayed by the world's opinion, but by that of heaven, which is reached through the instructions of confessors as well as through privations and sacrifices and not through worldly glory. Despite this, Father Ferrando understood and stimulated his interest in the monstrance, which he should consider only the fruit of his devotion.

Immersed in such thoughts, still drowsy, he walked unhurriedly towards Montision without noticing the few pedestrians he came across. In the silence of the sleepy streets only the church bells had begun to propagate the joy of the day with the din of their bronze. He still had to wait a while before hearing Mass at eight, then, as he had told Polònia, and so far he hadn't lied, he would go for a stroll, just long enough for it to be ten o'clock sharp, the time his confessor expected him. He might show him into the parlor and who knows if he might receive him in the garden, since the day was agreeable. Thinking again about the testimony against his relative, reassuring himself that he wasn't an informer but a good Christian, Costura did not realize that the person approaching was none other than Gabriel Valls, until he stood in front of him. Almost without noticing that the latter was staring at him with his steely, deep blue eyes, so different from the cowardly blue, meek lamb's eyes most of the inhabitants of the Street had, Rafel Cortès doffed his hat, whereas Valls merely tipped his. Both stopped and Costura was the first to greet him and strike up a conversation. A conversation about the weather, the good weather of that first week in June that had nothing to do with last year's, with its raging winds that tore down trees, attacked orchards and damaged walls and roofs, served to take up the first minutes of their meeting. The fact of bumping into Gabriel Valls as he went to fulfill his Christian obligations, far from disturbing him, struck Rafel Cortès as extremely auspicious, because he wanted to see him and did not dare to go to his home. Since that business with Harts, their relations had worsened. Casually he admitted that he wished to consult him about the debts of his cousin, Cap de Trons, who in his opinion was going mad. And it was then that Valls replied that he also would like to talk to him about Cap de Trons and that is why he had been looking for him and it was his maid Polònia dawdling on the doorstep who had given him directions as to where he could find him. "I invite you to lunch," he said without taking his eyes off him, perhaps so that he could better gauge the impression his words had on Costura, "my sons will be there, the Consul, Pons, the merchant Serra, Josep Valleriola and Pere Onofre Aguiló, who's visiting and has interesting stories to tell. You'll enjoy the spread."

Unable to explain that he had an appointment with the confessor, or to think up a convincing excuse to turn down his invitation, in case Valls should suspect something, Costura did not know how to wriggle out of it. He was also afraid that, if he put off the conversation about his cousin's debt to another day, Valls would be less inclined to help. There was no way he could squander this opportunity that fitted him like a glove, even if it made him look bad in front of Father Ferrando, whom he had no way of telling that he would miss the appointment, unless Valls left him alone. To tell him that he had a meeting with the confessor on a Sunday morning would have been foolish, since, if Valls had spoken to Cap de Trons, he could suspect that he planned to turn informer. *I can't refuse the invitation. Father Ferrando trusts me, he's shown it and as soon as I explain what's happened, he'll understand. Besides, this invitation to Valls' place is bound to reveal things I could never have hoped to find out.*

Gabriel Valls had never invited him to his home, even though almost everybody from the Street had been to lunch or tea there. During confession Father Ferrando had sometimes asked him if he had attended these gatherings, where, he had been told by officers of the Inquisition, they were supposed to discuss the law of Moses and receive instruction. Now he could answer him from experience. Everybody knew that Valls Major had bought the land a couple of years before, when business was going well, and hadn't wanted anyone to look after it who wasn't of their lineage and had problems finding a couple to come and be gardeners. The couple he hired, Pep Pomar and Miquela Fuster, came from Porreres. Madò Miquela had green fingers and the flowers she sowed were the envy of all. Her rose bushes gave fleshy roses with buds that suddenly burst with a sweet, intoxicating perfume that filled the air with a welcoming fragrance and, as if it had a medicinal effect on people, seemed to heal rifts and soothe friction. Under the scent of the rose bushes, in the pleasant shade of the vines, Gabriel Valls had the table spread for guests who on holidays, in the good weather, took delight as much in the food as in the garden's sweet mellowness. He not only seated relatives and friends at his table, but also invited other people, travelers passing through Majorca or merchants from outside the Street who had long been considered Christians and with whom he had dealings, a fact that contradicted malicious rumors that only Jewish conclaves were held in the garden.

Costura, as soon as he decided that to make Father Ferrando wait was a lesser evil compared with the benefits he could derive if he accepted the invitation, concluded that chance was on his side. He had heard a lot about these feasts and was very happy to be able to verify with his own eyes whether the famous vegetables really were so fresh as everybody said and the vines gave the delicious shade their master was so proud of.

He heard Mass next to Valls, watching how the latter followed and seemed to do so mechanically, for the sake of appearances, without his face showing the devotion he believed his own to reveal. At the end of the ceremony, so that everybody could see he had gone to church in the company of Valls, he beckoned for him to go first and offered him holy water as inferiors did to their superiors and youngers to their elders. Gabriel Valls was almost twenty years older than Costura and highly thought of in the Street. His reputation as a just man who understood about a lot of things had spread beyond the limits of the district where many new Christians had settled after the mass conversion of 1435, when they abandoned the Jewish Quarter, and on several occasions leading figures had sent for him to propose business or ask for money.

When they came out of the church, they decided to go to the Street before heading to the garden, because Costura wanted to let Polònia know that he wouldn't have lunch at home, and then, their cloaks folded over their arms because the sun began to bother them, they made for St Antony's Gate.

"Your cousin Cap de Trons sent for me to tell me you've threatened to report him to the Inquisition," Valls interjected.

Rafel Cortès blushed. Trying to disguise the anger that coursed through his veins and above all to control his voice, he declared that if he had threatened his cousin, it was so that he would stop pestering him with false apparitions of archangels. But Valls, ignoring the excuses Cortès gave, continued in the same deliberate and forceful tone he had adopted.

"I don't advise you to accuse him. If you report him, you'll never recover the debt, because they'll open proceedings, you can be sure about that . . . The debt's substantial, I know. He's prepared to make an effort and search for at least some of it under the stones. I'll stand surety for the rest. He'll pay it back in a period of three years. I imagine that you find the deal acceptable . . . That you agree . . ."

Before answering, Rafel Cortès, Costura, instinctively placed his hand on his chest, in the exact place he had hidden the document, to make sure that it was still there, protected tightly against his own body, and that the clothes he wore had not turned transparent, allowing Valls to see the accusations written against his cousin.

"I find it acceptable," replied Costura, attempting to conceal the confusion he felt. "We all consider you a man of your word. It's not for nothing everyone respects you," he added, hoping to flatter him. "And I'm very grateful for your help. I had even thought to ask you for it. Cap de Trons is crazy, but he's always listened to you."

"Not always, I'm afraid. I would never have advised him to do what he did. Aside from the harm caused he's put himself in an embarrassing position. Juli Ramis must already have told Canon Amorós by now. Which means we'll have to be more careful than ever . . . Cap de Trons had an attack of madness, I imagine you agree with me. You referred just now to the angel's apparition. The angels have never picked idiots to convey their messages either among Jews or among Christians. You only have to read the Bible . . . Anyway, Cap de Trons is old and he's sick. Let's say the angel is a product of his dotage. The apparition is a lie, that's obvious, nobody would believe it. There's no need to give it importance, but it sets off a chain of events that are very serious. The boys are recovering from their wounds. Aina is outside the city, I saw to that myself. The Bailiff's men want to take a statement from her to see if everything is true they were told by the sailor they arrested, a good Samaritan who was taking her home. I understand from Isabel Fustera that you expressed an interest in him . . ."

Costura deliberately seized the bait Valls offered him, keen to steer the conversation away from Cap de Trons' butchery, the most forceful part of his accusation, which the other seemed to guess at.

"I happened to catch sight of him when he was carrying the wounded Aina in his arms. And I asked Isabel Fustera what she knew, why she refused to help him. Which I found quite unfair."

"She must have had her reasons."

"She told me the foreigner was a friend of Captain Harts and so she wanted nothing to do with him."

Suddenly Costura's words carried Valls back four years, as if he had mounted a magic horse galloping at full speed, to a night at the beginning of June, which he insisted on pushing into the shadiest corner of his mind, because he would never have been able to imagine with what delight he laid into the captain, with greater force than the Consul, much younger than him, and than his son Miquel, who had the strength of an ox. He remembered how they fell on him by surprise, without making a sound and without letting him escape or cry for help. They beat him to a pulp, so much so that when they stopped—

because they didn't want to skin him alive—he was a bloody mess that would have scared away the scarecrows. He remembered that while they were hitting him, while with clenched fists they were striking the body of that man they gave no opportunity to defend himself, he didn't feel fear, or nausea, or even compassion, as he supposed he would, but only rage, an intense, compact rage, not because of what Harts had disseminated, a big-mouth like few others, but because as he hit with rage his fists turned into iron, stronger and more powerful than he could ever have imagined. He remembered how this sensation disturbed him for a long time, because it made him see to what extent he, who considered himself a peaceable man, quite passive and not at all aggressive, harbored a violent instinct and even, like a rabid dog, a hidden taste for blood. Costura also thought about Harts. Harts had sold him diamonds and the last time he came to see him, he wanted to know how much he would give him for a ring engraved with some compromising initials. But he wasn't interested and directed him to Bonnín, and didn't tell Valls or any of his own people to warn them. He only told the confessor.

They were passing in front of the Church of Consolation when they bumped into the chronicler Angelat, his brother Príam, who had just said his first Mass, and the notary Selleres. Only Angelat returned the greeting that Costura had given obsequiously. The newly ordained priest averted his head and the notary gave them a scornful look.

"They only offend themselves!" exclaimed Valls without giving it importance, but loudly so that they could hear. "Virtue makes a man noble, and not his lineage."

"Don't take it like that, today they must be in a bad mood," suggested Costura mollifyingly. "They've always greeted me before."

"Bad times are coming," continued Valls.

"How do you know?"

"I can smell it. Adonai gave us big noses for something . . ."

In the garden, enclosed by walls over which projected only the tallest branches of the oranges, they were welcomed by Valls' wife, Maria Aguiló, and the couple's sons, the elder, Miquel, who happened to be in Majorca, but had settled with the necessary safe-conduct in Alicante, where he had established a second-hand clothes business, and the younger by fifteen years, Rafel Onofre. Costura was taken aback by the natural way in which everybody greeted him as if this casual invitation had been planned long before and he was joyfully expected. Maria Aguiló immediately offered him a glass of fresh water that the maid had just brought from the cistern. He drank it with delight and took shelter from the sun. In the distance he could hear the steady progress of a mule turning a water-wheel. The music of the water was interrupted at intervals by the blows of a hoe used by a laborer to loosen the soil. *They're not ashamed to work on a Sunday,* thought Costura, surprised by the natural way in which Valls' gardeners carried on working when there were guests.

"We're very lucky with the water in this garden," said Maria Aguiló as if she had read his thoughts. "It comes with the old agreement. When it's our turn, we have to make the most of it, even if it's Sunday. The Curia does the same . . ."

Maria Aguiló spoke nasally and shaped her mouth like a hen's bum, perhaps so that the holes left by her fallen teeth wouldn't show. Being a vain woman, despite her forty-something years, she dressed in silk, ignoring the fact it was prohibited, and had rings all over her fingers. With a welcoming gesture of her right hand, a gesture replete with pearls and rubies, she invited Rafel Cortès to sit down on the stone bench where she and her mother, Caterina Bonnín, were seated.

"I think you all know each other," said Gabriel Valls, viewing the guests who had arrived before Costura. "We're all the same here," he added, deliberately addressing Cortès, "except for Pons, the saddler," and he looked at an old man who smiled, revealing gums the color of watermelon, made as if for a joke, "and Jordi Serra. They're both good friends," he remarked kindly.

"Friends, friends . . ." Caterina Bonnín monotonously repeated, as if reciting a litany. No one paid any attention, convinced that she would carry on saying the same thing for a good while, until some other words, also plucked at random from the conversation, made her change her tune. In this unusual way Caterina Bonnín would occasionally take part in her family's conversations. There were times, however, they had to shut her away in the furthest room of the house because she shouted and turned violent, claiming that the witches were after her to carry her off on a leaf after stealing everything.

The sun's sharp light filtered through the vines and fell, tenderly almost, on the faces of the guests. A white linen cloth covered a long table where Marianna, the gardeners' elder daughter, had just put some plates of green and spicy, black olives and two jugs of white wine—wine from the vineyards of Binissalem that belonged to Gabriel Valls, fruit of his brother Pere's inheritance.

"I'll slice some bread," said the girl who was serving, "or there's cake if you prefer. It's made by us," she continued, seeing that no one made up their mind, "prepared by clean hands, it's quite safe."

"With a strong taste of oil, no doubt!" the saddler Pons remarked with a smile.

"Try it," answered the girl, who had noticed the comment, but did not take offence.

The fragrance of the roses blended with the scent of basil, which grew in thick clumps inside the cracked tubs that surrounded the stone benches where they were seated. The green of the seedlings planted everywhere and the gurgle of the water in the ditches merged, as if holy oil trickled idly, slowly, down Costura's forehead, giving him the calm he so needed to be able to discern what he should explain to the confessor about all he had seen and heard, and would yet see and hear, and what he could keep quiet without sinning by omission. He didn't want to leave anything out, but so far only the fact of using the water was reprehensible, though a venial sin, given that, as Maria Aguiló had pointed out, the Curia, the friars and nuns, did the same in their gardens. It was much more serious, for example, that the nuns of St Margaret's kept what did not belong to them by damming up the ditch with bits of old habit . . . At the moment he had nothing to say against these companions who received him in the quiet of the garden to celebrate Sunday among friends. Pons' comment about the lack of lard in the cake was a joke and not to be taken seriously, and if true, affected the gardeners more than Valls. It might be useful to him if there was nothing more important. But he did not want to lapse into last night's misgivings, the minute analysis of any detail that could be of interest to the confessor. And in order to forget his obsession he tried to butt in on the general conversation, but nobody listened, because at that point the Consul and his sons Josep and Mateu arrived, the only guests who were still missing.

Josep Tarongí, called the Consul, which he had been for the English for some years, greeted everybody and embraced Pere Onofre Aguiló, a close friend since long before the latter was granted a safe-conduct to leave Majorca, representing merchants and nobles of the island in the business of exporting oil and importing rolls of linen. The merchant had arrived in Majorca only a couple of hours previously and would depart very soon, entrusted by the authorities with setting up a treaty between the ports of Majorca and Livorno to foment trade between the two cities, since he was highly regarded in that

Republic, where he had a house and where he had left a wife and children.

The Consul's presence was the spring that activated the tongue of Aguiló, who while waiting for him had barely opened his mouth, and he started to relate his adventures and in particular the latest marvels he had witnessed. While sampling the olives, he told them how in the port of Genoa—and he explained exactly where it had taken place—in an oratory dedicated to St Elmo, a preaching friar had, in front of his very eyes, revived a man who only an hour before had been struck down, foaming at the mouth, after he had branded as false the relics that the friar was using to beg for alms, offering consolation to those who needed it. They had never belonged to St Luke, they were bones stolen from some cemetery, the bones of a poor, anonymous person whose grave had been profaned to swindle people of good faith. The friar was recollected in prayer for a long time, asking God to pardon the liar's miserable soul, and then laid the deceased's tibia on the man's head and suddenly revived him. With tears in his eyes the man confessed that everything he had said was untrue and praised God, as did all the parishioners, who filled with coins the saddle-bags of the friar, who did not stop giving thanks to the Lord.

When Pere Onofre finished his story, only the Consul remarked that the friar and the revived man could be partners in the same business, because he'd heard that story before. And it was Gabriel Valls who added that there were many falsifying and lying priests and friars, because there were countless poor in spirit on the earth.

When they started to have lunch, Aguiló's bowl of scalding soup went cold without him touching it. He described how in Marseilles he had met a corsair captain who had a monkey that attended to him much more carefully than the best slave. And this captain, a native of Flanders by the way, had a servant who with a single high-pitched scream, accurate as a well-shot arrow, cracked glass and, as if it were a newly sharpened knife, smashed it and broke it into a thousand pieces. But his powers, acquired at birth due to who knows what strange and unknown causes, went further than breaking glass with his voice, since he could also bend silver cutlery just by concentrating his gaze. Between the starter and the main course he told them how he had met a man whose burning ambition was to fly and who had stored a heap of feathers in his attic with the excuse that they were for making mattresses, so that nobody would suspect his intentions. He had almost completed his project, because having carefully observed the flight of birds, from pigeons to vultures and eagles, and studied the exact proportion of flesh to plumage, he had performed tests to apply a paste to his own body and prepared ties to secure the wings, which he would propel with his arms.

It was the story of the flying man that most interested the gathering and everybody asked questions and sought details. The Consul was well informed, since he knew a book published in London by one Francis Goldwin, which related the exploits of a man from Seville called Domingo González who had reached the moon flying.

"But not in the way your man would like to," said the Consul very seriously, "nor borrowing wings from eagles as some ancients did, but in a large basket linked by means of pulleys to twenty-five trained geese, which shared out the weight and because they were so many, almost didn't notice and could fly easily."

"All that's a fraud, or inspired by the devil," interposed the saddler Pons.

But the Consul ignored him and assured them that he had read it and could even show them the book.

"You won't understand because it's written in English," he added, "but I can translate it if you like."

"Now I get it," Pons again interposed. "You're not so proficient in this language and you've read it wrong."

"And did Domingo make it to the moon?" asked Miquel Valls in fascination, overlooking the saddler's ironic remarks.

"Of course he did, and there he discovered another, marvelous world, a world much better than ours. The Selenites, as the satellite's inhabitants are known, are taller and stronger than we are and better, much better. They never tell lies and their greatest virtue is loyalty. No brother has ever betrayed his brother, no friend his friend . . . When a child is born, they can tell by its appearance if it will be good-natured and practice this virtue, and if they see in it a harmful tendency, they secretly come to Earth and swap it for one of ours, for one of the best of ours . . ."

"You mean to say you believe all this, Consul?" Now it was the merchant Jordi Serra interrupting. "I think old Domingo must have been round the twist and Goldin, Golvin or whatever he was called who swallowed the story and wanted to write it up, stark raving mad."

"I didn't go with them, obviously," replied the Consul, "but nobody would ever have believed Columbus, you know, and he got to the Indies."

"By sea, in caravels, as you'd expect," Serra again insisted. "The air wasn't made for man to go through it. It belongs exclusively to the birds."

"That's not the case," Valleriola's strong voice made itself heard. "I don't know if you know that the prophet Habakkuk was flown through the air from Judea to Babylon by an angel to go and help the prophet Daniel. Angels, demons, witches can fl—"

"Witches, witches," shouted Caterina Bonnín, interrupting him. She had been quiet up until that moment, but this word had suddenly excited her beyond measure and she struggled to rise from the table and leave the meal.

"We won't see it, but the day will come when man, as he controls the sea and the earth, will control the air and there will be ships that cross space. You can believe it," opined Valls.

"And now that you've mentioned travel books, Consul, I once read in an old book," said Aguiló, "the story of a rooster that reached heaven and there discovered the mysteries of the creation of nature. It knew about the lighting of the stars and the change of the moon and the cause of earthquakes and storms, but kept it secret."

"What are you talking about," resumed the Consul, "the rooster's travels, that has to be a joke! I suppose you believe what Sopete says, that when animals had the power of speech, there were eagles that reached heaven and not only eagles, but camels as well and even beetles."

They were already eating quiddany when Costura, his eyes on stalks, ventured to ask Pere Onofre more details about the man who wanted to fly, if he could say his name and where he lived.

"His name, no, I cannot. He's not from Majorca, but if what you want is to escape, I suggest you apply for a safe-conduct and go by sea, which is the safest way I know to get off Majorca."

"I don't mean it for me," Cortès quickly added, feeling uncomfortable. "I have no need to travel. I mean it out of curiosity, my friend, that's all."

"I know you do," Pere Onofre cut him short uneasily, perhaps because with all these remarks he saw no way to continue telling his stories. "Talking of the sea," he immediately added, in order not to be interrupted, "talking of the sea, did you know that in Holland some sages are working out how many sponges are needed to soak it up and make it recede a bit?"

"They'd do better to use suckers or pumps," proposed the Consul, "they'd make more progress."

"If they have to invent something, why not invent a machine for soaking up bad thoughts?" intimated Valls.

"And another," Pere Onofre resumed, "for reproducing our words with perfect accuracy . . ."

"A machine," continued Valls, "that recorded everything without missing a thing, without altering a single word. That way we'd always be sure of what we did or didn't say. It would help a lot in front of the courts." And he deliberately eyed Costura, who, however, did not notice, because he was having seconds of quiddany and greedily devouring the last mouthful, concentrating on its exquisite taste.

The afternoon was just drawing to a close, its light swallowed up among clouds, when Costura left the garden in the company of Pons. In silence, because the saddler was a man of few words, they entered the city by St Antony's Gate and quickly reached the Quarter, where they took their leave. After that Costura turned round three or four times to see if anyone was following him, because he had decided, instead of going straight home, to head for Montision in case there were still time for Father Ferrando to receive him. He would simply apologize and explain the reason for his absence that morning, but he wouldn't hand him the document. What he had heard over lunch, especially the story of the flying man, struck him as sufficiently interesting to be included, but he would tone down the accusations against his cousin, since he couldn't take them out altogether, as Valls had advised him, because of his arrangement with the confessor. He decided not to walk past his house, however, because he suddenly thought he saw the figure of Pere Onofre behind him and to see if it was him he waited almost at his doorstep. Aguiló greeted him warmly, but turned down the invitation to come in that Costura gave with the key in his hand.

"I suppose we'll still have time to see each other. When was it you said you were leaving?"

"The day after tomorrow."

He knew about it, reflected Costura after taking his leave. *With the excuse that he always returns, he gets safe-conducts easily and quickly. And they say his business is going well. At least he seems rich and fat and has traveled a lot. He's seen the world. It's quite possible he could take off with false wings like the man he talked about. Who knows if it isn't him . . .* Costura informed Polònia that he was so full he wouldn't have dinner and shut himself in his room. He didn't even pace the terrace that night. Being so tired, he decided to go to bed soon to see if the accumulated lack of sleep helped him and he finally managed to rest. He undressed carefully, because he was wearing his Sunday best, and put on his nightshirt. As he folded his clothes, the document he had carried all day like a scapular against his chest fell at his feet. He put it under his pillow. He placed a candle on the bed-head, lay down, retrieved the document and began to read:

Jesus, Mary and Joseph,

At my confessor's request I, Rafel Cortès, nicknamed Costura, begin to write this document on the night of the first Saturday in June, in the year of our Lord 1687, to unburden my soul, may God keep it.

Last Thursday my cousin Rafel Cortès, nicknamed Cap de Trons, sent for me at home to explain how the angel St Raphael had appeared to him to tell him he had to warn me about not observing the Old Law. And to tell him he had to circumcise his sons. I found out he circumcised said sons on the same night his daughter Aina was seen wounded in a sailor's arms, as your reverence is aware. So I told Cap de Trons to stop pestering me and not to threaten me, because I was Catholic, Apostolic and Roman and would never believe in the law of Moses again, and that's why I don't keep Saturday, but Sunday, and eat pork and don't care two hoots if the fish has scales or not. And that's what Cap de Trons and I talked about last Thursday in his shop, without any witnesses. May the grace of our Lord be with me and the Blessed Virgin Mother of God have pity on me.

Signed,
Rafel Cortès, Costura
Seventh of June, 1687.

Now, however, after that Sunday spent in the garden and above all after Valls' offer to stand surety for the debt, and Cap de Trons' promise to pay back some of the money very soon, he wasn't sure how much the report made sense. In fact, if proceedings were opened against his cousin, as Valls had made clear, he'd never get the money back, because Cap de Trons' goods would be confiscated at once. No, there was no way he could make reference to the circumcision. He needed to moderate the accusations against Cap de Trons by all possible means. But perhaps if he acted like this, Father Ferrando would consider him guilty for covering up, and not only would the monstrance be at risk, but also his property and possibly even his life. He had no option but to give up the money and follow his Christian conscience, which, as the confessor had reminded him so often, obliged him to act in accordance with the interests of the Church, which did not want to persecute Jews, but to teach a lesson to those bad Christians who, having accepted baptism, turned to heresy by renouncing the grace of Christ.

There has to be a way, prayed Costura, *there has to be a way, Lord, for your justice to show itself without my having to turn informer. What if Father Ferrando, who understands the workings of the Holy Office very well and is perfectly familiar with its ins and outs, could persuade the court to return the money owed by my cousin in exchange for this document?*

He hadn't discussed the question of the money with the confessor in case the confessor concluded that he was motivated by a desire for revenge. Now he would tell him everything. Cap de Trons had only ever been a nuisance throughout his life. Besides, he was old and the proceedings would take some time . . . *I won't gain anything by not accusing him,* thought Costura again, becoming more convinced, *however much Valls asks me not to and invites me to his garden and subjects me to stories of flying men.*

Of that Sunday in the garden, of those relaxing hours and the good food on offer, Costura was only prepared to say that they used the water, that the saddler had cracked a joke about the cake not tasting of lard, something he hadn't noticed, and that Pere Onofre knew a man not from Majorca who was making himself some wings. Exhausted by so much uncertainty, still holding the document, he closed his eyes and fell asleep. He woke up at midnight, in a sweat and terrified because he had just dreamed that some big men, tall as giants, had surreptitiously swapped him for a child sleeping in a cradle, when the wet-nurse wasn't watching, who was too young to make sure no intruder came up to the child and replaced it. Upset by such a strange dream, Costura got up and checked in the mirror, afraid that the dream had been real and that night somebody from the moon had been swapped for the person he believed himself to be.

IV

GABRIEL VALLS BID FAREWELL TO THE LAST GUESTS AND entered the grove of oranges, seeking the cool of evening, accompanied only by the Consul. The Consul was the first to speak once they had found a suitable corner to sit in, under the thickest fruit trees, where it was difficult for them to be overheard. He told him he had been biting his tongue all day to avoid asking him how it was he had invited Costura, whom he would never have expected to come across in this place. But given that he knew him, he imagined there had to be a reason that escaped his notice. It was not for nothing that he also considered him the spiritual head of the Majorcan Jews and called him Rabbi, as the others did in private. That is why he had kept his mouth shut, seeing the deference with which Costura was treated. Gabriel Valls smiled at his friend's misgivings and did not interrupt him. Only when he openly asked him, "Have you converted him, Rabbi? Will he become one of us again? Will he return to the Old Law?" did Valls decide, with the promise that he wouldn't tell anyone, to explain that Costura had threatened to report Cap de Trons to the courts and he had gone looking for him to find out how far his mad cousin was telling the truth. He told him that he had invited Costura to the garden for two reasons: first, to gain his trust, so that he didn't feel completely rejected, and second, to show him that the best known people of the Street devoted their Sundays to the same pleasures as people from outside the Street. So Costura had been able with his own eyes to confirm that in the garden, at least on Sundays, there were no Jewish meetings, as some clergy suspected. The presence among them of the saddler Pons and the merchant Serra was telling, as he himself had tried to make him see before the Consul arrived. Of course he didn't like Costura. For him, believing as he did that men proved themselves above all in their loyalty to their lineage, to the age-old, shared traditions, Cortès was a wretch. That's why he had been deeply grateful to the Consul for his references to the Selenites, which Costura had surely noticed like a serpent's venomous bite, despite not paying attention. Valls admired in the Consul his ability to make a suitable reference at the right time and envied his knowledge of so many things, almost always drawn from books that he could read in different languages. That said, he disliked his intrusive nature and the way he used to scrutinize everything.

For a while after Valls had explained his reasons for inviting Costura, the Consul didn't stop speaking, inveighing against the silversmith with details that Valls knew inside out, insisting on his piousness, his priestly way of rubbing his hands or his hermitic air of compunction when he was praying. The rabbi barely listened and endeavored to interrupt him, to question him on the matter for which he had asked him to stay a little longer alone with him. At the same time he was afraid of what he might hear and waited for the Consul to broach the subject. He knew that without fail the conversation would disturb him, tickling him with old sensations. Because, in spite of his years, when he remembered Blanca Maria Pires, a strange weakness still seemed to slacken his limbs and take control of his whole body, softening his bones to the marrow, as if all his insides were being macerated and, steeped in aqueous humor, would end up turning to liquid. For Valls, who even as a young man had never allowed himself to be carried along by such sensations and had refused with all his strength to be taken in by images that could arouse his lust, the realization how far the memory of Blanca touched him was completely unacceptable. Endeavoring to control himself and taking advantage of a pause in the Consul's attack on Costura, he abruptly asked him if he had been able to talk to the sailor.

"Yes, this morning I managed to persuade the Warder to let me in. I felt sorry for him. He's a poor Portuguese boy by the name of João Peres who's come from Antwerp. He thinks he'll rot in prison for the rest of his days. You've no idea how many times he thanked me when I told him that his captain had asked me, as Consul for the English, to do all I can to free him. Tomorrow or the day after tomorrow a small galley will set sail for Livorno and if everything goes according to plan, I shall convince Giacomo Tadeschi . . . do you remember him?"

"Consul, all this is very well and confirms you as a just man, but what I want to know is what he told you about Harts and above all what he told the Bailiff."

"It's the first thing I asked him, Rabbi, the first," he repeated vehemently, "what he knew about Harts and if he had sent him. He told me he met Harts in Antwerp, who described how on his last visit to Majorca he had enjoyed the favors of a lady whose beauty coincided with that of a lady he had been able to contemplate many times in dreams and for that reason, owing to the coincidence, and convinced that he would have better luck than Harts, he had come to Majorca. But Harts never told him the lady's name and he couldn't ascertain it, and this is what he confessed to the Bailiff. I assured him that the captain must have deceived him, that here, in the city, there is no lady like the one he described and that I've heard a pile of such stories from sailors about seductive, cruel ladies who send their servants to solicit the presence of strangers to enjoy their favors."

"He must be an innocent boy, if he's telling the truth!"

"I think he is. He was greatly disappointed when I denied the lady's existence. He had hoped to do better than Harts . . ."

"Blasted Harts! Shameless cur! We should have flayed him."

"Rabbi, you know what I think about what happened. Harts was not entirely to blame. I'm not sure what we did was right, the lady . . ."

"Consul, I won't permit you . . . Maybe I can't make you change your opinion, but I can at least shut you up. Blanca Maria Pires risked part of her fortune and her good name to help us. She deserves our gratitude and respect."

The presence of a laborer coming to find the Consul and accompany him to St Antony's Gate, which was due to close very soon, ensured they didn't become embroiled in an already old argument. Valls bid farewell to his friend and again entered the orchard to walk for a while by the seed-beds, to listen to the night just beginning and gaze at the stars alone. He did this as often as he could before saying his evening prayers. But the stars, which in the June sky seemed brighter and closer than in other months, did not calm him; on the contrary they sharpened his unease because on a night like this in early summer for the first time he had spoken to Blanca Maria Pires long enough to realize that this woman was not like any other he had known, and not just because she had violet-colored eyes and the thickest, hardest rays of the midday sun in August had sheltered in her corn tresses, but because her courage and valor also set her apart. He had seen her several times before the night he had to bear sad tidings, because her husband and he were in business together, but he had never noticed anything other than her beauty and pleasant mien. But that night, when unfortunately he had to ask the servants to open and beg to be received, he was able to witness her fortitude and intelligence. She guessed before he told her that the news concerning her husband was painful, but only when he returned the wedding ring inscribed with her name did she burst into tears. But she didn't cry out or tear her hair as women he knew had done, nor did she summon her maids. She wept for a long time, without groans or sighs. Overcome by grief, she seemed to forget that Valls was seated next to her and that his arms held her for a moment when he thought she was going to faint from the shock. It was then her hair brushed against him and he smelled jasmine and feminine warmth, and the mixture of smells was engraved on his memory and, whenever he remembered Blanca Maria Pires, he was assaulted by that perfume that was the perfume of Judith's hair, even if the Bible made no mention of jasmine. Jasmine anywhere would always take him back to the tresses of the widow of his former partner Andreu Sampol, whose interests he watched over even more carefully than his own, since he had asked him to.

At such times, as whenever he was tempted to recall the past, Gabriel Valls repented and thought what would be a fair punishment to mortify his flesh, which, old and withered, still seemed ready to blossom if a little sap nourished its roots. He realized, however, that he was unfair to his body because the waves of desire it experienced came from another, more hidden, much less controllable place, from a faculty of the soul, memory, he didn't know how to mortify to force it to consign to oblivion everything it showed him so precisely. Because often past, disquieting images would suddenly put in an appearance, although he had not the slightest intention of going in search of them, at the most inopportune moments, when he thought he was concentrating on his prayers to Adonai, when he was closing a business deal or trying to teach his sons the law of Moses. These memories mortified him because they made him feel weaker and much more sinful than he had ever considered himself, since he believed that lust belonged to unworthy men, men who were closer to animals, and it humiliated him to recognize this in himself. At the same time he tried to exercise his will and by dint of will overcome the impulses of his own memory. Intellect watched while the two powers maintained a single combat, which will almost always won, prevailing over the battered memories. Will afforded him the opportunity to esteem Blanca as a friend's widow, as a sister with whom he could share not only loyalty to the departed, but also a lot of common interests, which ended up being more spiritual than temporal. They had spiritual conversations about the soul and Paradise, and even about love, which they often discussed, love of souls, it was Blanca who said it, free of physical ties, pure love that through its purity led by the secret ladder to heaven. Souls, she insisted, are neither male nor female. No doubt souls are equal and under the same obligation to become perfect. It is the fact of inhabiting a separate body that can seem to make them different. He found all this daring, even dangerous, and so preferred to steer the conversation towards more familiar terrain or at least to touch on areas where his convictions were absolutely secure, such as his trust in the coming of the Messiah, which he had reason to believe was very close.

"Explain this to me, Rabbi, because if I ever saw it, I'd be the happiest woman on earth." And her eyes shone even more.

Then he would start by quoting the prophet Daniel when he says that the final redemption will only begin when the people of Israel are all in the diaspora, and refer to a text from Deuteronomy that spoke of the dispersion being universal, from one end of the earth to the other. And as he had been able to find out, and he even had written proof, a traveler of theirs, a Marrano, Aaron Levi Montesinos, Antonio de Montesinos other people called him, in 1642 near Quito, Ecuador, had come across some natives belonging to the lost tribes of Reuben and Levi . . . In England, at the world's end, the Jews began to enjoy certain rights. Cromwell welcomed back exiles who had gone to

Holland . . . If in England the Jews could freely practice their cults, something the Consul thought more than likely, the dispersion would very soon be complete and the Messiah's liberation imminent. With the arrival of the Messiah, their hardships would be over for good.

"The Messiah will gather the Jews from the four corners of the world and return them to the promised land, and the temple of Solomon will be rebuilt. The Messiah will give us a new heart, without wickedness . . ."

At such moments, however, he was forced to admit, as the Consul had informed him, that the settlement of a Jewish community in England had been tolerated, not authorized. And this was not the same, which meant it was still some time before the desire for the Messiah's coming ceased to be a stubborn hope. But he, Gabriel Valls, known as Rabbi, Gabriel Valls de Valls Major, son of Miquel Valls, merchant, grandson of Gabriel Valls, of the same profession, great-grandson of Miquel Valls, surgeon, great-great-grandson of Gabriel Valls, physician, also called Absalom, descendant of Jafuda Cresques the cartographer, did not want to question such hopes, since neither had his father, his grandfather or his grandfather's grandfather questioned them, convinced as they were that keeping the Old Law in times of humiliation and shame, in times of so much misery and disaster, times of wolves, hard times, times of ignominy, times of serpents, was only in times of waiting, times of trial that Jehovah the Almighty, God of heaven and earth, sent them. He didn't deny it, like Costura, who renounced the law of his ancestors, nor did he question it like Miquel Miró or the Valleriola cousins; he knew, because he carried it engraved in his own heart, written on his own skin, stamped in his soul, that this was the only path to salvation. That the Christians, who trusted in that heap of images filling their churches and lit candles to them and gave them alms and made relics from their remains and garments, were just a bunch of idolaters who were mistaken, immolating sacrifices, offering hymns and praise to the golden calf instead of worshipping the true God. He was fortunate enough to have been born a Jew, like her, like Blanca Pires, and like Blanca, who thanks to his intervention had returned to the straight way, he wanted to die a Jew. And he felt proud of his origins, which were older and nobler than those of all the city merchants who by their money had obtained coats of arms and by their profits from privateering could maintain the nobility they themselves had invented, false descendants of the Catalan conquerors who arrived in Majorca when the Jews were already settled there and had good houses and good property and good professions with which they earned an honest living and kept open a splendid synagogue. For this reason, if anybody owned this land, this dear island, a small paradise risen by a miracle from the blue of the waves, this closed kingdom like the Ark of the Covenant, this promised land, the only promised land possible, as his father declared in the lowest moments, it was them, the Jews, and also those called Bennàsser, Arrom, Alomar, Aimerich, Maimó, even though everybody he knew with such lineages looked at him like a madman, sent him packing and obliged him to shut up when he dared to tell them they could feel proud to descend from Moors, from real Moors, from honest people and not pirates, not from those who almost always coming from Algiers, with their razzias terrorize coastal villages, bloodying and burning everything they find, respecting only the lives of those they plan to sell as slaves. Not from these Moors, but from the Moors who were lords of this land, lords who lorded it over this land, who allowed them to live and practice their religion in peace for so many years. But he won't ever dare to imply this to somebody by the name of Bennàsser or Arrom again, however good a friend he might be, however much he respects him and believes that by sharing this with him he will bring them even closer together, by referring to a common past much more glorious than the times in which they happen to live.

Llorenç Bennàsser is fourteen years old like him, they've known each other since they were children, since Gabriel Valls taught him to hit geckos with a stone and gave him the weapon the other boys so envied him: his sling. But Bennàsser didn't understand him. "Me a Moor?" he said and tried to shove him without managing to move him, because he's shorter and weaker and has thin bones like a girl's. "Take it back, animal, shithead. I suppose you think I've something to do with you, Jew, with the nails you used to crucify Good Jesus! Jew, you're just a Jew!" And Valls pushes him off and even tells him not to take it badly, he didn't mean to offend him, he's the one who's insulting him, who's offending him. But Bennàsser doesn't take any notice and, shouting and sobbing, moves away and suddenly turns and spits at him that one day he'll force him to show him the tail his father says all Jews have, a tail hanging from their bum, a demon's tail . . . Valls is chased by a gang of boys, Bennàsser's neighbors, through St Antony's Gate on a Thursday there's market. He tramples vegetables, dodging earthenware pots, plates and bowls, scaring hens and turkeys, rebuked by the vendors who, despite the uproar, think it's just a reckless game, children mucking about. He tries to squeeze through to Butseria Street and make it home in a flash, and take refuge in the furthest room, behind his father's shadow, under his mother's skirts if need be. He's afraid. Very afraid. But he doesn't fear a beating. He fears humiliation above all, that they might lower his pants and take them and not give them back and like this, with his bum in the air, he might have to go home and receive a dog's thrashing from his father. He already knows the sharp strokes of his belt, which he certainly doesn't want to get used to. He runs like mad, pursued not only by enemy legs, but also now by the shouts of "Jew! Let's see your tail!" The farmers join in, no longer thinking it's a reckless game, but some of their lads wanting to lay into an adversary, and to the gang's voices is added their laughter, the remark of a fat voice, of a thin, piping voice, of a master's voice, a servant's voice, a mistress' voice. And now six or seven voices as well as the pursuers' hunt him down: "Come on, lads, get him!" But he carries on running, he runs with all his soul, like a soul the devil's taking. He can't confront them. It's five against one. "Jew, Jew boy, show us your tail!" They're about to fall on him, they're only twenty paces away, maybe fifteen, they're already on top of him. They struggle to remove his clothes, they rip them off, tearing them to shreds. They bare one thigh, his buttock, his bum. "No, no, leave me alone. That's enough!" He's had enough. He doesn't want to see himself on the ground, kicking, punching, spitting out phlegm and curses. He pushes back the images of himself as a teenager, humiliated almost in front of his home, pushes back Llorenç Bennàsser's greasy hand about to touch his penis. No, he doesn't want to see them again. Not because of pity or piety. He's never had a lot for himself. But because of revulsion, the infinite nausea they cause him. That's why he drops them into the darkest well, puts them in the most secret hiding place. They hurt him, fill him with a confused feeling in which hatred and revenge merge in a dreary magma. His law protects him. Adonai does not condemn him. An eye for an eye, a tooth for a tooth. Repayment in kind. With the exact same rigor. Now it's Llorenç Bennàsser who's running with his baggy pants down in the direction of Nova Square and Gabriel Valls who's chasing him with a stick, a stick to thrust right in his shit-hole to make him understand how scoundrels can acquire tails. "Kids' stuff," says the Assistant Bailiff, almost without giving it importance, because on the previous night much more serious events took place in the city than a tussle between boys, even if one of them is from the Street. The Assistant Bailiff, half asleep, still has all the bells of all the city churches ringing inside his frame. All the bells sounding the alarm, echoing the bell of the nuns of St Magdalene's, which roused the city after midnight with the din of its bronze. Gabriel Valls, who was still awake, heard how it was answered by Figuera in the city and the Cathedral Eloi, then, almost in his ear, by St Eulalia and then St James, St Nicholas, Holy Cross . . . "What's going on, what's going on?" asks his poor mother, pacing up and down the house in her nightdress, shaken by the uproar that has jarred her awake. "It's the French fleet attacking us," says his father, "but I can't hear any cannons." They soon find out that the disturbance was caused by the Count of Ayamans trying to abduct his wife, who sought refuge in St Magdalene's Convent when he abandoned her to go to Court, ignoring her pleas. And while the count takes flight and hides, and the Bailiff's men remove the ladders used by the group of bandits accompanying Ayamans in the assault, Gabriel Valls thinks that tomorrow, or rather today, because it's almost three o'clock in the morning, will be a good time to go after Bennàsser, because even if he reports him to the authorities, the Bailiff will be too busy to pay attention.

No, nor does he like himself now, with the stick in his hand, chasing the terrified Bennàsser, who almost didn't put up any resistance, because he's a coward and he's all alone. He made him kneel at his feet and follow the orders he gave him while he whimpers and complains, but does not dare to disobey him. It was Llorenç Bennàsser himself who lowered his pants and proffered his bottom to Gabriel Valls' stick. With rage and loathing Valls sank it in between his buttocks till blood spurted out. Then he made him run in the direction of St Nicholas', where his father has a cellar open, and saw him enter, covering his bum with his hands. No, no, he repels these images even more forcefully than the others, even though he acted justly. He gave him the punishment he deserved and did so alone and without help.

His father didn't tell him off, but he feels false, uncomfortable, dissatisfied. And from a distance of so many years he continues to observe Bennàsser's frightened eyes looking at him, the humble eyes of that lamb who did everything he commanded, those eyes in which he thought he saw the flicker of a dark pleasure, of a hidden desire. As adults, when they met, they pretended not to know each other, but Gabriel Valls noticed that Bennàsser watched him out of the corner of his eye as soon as he moved away. One morning the city woke up to the news that the bachelor wine merchant of St Nicholas' had been stabbed to death. The perpetrator, who immediately confessed, was a Moorish slave from Can Torrella, who killed him to protect himself against his acts of sodomy. The excuse was to no avail. They hanged him and his head was displayed on a spike of the prison as a lesson to wrongdoers.

He didn't know why in the quiet of the garden, under this June sky, he was suddenly assailed by these turbulent images, nor how he had gone from the upsetting, but always pleasurable memories of Blanca Pires to those of his youth, those of his first confrontations, of his first troubles on account of his condition and lineage. Throughout his life he had been forced to learn not to be accepted, to consider himself different. And he was different, and proud of it because, like the other Majorcan Jews who had arrived after the diaspora, he descended from those Israelites to whom Adonai, their sovereign Lord, sent manna as nourishment. Feeding them with nectar and ambrosia directly from heaven, he granted them a much brighter intelligence than other mortals. But this, and Gabriel Valls always emphasized this to his followers, was not through their own merits, but because Adonai had the immense generosity to choose them as his people. They ate manna in the wilderness, manna sent by God, to whom they had to be grateful, even in shameful times like these, in which God seemed sometimes not to hear them, as if he were distracted. Not many years before, some of them had suffered prison, their goods had been confiscated, but when they came out of the Dark House they had started anew and by their efforts had recovered, whereas anyone from outside the Street would only have been able to live off alms or crawl into a corner to die. They, God's people, Elohim's people, by his grace would again escape from the captivity in which they lived, as they escaped from captivity in Babylon. There was always someone in their lineage ready to lead the others who needed guidance. And suddenly he remembered Esther and he remembered Judith, the Widow Sampol's favorite examples. Her queens. And again he was confronted by the lady's face, framed by the thick hair that gave off the heady aroma of jasmine. He instinctively searched for the stars. The silver-skinned animals of heaven sparkled, high for fear of seeing themselves in the sea, as his friend Sampol used to say when from the bow he watched how the captain steered the ship. From his journeys, from his travels all around Europe, Valls derived a taste for freedom and improvisation, which on returning to Majorca he lost. But those journeys were more than thirty years ago. Things were different then. He could easily have stayed in Ferrara, protected by the descendants of the Mendes, or even have settled in Bordeaux, but he knew that he would be unable to stand the empty hours at the end of the day, the dark hours without his own people, and that he would die of melancholy without seeing his parents, who were too old to leave the island. Some time later, when his parents passed away, his only concern was to go, to go where he could freely bear witness to his religion and not have to hide, pretending to be Christian to the outside world, forced to live two lives, forced to lie. But it became impossible to leave. Safe-conducts were no longer available to abandon the kingdom and settle in Europe. Pere Onofre's safe-conduct was a gift, a stroke of luck he owed to his partner Pere Desbrull, who needed him to come and go freely. But aside from him, nobody else had obtained one. Everybody was forbidden to leave, to escape from the mousetrap, to abandon the lair. They wanted to keep a close eye on them, to make sure they didn't go back to being Jews. That was the excuse, they wanted their money, that's what they wanted, to get it with impunity, to steal the fruits of their labor.

"In Livorno," Pere Onofre had told him, "everybody is rich. I don't have a large fortune, but I can keep a carriage." Here no Jew can have one. They aren't allowed any luxuries. Not even silk. In Livorno Aguiló drives to the doors of the synagogue in a carriage. "You don't have to hide from anyone. That's real living," he reiterated. "We should find a way for you and the Consul . . ." But Gabriel Valls thinks that more should benefit from the escape. Everybody who needs to at least . . . There's no place like Livorno. That's where Blanca Maria Pires lives. From there he's received presents and greetings through common acquaintances and friends, but no written word, no handwritten note he would have learned by heart before tearing it and consigning it, on a night like this, to the tall, mute stars.

V

Father Ferrando received Costura quickly and took his leave quickly. He almost didn't allow him to explain the reasons that made him miss the appointment and he almost didn't pay attention to the details Rafel Cortès gave him about the meeting in the garden. Contrary to what the silversmith expected, he didn't extol his behavior or tell him that the Lord God would reward him for helping to stop the harm his enemies were doing the only true religion, nor did he mention the monstrance, as he had done on the previous Saturday.

While Costura left in disappointment, slowly, not knowing which way to go, because he thought that interview would last a lot longer than a few minutes, Father Ferrando swiftly perused the document Rafel Cortès had just given him and put it back in the pocket of his cassock, next to the breviary he always carried with him. He hurried towards the second floor, towards Father Amengual's cell, where, as on every Monday, at exactly four in the afternoon, a conversation began in which the two of them took part, together with the chronicler Angelat, the Judge of Goods Confiscated by the Holy Office and the Viceroy's nephew. He wanted without witnesses to inform Father Amengual, his nearest rival for the position of rector of Montision Convent, that as of this moment he had a guarantee that was bound to win the support of their superiors. By means of "the power of his word inflamed with love for the Redeemer," as he put it, he had persuaded Rafel Cortès, Costura, to sign a document reporting his cousin Rafel Cortès, Cap de Trons, to the Inquisition, which made it possible to initiate proceedings and prove that none of those reconciled ten years earlier had remained faithful to the Catholic religion, but they had relapsed. And given that he would be handing over the document immediately, he had come to ask him to withdraw his application for the position of rector. Father Amengual did not answer. Standing at the window, he watched the signal tower and a broad patch of sea. It was five years since he had been assigned, or rather sidelined, to the city of Majorca, after a brilliant career begun in Valencia and ended in Manresa, where, without knowing the reason, he had fallen out with his superiors.

At this very window Father Amengual had often wondered why at the moments in his life when he was about to achieve a post, a prebend or a promotion, without anybody's help, purely through his own merits, said post, prebend or promotion vanished from before his eyes as if by magic and was awarded to an undeserving upstart who by chance or by mistake was in the place where only he should have been. And it seemed this was going to happen to him again. Now, after five years of doing exactly what his superiors told him, of writing lives of saints on behalf of the convent's benefactors or memoirs and reports by order of the provincial Father-General, now that everything seemed to have been arranged and pointed to him, Father Ferrando had turned up and wanted him to surrender what was his by right . . . This time, however, he was not prepared to give way. He would appeal to the Father-General if need be; he would move heaven and earth. What's more, this time he could offset all his hard work over five years against any recommendation Father Ferrando might come up with. His merits were obvious and he had tangible proof that could be found right there on his desk. Scattered about were almost all his papers, the result of his late nights, of his private research and inquisition and also of corrections and emendations, so that his work was not only a song of praise to God and an example for sinners, drawn from the holy life of the Venerable Sister Eleonor Canals, but also a set of stylistic rules that in such books he considered extremely useful to fulfill the Horatian precept of *prodesse et delectare. And this is something that scoundrel Father Ferrando has to recognize, even if he is a brute and of less than average intelligence. Really, what work has he written that can be offset against mine? The man can barely string a sentence together! Read, fool, read my manuscript while I pretend not to realize, as if I were admiring the view, rooted to the spot in front of the window . . .*

This most exemplary nun's virtues were so many and so sound that they made up the living image of perfection of such an irreproachable life that seemingly owed nothing to a daughter of Adam. When she was only a few months old, she would refuse her wet-nurse's breast on fast-days, and her first words were: "I want to be a nun."

"I see you're already correcting the Venerable's life. That means you'll be publishing it soon, Father Amengual . . ." remarked Father Ferrando unashamedly.

"I believe so, and I hope my own writings will serve as guarantee. I do not, unlike your fatherhood, Father Ferrando, rely on what other people write."

Father Ferrando remained silent as if he had received the blow and, before responding to that shot that had hit him full on, sought a better position. Unlike Father Amengual, Father Ferrando had not been born on the island. He hailed from Valencia, but had lived in the city for more than twenty years and was extremely well known, not only because he confessed many people, especially from the Segell district, but also because he wielded influence and had done so even more in the past, when the former Viceroy took him as spiritual director. If he aspired to the office of rector, it wasn't like Father Amengual to make swift progress to another, more important place and get on in his career, but because his brother, almost eight years younger than he was, had been rector of Zaragoza Convent for three years and, although he would soon turn forty-five, Father Ferrando had never managed to be anything other than a reputed confessor.

"I suppose, Father Amengual, that today you'll delight us, as you promised, by reading the opening paragraphs of the book. Has the Viceroy's wife seen the manuscript? I suppose everything you've attributed to the sanctity of Sister Eleonor has been carefully checked . . . I say it for your own good. At times like these the slightest error can be dangerous. And that bit about fasting from such an early age . . ."

"I was told this by the wet-nurse's daughter, who's still alive. She's a good woman, a peasant from Algaida, of very pure blood, really. Why should she lie?"

"I'm not saying she's lying. I'm only saying that simple, rustic people like this young woman will believe anything. For example, that pigs might fly."

"I don't know if they'd believe that pigs might fly, but stranger things are happening right now. I've no doubt, Father Ferrando, there are pigs that talk."

"And others that kick and squeal as well."

He was clever this time, thought Amengual. *He deserved it. What was he thinking? Pigs indeed!* reflected Ferrando. The two fell silent as if waiting for the other to attack first. They might have stayed like this for a long time had they not heard the sound of chatter coming from the corridor. The voices belonged to the chronicler Angelat and to the Viceroy's nephew, Captain Sebastià Palou, who was responsible for supervising repairs to the bulwark of St Peter's and, contrary to what some might think, admiring his well-set frame, more in keeping with a man of action, was *letter-sick*, though not so much as the chronicler.

Father Amengual went out to meet them, attempting to disguise the nervous state Father Ferrando had put him in. On the contrary, he summoned the most appealing gesture he could find and, tugging his forelock and rubbing his hands, showed them into his cell, where a lay brother had recently arranged the five chairs the collocutors would occupy. Father Salvador Ferrando, not to be outdone by Father Vicent Amengual and to prove to him that he was not only at his level, but even higher, received the guests with an almost beatific smile.

"Both Father Amengual and I, or rather most of all I, who am much more ignorant than Father Amengual, are deeply indebted to you, gentlemen. Your lordships enlighten us, most of all me, every Monday with your wisdom. Thanks to your lordships we often know how the affairs of this world are going . . ."

"Father Ferrando," interposed the chronicler, who was a sarcastic man, "please do not exaggerate. I do not think the Jesuits are enclosed nuns."

"I didn't mean that, Mister Angelat, no," Ferrando immediately clarified, above all because he noticed his rival looking daggers at him, "but it's very different to live in the world than to be withdrawn, like Father Amengual and I, in the peace of this convent, far removed from external matters."

Father Amengual did not reply, but invited his guests to sit down and, when they were seated in their easy chairs, asked the porter who had accompanied them and was awaiting orders to let in the Judge of Goods Confiscated by the Holy Office as soon as he arrived and to tell the lay brother Jaume to bring up the iced cakes the Clares sent him every Monday and he was kind enough to offer his collocutors.

The chronicler Angelat, who sometimes burst out laughing for no apparent reason with the same sound a plate makes when it smashes on the floor, was delighted as almost always at the mere mention of the Clares' cakes—"the city's finest," he said—so exquisite that he had referred to them in the *History of Majorca* he was about to complete in Spanish and that would, it seemed, be his masterpiece. *The island of Majorca,* so it began, *is more beautiful than all those that rise from the waters of the Mediterranean. The variety of its lands, the height of its mountains that almost jostle with the clouds and the extent of its plains, together with its forests and irrigated lands, make it a microcosm in which divine providence generously opened its hand . . .*

This incipit, read at the gathering not long before, had been highly praised by everybody, in particular by the Viceroy's nephew, who had already found the rhymes for the ten-line poem that would head his friend's book, together with poems by other local talents, including the Reverend Father Amengual, who had also tried his hand because he liked to do things in good time.

Sebastià Palou envied Bartomeu Angelat his ease with the pen, which he lacked, despite his stubborn appeals to the Muses. Not a single verse had come to him without effort. *The dry teat of the milked breast,* he once wrote with reference to the suffering he endured drawing on his own inspiration. The words he chose rotted in his hands, he spent so long toying with them to no effect. And his poetic labor always gave pale, vigorless, almost deformed creatures, fruit that to be complete needed a lengthy gestation, that of a she-ass more than a woman, and full, therefore, of kicks, jolts and shudders. And it's not that Sebastià Palou was stupid or more stupid than the chronicler Angelat, the most important local writer, author also of two comedies and two volumes of poetry—one of which had been very well received at Court and praised by the greatest poets, such as Calderón, who had honored him with his friendship for some time—but simply that God had not called him to the path of letters. His uncle, the Viceroy, had warned him not to torment himself with hateful comparisons to the chronicler. And although for some time he had laughed at his nephew's tendency to sit in on priestly conversations, the only ones in the city where poetry was discussed, and had urged him to take his military career more seriously, where no doubt a better future awaited him, now it suited him really rather well that Sebastià should remain faithful to his obsession and continue to have dealings with such people. His nephew often rejoined that it was possible to be both courteous and brave and that if Garcilaso de la Vega, whom he considered a distant relation and could therefore claim as an ancestor in terms of family, poetry and military, had managed to be both things at once, taking now the sword, now the pen, he didn't see why he couldn't do the same. "Stop piddling about, nephew," asserted his uncle, "and watch out, all that about the pen reeks of pettifoggers, judges and priests and, if you press me, the odd bluestocking, but has nothing to do with real men like you and me. If you need verses to send to a lady, borrow them like everybody else. They don't care, and the results can be even better with second-hand verses . . ."

Sebastià Palou rose with the chronicler Angelat and the two Jesuits as soon as the Judge of Goods entered the cell, followed by the lay brother with the tea tray, which he placed on the desk. Father Amengual made room for him, removing the pages given over to the life of the Venerable Sister Eleonor Canals, which he wanted this afternoon to subject to the analysis of his collocutors, whom he also wanted to ask for some opening verses, although books of devotion didn't need them.

The Judge of Goods, the Very Reverend Canon of the Cathedral, Jaume Llabrés, had highly developed taste buds, like the chronicler Angelat, so much so that his mouth seemed to protrude in a kind of double chin. The other guests had sometimes remarked that what interested both men most about these gatherings were the iced cakes, especially if, as this afternoon, they were accompanied by biscuits and jujube jam that only virgin hands, hands consecrated to God, like those of the Clares, could make.

The Judge of Goods greeted everybody, breathless from the effort of having to shift almost twenty stone to climb the stairs, especially at a time other mortals, which for him meant the members of the Curia, devoted to the siesta, out of habit more than the need to rest from any effort. The canon came from home, but before that had been in the Cathedral and that same day had lunched at the Palace. For that reason he could give them lots of news, first-hand news, always highly prized, fresh from the mouth of his Most Reverend Eminence, the Lord Bishop of Majorca.

"Really, what good things does the Lord Bishop have to tell us?" the host immediately asked while handing round the iced cakes and biscuits to his guests.

"Well, first and foremost, that he too, like the Lord Inquisitor, has received a ticking-off from the Holy Tribunal of Aragon."

"Really?" Father Ferrando exclaimed with great interest, without realizing he was aping his enemy.

"Really," the Judge repeated in a mocking tone. "For a couple of weeks now it's been complaining to the Tribunal of Majorca that we turned a blind eye, reconciling so many Jews, that we're not being zealous enough in protecting the Holy Catholic, Apostolic and Roman Faith, that we're lacking in enthusiasm. As your lordships can imagine, the Lord Bishop and most of all the Lord Inquisitor are not best pleased about all this."

"His Most Reverend Eminence does well to express concern," interjected Father Ferrando as soon as he could swallow the piece of cake that prevented him from talking, "but not all of us on this island are asleep, dear Judge. For my part and with all humility, of course, because for some time now I've been confessing people from the Street, I've been trying to tease out of them to what extent they're fervent Catholics or have gone back to being Jews. Now your lordships know that I'm confessor to Costura and by the way, Master Sebastianet," he added, addressing the captain who was spreading a generous spoonful of jujube jam on his biscuit, "perhaps you could remind your uncle, the Lord Viceroy, about the monstrance he's supposed to be ordering . . . Anyway, as I was saying, gentlemen, I've managed to get out of Costura, whom I believe to be a good Christian, let it be said, everything he knows after all the disturbance last week. And Costura has given me a document that I would like you, Lord Judge of Goods, to be the first to see, before you hand it to his reverence the Inquisitor-General from me."

Canon Jaume Llabrés with sticky hands took the document Father Ferrando had just pulled out of the right pocket of his cassock, folded into four. He did not read it and as best he could, so as not to dirty it, he held it with his fingertips and put it away. It seemed to him rude to unfold it in front of everybody to see what it said. That would have been to reveal something that should have remained a secret. It was enough that the Jesuit, to create a good impression before the others, should have given the name of his informer. He never would have thought that in such a delicate matter as this Father Ferrando could be so indiscreet. *I'm missing something here,* suspected the Judge, wondering how he could lay hands on the last cake without the chronicler, who also had his eyes on it, noticing. But while he made up his mind, Angelat was quicker, snatched the prey and gobbled it down almost without chewing, as if he feared the Judge might claim at least a part. Irritated as much or more because he hadn't gotten to that sugary delight in time as by Father Ferrando's inopportunity, the Reverend Don Jaume

Llabrés simply declared that the document would reach its destination the very next day.

"Of course," continued Father Ferrando, who seemed not to have realized that the Judge did not like this errand, "should the Lord Inquisitor wish to see me, I am at his service, needless to say."

"Your zeal has amazed us all, Father Ferrando," Father Amengual now intervened, too obviously sarcastic for everyone not to notice.

"Well, I saw Costura on Sunday, around ten o'clock," said the chronicler Angelat, whose mouth was no longer full and whose appetite was not satiated, since he sprinkled the others with a glut of saliva, "he was walking along very happily with Gabriel Valls, I suppose they were going to a garden party . . ."

"They must have filled the air with their stink," added the Judge of Goods, laughing.

"The stink is not from them. I mean they don't make it. It's the stink of frying, of reheated oil, from not using fat," declared the chronicler, looking at Sebastià Palou, who nodded his head.

Like the other guests, though not so much as Angelat and Llabrés, Sebastià Palou had tucked into the tea. But however greatly he appreciated the sweets that the Clares' virginal hands had made, he was much more inclined to picture those divine extremities—*melted snow if not glass,* he had written in his best poem, devoted to other themes. Despite this, the Viceroy's nephew felt full and, like the others, prepared to while away the time in conversation.

Father Amengual decided he should take the initiative at once and stop Father Ferrando reasserting himself and so, having carefully wiped his face in case the tiniest amount of sugar tempted him to lick his lips, something he thought very ill-mannered, he stood up to take the manuscript and read the paragraphs he was most pleased with to his friends.

"As I understand it," said Father Ferrando as soon as he saw that his rival was gathering the papers, "the Venerable Eleonor Canals is related to his excellency the Viceroy, isn't that so, Don Sebastià?"

"She's my aunt's aunt, Father Ferrando. She and I are not directly related, if that's what you mean. I don't have the makings of a saint," he added with a smirk.

"I've seen greener fruit ripen, Don Sebastià," said Father Amengual. "Really your lordship can't be saying you've the makings of a demon, that's something we wouldn't believe. Now if you'll allow me . . ."

The chronicler Angelat tried to discern whether the ship almost on the horizon, at the back of the cell's window, disappearing in the last blue, was a xebec or a galley as Father Amengual began to read:

> *This most serene pearl and highly precious daisy, enclosed in the shell or religious cloister, took shape with the heavenly dew that God the Father Almighty directly gave her. Her zeal was so strong that to obey the novice-sister with greater haste she jumped out of a window to reach the courtyard more quickly without hurting herself at all, although it was a distance of more than fifteen feet, something the Mother Superior considered most miraculous, believing the heavenly angels must have helped her . . .*

"It's lucky she fell on her feet," remarked Don Sebastià sarcastically, "because had she fallen on her head, she wouldn't have lived to tell the story . . ."

They laughed and no one rebuked him. There were some things the Viceroy's nephew could get away with.

Other times she was called, she obeyed so readily that were she speaking, she would interrupt her word, her task and even her foot-

steps . . . As for the other virtues, she practiced them all, especially those to do with mortifying the senses. So for her food to have the worst possible taste, she would mix in pieces of bitter oranges and wormwood . . .

"I couldn't do it," interjected the chronicler, exchanging knowing looks with Sebastià Palou.

I don't think my uncle would like such sniffling acts of humility at all, reflected the captain. *My aunt, who knows? She's so devout! She's already commissioned a painting of her Venerable relative. She'll see they make her a saint. Meanwhile if as she said I have to go with her to Rome . . . With the excuse of Rome and being in Italy . . . Livorno . . . Pere Onofre says she leads a secluded life, hardly ever goes out . . . Love has no doubts what he should call the color, / Blanca is the dawn, Blanca the aurora.* It had not been easy to write these verses and he would send them to her today.

At the age of fifteen, after taking the veil, she decided she would not take her eyes off the ground unless it was to gaze at her Sacramental Husband. Her humility was so great she was heard to say she felt sorry that the nuns loved her and wished nobody would remember her or value her, because she considered herself to be the vilest, basest creature in the world. "I should like to be less than worthless and for all creatures to despise me. How it hurts me to see everybody loves me so! I should like to be despised and forgotten as my Husband is despised and forgotten by souls . . ."

"We should take lessons from Sister Eleonor!" said the Judge of Goods, who couldn't bear to listen to any more of the Venerable's life that Father Amengual read at times in the haughty voice he used for preaching sermons and with the most theatrical intonation he could find and at others, identifying himself with his biographical subject, conjuring up a voice like a ventriloquist, thinking it was Sister Eleonor's voice he copied. For this reason everybody had to suppress their laughter when in the mellifluous tones of a nun in choir he read out, *I should like to be less than worthless and for all creatures to despise me . . .*

"I think your reverence has done a wonderful job," remarked the chronicler Angelat. "I suppose you've considered publishing it in Latin. I advise you to do so. My *History of Majorca* will also see the light in this noblest of languages, which all the others should imitate. Have you never written verses in Latin, Sebastià?"

"No, to tell the truth, I haven't . . ."

"Well, I recommend you try. I'm sure you'd find they're not so difficult. Your admired Garcilaso, your relative, I mean, if I'm not mistaken, wrote some. If I had to choose between the Latin classics and all the others, I'd choose the former. There's no comparison. Don't your lordships agree?"

"Yes, really, I do," said Father Amengual. "They are on Olympus."

"That depends," barked Father Ferrando, who had been quiet for a while as if lying in wait. "Compared with profane authors in the vernacular, obviously, but not with the Bible. I value a word inspired by God more than all Virgil's *Eclogues* put together."

"The Bible's something else, my good man. Don't be so finicky," countered the chronicler.

"He does well to be so, he does well," said the Judge of Goods, who was getting bored. Besides, Monday was the day this gathering stopped him taking a siesta. He would end up not coming. That said, there were the cakes . . . "At such times the bull can catch us when we least expect it."

"Are you calling the Holy Tribunal a bull?" asked Father Ferrando in horror.

"I didn't say such a thing, Father Ferrando, it's you who imagine it."

"And is the Holy Tribunal planning to look again at old cases," asked the Viceroy's nephew, "or to open new proceedings? I mean, will they use old investigations or start anew?"

"I do not know," replied the Judge forcefully. "We've a meeting tomorrow. We're awaiting orders from our superiors. Of course the Viceroy will be kept informed."

"I didn't mean that, canon. For the love of God! I was thinking about the wretches whose goods were confiscated. If they're taken again, they'll die of hunger."

"You seem very concerned about the Street people, Don Sebastià," said the Judge of Goods. "You're like your uncle," he dared to imply, "who's defended them whenever he can."

"When they deserve it," answered Angelat, "the Viceroy has acted justly."

Sebastià Palou said nothing so as not to complicate matters. Everybody in the city knew that the Viceroy, the Most Excellent Lord Marquis of Boradilla del Monte, like many members of the nobility, had prosperous, if underhand, business dealings thanks to privateering, which he shared with some of the leading figures in the Street.

"Allow me, gentlemen," insisted Father Amengual, "to read you the final paragraph, so that your lordships can tell me the weaknesses in my book that need correcting. Really, if afterwards you wish to . . ."

"Don't worry, Father Amengual, don't worry. We'll tell you the good bits as well," remarked Angelat, who seemed to know him well.

"If there are any," he replied with delicate humility he seemed to have caught from the cloister flower he was working on. "If you don't mind listening, I'll read the final part . . . *On her death God showed his great affection, giving lively expression and singular proof on her corpse of how much her soul and spirit pleased him, for in life she was not beautiful or fair to look upon, but in death her body received a singular luster, a beautiful glow and the radiance of having been the precious mount for the rich diamond of her most perfect soul.*"

"Does that mean my aunt's aunt was ugly?" asked Sebastià Palou. "Oh, Father Amengual, she won't like that! Couldn't you pass over that point?"

"Don Sebastià," said Angelat in a fatherly fashion, "if she was ugly, Father Amengual cannot make her pretty, even if she was a saint. The first thing a historian has to do is to be faithful to the truth. Lies are meant for you poets . . . We are obliged to relate what happened, without adding or taking away. And though I have written verses, as you know, I'm speaking to you as a chronicler . . ."

"Well, chronicler, I think that Father Amengual has added and taken away to his heart's content, anything to please my poor aunt, a great benefactor of this and other convents, like her sister . . ."

"Not at all," retorted Amengual with displeasure. "I carried out research before writing. I've sheets full of statements. Really, I asked inside and outside the convent, you can be sure. And what do you think, Judge of Goods?"

"I think, Father Amengual, that you have written the wonderful life of a saint in the appropriate style, so that devout souls like hers, devout and simple souls, can understand it. Given the audience you are addressing, I think you have managed perfectly to keep decorum. Now that is not to say that your pen can't glow more deservedly on a more sublime theme, a more, how can I put it? . . . a broader, more breath . . ."

"Thank you, thank you very much, reverence. Your fatherhood understands me. Of course I have every interest in finding a theme that is also religious, naturally, deserving of the ardent zeal of my pen, ever at the ready for God . . ."

Ever at the ready for God, he repeated in his mind, content with this last phrase that had come out perfectly. Really, as soon as they left, he would jot it down. No doubt he would find it useful to write or pop in his next sermon.

"Should your lordships like a little fresh water," suggested Amengual, "I think the lay brother is coming."

Some light knocks at the door, asking permission, preceded the same lay brother who had brought the tea tray.

"Thank you, Brother Nicholas. You may take the plates. A glass of water, gentlemen? If you wouldn't mind . . ."

"Of course, Father Amengual, but I didn't come to clear away, though I'll do it to avoid wasting the journey. I came because, Father Ferrando, there's a gentléman downstairs who would like to see you, he says it's urgent, a matter of life or death. He pleaded with me so that I had no choice but to come up. I don't know what's wrong with him, but it must be serious. Very serious given the state he's in."

"Who is it?"

"The same gentleman you took your leave of only an hour ago. I believe his nickname is Costura . . ."

"Judge, give him back the document," whispered Father Amengual. "The thing is he's repented and come looking for it. You'll have to persuade him better, Father Ferrando." And he tittered. "Your guarantee's not worth much."

Father Ferrando was furious. Red as a beetroot, he did not reply. Without saying anything, without even apologizing for interrupting the conversation, he quickly left the cell, hoisting his cassock so as not to trip on its skirts, which always seemed to get in the way when he was nervous. He descended the stairs two by two, resolved to confront Costura. There was no way he planned to give him back the document, even if he swore that the accusations were false. Besides, why make a fuss now? He came across Costura in a corner of the porter's lodge. He was in quite a state, whimpering and sobbing, unable to speak.

"Come now, my good man, what's the matter? Could you kindly tell me? I had, I have, a very important meeting with eminent people, which I have been forced to leave. Tell me what's up."

"Cap de Trons, my cousin . . ."

"What about him? What's wrong with Cap de Trons?"

"Cap de Trons is dying, Father Ferrando." And he burst out groaning.

"How do you know?"

"I've just been told. It's absolutely certain. Before going to see him I've come at once to ask you to administer the viaticum. It's all I can do for him. Oh, Rafelet, Rafelet, you'll go to hell. I can't let him be damned, Father Ferrando!"

"What bad luck!" exclaimed the Jesuit aloud, giving away his thoughts. If Cap de Trons died before proceedings were opened, his apostolic zeal would have unforeseeable consequences. The Inquisitor did not like trials against the dead.

"My testimony is useless, Father Ferrando, there's nothing I can do now for his soul," moaned Costura, weeping and sobbing.

"That's not true, intentions are what count."

"Can you come with me, Father Ferrando, and help him to die well?"

"You'll have to inform the parish office, Rafel, the vicar might take it badly. You should go right away."

Standing in the doorway connecting the lodge and the courtyard he had just crossed, he waited for Costura to compose himself so that he could go out into the street, while he thought that now he needed his help more than ever. He needed Costura to give him proof, any proof, that served the Inquisition's noble cause and also, of course, his own. And when the silversmith finished blowing his nose and mopping up the final tears, Father Ferrando leaned over and whispered in his ear:

"By the way, Costura, I know that now is not the time, you're not in conditions, but Don Sebastià, the Viceroy's nephew, has informed me he thinks the monstrance will almost certainly be for you . . ."

Costura looked at him, transfixed with gratitude. His hands

wet with snot and tears, he took Father Ferrando's hand, still a little sugary, and kissed it with unction a couple of times before Father Ferrando, despite his nausea, could avoid it. Rafel Cortès noticed a sweet taste on his lips and thought it was the taste of sanctity.

VI

COSTURA RAN LIKE MAD TO THE PARISH OFFICE OF ST Eulalia's, but his zeal to arrive first so that Cap de Trons could receive the sacraments was in vain, since they told him in the parish office that somebody had come before him. Cortès' middle son had just informed the vicar, who was putting on an alb to leave. Standing next to the door he waited for him to come out, preceded by the acolyte ringing the bell, and followed just behind him, calmer, praying softly. He accompanied the viaticum into his cousin's house and climbed to his bedroom. Death was already brooding in the body of Cap de Trons, who at times stirred and threw off the covers in a weak attempt to rise from bed. His bleary eyes must have confused shapes, because he failed to recognize the priest and possibly this is why he did not receive him rudely. Nor did he protest when the priest prepared to confess him and asked everyone to leave.

Outside that dark room, behind the door, trying to listen to everything his father might say if he suddenly regained consciousness, Josep Joaquim Cortès de Cap de Trons kept vigil. The others had gone to the kitchen, where water boiled in a large pot, ready for when it was needed. The vicar, used to dealing with the dying, immediately realized that Cap de Trons' condition was very serious and he would barely come to. Seeing there was no hope of extracting a confession, he left the room to inform the family he would give him extreme unction and to administer this sacrament he required everyone to be present. Cap de Trons stirred uneasily while the priest anointed his limbs with holy oils. With a waxen face projecting a hooked nose, the dying man took his leave of life, gasping like a fish. He was clearly lacking air and suffering, because between death-rattles he emitted deep groans and clasped his ribs. As soon as the priest finished the ceremony, Costura went up to ask him if he thought that extreme unction could work the miracle of reviving him, as had happened before, but the vicar, although he believed in miracles, was of the opinion that the hours of Cap de Trons' life were numbered and the water simmering on the stove would soon be used to wash his corpse. Costura left behind the priest as he came, though he did offer himself to the children should they need him for anything and told them he would return. In the street, not knowing what to do, unable to shut himself up at home and certain that if he went to see Father Ferrando again, he would not be welcome, he took the road leading to St Antony's Gate in order to walk for a while outside the walls.

It was scarcely an hour since Father Amengual had bid farewell to his guests from the lodge, accompanied by Father Ferrando, who was weighed down since Costura gave him the news he had to impart to the others. As he had foreseen, the Judge of Goods pulled a long face because he didn't like complicated posthumous trials either, let alone all the business of unearthing the remains and consigning them to the flames. Father Amengual, however, was delighted and looked extremely smug. He predicted that instead of thanking Father Ferrando for his good work by recommending him for the position of rector to his powerful friend the provincial Father-General, the Inquisitor would fly into a rage as usual and even order Father Ferrando to retract Costura's testimony.

When they were alone, Father Amengual could not help expressing his opinion, because he knew how much this tormented his rival, but he had to let it go, because Father Ferrando very delicately insinuated he had reason to believe there was some doubt about Father Amengual's relatives, which, if the Inquisition was really becoming more zealous, as the Judge of Goods had declared, could prove highly suspicious.

Captain Sebastià Palou accompanied the canon as far as the Palace. There he left him to crown the afternoon next to his Most Reverend Eminence, the Lord Bishop, tasting some other mystic sweet. He then quickened his pace towards the Almudaina, trying not to stop to talk to any of the acquaintances he greeted, doffing his hat or waiting for the other to take the initiative, according to the respect he thought they were due. When he arrived, he asked first for his aunt, who, as every afternoon, was engaged in conversation with the city's noblest ladies. Being bored, they had no option but to pass the time with as little effort as possible, amusing themselves with gossip and hearsay. During this period they were particularly interested in the arrangements being made for the beatification, at long last, of the Marquise's aunt, the holy nun Eleonor Canals.

"There's only one thing I regret," he heard the Marquise say in her canary voice, before the servant announced him, "that my aunt wasn't my mother."

"My dear Onofrina, that would be impossible!" exclaimed the High Judge's wife. "She wouldn't have been a virgin . . . wasn't the saint a virgin?" she asked with feigned innocence that made Sebastià laugh.

"Had the Lord our God wished, she could have been a virgin and a mother, like the Virgin Mary," declared Lady Onofrina with a smile that was meant to be naive. "You know how devoted I am to the Virgin Mary. I believe firmly in her Immaculate Conception. St Anne, Good Jesus' lady grandmother, was also a virgin. This kind of motherhood must be a delight, a real gift of the Lord." And she sighed in relief, almost as if she had just given birth.

"Children are a constant headache, Onofrina," remarked the Countess of Bellumars, who had five unmarriageable daughters. "If God did not want to give you any, you can be satisfied."

"But Joanet . . . I'm his godmother . . . I love him like a son . . ."

The room in which the Viceroy's wife received her guests had a stuccoed ceiling and the whitewashed walls were covered in paintings. The last ones had been hung less than two years previously—she remembered it well. A thundering Zeus with the Viceroy's features, everyone could see the resemblance, a real honor for the Lord Marquis, and a Danae pleasurably receiving the shower of gold, in which the Marquise's poorly molded features also seemed to have been copied. Rumor had it that the opulent figure hiding her abundant flesh behind some rather thin veils was just like her. The painter, a Venetian the Viceroy himself had sent for from that Republic, it was claimed, had portrayed both the Marquise's face and her body, the measurements of which he had taken inch by inch. For a long time the memory of Maestro Chiapini filled the Marquise's empty hours. In Gaetano's company, in his conversation, she found an important incentive for her life as the bored wife of a husband who went far from home in search of a little amusement that she had never known how to give him. The painter not only let her speak, but also seemed to listen to her gladly.

The year and a half he lived in the house, working on a couple of paintings as well as some frescos in the Throne Room, was the happiest time for the Marquise, who was about to turn forty and for the first time felt solicited with the wit and consideration she had always thought she deserved, but nobody had ever been able to show towards her. Chiapini did his best, however, not to have to supplant the Marquis in his marital duties. It was not worth his while risking his position for an ugly old woman he didn't like. Besides, what he needed was not to squander his energy, but to save it. The Marquise's chambermaid displayed an enthusiasm for him he was hard pushed to satiate. So he tried to satisfy the lady only in the art of conversation and to disguise his lack of interest with the most exquisite courtesy. She accepted this. Thinking the painter refrained from entering her bedroom to avoid compromising her, she imagined him lying awake, torn between the desire to possess her and the need not to affront her honor, because above all, as he had insisted so many times, he considered her the most exalted woman on earth, upright, faithful and very pure. *Un angelo di Paradiso.* Only when the chambermaid was forced to confess that she was expecting and that the father of the creature making her womb grow with such provocative stubbornness was Maestro Gaetano, did she suspect that everything he had told her, repeated and re-repeated, and she had listened to with the same delicious expectation as in the beginning, as if each time were new, unsuspected and different, was just a big sham. But once again, when he knelt at her feet, kissing now her hands with a passion that made her tremble, then burying his tear-stained face in her skirt, asking forgiveness and declaring that, yes, he had possessed Inès, but while this was going on, his body, his desire, all of him, possessed the woman who filled his mind, his *angelo*, she believed him and forgave him. Gaetano was fortunate that the painting of Danae was missing only the finishing touches, because the Marquise's long abstinence, together with the affection that his words had gradually brought about, provoked in her such an overwhelming passion that he was quickly exhausted. He hastened his departure, forging a letter in which his chief patron, the Doge of Venice, sent for him urgently. When they took their leave, early one morning, in the secret of her bedroom, with a furious and jealous Inès keeping watch, Lady Onofrina swore to devote her whole life to God, spurning men's love for ever. And he, trusting in her generosity, asked her to protect the child about to be born, the child he would have liked to sow in her womb and that all the same, spiritually, belonged to her.

Joanet, the chambermaid's son, who was the spitting image of his father, and the cause of beatification of her Venerable relative, whose painting she had already commissioned, were her only obsessions, after she got over her desire to leave the Viceroy and enter a convent, something the Viceroy, though he didn't really mind losing sight of her, was not prepared to accept.

Sebastià Palou kissed his aunt's hand and courteously greeted the other ladies, who welcomed him with open arms, wishing to hear about something that wasn't the boy's charms or Sister Eleonor's miracles. The captain declined to sit down. He remained standing next to the High Judge's daughter, a sickly girl he courted from time to time to avoid disappointing his uncle, who advised the match. She blushed when he bowed so politely that the tip of his sword touched the ground. "Your disdain is killing me, Lizzie dear . . ." he then remarked, in private, recalling a sonnet he had sent her some time previously, which everyone in her home had read, expecting other, more compromising notes to follow. Poor Lluïsa Orlandis, however hard she thought about it, never understood what disdain Sebastià Palou had in mind, because she had always endeavored to be very open with him.

"Don't let me interrupt your conversation, ladies," said Palou with a smile that was intended to be pleasant, "fear not, I shan't stay long."

"Oh, Sebastianet!" cried the mother-in-law-in-waiting, closing the fan she thought she handled graciously. "What things you come out with! Can't you see we want you to stay for a while?"

"Your ladyship is right, a while, just enough time to inform my aunt that Father Amengual has already finished the life of her ancestor."

"Praised be the Lord!" exclaimed the Marquise with delight. "Why didn't he notify me immediately? I'll send for him right away . . ."

"He hasn't had time to make a copy yet, aunt. I suppose that's why. He can't have finished it more than twenty-four hours ago. This very afternoon at our gathering he read us the main paragraphs. Ladies . . ."

"Oh, how I should like to go to Rome!" sighed the Marquise with feeling.

"And how I should like to go with your ladyship. That would mean she gets put on altars, aunt. Ladies," he said again with a bow, "I do not wish to be a nuisance, now that I have had the pleasure of greeting your ladyships."

He made a long, slow bow and left the room with the same air of a martial cock he had come in with. Sebastià Palou was more interested in seeing the Viceroy than in chatting with these gloomy ladies, who held no interest for him, even if they included Lluïsa Orlandis, whom one day—as late as possible, if he had anything to do with it—he would have to marry. So he left at once and having passed through six more rooms furnished with austere luxury in the Majorcan fashion, preceded by the servant, who opened the doors, he entered the Palace library, where the Viceroy used to withdraw, he said to work, but everybody knew it was to be left in peace and not to be disturbed with banalities.

"Welcome, nephew," said the Viceroy, a little surprised to see him at this time. "Is anything up?"

"That depends, uncle. I've just come from our gathering and have two pieces of news that could be important, one for my aunt and the other, you know, for your lordship."

"Well? What did you talk about today?"

"About the Venerable, first of all, but I've already told aunt about this. Then about the Inquisition. The Judge of Goods said they've received orders to open proceedings and it looks serious. At the same time, in front of everybody, Father Ferrando handed over a written testimony against someone from the Street and told us who the informer was."

"And who's the sneak?"

"Rafel Cortès, the silversmith."

"Costura?"

"The very same. Which reminds me, Father Ferrando again asked me to recommend him for the monstrance you said you would pay for . . ."

"Rome does not pay traitors, nephew, certainly not at the moment. Father Ferrando's gone mad. Is there no way of knowing who the wretch is accusing?"

"I think there is, that it all has to do with Cap de Trons, but Cap de Trons is dying, as I understand . . ."

"I'll send for Gabriel Valls and we'll get to the bottom of this. Is there anything else, Sebastià?"

"No, nothing. Angelat defended you against Llabrés, who thinks you look out for the Jews too much . . ."

"Fool! I look out for myself, or rather for my wife. I'm poor, doesn't he realize that?"

The Viceroy reached for a bell and tinkled it noisily. A servant appeared at once, making bows.

"Send Toni to fetch Gabriel Valls. And tell him to come immediately. Tell him it's urgent."

The servant retreated with his bum to the door and before leaving the room bowed as devotedly as if it were the Host and not the Viceroy in front of him.

"I have to go, uncle. Pere Onofre Aguiló's off tomorrow, and I've a couple of orders for him."

"Silk? Spices? Tobacco? You won't get anything in exchange for verses. You should see about getting married, nephew, and stop messing around. Livorno's too far and besides you won't get anything out of her . . . She's cold and more stand-offish than a princess. She's not right for you. Come again one of these days and I'll show you something you'll like . . ."

It was some time since Sebastià Palou had left the library, where the Viceroy was seated in the same position his nephew had found him in: he held a document in his hand that his secretary had asked him to sign urgently, but when he tried to focus on what it said, he could only read a few words: "We order that wheat be taxed at the rate of eleven . . ." He immediately became distracted as he evoked the voluptuous delights he had enjoyed the previous night from those two slave-girls, perfectly trained in an Alexandrian harem, the gift of a corsair captain who was especially grateful for his kind favors. Until the day before, his excellency, used first to the skinny body of his first wife, who went to dine with Christ only a year after their wedding, and then to the robust and unattractive body of Lady Onofrina, and in between whiles to the uninteresting bodies of his lovers, had not discovered that one of the greatest pleasures life had kept back was the contemplation of naked beauty, embodied in the youthful shapes of those creatures, who had meekly, without shame and yet with delicate modesty, undressed in front of him and while baring an increasingly large amount of flesh before his delirious eyes, while dropping the veils that covered them, danced softly, as Salome must have danced in front of the Tetrarch, confident in spite of their tender years—thirteen or fourteen—that they exercised over the years that contemplated them the same fascination as a snake-charmer exercises over his prey. After the dance, when they were only wearing the bracelets on their ankles, impossible to take off without breaking, since they had put them on when they were small, they bowed invitingly before the Viceroy, ready to indulge his every wish. But Antonio Nepomuceno Sotomayor y Ampuero only asked them to dress again so that they could undress and repeat every single gesture exactly as they had done the first time. Knowing that he was lord over those bodies in his own right, he was in no hurry to possess them. What's more, he was prepared to let a few of his closest friends enjoy this pleasure, so long as his wife, who had shown absolutely no interest in the arrival of the girls, didn't find out. If she realized, the news would reach the Curia, which, highly satisfied at having caught him out, was capable of causing a real scandal, something that would damage the Viceroy.

Life had not been unkind to him and perhaps this is why he didn't expect much more from it. God had not wanted to give him children from his two marriages, but he had two healthy, strong bastards doing well at Court under the protection of the Most Serene Queen Mother, with whom he had always maintained very good relations, especially since the King died. He was in Madrid at the time and managed to get her Majesty, Lady Mariana, to accept his condolences in the form of the gift of a health-giving stone, a stone set among diamonds that the Queen had done him the honor of wearing. Not just that: in an audience while she was regent of the kingdom, she told him that from the moment her finger had been made prisoner of that ring, the headache that always plagued her had abated considerably. The Queen protected him, that much was clear, and proof of this was the viceroyalty, of such interest to him after he married his Majorcan relative. He intended to use the office to increase the profits of his wife, whose affairs he managed, not because he was a venal man—anymore than others—and wanted to sell favors or influence, but so that he could keep a much closer eye on corsair activity, an extremely important source of income for the Marquise of Llubí, who as heiress continued in the same maritime business that enriched her father. His father-in-law, like much of the island's nobility, was involved in corsair activity under the cover of his Jewish partners, who saw to their own interests. But if things turned ugly, he would have to switch alliances, even though Valls was completely reliable, and the sooner he knew this, the better. Except for the days after his arrival, when some old rivals, out of envy, nothing else, were rude enough not to stop their carriages when they found him out walking on the quayside, the rest of his term had passed without incidents, perhaps because from the start he had exercised his authority and, following advice in an audience, had banished to the Castle and Fortress those nobles who had behaved badly and locked up in the Angel Tower a couple of coachmen the nobles blamed for being absent-minded.

The news brought by his nephew—the best spy he could ever have wished for, and also a friend, a son almost—which at another time would have worried him considerably, forcing him to think long and hard about a possible line of attack, or at least of defense, did not, however, prevent him recalling the softness of those sweet shapes . . . *I shall wait for Valls to arrive,* he said to himself. *What's the use of anticipating events?*

Costura wandered without knowing what to do along the tracks that led from St Antony's Gate out of town. He was dressed in the solemn clothes of formal visits and his figure attracted the attention of the farmers entering and leaving the city on foot, astride mules or seated on carts. Costura seemed to come from nowhere and be going nowhere. He walked mechanically and dreamily down the middle. He only halted or stood aside when he was about to bump into somebody or heard the sound of cart-wheels or hooves too close. He didn't even protest about the splashes of urine from a mule that stained his pants everywhere and provoked first the laughter and insults of some lads watching what was going on, and then a shower of stones he could barely avoid. One stone hit him full on the leg, and Costura tried with difficulty to move away. He didn't dare to head back to the city, since that was the road his assailants had taken, but limped in the direction of Valls' garden, the only place he knew nearby where he could seek help. He asked for the master as soon as he passed through the gate, but a laborer told him they hadn't seen him all day. The gardener was there, however, and the master's younger son would soon arrive. The laborer wasn't too concerned about Rafel Cortès' excited state or his appearance, and did not ask him if he was limping as a result of the wound that with a trickle of blood was soaking his pants. Costura hobbled along, noticing the pain ever more acutely, and sat down on a stone bench. Resting for a while in the shade of the vines, he felt comforted. *The place must have health-giving properties,* he said to himself and breathed in, gulping down the air as if that balmy air could heal the wounds that plagued his soul. Cap de Trons was dying. He clearly was not going to pay the debt. Only Gabriel Valls, who had stood surety, could make his cousin's sons agree to pay it, but that would involve time and a lot of complications. Worse was the knowledge that Cap de Trons would die, there could be no reconciliation with Jesus Christ and he would burn in hell for ever. And what had he, Costura, done to help save his soul? Fetch the confessor, but the confessor had arrived late . . . Who knows if Cap de Trons had already given up the ghost, facing the wall, as he had watched his mother die, unable to do anything to avoid it?

"Are you hurt?" he heard a young, almost childish voice say.

"Just a little, a stone some scoundrels threw at me when I was walking near here."

"Don't move, I'll call my mother and we'll put on a bandage. We've an ointment that doesn't sting, made of honey . . ."

"You're the one who's made of honey, my darling," he said, almost talking to himself, because the girl's hair tied in a thick plait seemed to have been made by all the bees in the garden, it was so golden, and her voice to have been poured directly out of the flowers. *She's a little saint,* thought Cortès, who did not recall having seen her the day before, though he supposed she also was the gardeners' daughter.

It was she and not her mother, who only held the bowl, who washed the wound, spread a healing ointment she took from a small jar and put on a bandage.

"You'll see it'll soon stop stinging and you'll be well . . . I wasn't here yesterday, that's why you don't know me," she clarified as if she had read the question in Costura's mind. "I was at my godmother's. On Sundays she likes to have lunch with me. Now, see if you can walk a bit . . ."

And she herself helped him to stand up and offered him her arm. Costura felt better, but the leg still hurt and he limped.

"I'll bring you a stick," and again she disappeared towards the houses.

"Your daughter's a treasure," remarked Rafel Cortès to the gardener. "Bright as a spark!"

"Do you think so? Thank you. You can stay here tonight if you like. Tomorrow, when the servant goes to market, you can hitch a ride. The road is a bit long for you in this condition."

"I would prefer to go now, but I appreciate your hospitality very much. I'll see if I can walk with the stick. I'd like to stay at home if I can . . ."

Father Ferrando was unable to concentrate on reciting the breviary, thinking about everything that had happened that afternoon and waiting for news of Cap de Trons' death.

Father Amengual, on the other hand, felt satisfied. Events were on his side and this filled him with optimism. He had rattled off a ten-line poem to head the chronicler Angelat's *History of Majorca* and now, reading it aloud:

Majorca, that golden morn,
for such great deeds does not know
if to your pen she will owe
more than to the mighty sword.
She sees how through you her form
is made solid, and not hollow,
and thanks you because you follow.
She has with effort and art
a thousand trophies from Mars,
but you give light like Apollo.

he paced up and down his cell, pleased with the result, though it was way over the top, because Angelat, short-legged and pot-bellied, wasn't a bit like Apollo and as for the light that would exalt the island, his book on Eleonor Canals would no doubt make a better beacon, since it dealt in particular with divine grace, with mystic cautery, with the Holy Spirit's tongue of fire. But he didn't care: he'd written it, and that was that. The chronicler should be grateful, very grateful indeed, for such high praise.

Angelat, on arriving home, was surprised to find a present a friend of his in Barcelona had sent him. On opening the package he confirmed that Agustí Pons had finally fulfilled his promise to get him *La pâtisserie française, où est enseignée la manière de faire toute sorte de pâtisseries très utiles à toutes sortes de personnes*, having highly recommended it, especially on account of the wonderful results his cook had managed to produce, after he, naturally, translated some recipes for her. Angelat noticed how his mouth began to water as soon as he thought about all the possibilities of pure delights that the book concealed. But when he started reading the recipes, he realized that he barely understood a thing. The meaning of the majority of words was foreign to him. And without knowing precisely which ingredients were necessary, Joana Maria would not be able to use it. So the jet of saliva his glands had begun to secrete in honor of future delicacies was in vain. *I'm sunk, how can I ask for help when I'm supposed to be the one who knows French best in the city?* And while his greedy eyes read here and there *Oranges à la neige de claire avec soufflé* or *Biscuit flambé au vin doux*, *Omelette farcie aux cerises*, his imagination overflowed with trays and dishes laden with sweets.

Gabriel Valls Major, a little frightened by the urgency with which the Viceroy wished to see him, ran to the Palace. He had just been announced by the butler and was already bowing respectfully in front of his excellency. The Lord Marquis welcomes him in his warmest tone of voice, the same he uses to address those he considers his friends. Seated opposite the desk on which the Viceroy has just placed the document he has been holding for so long, Gabriel Valls wipes the sweat from his face with his handkerchief and apologizes to the Lord Marquis for making such an improper gesture in front of him. But the beads that glisten on his brow and roll down his cheeks make him feel uncomfortable and prevent him concentrating the five senses on what the Viceroy has to tell him: a grave matter, no doubt, or at least important, given the manner in which he has been summoned.

"I sent for you, Gabriel, to inform you . . ." the Viceroy begins and pauses. The Cathedral bell has just struck six in the evening.

Sebastià Palou took his leave of Pere Onofre with an embrace in front of the startled gaze of the peasants waiting to be served at the counter of his mother's shop. This public display of affection by the captain to a man so inferior in status and above all of *contaminated* blood amazed them all. Sebastià noticed, but was not sorry. His gratitude to the merchant for the many favors he owes him is above any other consideration. Thanks to his friendship Valls lent him a hundred Majorcan ounces without interest. And he still owes some of that money. Aguiló is an intimate friend and that's why he has just been given a sheaf of scented papers fastened with a velvet ribbon to deliver to Livorno.

Costura agreed to stay the night, because lame and hurting all over he didn't feel up to walking home. Besides, the presence of that sprightly girl who can't have been fifteen fills him with an ancient, buried tenderness he had not felt since meeting Joana when she was a girl, a tenderness that makes him forget the worries that beset him.

This evening he still has a few hours of life and a lot more breath than Cap de Trons seems to have, who's in a tight squeeze. Everything is ready at the doors of the death-room. Madò Grossa appeared some time ago with the mortuary equipment she has been handling for more than twenty years with such naturalness and diligence that she has sometimes received requests from people outside the Street to attend the dead. The cloths to dry the body and the shroud in which to wrap it are waiting on a stool. Madò Aina Grossa produces a figure of Christ she will place in Cap de Trons' hands while he lies in state, under the watchful eyes of possible informers, and then, when they close the coffin amid tears and groans, she will take it and offer it to the middle son as a relic. This will stop Cap de Trons appearing with that forbidden image before the face of Adonai, who would rebuke him for it.

The boiled eggs and olives for the funeral repast are already in the pantry: the woman next door has just brought them, realizing that the daughter of the house is missing and men are not up to cooking or selecting olives, least of all in such circumstances. Madò Grossa only had to check that in the house there was no more water, in tub, bowl, basin, cup, glass or pot, than that remaining on the stove to wash the body, she didn't want Cap de Trons' soul to be held back in the water and not to make its journey to eternal rest. "No, the only thing here is a sad mirror," she murmured. "This lot are poor or would have me believe it. This isn't Sampol's house," and she remembered how Lady Blanca had all the mirrors in the house covered with transparent veils, veils of black lace, when her husband died and they stayed like this for half a year in sign of mourning. That was something worth seeing . . .

Gabriel Valls retraced his steps and headed quickly towards Segell, taking a short cut down the alleyways that led from the Viceroy's Palace to the home of Pere Onofre Aguiló. Worry was etched on his features. On entering the mother's shop he didn't even notice that there were people looking at him in surprise, since almost without a word of greeting he simply asked where he could find the traveler and, on hearing he was upstairs, climbed up to his bedroom, shouting for him.

"What brings you here?" asked Aguiló.

"We haven't a moment to lose," answered Valls in a sweat.

"Rest for a while," said Pere Onofre, offering him a chair. "What's up?"

"Costura has reported one of us to the Tribunal. Canon Llabrés has a document Father Ferrando gave him from the informer."

"You must have been expecting this. You already suspected Costura."

"Yes, he threatened Cap de Trons, but I didn't know he would move so fast."

"Cap de Trons is dying, he won't last long. There won't be time to open proceedings against him."

"Not when he's alive, but dead . . . I've never liked him, but there's no way I want to see him dug up and thrown on the flames."

"Proceedings are slow and Cap de Trons is poor. They fairly cleaned him out the last time. If Costura has only reported Cap de Trons, then . . ."

"Yes, but we don't know that. Besides, one accusation leads to another . . ."

"How did you find out about all of this?"

"The Viceroy sent for me to inform me. Don Sebastià Palou, his nephew, attends the gathering at Montision."

"He was here not long ago. You see these papers? They're for her. She won't pay any attention, I'm sure of that. I already told you she doesn't see anyone. She doesn't go out. All she does is pray."

"Now we'll need her again. Tell her this from me. If things turn ugly, it won't be like ten years ago. The Viceroy has heard the Tribunal is getting ready. They need money and want to teach us a lesson. We should try to leave again . . . We don't have any other choice."

"It won't be easy. After what happened with Harts, there aren't many captains I trust. Except Willis . . ."

"We'll have to risk it. I won't be able to get much money before tomorrow, but I'll do what I can. Tell the lady to give you what you need. She'll get it all back, of course. I'm relying on you, Pere Onofre."

"If it were you and your family, everything would be much simpler. You and the Consul with his children. But if, as you asked me the last time, I have to find places for lots . . ."

"People are implicated. We can't just abandon them."

"I understand, but the more of you there are, the worse it'll be."

"That's why we need to get a move on. We don't have much time. We need to do this before they open proceedings. It won't be possible from prison . . ."

"They may not act immediately. And, besides, we don't know who Costura has reported. He may not have accused any of us."

"Think about it! Anyway, Costura's days are numbered. I can tell you that."

"Be careful, Gabriel. Any suspicion would be very dangerous."

"I know. That's why we need to find a way to escape as soon as possible. Our people are tired. Any more years in prison, and they'll start accusing each other. Complicity helped us a lot, but it wouldn't work now. Besides, the Viceroy is right: things have changed. The Inquisition's zeal is much stronger. They need money, lots of money, and they won't stop till they get it. They'll turn this into a carnival, I assure you. With fire and smoke and lots of jamboree . . ."

The gardener offered Costura a room overlooking the back of the garden, above the paths lined with pomegranates. Costura accepted the invitation to dine with his hosts in the kitchen and preferred not to be served in his room, where he had been resting for a while. With the aid of the stick he descended the few steps down to the kitchen and sat in front of a bowl of soup.

"Would you bless the table," asked the gardener, "since you're the guest?"

"I'd be happy to," he replied, surprised at her display of religiosity.

Then they ate in silence. As at lunch the day before, Costura was full of praise for the cooking.

"It's good and tasty," he said, having seconds, most of all because he had been warned there was no dessert.

"Dried figs. We do have those," suggested the husband, who had just arrived for dinner, "and we like them a lot. They're not for the pigs, they're not."

Rafel Cortès, with the excuse that the wound smarted, retired at once. The following day they would call him to take him to the city as soon as the horses were harnessed, around five. *If only I could go for a walk in the garden,* he mused, but in his condition he shouldn't even try. He said almost a whole rosary and was just reaching the final mystery when he noticed his muscles slacken and his eyes fill with sand . . . However, the sweet feeling of giving himself up entirely to sleep lasted a few seconds. He opened his eyes again because he thought he heard the sound of a guitar coming from very near his window, accompanied now by the voice of a boy singing softly:

You who kill with a look
kill me only by looking at me,
who prefer you to kill me than to live
if you do not look at me.

He intones well, and it doesn't sound like the voice of a farmhand. And who can she be? I bet it's the gardeners' younger daughter. I'm not surprised she's serenaded . . .

Curiosity got the better of the pain in his leg and laziness. He approached the window without making a noise. In the moonlight he recognized Gabriel Valls' younger son, who had stopped singing. With his face raised he was looking at the window just above Costura's and calling something. Softening it as if kissing it, he was gently repeating a name: "Maria, Maria . . ."

VII

TO THE RIGHT, ON THE HORIZON, THE FINAL PROFILES OF land disappeared from view. On both sides of the galley, port and starboard, the waters, a deep blue, were turning nasty. In the sky some dark clouds, with faces like scarecrows or ruffians, seemed to watch over their dominions like sentinels, dissuading the birds from flying near. In the hold the sailors checked the ropes were secure to protect the cargo from probable upheavals. On the bridge the captain prepared to confront the storm he had seen coming as soon as they rounded Cape Blanc and he observed the first red stains in the sky and felt the assault of the wind veering to the north and rousing the waves.

Night was falling quickly with its drums of shade that now, moments after the sky was opened with a bloody rip, rolled with all their might, as the sails began to creak and the ship resisted the swell as best as it could.

Pere Onofre Aguiló woke up suddenly without knowing what was going on in the dark of his cabin, because a sea-blow threw him from the bed and knocked him to the ground. He did his best to stand up, returned to the bed and tied himself in. He closed his eyes, clung to the sides of the berth to try to ride out the storm without falling out again. Aguiló was not a seafaring man, but long journeys across the Mediterranean had taught him to endure the treacherous acts of the wind and waters with patience. He much preferred the galley to have to fight against the storm than against corsairs, whose attacks would have put everyone's life at far greater risk than that posed by an irate nature that always ended up being happy with a few hours' torture, but, when it cleared, would not take them hostage or steal the cargo and would shortly send them hours of fair weather to make up for its ferocity.

One of the worst memories of his life was of a confrontation with corsairs when he was sailing with Captain Esteve Fàbregues on behalf of the Suredas, with a letter of marque granted by the Viceroy Ponce de León. Everything seemed to be in their favor, because they were the ones who spotted the enemy first and opened fire, thinking the surprise attack would bring them substantial booty. But luck turned against them: the ship they boarded was a decoy, alluring and without cargo, the captain of a small Moorish squadron had sent ahead to attract the attention of ships sailing in the area, which would then be sunk by their powerful cannons and their crews captured and sold in the slave-market. He would have been bought by a Turk in the port of Tabarka, where they were taken from the Gulf of Genoa, and been branded by his new master had it not been for the great mercy of Adonai, who made use of chance and sent him a friend, a merchant of his nation who paid the corsair captain three times what the Turk was offering and never wanted to receive back the money, which Aguiló insisted he would pay as soon as it was possible.

"Since I owe you my life," he said when taking his leave, "permit me at least not to owe you money. I couldn't bear the thought that one day you might change your mind and claim me as your slave."

Salomó Abrahim, who could never have forgiven himself for not helping a fellow Jew, was generous towards Aguiló and with letters for the community of Livorno sent him to this port, suggesting that he work for him instead of for the Majorcan nobles.

Pere Onofre Aguiló did not wish to sever relations with the nobles of Majorca and sent letters from Livorno explaining the unfortunate boarding, the loss of *Our Lady of Help* and the capture of its crew, while expressing his indebtedness to Salomó Abrahim, something that made him his tributary, at least for a few years, and obliged him, as Salomó had proposed, to settle in the Medicean port, from where he could continue to look after the maritime business of his Majorcan lords. Don Joan Josep Sureda was delighted with the idea: having an agent in Livorno who also maintained close contact with the port of Tabarka made his business of importing wheat a lot easier. He himself obtained from the authorities the permit that allowed Pere Onofre to be away from the island for a time and to come back whenever he wanted, with absolute immunity, without being liable for his prolonged absences.

Pere Onofre Aguiló was twenty-five when he disembarked from *The New Jerusalem* in the Medicean port, with references from his patron for the Jewish community of Livorno. Although he had been sailing with Captain Fàbregues for a year, he had never called at Livorno. Like all sailors, however, he knew how important it was becoming and how much of its power was due to Marranos who had emigrated from Spain and Portugal, some of them via Antwerp and Ferrara. For this reason, throughout his life, he never ceased to give thanks to Adonai for the meeting with his savior, who also put him on the road to freedom.

Shaken by the violence of the storm, which shoved the ship along, not caring whether it sank it almost or raised it to the highest crest, Pere Onofre Aguiló thought about his family. It comforted him to know that they were safely installed in Livorno, fearlessly faithful to their God, well considered by everybody, even by Christians, who would never think to bother them, wealthy without forgetting the poor, especially those underprivileged and persecuted like their brethren in Majorca.

With his eyes closed he continued clinging with all his strength to the sides of the berth. But rather than with the strength of his arms, with the strength of his will and memory he clung to the good times he had just experienced on the island with his friends, with the Consul, recalling the sweet days of their shared childhood, when they had yet to discover their condition and their families' good reputation as prosperous traders protected them from any danger of uncertainty. With sorrow he remembered his widowed mother, whom he had embraced only a few hours before, afraid that this would be the last time he held that body diminished by the years, that young pigeon's body, with its brittle bones, almost without fat, covered with wrinkly, gnarled skin, all of her on the verge of disintegrating into sawdust. "Don't worry, Onofre," she had said to him. "The Lord our God will have pity on his servant and will give me a good death." She said it without hurt, convinced of the infinite mercy of Adonai, whom she had humbly served as well as she could, attempting to pass on to her children the secret, which from generation to generation, after they were forced in a mock baptism to pretend, mothers passed on to their children just when these awoke from the dream they had been in as sleeping babes.

Pere Onofre turned thirteen the day his mother, on wishing him a happy birthday, told him she had a present for him, a jewel she had kept for him since his birth, waiting for this great day of festivity and grace that would change his life, not only because he was a man now and as such different things would happen to him, but also because he was a Jew. A Jew like his parents and grandparents, and great-great-grandparents and the parents of his grandparents' great-great-grandparents, descendants of the tribe of Levi, aristocrats, therefore, among the twelve tribes, Jews in secret because of the Christians, who never took their eyes off them and forced them to observe Catholic rituals. A Jew, which meant one of God's chosen people, whom, despite the sufferings of exile, he would never cease to protect. Pere Onofre's eyes were still full of the gold Star of David his mother gave him, kissing him on the forehead. It seemed to him the shiniest and heaviest jewel he had ever seen. Often of an evening, without anyone knowing, seated on a stool beside his mother, he received lessons in the new religion that, as of that moment, he swore to be the only religion, as the Consul, his best friend, did shortly afterwards, though he didn't have such a valuable present. When he settled in Livorno he wore it over his heart, hanging not on the thick chain his mother gave him, but in a linen pouch where he kept his money, hidden under the folds of his clothes, next to his skin. He mechanically placed his hand over his heart, where he wore the same purse full now of the gold ounces Gabriel Valls had managed to collect, which he didn't want to lose for anything in the world.

Only once had the cargo carried in that intimate hiding place not reached its destination. But only he knew this, it was the best kept secret of his life that nobody could find out if he did not choose to reveal it, although there were times, on this last trip in particular, he had felt the urge to explain it all to his mother, at whose request he ran that risk that afforded him such respect in front of the Majorcan community. In the end, however, he decided not to, because to ease his conscience would have meant dealing the poor old woman a huge blow, from which she might not have recovered. And again, as always happened when he was in danger, the goad of remorse began to lay his faults before him.

I was frightened, Lord, he mentally answered the charges brought by his conscience. *Frightened, much more than now. Frightened that I wouldn't be able to defend myself, to fight to protect myself, to offer anything in exchange for that treasure that would be mocked, thrown, scattered and trampled, and I would have to accept it. Accept in front of them my condition as a Jew, for*

which I would be sentenced. But I tried. At the last moment,
I left, convinced that they would take me and, on searchi
find the purse, which clearly accused me. Frightened, Lord,
more of the hands breaking the strap of the bag around m
than of the wild nights spent in the woods, out in the open,
ed by the fangs of wolves and thousands of watchful eyes o
staring, motionless, like souls, like souls come back to life t
me away when I was almost there and had overcome other fe
bandits on crossing the Tossa mountains and of famished so
the group of deserters raiding the inn . . . Frightened, Lord, o
beasts and sharp fangs and men, of knives, needles and arms
ing arms till they break, of the flames . . . But you, Lord, are
ciful and know that I tried, I did everything in my power a
penance will do everything I can and more to accomplish
Valls wants, but I need your help, Lord, Adonai, my God . .

Pere Onofre gradually calmed down, stopped prayin
began to think about how he could get his brothers and s
off Majorca before proceedings were opened. And how he
persuade his friend Salomó Abrahim, whom he always end
asking for advice when things were difficult, to take part i
expedition and how best to arrange the charter, whether fr
port in Tunisia or from Livorno. He imagined that the W
Sampol would agree to help with the necessary money,
though she no longer seemed so close to Gabriel Valls as she
in the beginning, but confided more in a rabbi from Livorno
visited her frequently. He didn't dare discuss this with
however, or how Moashé wielded ever greater influence
Blanca Pires, as he did over other women in Livorno who
lowed his doctrines with elation. For a time, more than anyt
because of his wife, who believed firmly in the doctrines put
ward by Jacob Moashé, he also considered himself a followe

this man, who in turn had been a follower of Sabbatai, whom he took to be the true Messiah.

Precisely in the year 1666, appointed by the Zohar as the Year of Redemption, the year of the new era, in which Sabbatai would be made King of Jerusalem, Pere Onofre Aguiló had just returned to Majorca from the first of his long journeys around the ports of Europe, where he had heard from very different members of the Jewish community the good news that also excited much of the Majorcan community, filling them with hope. But, unlike their brethren in Antwerp, Ferrara and even Salonica, the Majorcans did not prepare to return to the promised land. They knew that the laws prevented them from emigrating and they also knew that if they put their goods on sale, they would give away their intentions and without money they had no way to bribe the captain of a ship so that they could escape. And besides not everybody was convinced. Many doubted. They suspected it could be an impostor's skillful maneuver to win support, and who knows if the Inquisition wasn't meddling in matters to set them a trap and make them fall more easily? Pere Onofre felt annoyed when he had to contradict them, because he had seen how firm was the hope of other communities, much more observant than the Majorcans and much more attentive in adhering to the laws. He had even quarreled with Gabriel Valls, who had received other information from the community in Bordeaux, contrary to Aguiló's, according to which he maintained that Sabbatai was a madman, a visionary whose exaltation everyone could end up paying dear. And when Sabbatai converted to Islam on pain of being burned alive by the sultan Ibrahim of Constantinople, whose throne he wanted to take, Valls supposed that Aguiló would no longer have arguments to defend him. But this wasn't the case; like other Jews in the diaspora, Aguiló accepted Sabbatai's message—"God made me a Muslim. He ordered this, and this happened on the ninth day of

my new birth"—and even accused Gabriel of being ignorant. In Antwerp he had heard how one of the most prestigious rabbis, Jacob Judah, interpreted Sabbatai's apostasy according to the cabbala and presented this treachery as proof of his Messiahship, as the true Passion of the only, true Redeemer, who, to atone for the sins of his people, a lot of whom had also converted to other, abominable religions, had committed the terrible sin of renunciation. From that moment apostasy would be his martyrdom, his cross, but also his most important act and his great merit. No doubt Isaiah referred to Sabbatai in the words Christians unjustly applied to Christ, "a man of sorrows," since with his own sorrow he redeemed the faults of those who had also had to apostatize. But Gabriel Valls did not accept this argument, he thought it flippant and did not understand how Pere Onofre as well as the rabbis he quoted as authorities from different sides of the world could defend it. For Gabriel Valls the Messiah, being one of them, could not be like them, hypocrites, who in public lived like Christians and only in private, in the shady secret of their homes, showed themselves for what they really were.

"It's the only way to survive, they haven't given us any choice," Pere Onofre almost shouted, upset before his friend, who listened to him carefully, a little perplexed. "The Messiah comes from us and is like us!"

Aguiló suddenly heard his discordant voice of years before, a slightly nasal voice, not so deep as he would have liked. He heard it in the sooty muddle of his memory over Valls' softer voice, which sounded more convincing, perhaps because it was much less nasal and more amorous. And on recovering the voices he also recovered the exact words of that quarrel with Valls about Sabbatai's Messiahship at the end of 1666, when on returning to Majorca from Bordeaux, having been on that mission that only he knew he hadn't carried out, he brought first-hand news. While the storm gradually subsided and the galley seemed not only to be governed by the forces of the sea, but little by little to be responding to the movements of the rudder, far from those dashed hopes, he reflected that Gabriel Valls was absolutely right: Sabbatai Zevi was nothing but a fraud, a demoniac madman who had dared to order that the Ten Commandments given to Moses directly by God on Mount Sinai, in which the Jewish people had believed through the centuries, be replaced by his eighteen rules, one of which commanded that he be considered the only Savior.

For this reason, because it had all been a terrible lie, it was necessary to continue waiting for the Messiah's coming, and Jacob Moashé, precisely because he had been a penitent follower of Sabbatai, believed he could recognize what other true signs the Savior of the Jewish people should embody, something he was prepared to reveal only to the chosen, which included the real Messiah, who had yet to reach adulthood. Everyone in the community of Livorno understood that the rabbi was referring to one of their children. Pere Onofre's wife began to suspect that it might have to do with their first-born, Samuel Pere, and told her husband this, who was more worried than overjoyed by the news. His remorse at not having fulfilled the mission he had been entrusted with assailed him more strongly than ever, and he was sure that this fault transmitted to his son when he was begotten would be what stopped Adonai granting him the grace of his election. For this reason he tried to dissuade his wife from thinking she might be the Messiah's mother and pointed out that their thirteen-year-old son's character was not right for the Savior. Samuel Pere showed the same entrepreneurial spirit as his father, if not more so. There were times he had suggested storing most of the wheat instead of shipping it immediately, waiting for the price to go up. Also, when he was away on a trip, his son kept the books, noting down profit and expenditure with strict, faithful punctuality. These virtues, which filled him with pride, were not, however, those of the future Savior. Nor was Samuel's mocking air, always close to laughter, especially at someone else's expense, a trait he inherited from his Majorcan grandfather, who was nicknamed the Joker because of his fondness for teasing people.

"Times have changed since the Bible," argued Pere Onofre's wife. "And Adonai can work wonders," she added when her husband informed her that Samuel was chasing the maidservants at home and displayed an enthusiasm that was understandable in a boy for his first amorous discoveries. "The Lord's ways are inscrutable," insisted Esther Vives, who was delighted with the idea that the Savior had come out of her insides after nine months' exclusive residence in her blessed womb. What's more, she was still in time to redirect her first-born along more religious paths, to make him walk straight, to persuade him of the need for a strict observance of Mosaic law, to imbue him with knowledge of the Torah, sending him to Jacob Moashé's school. Seeing he was on the wrong tack, Pere Onofre reminded his wife that the rabbi had never specified anything. He had simply hinted at the Messiah's presence among a group of Livorno boys, which included Samuel Pere, and so he did not allow a change to his son's life, as his wife wanted, and forbade Esther Vives to talk to him again about such fantasies. And now, some time later, he rejoiced at his decision and the firmness with which he had enforced it, ignoring Esther's pleas and tears. Not even when he remarked that Jacob Moashé's close and frequent contact with Blanca Pires and private tuition given to her only son indicated that the rabbi had already decided who the chosen one was, was she convinced. There was only one minor defect with that Messiahship, argued Pere Onofre: that the father of Josep, the future Savior, the merchant Sampol, was not of Jewish stock, he was a Christian, a descendant of old Christians on all four sides. The rabbi, however, might overlook this fact, considering the possibility that Blanca Pires, as the Christians maintained about Mary, was a virgin before and after the birth. But all this was idle speculation, and his wife had much more time than he did to spend theorizing and milking commentaries with friends on the Widow Sampol. Because in the end, and Pere Onofre pointed this out to his stubborn wife, Jacob Moashé had yet to say who he thought was meant and, if he gave special lessons to the lady's son, it was because she had asked him to. But, all considered, there was nothing strange or suspicious about this. However rich she might be, the lady was alone and could be expected to entrust what she most loved in the world to people of proven wisdom and moral standing, nor was it at all odd that she should spend the most agreeable hours of the day with the person who directed her son's education, so that he might turn out a good Jew, discussing both Josep's spiritual progress and the interpretation of Scripture. And if all this went on not in the synagogue, but in Blanca's home, palace almost, one of the most luxurious in Livorno, it was just because the lady hardly ever went out. What harm was there in the fact that every evening she walked in the grove of oranges, protected by cypresses, that in imitation of her grove in Majorca she had planted in Livorno as well, accompanied by Jacob Moashé, as she once was by Gabriel Valls? And besides wasn't she paying for the building of a new synagogue from her own pocket? With his eyes closed, still clinging to the sides of the berth, but encouraged by the direction the storm was taking, Pere Onofre Aguiló recalled the sour grapes of his wife, who was jealous of Blanca like all the women in Livorno, when forced to admit that the widow was extremely swift to perform charitable acts. "That may be true," Esther Vives finally conceded, "but she has too much of a twinkle in her eyes to be devout and paints them too much not to be interested in worldly affairs. What she wants is to fell all of you at a single glance."

Esther Vives, who arrived with her family in Livorno after a long pilgrimage from Valencia to Antwerp and from Antwerp to Rome and later to Ferrara, was not easily hoodwinked. This quality, together with her manual ability to turn the coarsest horse's mane into a skein of silk, attracted the attention of Pere Onofre when he was looking for a woman with whom to settle in Livorno and establish a family. So everything Esther said about the Widow Sampol, however much envy might distort her view, was not so misplaced. Even he, who had never felt drawn by those heron's eyes or aroused by her deep gaze, thought Blanca Pires was of an unusual beauty and possessed the secret power of snakes to hypnotize birds just by staring at them. Pere Onofre smiled to imagine his wife's anger if she knew that amid the chaos of the storm the Widow Sampol had come and gazed at him as only she could. Aguiló was lucky to have gotten the only single cabin on the ship, apart from the captain's, kept for distinguished travelers, nobles or authorities, which this time he had managed to reserve for himself in the absence of anyone more important. If there was one thing he hated, it was having to share the reduced space of ships during a storm and having to endure the fear and vomit of the other passengers, fear and vomit that always became contagious, especially on his first voyages, when the storm had caught him crouching between others who wept and groaned with spewing and swearing, others whose faces were transformed by the swell and turned from white to yellow and green and then vinegary and purple, colors of gastric juices with whitish, bilious spit trickling from the corners of mouths, accompanied by spasms, coughs and retches. As if all of them, himself included, were a bunch of lunatics shut up in a dark room, a load of idiots, wet, slimy flesh stinking up the room with a dense, heavy, particularly acrid smell, which continued after the effects of the storm had returned people to normal and did not go away for days, even if the same passengers tried to wash it away with buckets of seawater and opened the portholes to allow other, less offensive sea smells in.

Whenever he embarked again, he understood his mother's fear of leaving Majorca and strong resistance to crossing the sea. "The sea robs Peter to pay Paul," she would insist whenever her son proposed finding a way for her to leave. And however much Pere Onofre tried to convince her that storms did not always seize the waters and traveling in fair weather, with a good wind filling the sails, was pure delight, Aina Bonnín did not wish to give it a go. She was sorry because she would have liked to meet her grandchildren, but her fear of the sea was stronger than anything else, even than her fear of the flames. *If I get the galley Valls wants,* thought Pere Onofre, *I don't know how I'll manage to persuade her to embark as well. Stubborn as she is, she'll probably prefer to stay on the island and then, if things turn ugly, who knows what will happen?*

The rumble of the sea, which seemed to be bubbling away, like a pot that has been warming on the stove for ages, and the increasingly tame roll of the ship made Pere Onofre, who was exhausted by the storm, sleepy. *Perhaps I'll wake up in the first port,* Aguiló wished, squeezing his eyes shut in the hope of resting for as long as possible.

He was already half asleep when he heard a groan that made him open his eyes and prick up his ears to work out where it came from. But he only heard the familiar rumbles of the sea and the bustle on deck. He closed his eyes again, resolved not to pay any attention to that sound he had exactly identified as a human moan emitted not far away, as if somebody else were traveling in the same cabin, somebody who hadn't yet dared to show themselves. But he reopened them a few seconds later, having heard the moan again, now perfectly clearly. The merchant did not understand, if somebody had hidden in his cabin, why they had taken so long to complain, missing the opportunity to do so in much more terrible circumstances than the current ones, since the storm had slackened off.

"You'd better tell me who you are and how you got in here," demanded Aguiló without receiving a reply. "You wouldn't be a fish now, would you?" he carried on, seated on the bed, struggling to undo the straps, reach for the oil lamp that had gone out and been hanging from the ceiling and find out where the person might be hiding. While he groped in the dark, he thought about the man he was shown in the port of Genoa who survived the wreck of his galleon for more than two months, being carried along by the currents and living off the fish he swallowed, and when he was finally saved by some fishermen who caught him in their nets, only let out a groan, having lost the power of speech. But this case was not so unusual if he compared it to what happened in Catania, in the kingdom of Sicily, which formed part of the exploits he was so fond of recounting when he had a big enough audience and which he himself had heard so many times. Everyone agreed that from an early age Cola, nicknamed the Fish, displayed such affection for the sea that not a day went by when he didn't go swimming in it for hours and hours and when some obligation prevented him, he became so sad it seemed he lacked the desire to live. When he grew up, his affection did not wane, quite the opposite. He told anyone who would listen that the sea seemed to him much more beautiful than the land and in the waters he discovered wonderful haunts not even the sweetest meadow could offer him. And his ability as a swimmer was so very strong that, even if there were a storm and waves the size of belfries, he wasn't afraid and disappeared out to sea and didn't come back for two or three days.

He was remembering Cola's story, as he continued to search blindly for the oil lamp, without finding it, when he noticed footsteps in front of the door and heard a knock.

"Open up, sir!" asked a young voice. "It's the topman Arnau Mulet. I don't wish to harm you . . ."

"I should hope not," replied Pere Onofre, unbolting the door. "Tell me what you want," and happy to see that the boy held a lamp in his right hand he added, "Before you go any further, let me look for my lamp with yours. This weather has made a fine mess of things. Do you know what I was doing? Trying to work out where some groans I just heard were coming from. They weren't yours from behind the door, were they?"

"No, sir, but I think I know whose they are and where they're coming from. That's why I came to free the person who embarked in one of your trunks."

"But that's an abuse! I shall complain to the captain!"

"It doesn't matter, sir, the captain already knows. We didn't expect this storm. I myself was ordered to come as soon as we rounded Cape Blanc, to free him and apologize on behalf of the captain and give you this letter," and he produced a sealed letter from inside his shirt. "It's for you, sir. If you've complained, you're still alive," he added, addressing the trunk. "Let's get you out of there. You must be petrified, my friend."

"I should like to know whom I have had the honor of hosting," said Pere Onofre, breaking the seal and seeing it was the Consul's handwriting.

"You'll know right away, sir. What's clear is he's escaping from Majorca."

VIII

JESUS, MARY AND JOSEPH,

I, Rafel Cortès, nicknamed Costura, truthfully declare that on Monday in the first week of June, in the year of our Lord 1687, with my cousin Cap de Trons on his deathbed and unable to do anything to help the said Cap de Trons after he received extreme unction, I went for a walk out of town and from there, after some lads threw a stone at me and because of the said stone my right leg began to hurt, ended up in Gabriel Valls Major's garden, which was not far from the scene of the occurrence. I declare that I went there seeking help and also because Father Ferrando, my confessor, asked me to keep my eyes open to see if it was true that in the said garden things were taking place that contravened the true religion of Christ our Lord. I had been invited there by Valls the day before, I was there with the Consul, the merchant Serra, the saddler Pons and Pere Onofre Aguiló, who spoke of events that occurred outside Majorca, where some experimented with flying machines as I already explained. But I saw nothing that night to indicate that the gardeners, the only ones to spend the night in the garden, and their servants had become Jews. But during the night, around midnight, I heard how Gabriel Valls' younger son sang under my window and called to a girl by the name of Maria and how she appeared at the window and how with amorous talk he made her say a prayer that I understand to be Jewish and that goes as follows:

Almighty Father,
who work wonders every day,
great God in heaven,
have pity on our simple sheep
stung by bees
in such great weakness.
You who are the true God,
have mercy and pity on them.
Hallowed be your name
now and always.
Our Lord, do not hide
your light any longer.
If your people
have erred in the past,
you, O Lord, have pardoned
according to the sacred law.

Which I wish to make manifest to unburden my Catholic, Apostolic and Roman conscience and that the Holy Tribunal of the Inquisition might act accordingly, given that the suspicion the said Tribunal entertained I'm afraid can be confirmed, since they suspected that the law of Moses was being taught in Gabriel Valls' garden and what I heard and saw on the night I was lame was Rafel Onofre Valls de Valls Major indoctrinating the gardeners' younger daughter, Maria Pomar, daughter of Pep Pomar and Miquela Fuster, natives of Porreres.

And if the Lord Inquisitors wonder how I know this Jewish prayer so well, it's because others chose to teach it to me and I know it, but I have never used it because I'm Catholic, Apostolic and Roman.

On the said day I stayed in Valls' garden, unable to find out anything more important concerning errors against the holy Christian religion than what I have already explained, I did not wake up at the crack of dawn as I usually do, when she often catches me working because sleep has never kept me company me for long, either because the pain in my leg had exhausted me or because the tranquillity of the spot afforded me better rest. Nobody woke me either and the servant must have left without me; so Gabriel Valls found me still in his garden when he turned up at around ten o'clock and warned me again, as he had done on the way to his garden last Sunday, that I shouldn't pay any attention to the behavior of Cap de Trons, who was not dead yet, and after saying this, in a low voice, looking at me as though he sought out my soul, he said I had been wrong to accuse Cap de Trons, my cousin. I didn't reply, but by the way he said it, I suspected he could see straight through me and I think I went red as a tomato. Before having a horse harnessed to take me to the city, he ordered the gardener to serve me sponge-cake for breakfast and, when I praised it highly, told me to take home a large piece. From this present I deduced he wasn't angry with me, especially since he has continued sending me cake while my leg has been bad. The pain has not died down, quite the opposite, rather than abating it has increased and now my whole stomach hurts and tortures me, but I endure with holy patience since the Lord our God sends it to me and my sufferings are as nothing compared to the Passion of Christ.

I declare that everything I have written is true and sign it in my own hand today, Friday the twelfth of June, in the year of our Lord 1687.

Rafel Cortès, Costura

The Very Reverend Inquisitor Nicolás Rodríguez Fermosino finished reading the documents Father Ferrando had given him in person and while putting them away stared at him without saying a word. Seated opposite the desk behind which the Inquisitor looked at him, the Jesuit waited for Don Nicolás to pass judgement. He wanted to work out from the tone he used, if it wasn't obvious from the words, whether now would be a good time to discuss his personal affairs or whether he should ask Rafel Cortès for more accusations with which to further his help to the Holy Office. But Rodríguez Fermosino must have enjoyed making him wait because he delayed opening his mouth for a few more minutes. He stroked his chin. He carefully removed his glasses and stood up without taking his eyes off Father Ferrando. He slowly pushed back the easy chair so that it didn't rub against the newly whitewashed wall, moved to the middle of the room and began to pace from the door leading to the cloister to the window opposite, open to the terraces and swifts. Sharp as a weasel, he had immediately noticed how Father Ferrando was desperate to hear his opinion and allowed him to get nervous, enjoying this silence that vexed the Jesuit. The Inquisitor was used to interrogations and knew how much defendants hated pauses that suggested evil intentions, even more captious arguments, heralding terrible tortures. He believed that silence could be much more eloquent than words and was in the habit of using it as one of his most effective tactics, even though during these pauses, this time out, he did not weigh the pros and cons of the accusations or consider the defendants' guilt or pay any attention to what was going on in the courtroom. On the contrary, he used these moments to rest and, though he did not take his lively, piercing eyes off his alleged victims, with those of his memory he gazed at other places and looked on other people. A word from someone else, from the judge or the alleged offender, could be a good start. This word, as if it had wings, took him to other words uttered by other people and then, holding on to these terms, like a short prayer to ward off bad thoughts, he left the place where he was. Other times, if the recesses were longer—something that definitely unnerved defendants—he rested for a sensible interval, thinking only about his affairs, as if meditating—his head in his hands now—recalling much more pleasant periods of his youth, and he would often anchor for a while in his stay in Rome in Cardinal d'Angelioto's service. At the moment, without settling on any word that might be beneficial or any image that might amuse him, he simply enjoyed the discomfort of Father Ferrando, who was anxiously rubbing his hands and about to explode.

"Your reverence will say what he thinks I ought to tell Costura," the Jesuit snapped in a whisper.

The Inquisitor smiled with satisfaction—*You'd burst if you didn't speak*—and answered Ferrando with a question.

"And what do you think about Costura's declarations? You know him better, you're his confessor."

The Inquisitor had sat down again and done so noisily, on purpose, flopping his heavy bones on the easy chair, whose leather creaked in return. The Jesuit was not expecting the Inquisitor to begin by interrogating him, as if he also were under suspicion. In fact his walk around the room could already have told him that things were going badly. The Inquisitor was in the habit of standing up when he felt uneasy, without caring that it might seem rude. But Father Ferrando preferred not to take offence at his behavior or the question and for encouragement considered the possibility that Fermosino valued his opinion in such a delicate matter. *I shall take it as a compliment,* he said to himself and in humble tones, groveling, answered that he considered Costura a good Christian and believed everything he said was true. What's more, he was sick not just because of a leg wound that refused to heal, but also with a terrible stomachache that gave him no rest. For this reason, because he feared for his health, he would not dare to tell lies. But these pains, interjected the Inquisitor, might lower his spirits and who knows if he was clear-headed or seeing things and confused? Father Ferrando rejoined that Costura was prepared to testify long before the unfortunate accident, precisely because as a good Catholic he believed that some of his same race, if not religion, had gone back to being Jews after the reconciliation, something as a Christian he could not tolerate. The Inquisitor felt a strong aversion to Ferrando. He had never liked this stunted Jesuit who curried favor with him, unsuccessfully, by confessing people from the Street. *You're not motivated by apostolic zeal, brute,* he said to himself, *it's the position of rector you're after with all this wangling. Let them skin me alive if it's not . . .*

"Your reverence," continued Ferrando, "has seen how Costura's first testimony, the one I sent you through the Judge of Goods, coincided with Juli Ramis' declarations. Costura is telling the truth, I'm sure."

"Juli Ramis is a worthless wretch, Canon Amorós told me this himself. Who's to say he's not lying? If he accuses Cap de Trons of these crimes, the insult to his own honor is mitigated. Father Ferrando, if I were an affronted father, I would adopt the same castrative measures against the defamer of my blood."

The Inquisitor again fell silent and this time did travel far on the back of his own words and saw himself galloping through the gate of a walled city, chased by another horseman. Could someone in Siena call him father as they had led him to believe?

"Reverence, Cap de Trons circumcised his sons, or at least tried to, before coming across Juli Ramis in his own daughter's bedroom, there's no doubt about that."

"Did you see it, Father Ferrando?" asked the Inquisitor, standing up again, this time to straighten the painting of St Dominic, which seemed to have slipped to the right. "Has your fatherhood examined their private parts?"

"Obviously not," replied Ferrando, not at all happy with the direction the interview was taking. "He may not have actually circumcised them . . . but it's the intention that counts and his wish, I'm sure, was clearly circumcisional."

"Cap de Trons is dead, Father Ferrando. We can throw his bones on the fire, but not question them about their mistakes. As for his sons, it won't be difficult to prove how far their father's madness went."

The silence became as thick as heat. The Jesuit wiped his brow with a handkerchief. Beads of sweat drenched his face. The sultriness was almost magmatic. Father Ferrando felt trapped for two reasons: he was uncomfortable and could not see how to ingratiate himself with the Inquisitor. There was no way he dared to ask him for the reference he wanted. It seemed to him that Fermosino, instead of attributing his conduct to the good zeal of a fervent member of the Catholic Church, saw him as a dung-beetle that had fallen into an aromatic, steaming soup. If the Inquisitor were not so powerful and not considered so incorruptible, he could find a way to report such unclear, such—why not say it?—suspicious behavior . . .

"Do you think it's a good idea, reverence," Father Ferrando finally ventured, "to ask Costura to keep writing down for us everything he knows, or do you think . . .?"

The Inquisitor again turned his eyes on the Jesuit.

"You'd be a poor Christian and what's worse, a poor priest, a poor minister of Christ, if you did not watch for the triumph of our Catholic faith. And now, if you don't mind," he said, ringing a golden bell, "I have several urgent matters to attend to."

They both stood up. Before leaving Father Ferrando still had to thank the Inquisitor for receiving him and, returning the courtesy, the Inquisitor told him to come whenever he wanted, he would always be welcome.

Don Nicolás Rodríguez Fermosino put his glasses back in place and again leaned over the documents covering his desk. He opened a dossier he had been working on before the Jesuit's visit. Now that he was alone, he also wiped his brow with a handkerchief and then wiped the collar of his cassock, attempting to free his skin from that clamminess that prevented him concentrating on the protocols he had to examine that afternoon, which, if he was honest, irritated him a lot. For more than two years, since his mother died in a corner of Galicia before he could get there to close her eyes and kiss her for the last time, his inquisitorial passion that earned him a deserved reputation for being strict and incorruptible had been on the decline. It's not that he didn't take his obligations seriously, but he found it harder to work at the same rhythm. Promising to undergo the most severe privations, he had asked God for the storm to abate so that the galley on which he finally managed to embark for Barcelona could continue on its way. But the waves were so wild that the captain had no choice but to seek help in the port of Sóller, where for two and a half days they waited for fair weather, which didn't want to come. When it finally arrived, the calm again made the journey more difficult, so that it took longer than usual. The Inquisitor disembarked in Tarragona and on horseback, without waiting for a mail-coach heading north, with only a spare horse for company, galloped apace, stopping only when he had to because of the dark. He rode for four days, his only concern to get there on time, and when, exhausted, he finally made it home, the worms had been courting his mother in the grave for two days already. His pleas, promises, spent limbs, were of no use. "The Lord our God took her soul at the crack of dawn on St Matthew's Day," he was told by the priest, who looked after two other parishes aside from this one. "She'll carry on praying for you in heaven, you can be sure, as she did on earth. She was so repentant of her sins, leaving everything she had for Masses, they can flay me alive if she's not in glory."

Don Nicolás Rodríguez Fermosino decided to buy new horses to return immediately, but stayed more than twenty days in the village where he had been born one Christmas Eve, also almost miraculously—his mother was only thirteen and everyone considered her a virgin. The softness of the green, the sponginess of the meadows and that juicy land where chestnuts grew, kept him prisoner as if he had been exorcized. They had to send for him with an urgent mail from the Tribunal of Aragon, reminding him that his predecessor had been punished for his improper conduct. And that things in Majorca were not going well and required the Inquisitor's attention. The familiars were being driven to distraction by Sara de les Olors' apparitions, which had started again and he had chosen to ignore because he thought her a poor madwoman, even though Cabezón had opened a file on her. He obeyed and returned, but those days were decisive, as was his mother's death. "Let me close her eyes, Holy Virgin, and I promise I will tighten a belt of thorns around my right thigh every Friday of Sorrow to accompany you in your sufferings. You spurned me," he said to her after hearing the news, annoyed as if talking to a lover. "You could have delayed death by asking your Almighty Son." "I could have, but I didn't," came the reply. "I don't like to be put to the test. Haven't you often insisted in your sermons that it's a sin to judge Providence, that God always arranges the best for everybody? And what if your mother on her deathbed had confessed to you the truth of your origin? Had told you that, instead of being begotten by a bishop who continues to protect you—look where you've gotten to—you were by the first wretch to get her on the floor?"

The Inquisitor of Majorca crossed himself before attending to the documents, in this way regained the concentration he lacked on such a sultry afternoon, but again, on re-examining the declarations of witnesses, as had happened to him since the case was opened, heard the pitter-patter of rain falling on the thirsty fields, on the porous, soaked land, mother land in which any seed sprouted. *It must be the heat,* he thought to himself, *it must be because of this unbearable heat, this hellish month of June. O God, what shall we do in August if it carries on like this? We'll burn as if we were all in the flames . . . And what if the witnesses, as so often, proved false? What if it were revenge again? How to make them understand that the eyes of God, infinitely merciful, see and look at everything with much more care, much more clarity than human eyes? Hadn't Christ said to consider first the beam in our own eye and then the mote in our brother's?*

On said day in the month of May, 1687, the said Margarida Antich, Pere Antich's wife, came looking for me to say with her the prayer of St Helena, which goes as follows:

> *St Helena, king's daughter,*
> *you who satisfy the sea,*
> *who cross the sea,*
> *you who go to Bethlehem,*
> *you who laid a table with the apostles,*
> *you who cleared a table with the apostles,*
> *you who called to Judas,*
> *Come here, Judas,*
> *tell me where Christ's three nails are.*
> *Helena, go to Mount Tabor,*
> *you'll enter three times*
> *and find the three nails:*
> *you'll throw one in the Red Sea*
> *and stick one in the heart of Sion*
> *so that it can't stop or rest*
> *till it's at my feet,*
> *may a bad fire burn it as it will me,*

because I wanted and asked her for a way to stop my husband leaving me. Then she made a heart of paper and stuck it in the ground with a nail, banging it, and then taking the heart and dip-

ping it in water, she wrapped it in a dry piece of paper. Then she lit a candle and repeated the said prayer and said "Sion, Sion, Sion," and made me say it. And she gave me the wet heart, which, because it was wet, was not consumed by the flame, and made me put it under my husband's pillow and asked me with my hands to take a little of Sion's seed and tell her why I needed it . . .

The thin rain fell on the protocols strewn over his desk. The rain, like sand, impaired his vision. He closed his eyes and took off his glasses and rubbed his eyelids and saw much further, much further away, the green fields again and the moist meadows. In the afternoon's lazy, diffuse light appeared the attic window from where he had so often watched how a bit of field, a bit of bell-tower, lost in the valley bottom, came in. He saw himself, what he was no longer, but had been, sprawled on a bed of straw with his eyes half-closed. Near him was the body of Margariña, who cried softly, accompanying the sweetest rain. "Don't cry, woman," he told her, "there's nothing we can do. I'll never forget you, you can be sure of that." "I am sure," she replied while showing him a heart of paper her mother had given her to pass over her pubis after accomplishing the act with which he had possessed her. And she began to intone softly:

> *Lady St Helena,*
> *beloved of God and of his mother . . .*
> *. . . you laid a table*
> *. . . you cleared a table*

Antich's case was not the only one he had to look over that afternoon, but it was the one that irked him most, because it forced him to face a period from his past he did not like at all, since it made him realize he would judge Antich and also that witness with far more rigor, far more severity, than he used to judge Margariña's mother, who encouraged the spell, worried about her daughter's misfortune, and her most of all, whom, as the rain fell down, summoned by a memory as juicy as those lands, he remembered despite the years and distance. He looked for her on that last trip and one night at a crossroads, after visiting a friend, he thought he recognized her among others. He vigorously rubbed his eyes to try and avoid that rain like sand and concentrate again on proceedings. First, however, to ease the heat, he wiped his face with the handkerchief and stood up to see if the shirt he wore under the cassock would come unstuck from the body it seemed joined to. When he sat down again, he put away the protocol containing Antich's case, as if he had changed his mind and was not now keen to examine it. He closed it, tied the file where it was kept with strings and retrieved Costura's documents. As was his custom, he wet the pen to have it ready in case on a separate piece of paper he wanted to jot down some aspect that caught his attention, before deciding to give the order to open proceedings, something Father Ferrando had such interest in. This is what annoyed him most. He was sure that Father Ferrando, although he had been tactful enough not to mention it, wanted to use that decision to obtain his recommendation for the post that Amengual was also after. He thought the two of them were equally despicable, but at least Father Amengual had never troubled him. He trusted in his lives of saints as his greatest merit. But Costura's information, if it proved reliable, could not be taken lightly, especially now that he had been warned by his superiors, who had empty coffers and lots of cracks in the house. Costura's testimony, however, bothered him and he pushed it aside. Nervously he took another file that had been open for months, that he looked at whenever all the others were too distressing for him. Sooner or later he would have to take a decision. The case connected the former bishop with a prostitute from the brothel, who had been involved with the Inquisitor before him. Fermosino reread:

I saw slugs and worms enter and leave the holes of those souls, thick as ants, and my vision was blurred with smoke. The demons howled, the beasts roared, the dragons bellowed like bulls and the poisonous snakes hissed, and all of them together helped to create that extraordinary music.

I saw great tempests, great winds, great storms and squalls, lots of thunder and lightning, awful lightning that fell on the damned and seemed to smash them in pieces.

I saw souls of all the Church's religious orders and high dignitaries, cooking like a joint in the oven. Popes and cardinals were seated on thrones and chairs of fire. There they were, dignitaries and favorites abandoned and crestfallen, wearing cuirasses instead of mitres, and often others took them and stuck them in boiling pots and lakes of foul water. They also ordered them to wallow in a broth of mire and demons' excrement. But far worse was what befell those in the final circle, touching the bottom of the flames, who are constantly tormented by demons' tongues, tongues and terribly hot logs exhaling a stench that covers everything . . .

I saw this as clearly and surely as my name is Benet, Bishop of Majorca, sinner that I have been, committing sins with all the parts of my body, especially with the said privates. In repentance I confess and wish Beatriu Mas to confess, nicknamed Limp, prostitute in the brothel, with whom I had carnal relations for ten years.

Part Two

I

THE MORNING FOUND THEM AWAKE. THEY TASTED THAT dawn like a bitter-sweet dish. Most of them worked all night and prayed. In a very low voice, in their own homes, they intoned psalms of praise and thanksgiving. They unearthed tubs, searched hiding places, rummaged in drawers. Anything that might be of use was put to one side: money, gold, jewels. The women sewed pockets and pouches, added worsted linings to skirts. They kneaded and baked bread, prepared cakes. But when they heard Eloi, they put down their needles, extinguished fires, closed workshops and changed into the best clothes they had to attend Mass.

They took holy water and prepared to fulfill their obligation. Dotted about the church, they do not stint in their devotion.

At the end they returned to Segell and Argenteria, but nobody changed into work clothes. They kept on their fine clothes, their Sunday best, to go for a stroll. The women took a bundle with the bread, having decided to make the most of the fine day, a clear day with a glorious sky, to lunch on the seashore and enjoy a spring that seems to have come two weeks early and promises sweetening softness. They didn't leave together. They left in small groups, some with their family, others on their own. Nobody attracts attention. They greet acquaintances, bow right down in front of lords and ladies and even kiss the bishop's precious amethyst when they bump into him on his way back to the

Palace. The bishop blesses them and pats the children who come up to him. The children walk alongside the women, jumping and shouting. They look clean, with a perfectly straight parting. The men on reaching the King's Garden pass in front of them. They gather and form a solid group. They precede the others through the sea gate, look to see where the best place to rest would be, what people they might meet on the shore. Some of the old ones lag behind, dragging their feet, limping, going as fast as they can, afraid that they won't be on time. It's cost them a lot of money and a lot more words to be accepted and they can't believe that the time has come at last. They're weighed down. They're carrying all they have in pouches stitched into their shirts, which are tight because of their vests; in their baggy pants, disguised by the folds, they're hiding the richest merchandise.

On the shore, among the rocks, the first to arrive select the best place to lay out the tablecloths and calmly prepare omelets and cakes, as well as buns, to eat. But not everybody is hungry. There are families where nobody has managed to swallow anything. Anxiously they look towards Port Pi and the English ship, a dark xebec with the hull painted green and black, which has anchored in the port before, and then towards the city, huddled to the left, golden like Santanyí stone, the city split in two by the river, guarded by belfries like watchtowers, protected by walls and bulwarks. The hostile city that rejects and casts them out, but is theirs nonetheless. The city of their parents and their parents' parents and their great-grandparents and great-great-grandparents and even further back: the city reached by their first, ancient ancestors when the diaspora began. They are familiar with its stones, its walls. Eyes closed, they picture its streets, know by heart the splinters, cracks, marks on its façades. They've eaten the fruits of its gardens, grown used to the wind that at times wages war and blows everything down, to the lack

ken a ban. No one can accuse them of having done
iiss. They fulfilled their obligation on a Sunday and
ating buns and, the most fortunate among them,
uit. In a short while, having gathered their provi-
folded the tablecloths, just as they came, *gento con*
reach Port Pi. Other Sundays they've chosen the
t's hardly surprising they should have gone back
e the most of the day. The sea air fills their lungs
e appetite.

lready standing up. Some are already beginning to
cry, Isabel," says Rafel Tarongí to his sister, who
t has been struggling to hold back her tears. They
to head for the quayside, because she doesn't want
ee her in this state. But there's nothing she can do.
's left two children, what she loves most. "Right
laims, having heard Eloi strike two in the after-
have woken up from their sleep. My mother-in-law
to control them. And Tomeu will be asking for me
turn around," her brother tells her. "Don't think
husband is a bit scatterbrained, but he's not a bad
be sure he won't abandon them," he gently takes
m and notices how she trembles. "You'll see them
ee how Jehovah watches over them. And you were
dear. The children are too small to run into trou-
n't come to any harm."

wearing her best headscarf. Although this is for-
ade of silk embroidered with gold thread. A ray of
the clasp and breaks up into other rays as if it had
the heart of a St Savior or Lady of Sorrow. "I'm
says Isabel. "Save yourself, Rafel. I can't leave my
she gently disengages her brother's arm and takes
steps backwards. But Rafel does not let her, he
, protects her. "It's better for the children if you're

of rain and wild storms in raging September, like the one that made the river overflow and sweep up everything in its path. More than four thousand dead in a savage night. Swollen, rotting corpses floated in the bay the day after the disaster and carried on floating for two more days, warning of the plague that broke out, the ugliest of all the ills they and only they were responsible for . . . Many fellow citizens accused them of having provoked the floods, of having summoned the storm, of having caused that fierce rain that brought down turbid, violent waters. As if the power of their ancestors, taking revenge for that forced baptism, were like the power of Jehovah, Only Lord of heaven and earth, who has the power to send lightning and stop the sun.

The city is behind them. Next to the bell-tower of St Eulalia's, Segell and Argenteria, their streets; the others call them *people from the Street*. In some houses there's nobody. But there are dirty dishes in the sink, waiting for the maid to return at night, who won't be able to believe her eyes. The Christian maid in front of whom they pretend to say the rosary and eat bacon . . . The farce is over at last. No more pretending. That's enough comedy. They are leaving. Fleeing. Escaping. They know they're breaking the law that forbids them to abandon this land. They know that if they're caught, they'll be sentenced to death. But if they stay, as well. Since Costura died, since Father Ferrando during his final hours did not leave his side by day or by night, things have gotten complicated. Soon proceedings will be opened. Soon the Bailiff, with threats, will knock at their doors or hurriedly break them down without regret. He has men ready with the ax. He'll knock at a bad time, early in the morning, to frighten them more, to scare them more. Rudely he'll make them dress and will scatter the sleep still clinging to their eyes. They can hear the squeak of the iron bolts as they're drawn back and the cries and shouts of the children. He'll shackle them like beasts and lead them to the Black House, the Dark

House, and who knows if they'll come out of there cleared or to be burned alive?

They're leaving. They're going, but not giving up. *One day our children or our children's children will come back for what is ours, what we're leaving behind, what we haven't been able to sell so as not to arouse suspicion. Our houses and shops and workshops. Our tools, furniture and clothes.* They've shut everything up and taken the key. The key they mustn't lose, the key and title-deeds proving their ownership, even if all their goods are confiscated, as soon as the house is seen to be empty, and they, no doubt, are burned in effigy. *We'll never see you again, land of ours, stepmother rather than mother, given all you've done to us, all you haven't given us. We've kept warm with ashes, eaten snakes, drunk poisonous waters . . .* They relate exploits. Talk about everything to avoid talking about nothing, to avoid increasing their anxiety, fear of the crossing, the open sea few of them know, the attacks of corsairs, the storms that sink ships. They talk about the weather that is now so important to them, about the calm at sea, extremely worrying, because there's no breeze and, if there's no breeze, the sails can't be filled. "What do you think, Consul?" asks the tailor Valleriola, "I'm not sure we'll be able to leave." But the Consul doesn't reply. It's Gabriel Valls who answers with a scathing look. "It's a glorious day, a splendid day, sent to us by the Lord our God," he remarks before returning to his family: his son, his wife and the gardeners' younger daughter, who's engaged to Rafel Onofre; he's only missing the crazy mother-in-law he hasn't dared bring, because every day she gets worse, shouts and kicks and sees thieves and witches everywhere, and his elder son, who lives in Alicante and knows nothing about the escape. They'll have time to inform him from Livorno.

Only Gabriel Valls ate with any pleasure, praising his gardener's sponge-cake most of all, which Costura liked so much. The others picked at cakes without any enthusiasm. The rabbi outside and not dead, burned to a cinder. You have to escape."

Their uncle Costura told Father Ferrando that nothing could be done with them. "They're Jews and they'll die Jews," Rafel heard him say two days before dying, when the Jesuit, rather than confessing him, interrogated him about all those he considered worthy of suspicion. "I should have thought of a way to bring the children with me. Beleta will be looking for me all over the house," she sobbed. "I don't want you getting maudlin. I don't want to see those red eyes and that swollen face. You look ugly and you're supposed to be the most beautiful girl in the Street . . ."

Madò Grossa has almost caught up with them. She's walking nimbly despite her years. *She must be wearing all the skirts she has,* suspects Isabel. *She reminds me of the whale that swallowed the prophet.* Her sister and the two grandchildren are a short distance behind her. "If she's in the bow," says Polònia Miró, "the rest of us had better go in the stern. She's carrying all she has, can't you see?" Polònia addresses her neighbor, Rafela Miró, arm in arm with Xim Valleriola, who would much prefer to be chatting to the men and asking them about certain aspects of the journey he would urgently like cleared up. He is one of those who've contributed most money to the escape, and it's only fair he get a good place. Aina's son cries out for his mother's breast, and the Cortès brothers stop. Aina sits down on a stone bench and suckles that child who is her disgrace. At home they almost wouldn't look at him. He meant nothing to them. Only the youngest brother could bring himself to touch him and bought him a whistle.

The rabbi was one of the last to stand up. First he walked alongside his family, but then he waited for the Consul. The afternoon turns a patch of sky pale, but there's still no breeze. The sea is as flat as a freshly starched sheet. Only a rowing boat disturbs the calm. "What if there's no wind?" Valleriola asks

Gabriel Valls uneasily. "There has to be . . ." answers Valls without losing the smile that has accompanied him all day, giving his face an almost beatific serenity. "Man of little faith, how can you think Jehovah will not breathe for us? How can you think Jehovah will abandon us?"

And he tells them again what they already know: that Adonai's providence has been magnanimous, sending them that unsuspicious xebec that has anchored in the city port many times before and whose crew is even known to Pere Onofre Aguiló, who has done so much to help them from Livorno. Gabriel Valls praises the behavior of the captain, who only yesterday, less than twenty-four hours previously, visited the Consul's home and agreed that the following day, between three and four in the afternoon, as if they had gone for a walk outside the walls, as if they had happened to reach the quayside while stretching their legs, as on other Sundays if the weather was good—and the added fact it was Sunday was also a blessing sent by Jehovah, because nobody could suspect anything out of the ordinary—they would embark on a rowing boat that would take them to *The Aeolus*, anchored in the mouth of the port.

They've left behind the cluster of pines in Bellver, with such a wonderful fragrance of resin. They're almost there. The signal tower seems to welcome them. They advance with difficulty. They don't have hands, mouth, ears or eyes. Only smell. A precise sense of smell that moves their feet following the scent laid down by the rabbi, who represents the Most High. The boat is waiting. Now, perhaps because they wanted it so much, they manage to get a wind blowing. God has sent them this breeze that ruffles the waves. The boat will have to make at least three journeys, because not everybody will fit in at once. The children and women first. Then the old people and other women. Lastly, the men.

The city is just a whitish spot in the east. The sea has

changed its appearance and is nothing like the freshly starched sheet of a few hours before. Now the waves resemble wolves' jaws with gleaming fangs. The splashes and lather, like foaming saliva, catch them full on. They're all wet, and some are soaked. They have difficulty boarding. The sailors helped the passengers on the first two journeys. The men on the last journey board with more confidence, but also find it hard because the xebec doesn't stop moving. They were put in one of the holds. They're almost in the dark. The children scream in fear. They were made to sit on the floor, in a huddle, one on top of another. It smells musty down there. The whiff of spices merges with the stink of excrement. The Consul and Gabriel Valls go up on deck and tell the captain they've paid far too much money to be treated like slaves. He assures them that once they've weighed anchor and are sailing on the open sea, they can sit on deck or take shelter in the cabins. "I didn't know there would be children," he informs them. "We always spoke of a dozen people and there are more than twenty of you." "You can't deny that you've been paid extremely well," retorts Valls. "No, but I'm running a great risk," answers Willis. "If it wasn't for the fact that I'm a very good friend of Pere Onofre Aguiló, as you know, and he asked me, I wouldn't have taken you on board for all the money in the world."

They go down to pass on the news and encourage the others with the captain's promise. "The first thing we have to do is give thanks to God that we're already on board," cautions Valls. "We'll give him thanks when we're there," Aina Cortès blurts out. But nobody pays her attention. The rabbi's voice silences all remarks: *O give thanks unto the Lord, and call upon his Name, tell the people what things he hath done. O let your songs be of him, and praise him, and let your talking be of all his wondrous works* . . . The rest follow suit. The murmur of their prayer is heard on deck, where the sailors of *The Aeolus* are working to prepare the ship to set sail on the captain's orders. *Remember the marvellous works that he hath done, his wonders, and the judgements of his mouth, O ye seed of Abraham his servant, ye children of Jacob his chosen.*

The captain comes down in person to ask them not to shout so much, not to make their religion so obvious, they'll have time for prayers when they're in the last blue. "Pray in your hearts," says the rabbi, "without moving your lips. Pray with faith, thank God for the favor he shows us and the help he sends us. Pray also for the others still in the city, that Adonai may protect them."

Isabel Tarongí is unable to suppress a groan that rises from deep inside her. But it's not only her. Others do the same. "I don't want mourners on board," exclaims the rabbi in a firm voice. "Today is a day of joy, of thanksgiving, not of weeping. A great day for all of us. Adonai does not want weeping, he wants delight from us today. We're escaping so that we can freely obey the rules laid down by our religion, so that we don't have to hide, so that we can proclaim that we're Jews and we'll die Jews." "We're escaping to avoid being flayed alive," grumbles Cap de Trons' son in a low voice, who is reckless like his father. "You're right, for that as well, because Adonai needs us alive and not dead for his glory," Valls answers him. "Rabbi," says Valleriola, who had never called him this before, "haven't they told you when we're leaving? Because the wind's blowing with a vengeance . . ." "The wind's contrary," replies the Consul. "We won't be able to leave till it calms down." "Now what do we do?" cries Aina Cortès, who had no desire to embark. "Will we have to return to land?" asks Valleriola. "Then it *will* be obvious we're escaping!" says Madò Grossa's sister. "They'll arrest us quicker than if we hadn't left," Aina crows again. "Be quiet or you'll feel the back of my hand!" her middle brother warns her. "That's enough!" the rabbi raises his voice. "I don't want any fighting here. That's all we need! God will not leave us, you can be sure! God cannot abandon us!" "You seem very convinced," remarks Xim Valleriola in his unmistakable, piping voice. "What if God doesn't feel like helping us today?" The rabbi pounces on him: "Man of little faith! *The Lord is my shepherd, therefore can I lack nothing* . . ." "You answer us with a prayer we all know, Gabriel Valls, which is scant consolation," interjects Martí. "If we can't set sail, you'll tell us what you think we have to do." "Not put the cart before the horse, now at least, and wait for as long as possible. If we have to go back," suggests the Consul, "we should do so before they close St Catherine's Gate, which will be soon . . ." "Can't you hear the wind? It sounds like a hurricane!" exclaims Madò Grossa. "Consul, come with me," orders the rabbi. "We'll talk to the captain."

The captain is smoking in his cabin in front of a cup full of a dark liquid they have never seen and held upright by a ring. He invites them to sit on the bed while he clings to the porthole and struggles to keep his balance. The Consul has turned the color of a frog. His whole face is green and he can barely speak. "The wind is increasing, we can't leave like this," says the captain, tired of Valls' insistence that they weigh anchor immediately. "We'd sink for sure. We must wait till the storm slackens. It's impossible to leave the port and sail in the dark in such conditions . . . We must wait till tomorrow."

Lord God, Adonai, enlighten me, prays Gabriel Valls de Valls Major before opening his mouth, *show me what I must do.* He then asks Willis if they can stay in the hold, if he thinks they're at risk. The captain advises them to disembark: "If they're looking for you, they'll no doubt suspect you're here. There's no other ship in the whole bay. If they find you, they'll skin me even if I am a foreigner. When it calms down, I'll let you know. You must be ready tomorrow morning." "And what guarantee will you give us that you won't take off with our money?" asks the Consul.

"My word," retorts the captain, angry because he didn't like the Consul's question at all.

The children, who were so exhausted they had fallen asleep, are quickly woken. "Dear children, we're going back home," say the women, "you'll be more comfortable in your own beds." "May Adonai protect us!" repeat the old people, terrified at having to get back into the rowing boat, which is like a nut tossed about by the waves. "I'm afraid, I want to go with you and not with the women," says Maria Pomar to Rafel Onofre in a thin voice about to break. "You must go with my mother, but nothing will happen to you, my sweet, because I love you."

The forced disembarkation has struck them all like the plague, all except for Isabel Tarongí, who is the only one convinced that God has heard her. Immediately to see her children again is what she has been asking for since early this morning, since she leaned her gentle, pale face over her still sleeping babies to say farewell, with the excuse that she was going to visit a sick aunt with her brother.

"We'll go back the way we came," says the rabbi, "and we'll try to arrive before they close the city gates. If the patrol stops us, you know what to say: we were walking on the quayside and were caught by the storm."

The women and children disembark first. Their skirts and headscarves flap in the thick wind. They scream in fear, seeing how the boat is pushed against the xebec's hull. Old Aina Segura commended herself to both Jehovah and the Christ of St Eulalia's, just in case, that way there'll be two to help her, and on sitting down in the boat told this to Polònia, who severely scolded her. The children, protected by the women, tremble like poplar leaves. They pray and tremble. The sailors have to row hard to counteract the force of the waves, but are fortunate because the wind is behind them. The group's already there. Soaked they begin the return journey. The sun is still high, but will soon set. "Come on, why don't you sing a song?" Quitèria suggests to her sons in an effort to distract them. The boat goes back, without cargo it moves more nimbly. The second group is getting ready. The first to go down is Rafela Miró. Her husband has hung back to avoid going with her, in the hope of going with the men. Now it's Madò Grossa, who on setting foot in the boat almost tips it over. Aina Cortès does not wish to entrust anyone with her child, who whimpers no doubt because he's hungry. "He must be sucking bad milk," remark the other women, seeing the sour expression of Cap de Trons' daughter. He's been wrapped in a shawl against her breast so that her hands are free, but suddenly, halfway down the ladder, she loses her balance and the child falls into the waves. "I can't swim!" she cries. And shouts and groans and, as soon as she's in the boat, rips out her hair. A sailor dives into the water. He struggles against the waves to reach the child and, when he finally manages it and lifts him up on to the xebec, the baby's lips are purple and he isn't breathing. Isabel Tarongí presses him to her breast because his mother, in a fit of hysterics, doesn't know which world she's in. And it's Isabel who gets into the boat with the dead child and looks after the little bundle in her arms for the duration of the crossing. "We were walking along the quayside when the accident happened," says the rabbi to those returning to port. "A sailor dived in to save him, but was too late. Is that clear? There's no need to add anything else."

The rabbi thanks the sailor profusely. He didn't dare dive into the sea. He thought he wouldn't be able to save him, he would drown, and this worries him. The sailor displayed a lot of courage. Aina cries out for her son. With the dead baby in her arms she moves among the other women. Isabel Tarongí weeps silently. A golden sunset draws them in, tinged with violet ashes. They are accompanied for a while by the flight of seagulls, which twist and turn above their heads. The first swifts of the year fly by in flocks.

The last to leave the ship is Gabriel Valls. The Consul went down before him with his children, Pere Onofre Martí helping Valleriola, alias Xoteto, then Joaquim and Baltasar Cap de Trons and Rafel Onofre Valls de Valls Major. None of them is left on board *The Aeolus* and with that storm there's nobody out walking in Port Pi. "If no one's seen the boat come and go six times, everything will be all right." The rabbi hopes so. He's cold because he's drenched and is very tired, exhausted. But despite this he strides forward and asks everyone to hurry. All they need now is to have to sleep in the open! Then they would have problems explaining the escape!

Valls' face is grim and the expression of a flute about to burst into festive music has turned into one of somber panpipes. He feels guilty. He alone is responsible for the failure. He decided they would embark. He agreed terms with the captain, selected those most at risk, dictated who would escape and who would stay. He assured them that Adonai would not abandon them, he insulted them when they doubted, calling them "Men of little faith!" He asked Adonai for wind and God sent him wind, but it was a contrary wind. And if he, the chosen one, the rabbi, the master, had lost God's trust . . .? In no time at all everything has turned against him. Even the newborn's death is his fault. Didn't Aina Cortès ask him not to force her to come with that child? And didn't he persuade her not to abandon her son to an orphanage and oblige her to bring that child, her disgrace, and redeem him from evil in lands of freedom, where he himself had promised to see to his education, to make him a proper Jew?

The sun has reached its obsequies. Clouds streaked with red lay wreaths. The first group has already entered the city by St Catherine's Gate, is heading down Holy Cross, advancing along Vi Street and crossing Horlandisque Bridge. They hear Figuera strike the time. "Six!" counts Maria Pomar, accompanying her future mother-in-law. "What a long day!" says Maria Aguiló. "I wish we were home already!" They're in Nova Square, turning the corner of St Eulalia and Segell, when they stop short. They have no choice but to stop. The Assistant Bailiff bars their way on top of his horse.

II

IT WAS THE POOR, POSSESSED MADWOMAN WHO BEGAN TO shout. Screaming, she fumbled with keys, locks and bolts until opening doors and windows and denounced the thieves that were stealing everything, taking everything away. The thieves first, and then the witches who had put the evil eye on her. Neither her sister nor the two maids were able to silence her or managed to calm her down. She wanted to flee, to leave that haunted house so as not to be found by those enemies who had no respect. When they stopped her reaching the front door, she panted and pulled her hair and banged her head against the walls. She kept on blaming the witches for everything. "The witches, whores, have taken Maria and left me all alone, who ever saw such a thing?" "Don't worry, she'll be back soon," her sister tells her. "She's gone for a walk. It's Sunday today after all." "Where did you come from?" she replies. "Who on earth are you?" And she opens wide her roving, but inquisitive eyes as if wanting to place her somewhere. "Who do you think I am? Who could I be but Esther?" "Who are you and what are you doing here?" she asks again as if she hadn't heard her, while tugging at a loose lock of hair. "Do you know her? Her, her," she asks the maids, repeating the last word as she tends to. "It's your sister," Jerònia answers her. "I don't have a sister," she insists. "That's enough, Caterina, dear," says Esther, gently taking her arm. "That's enough, Caterina. Take a good look at me. Of course you have a sister!" "Aren't you dead then?" she asks after observing her as if she sought out her soul and in this search had found the gleam of an ancient memory that gave her confusion a little coherence. "No, Caterina, no, not yet. Can't you see how alive I am?" "See, see . . . It's the witches. The witches showing you in a shroud. Witches, witches, witches . . .!" She again repeats the word as if it were stuck in her throat, as if she only knew one that would open the doors of the secret room where the treasure is kept. "O God!" exclaims Esther Bonnín to herself. "What have I done to deserve this punishment? I don't know if I can bear it." "Witches, whores!" She varies the litany with another insult. "Caterina," her sister shouts again, "let the witches go, let them be, we don't need them anymore. Can't you see I've come to keep you company?" "It's the wind that's made her like this," declares Jerònia. "This devilish wind that won't blow us any good. I hadn't seen her so bad for a long time." "Witches, witches, whores . . ."

They shut her in her room and make her lie down on the bed, and she seems to become sleepy. They've given her an infusion of lime, mint and poppy flower, which calms the nerves, to see if they can assuage her fury. Her eyes are closed and she seems to be resting. So they tiptoed out and went downstairs. Esther sat next to the stove and Jerònia, the old housemaid, went back to the room she shares with her niece, Magdalena, who has been serving in the Valls' house for a year and, while she's not fond of them, is better off than in the home of Canon Amorós, who regulated her food and tormented her all the time. But neither Esther nor Jerònia manage to rest for more than ten minutes. Again they hear her climb the stairs and kick and stamp until opening the door to the terrace and from up there she makes an unholy racket, groans and cries out loud again and asks the neighbors to help her leave this haunted house. She's absolutely convinced that everything that is happening is because of spells and evil eyes. And she shouts out the name of Madò Grossa, the healer, and accuses her of having carried off her daughter on a leaf. "O witches, witches," she repeats wildly in the whistling wind that lifts her skirts and makes her look like a scarecrow. Neither Esther nor Jerònia, who has come up, accompanied by her niece, manage to subdue her. "Witches, witches, Satan's sisters, who took away my daughter. Ah, but I swear you'll burn for this!" "Come on, madam," says Jerònia, "it's no use being up here with all this wind. Won't you come down now?" The madwoman is silent for a few moments and waves her fists against the wind that has swiped her nightcap. Esther goes up to her and is about to place a hand on her back to lead her downstairs when she is attacked with scratches and bites. Jerònia and Magdalena attempt to defend her and also receive the sparks of her fury. "What a token, sister, to have been left behind with you!" exclaims Esther Bonnín in a loud voice and immediately she realizes there are outsiders with her, people from Can Peroni, and it's not good to let on. She'll have plenty of time to explain that madness the best she can. Caterina Bonnín does not wish to listen to reason. She kicks and scratches like a cat about to be skinned every time they try to restrain her. "We'll only catch her using nets," exclaims Jerònia. "You're right, aunt. What if we contacted the neighbors? They might lend us a hand. It's no use being up here in such a storm." "Thank God!" says the sister, seeing how Tomeu Aguiló has just jumped over the terrace's party wall. He lives two houses down and on hearing the rumpus climbed up to see what kind of madwoman was shouting out all those obscenities. "What's going on, madam? Don't you see the wind will snatch us all up in a moment? Come on, inside, inside. Quick, quick . . . You can go down now." Caterina starts to resist, but then, like a child, lets herself be led downstairs to her bedroom by the young man, without saying a word.

"This is a miracle, Tomeu," says the sister. "I don't know how to thank you."

There is a loud knock at the front door. "Open up. What's all this fuss about?" It's the Assistant Bailiff's gravelly voice that booms out, blunt and powerful. "All right, all right! Jesus and St Antony!" exclaims Jerònia. "What a hectic afternoon! What a bloody awful Sunday!" And she draws back the bolt and turns the key in the lock. "I heard Madò Caterina's shouts as I was turning into Segell Street. Where's Gabriel Valls? Or isn't the family at home?" Ripoll asks the housemaid in his typically harsh voice. "Why have they left this poor woman all alone on a Sunday?" "They've gone for a walk," replies the sister, who immediately approaches the door on seeing who the untimely visitor is, "and that's why I've come to keep her company. Besides, she wouldn't have been on her own even if I hadn't come. Aren't the maids baptized flesh and blood?"

Ripoll does not deign to answer, grunts and lifts up his head. A sardonic smile passes across his carelessly molded face. "Witches, witches . . .!" the poor madwoman shouts out again. "I'll get you, Madò Grossa, get you real good. It's you who put the evil eye on them." "She may be speaking the truth," hazards the Assistant Bailiff scornfully and wrinkles up his nose in a gesture of disgust before exclaiming, "It stinks of frying!"

Tomeu Aguiló finds him still at the door. "And what are you doing here?" "I came to help these women," he says, "when I heard the uproar." "Aren't you the good Samaritan, Tomeuet?" replies Ripoll mockingly while taking several steps back. "I don't want to hear anybody," he warns. "She's just a poor madwoman," exclaims Tomeu. "I said I don't want to hear anybody, least of all you. You're like peas in a pod, bloody Jews!"

Esther Bonnín turned the key again and waited by the door for a second so that the Assistant Bailiff would hear her: "Come on, girls, let's say the rosary!" With the Hail Mary on her lips she entered the kitchen. Her sister, calmer now, warms herself at the stove. "Witches, witches," she still says in a low voice, as if accompanying the prayer of the other women with her own litany. The Assistant Bailiff mounts his horse. "What a stink!" he exclaims and, while spurring on the horse, turns a threatening face towards the Valls' house and rebukes the women again, forcing his voice into a roar: "Try not to upset the street again with all this shouting or I'll have to come to a decision." He goes, but he only lets the horse take a few paces before reining it in. Even though it's Sunday, he'll use the fact he's here to visit the tailor Valleriola and wind him up a bit. He promised to deliver the cloak he ordered a week ago and as always has broken his promise. He dismounts and knocks at the door. There's no reply. Next he calls at the neighbor, Polònia, who, since Costura died of that stomach-ache that lasted eight days, has remained in the house all alone with the permission of his nephews, who haven't dared throw her out. He knocks, knocks again, kicks at the door, but nobody comes to open. "God save us, these Jews are always on holiday," he says in a loud voice to offend whoever's listening. "They must all be in the garden, having a good lunch. And I could bring the bacon!" "Blasted Jews who killed Good Jesus," adds the lackey, who has just appeared and is even more bad-tempered than Ripoll, because he is hunchbacked and has been treated like a workhorse all his life. "Why don't you go and call at Cap de Trons' house?" suggests his master. "I wanted to come tomorrow, but now that I'm here, I'd like to know how much they'll give me for this old cloak. Don't think you're getting it . . . I know you've had your eye on it, but honey isn't made for a donkey's mouth. Go on, Perot, that way we'll disturb them for a bit. Go on, hurry up."

Perot looks like a character in a pantomime with his big steps and the hunchback hanging like a sack down to his haunches. "Come on, quickly," orders Ripoll, "you look gorgeous.

Hey, girls, come on out here . . . Hurry now and feast your eyes on this wonder." "There's no reply," says Perot, having knocked loudly and kicked at the door. "Do you think I'm deaf, you idiot? I can see there's no one." "They must all be in the synagogue," remarks Perot right next to Ripoll's horse, which stamps and neighs nervously. "Didn't your mother teach you anything? Not today. That was yesterday, Saturday. But you're right in one respect: at this hour, with the wall about to close, if they're not at home, they must be up to no good!"

The wind is blowing strongly and sweeps up leaves and dust. The old bronze of Figuera is shaken by its onslaughts and has just struck six. The few people left in the streets quickly seek shelter. Ripoll is about to abandon the patrol, but the difficulties of Perot, who shields his eyes against the particles raised by the wind, make him carry on. They've reached the Quarter and, instead of heading for Banc de s'Oli or Sindicat, they go back to Segell. "That way we'll surprise them," says Ripoll to his lackey. The street is now quiet. Only the wind whistles in fits and starts. The Assistant Bailiff guides the horse towards Nova Square. They want to get to Portella to see if the wall has been closed on time, as it should. Suddenly they hear footsteps and on turning into St Eulalia come across the first group to disembark. "Whoa!" he addresses them rudely. "Where've you been at this hour, looking so black and blue?" "To the quay . . ." "The quay? Walking on the quay in such a storm? And what happened to you in Port Pi?" "An accident . . ." "An accident? What accident?" "Aina Cap de Trons' son, who drowned!" says Madò Grossa. "Must have been his mother, threw him in the water!" replies Perot with a laugh. "Where is Aina now? And the child?" Nobody answers. "OK, come on. OK, come on, all of you, we'll get to the bottom of this." "Let us go home," pleads Maria Aguiló, "and tomorrow you can take a statement. It's late now and we're tired." "Tomorrow's no good," answers Ripoll boldly, "there's been a death and you will have to bear witness."

The children are crying. The women start to groan when they see that the Assistant Bailiff has unsheathed his sword and spurs the horse to set it like a hound on that terrified huddle. "You see we're defenseless and that's why you maltreat us," says Maria Aguiló. "The men will be here soon." "Brave men you have," answers the lackey mockingly, "a bunch of cuckolds, bores, devils with tails!" "Tell them that to their face, Perot," says Madò Grossa, hot as red pepper. "Look who's talking, witch!" intervenes the Assistant Bailiff. "Watch out if you don't want to burn alive. You'd make a good fire. All that fat!" "Quieten down, Ripoll, we've known each other poorer," interjects the tailor's wife, who dealt with him as a boy, because his father was a saddler who opened a workshop in the district. "Quieten down, you don't know what you're saying." "I don't know what I'm saying? I know what I'm saying all right! Valls' mother-in-law was just accusing Madò Grossa of being a witch. We might just have to see if that's true. She was really shouting out from the terrace and very clearly stating you were flying . . ." "Where is my mother?" asks Maria Aguiló anxiously. "What have you done to her? The poor woman's out of her mind!" "Go on ahead now," replies the Assistant Bailiff. "And you, wait here, Perot. I'll send reinforcements. Stop everyone coming in." "Why do you have to do that, Ripoll?" exclaims Polònia. "What have we done wrong?" "I want to know where you've been, down to the minutest detail . . ." "We've been on a xebec," exclaims Miquelet, Quitèria Pomar's son. "Now I get it," says Ripoll, "now I understand everything. Wouldn't you like a ride on my horse? I bet you're tired, aren't you?" His mother turns pale. "For God's sake, Miquelet," she tells him, "don't fib. We went to Port Pi for a little walk . . ." "Come up on my horse, Miquelet," insists Ripoll. "I like you. You're a bright lad. Come on, tell me all about it." But Miquelet doesn't speak. Seeing how high he is on the stamping horse, he bursts into tears and sobs and calls out to his mother, who cries as well and pleads with Ripoll to give her back her son. "I'm going to get reinforcements," he repeats and gallops off with the child towards Nova Square. Quitèria Pomar has the good sense to whisper something to her elder son, who ducks and runs in the direction of Bosseria. He will try to find the men and warn them.

The Head Bailiff himself arrives with a group. "Everybody, stay where you are," he tells them, "or you'll be sentenced to death." The women go back into a huddle. "What are you going to do to us, sir?" asks Maria Aguiló. "Can't you see we can barely stand? Couldn't you wait till tomorrow and let us rest for a bit. We're worn out, what with all this wind!" "I'm taking you to the Black House," replies the Bailiff. "I've no choice. Were it up to me, I'd let you spend the night at home, but then I'd be punished." The Bailiff is still young. He looks as if he hasn't reached thirty. He addresses the women in soft tones. He's examined and appraised that merchandise at a glance. Nobody attracts his attention, except for Maria Pomar, who holds her future mother-in-law's hand, shaking and weeping silently. "Is this girl your daughter?" asks Don Gaspar Puigdorfila. "No, sir, but as good as. She's engaged to my younger son, Rafel Onofre." "All the same, you look alike," says the Bailiff, trying to work out what Maria Aguiló's youthful charms must have been, a trace of which remains. "Dear sir, for the love of God," insists Maria Aguiló, "I'm exhausted and this poor child can barely stand." "I'd be happy to leave it till tomorrow, madam, but I can't."

A tile fell in front of Don Gaspar's horse and smashed in a thousand pieces. The horse reared and almost threw the Bailiff. "Get a move on," he orders his men, "or the wind will finish us all off." The people of the Street watch from behind their windows. Marianna Martí, Pere Onofre Aguiló's mother, thanks God for the decision he inspired not to embark, because now she would be like those wretches, walking along between two lines of armed men, being buffeted by that wind. Esther Bonnín starts to cry when she recognizes her niece. The poor madwoman stands gaping as well and, on catching sight of her daughter, shouts aloud: "Where are you taking my Maria?" she asks. "Oy, Madò Grossa, look out, witches . . ." And she hurries downstairs. Now nobody prevents her from going outside. Esther Bonnín follows closely, but does nothing to stop her. *She might persuade the Bailiff to give us back Maria,* she thinks, *even if it's only for one night.* The Bailiff's men don't know what to do with the old woman running through the procession, spurred on by the blustering wind. With kicks and bites she fends off the guards and rushes at Madò Grossa, who looks at her in astonishment. "You carried her off, witch," she spits. Maria Aguiló is the first to break that heavy silence. "Don't talk nonsense, mother, and go back inside. We've just been for a walk. Madò Grossa hasn't touched me." Maria Aguiló hugs her for a second. "Go with your sister," she says. "And be good, mother." The madwoman clings to the wall, protected by Esther Bonnín, who exclaims, "Lord Bailiff, will you not have pity on this poor old woman and give her back her daughter?" But Don Gaspar Puigdorfila does not reply, his attention diverted by another group of women entering Segell Street from Nova Square, shouting and groaning much more than the others. In the light of the torches he ordered his men to kindle, the Bailiff scrutinizes the downcast faces. He is used to selecting the choicest, juiciest fruits and can easily imagine which features will regain their lost beauty with a rest and which will never be attractive, even if Morpheus were to take them in his arms for three centuries. So he is impressed by the sorrowful air and resemblance to Mary Magdalene of Isabel Tarongí, disheveled, without her headscarf, which the impolite wind must have swiped, her clothes torn, who refuses to move and has to be dragged along and shouts for them to let her go, she wants to see her children. He would love to release her, he himself would undress her and put her nightshirt on her and watch over her until she woke up. But he wouldn't do anything for Aina Cap de Trons, who with the dead child in her arms deserves far greater pity. "I don't suppose he received extreme unction," he says to her. "You'll be wanting him to go to heaven . . ." Aina does not reply. She carries the child against her swollen breasts, which hurt because they need to be emptied. "He'll be buried tomorrow in the proper way," Gaspar Puigdorfila assures her, "and tonight you can watch over him. Please accept my condolences." Aina remains mute. "Thank him, woman," whispers Aina Segura, walking behind her with her two grandchildren. The Bailiff overhears her and looks kindly at the old woman. "Sir, these children, won't you let them sleep at home? They're very tired." "Tomorrow, tomorrow, if the Inquisitor permits," replies the Head Bailiff while moving off.

The doors of the Black House, the Dark House, have been opened wide and oil lamps hung at the entrance. A gust of wind extinguishes a couple of flames, which the porter relights immediately. The fire stains the redwood beams propping up the high ceiling and speckles the faces of saints gaping from the dark of paintings. Three familiars are waiting to receive that band proudly led by Ripoll. "We were just going to bed when we got your message," one of them says to the Assistant Bailiff. "I had one foot in already, but this was worth staying up for." "I should think so," answers Ripoll. "It's a good catch and all thanks to me, since I'm the one who hooked them."

They direct everybody to the left, through two poorly lit rooms. In a third room with chairs against the walls and a writing-desk, they order them to stop. Madò Grossa, her sister Aina and the tailor Valleriola sit down. "No sitting down, you lazy lot! Remain standing, that's what you have to do, unless I tell you to kneel," barks Ripoll, who has accompanied the prisoners this far. And again they are put in a line, one behind the other, and separated from the children. "The children can follow me," says another familiar, who has just come in with a torch. "They'll get something to eat." "A bit of bacon!" laughs the Assistant Bailiff. "The children and you, Aina Cap de Trons, follow me." The children cross a courtyard and climb to the second floor, preceded by the officer of the Inquisition. Aina, no. Aina is led by a tall man in a cassock to a room on the ground floor, a long way away from the others. On entering she screams. In the middle of the room is a large coffin, surrounded by four burning torches. But the coffin is empty. "You're in luck," says the slippery man in a cassock. "This coffin is ready for Don Joan Montis, who's about to peg out. You can use it for your child till tomorrow. Tomorrow, before we bury it, we'll order a box from the carpenter. A box should do . . ." Aina remains silent. She lays the child in that oarless boat, which swallows his tiny body like a bubble. "Not much of him," remarks the broom in a cassock before leaving.

There's no chair, only a kneeler, but Aina does not kneel down. She does not want to watch over the corpse, nor can she. She's sleepy. Her breasts ache, she feels the dampness of the milk and the trickles soaking her bodice. Her head is burning. She approaches the coffin. She gazes at her son and with her right hand traces his features. He looks just like Juli Ramis. Nobody will deny he's the spitting image.

"I don't want to hear anybody," the others are informed by the Judge of Goods, who has just arrived. "I don't want to hear any groaning. If you're repentant, silently ask Good Jesus to forgive you, but don't cry." "What are you going to do to us?" asks Madò Grossa. "That depends," replies the priest, still short of breath, shaking his voluminous double chin. "Now," he tells them, "we have to make an inventory. The sooner we finish, the sooner we can go and lie down." "Will we be allowed back home?" inquires Isabel Fustera, expressing herself for the first time. "No, madam," answers Jaume Llabrés, "that's out of the question, there's no way you're going back home. You wouldn't be able to get in. You'll sleep here, in the Inquisition's cells." Isabel Tarongí can hardly breathe. Maria Pomar doesn't stop crying. "What about my grandchildren? They only have me!" groans Aina Segura. "Silence, I said! Didn't you hear me? The familiars will give you a hand and the clerk will make a note of everything."

The familiars, Bartomeu Sales, Antoni Papell and Tòfol Martí, are accompanied by the clerk, Miquel Massot. He's a skinny little man who hops about as if in another life he had been a sparrow. He greets the audience in an almost sugary voice. "Good evening, your reverence," he addresses the Judge of Goods, "good evening, ladies . . ." He sits behind his desk, hitches up his sleeves and dips the pen in the inkpot. He awaits orders and so writes nothing down, but points the nib at the paper and with his left hand adjusts the flame of the lamp on his desk. Meanwhile the familiars search the first women in the line, high and low. They feel them, grope them, look up their skirts and open their bodices. They remove rings, earrings, bracelets, buttons, gold chains. Their hungry hands reach the most secret hiding places and the money crashes to the ground. "I shall report your bad manners to the Viceroy," Maria Aguiló dares to say. "We're defenseless women and you're taking advantage." The Judge of Goods glares at her: "I wouldn't do that if I were you, woman. Who do you think you are? Besides, the Viceroy is not in charge in this house. Here only the Holy Office is in charge.

"You can start now, Miquel," says the Judge. "Right away, your reverence." The clerk has big handwriting in contrast to his reduced stature and quickly writes:

Maria Aguiló, married to Gabriel Valls de Valls Major, from the city, aged forty-eight. One ruby ring, one gold wedding ring, ruby earrings and buttons she was wearing. Item, hidden away in deep pockets sewn to her skirts, three solid gold chains and fifty Majorcan ounces, three buttons and one diamond ornament. Silk scarf and taffeta skirt.

Maria Pomar, maiden, daughter of Josep Pomar and Miquela Fuster, aged fourteen, from Porreres. Some gold earrings and one gold ring with a filigree flower. Seven sous in a pocket.

Rafela Miró, married to Xim Valleriola, aged sixty-five or sixty-seven, from the town of Sóller. Gold wedding ring, gold button and thirty ounces.

Quitèria Pomar, married to Pere Onofre Martí, known as Moixina, aged twenty-seven, from the city. Turquoise ring, gold wedding ring, gold button and, in a pocket sewn to her skirts, twenty Majorcan ounces and one gold ornament. Silk scarf and saffron-colored silk skirt.

Polònia Miró, spinster, from the city, aged sixty-nine. Gold ornament and in her pockets twenty-nine sous and one button.

Pràxedes Segura, known as Madò Grossa, widow, from the city, aged sixty-five. Gold chain, gold earrings set with a pearl. In two pockets sewn to her skirts, forty-one silver royal maravedis, twenty-five ounces and one button. Three bags full of rue, rosemary and mint to prepare infusions. Three linen skirts and three caps under her scarf.

Aina Segura, widow, from the city, aged sixty-four. Gold button and two gold wedding rings. In her pockets the title-deed of her house and seven ounces.

Aina Fuster, known as Isabel Fustera, married to Gabriel Fortesa, aged fifty, from the city. Gold wedding ring and one chain. In her pockets twenty-five ounces and four silver royal maravedis.

Isabel Tarongí, married to Joaquim Martí, aged twenty-

seven, from the city. Gold chain, gold wedding ring and in her pockets three ounces. Not wearing a headscarf. Silk skirt, torn.

Sara Bonnín, known as Sara de les Olors, maiden, daughter of Miquel Bonnín and Marianna Piña, aged thirty, from the city. Gold earrings set with a ruby, buttons and in her pockets four Majorcan ounces. Silk scarf and two gray taffeta skirts.

The inventory is finished. "Read what you've written," the Judge of Goods orders the clerk. Miquel Massot obeys immediately, but his voice is lost like a remnant at sea. All the city bells start ringing.

III

His head is bursting. The unrelenting wind has sunk its teeth into his brain. A famished pack of wolves that, howling, attacks the guard, pounces on the shepherd and doesn't spare a single sheep. A giant who threatens to raze belfries, towers, bulwarks, and demolishes walls with the strength of his arm. A whirlwind, a giant wolf. A whirlwind that uproots trees, drives carts, people, beasts, and scatters branches and tiles.

The wind and the bells. The bells of all the city belfries: Eloi, Figuera, Bàrbara, Antònia, Mitja, Nova, Tèrcia, Matines, Picarol . . . An uproar of bells inside his poor head, which is about to explode. The bells ring constantly. They ring to stop the wind, to chase it away from the city at least, to repel it with the strength of their more powerful sound. But the wind ignores the spell. The wind laughs at the belfries and bell-ringers and carries on blustering. It pays no attention to the din of bronze that must have woken up the few still sleeping, the few who were able to close their eyes without fear: newborn babies, innocents . . .

The din of bronze against the howling wind penetrates his body to the marrow. Although he's very tired, although he can barely stand up, he can't sleep. He's kept vigil for three nights now. Two nights of preparations, nights full of hope, brimming with expectation, so different from this night. Slimy night, putrid night, night full of sharp edges, topped with barbed wire. Dark night of the howling wind and bells.

He's alone. He's been left all alone in a windowless cell. To get there, he had to go down stairs. Forty steps. Not a streak of light reaches that far. He tried shouting. He beat his fist against the wall. But nobody answers him. Nobody shows any signs of life. It can't be long before dawn. And at dawn everything will change. He'll be able to locate where he is, what corner of the Dark House he's been led to. He'll be able to ask after the others. He'll try to send a message to the Viceroy. He's told them that he and only he is to blame. It was he who took them on a walk by the sea and didn't bargain for treacherous March, a month of so many different faces. It was a wonderful day early in the morning. Nothing pointed to the storm. In Port Pi, on their way back, they were caught by the wind. The wind is to blame for their misfortune. He didn't wish to admit even the possibility of xebecs and boardings. He feigned ignorance. He doesn't know what the others have declared. He doesn't know how many were able to save themselves. How many managed to shelter in the houses of relatives or friends. Not in their own. Not in their own, which have been shut and boarded up with planks and laths. Planks and laths nailed down with a hammer. They forced him to see it. They forced him to watch how they protected his house from certain robbery. "It would be tempting for the thieves your mother-in-law was denouncing," he was told, "knowing the master is not at home." "But the maids are there," he protested. "Jerònia has been with us for more than thirty years. Magdalena, her niece, serves us as well. The maids and my mother-in-law, the poor woman, she's out of her mind and sees witches and evil spirits. Where have you taken them? Where are they? I hope you haven't shut them up inside. Does the Viceroy know about this? Have you asked his excellency for permission?" "The Inquisitor is in charge here, not the Viceroy," he was informed. "I asked after my mother-in-law and the maids. Now that I think about it, you must have found Aunt Esther at home as well. She had promised to pay us a visit this afternoon."

"You're not wrong. She was there as well. We haven't shut them up inside. They've gone to old Esther Bonnín's house. That's where they'll be until the Tribunal decides otherwise."

Segell Street is illuminated as if it were a great feast-day and the Viceroy has ordered torches and lamps to be lit everywhere. The flames that the wind extinguishes or lessens from time to time, only to fan them a moment later, give light to the piece-workers, who hammer planks and laths to those doors marked with a sign of disgrace. All the goods have been confiscated forthwith.

From now on, from the moment a door is marked with a cross, nobody can go in, bring or remove anything. The Judge will dispose in his own good time. The house that belonged to Costura, where Polònia now lives, has already been branded. And the last boards have been nailed to Cap de Trons' front door. Others are starting work on the tailor Valleriola's home. The unusual lighting and the hammer-blows have attracted the attention of neighbors from outside the Street. The people of the Street do not dare come out of their homes, but watch from behind their windows, having blown out candles, and are unable to agree on all that awaits their imprisoned relatives. But those from outside the Street have formed groups, heedless of the wind and the risk they run being out in the open on a night like this. First of all they just gape, watch what's going on, albeit with a certain pleasure, pass remarks in low voices. But when they hear the boldest among them say, "That'll teach you, bloody Jews!" they begin to rain down shouts, insults and provocations. "Look, look, it's Gabriel Valls!" says a boy, raising a fist. And it's the men of the party leading him captive, the men who arrested him, who defend him and protect him from the assault of that crowd, who stop them with unsheathed swords. "Get back! Go on home!" says Don Gaspar Puigdorfila, now returning from the

Dark House, where the women have just been detained, and with his own eyes supervising the work of urgently boarding up the prisoners' homes.

Gabriel Valls is grateful for the arrival of the Head Bailiff, because he knows he'll push back those people, whose faces in the flickering light of the torches resemble the faces of demons, their clothes swept along by the dance of the wind, like those he's seen in the illustrations of devout books, surrounding a dying man, intending to take his soul to hell. He doesn't even ask, "But what have I done to you?" He's convinced that he hasn't done anything to them. Some he only knows by sight, others he's friends with and they owe him favors. He realizes, however, that whenever there's a problem, whenever there's some commotion, they're the ones who will pay for it, the chosen by the God of Israel to be his sovereign people over all the people on earth. They know what they're doing, even though they've no reason to do it. *But, Adonai, why do you punish us? I organized the escape relying on your help, feeling the strength of your arm, which gave me courage. Why have you forsaken us, Adonai? For which of my sins is this punishment? How can you wish me so much ill, Lord?*

Protected by the men, he walks towards the Black House. As they turn the corner of Carnisseria, they come across the Viceroy's carriage. Gabriel Valls tries to stop it with his hand, but can't lift his hand, having been handcuffed to two guards. The coach's curtains are drawn, but the rabbi thinks he sees the Marquis pull back the curtain to watch what is going on. "The Viceroy must have seen me. He already knows about our misfortune by now." A herd of pigs, disoriented by the wind, blocks their path, baring their teeth. "Make sure you don't kill any," says the Bailiff, riding behind them on his horse. "They're from the hospital." He goes up to them himself and the animals, grunting, move out of the way. "I bet you didn't enjoy that, did you, Valls?"

exclaims the guard handcuffed to his left with a smirk. "Where's my wife?" he asks. "Where do you think?" they answer him, laughing. He won't ask about anyone else. Certainly not about what he loves most: his son. "Go to the brothel," he advised him. "And when the gates are opened tomorrow, hide outside the city and see if you can embark from Alcúdia for Alicante," he told him as soon as Quitèria Pomar's son managed to find them on the other side of the bridge and, trembling, recounted what had happened. "Hide in the brothel," he insisted. He doesn't know why he suggested that din of iniquity he railed against to his sons whenever he could. He won't ask about the Consul either. "I don't want to leave you, Rabbi," the Consul said once he told them to separate. "You have to, Josep, you're quicker than me. You have to. I'm the first one they'll look for. Save yourself if you can. You'll be more use to us on the outside."

They disperse. Pere Onofre Martí lifts his son on to his back. The child is exhausted. He's run from Segell, out of breath, stooping, almost on all fours, to be confused with a beaten dog escaping in the dark, till finding them. Josep Valleriola envies him. He wishes someone would give him a piggyback! He can't go on and sits down on the first stone bench he finds. His cousin, the tailor Valleriola, enters Pep Barral's cellar. He'll ask him for shelter for a few hours. They've known each other since they were small. The others—the Consul's sons, Josep and Mateu, Miquel Bonnín, the Cap de Trons brothers and Rafel Tarongí—run in different directions. "May the Lord protect and defend you," adds Valls before taking his leave.

He's all alone. The wind does not stop howling. It raises his cloak and he has to hold down the little hair he has left. He's no longer wearing a hat. He lost it leaving the xebec. It doesn't matter which way he goes. He won't get far. So he can choose, head for the place he likes best. Home, after visiting the Viceroy. The Viceroy might take him in. He'd prefer to be in the Angel Tower than in the Black House. So he'll visit the Viceroy if he is lucky enough to get there. He's already turning into Almudaina Street. Everywhere is dark. The wind has blown out the torches the Viceroy orders the soldiers on guard to light every evening. "Who goes there?" he hears the sentry ask. "Who is it?" "Gabriel Valls, at his excellency the Lord Viceroy's service." "Halt, Valls. Take another step and you're dead." This voice is not the same as the one that questioned him before. It's not the sentry who gave the order, but someone who's just come up behind him, having heard him give himself away. "I've stopped," replies Valls, turning round. "I've stopped completely. Aren't there a lot of you to arrest a single man?" he adds on being surrounded by more than half a dozen armed men. "Besides, what do you want? What have I done, if I may know? I was just going to the Viceroy's Palace."

The constant bells. How long have they been ringing? On being led downstairs he imagines that down there he won't hear them, that the sound will be much softer, more bearable. But he hears them with almost the same force. While they searched him, while the clerk carefully noted down everything they took from him, he heard a familiar remark that the Inquisitor had been urgently summoned to a meeting, to which the Viceroy was also invited, to try to stop the wind with the bells' blessed ringing. *Your God didn't pay much attention,* the rabbi muses, and immediately tries to drive away the thought that disturbs him. He seeks a motive, a reason, to mitigate the responsibility for Adonai having turned his back on them. What has he done wrong? Who can have denounced them? Who denounced whom? he wonders. And he goes over the relatives of those who embarked and concludes that only Isabel Tarongí's husband is foolish enough to accuse his wife, knowing as he does that when proceedings are opened he too will be hurt. No, it can't be

Martí, it must be someone who talked too much, perhaps without meaning to. Someone who couldn't keep his mouth shut and unwittingly confided in informers . . . What about Aina? Aina Cap de Trons, who didn't want to embark? The Lord punished her with the death of her son . . . She could have confided in Juli Ramis . . . Everybody knows that, instead of hating her slanderer, instead of wishing him all the ill in the world for not keeping his word to marry her, she went looking for him, not to ask for her lost honor back, but to beg him to continue visiting her at night in her room. Valls knows this because amid laughter Juli Ramis talked about it in the city bars, repeated it in the brothel, told his mates. And even though Valls doesn't hang out in bars or brothels or have dealings with bandits, he knows a lot of people, people of all kinds who enjoy spreading news at the speed of light. God punished Aina, but Aina didn't love the child. She might be relieved by now to be free of her disgrace. A death like this is not a punishment, but a liberation. But Adonai cannot have rewarded Aina because Aina deserves no reward . . . Who is he to judge? What does he know about the acts of others? Aina wept with the dead child in her arms . . . He saw it. Where can she be now? She didn't want to embark. "There's nothing for me in Livorno. I prefer to stay in the city," she said with determination. "You'll start a new life. I'll help you." "A new life with a baby? On my own and with a dowry, maybe . . . I should leave him in the orphanage." "You wouldn't dare!" She must have thrown him in the sea. Can his own mother have killed him? He couldn't save him. A sailor tried, but was too late, he told the others to say. Hopefully the captain will give the order to set sail as soon as the wind dies down, and won't wait for them or send word. If he's questioned, they're done for. They didn't agree with him what they would confess and what they wouldn't, if the authorities questioned him. He never wanted to consider this possibility. He always rejected it. Adonai was on their side. Therefore could they lack nothing. The birds in the sky . . . The boarding was hasty, it's true. But how else would they have gotten away? In conditions of such extreme necessity they couldn't wait for a more suitable time. And it was up to him to decide. With the Consul's support. He could have postponed the escape, but he didn't. He thought the captain was an angel sent by God and the day, Sunday, could not have been more propitious. The moment, the great moment, had arrived. So he informed the others and gathered them in secret with instructions. The next occasion might be too late. They wouldn't be in time. Costura was pushing them, his accusations were forcing them to leave . . . What can Costura have said about him? What does Father Ferrando know about everything? How far did the informer go? Polònia Miró, Rafel and Isabel Tarongí, Costura's nephews are witnesses: Father Ferrando did not move from Rafel Cortès' bedside in three days and comforted him with prayers and the Holy Sacrament, when he wasn't rummaging about in his room in search of papers. What did Costura's testimonies say? Who did he inform against?

He's cold. He's wrapped in a stinking blanket he was given in exchange for his cloak, which was taken as well. He's seated with his head down and from time to time covers his ears with his frozen hands. He struggles to repel the image he has been watching with his eyes closed since he evoked Costura's death. He sees him lying in state with a swollen belly and a wince, his nasal bone jutting out. This is not the first time he sees him in a shroud. He's come to him on many nights, many, just another ghost, concrete and precise at the hour of countless, anonymous ghosts. And the only way he can get rid of him is through prayer. "I thought it necessary, Adonai," he repeats, "Lord of hosts," he says, "he himself came looking for me. He found me and by accepting the invitation to the garden he put himself in my way. But, Adonai, you didn't demand reasons or accounts. You had it written in your law: *An eye for an eye, a tooth for a tooth.* You are just, Adonai, not like Christ, who turns the other cheek and weakly forgives. You are strong, Adonai. You have said we will pay for our actions. You want justice and I was your instrument. Rotten fruit must be thrown away before it spoils the rest of the crop. It was right for the informer to pay with his life the price of his accusations that landed us in so much danger . . . The gardener's sponge-cake . . . How he liked it! The sponge-cake poisoned with yew-seed juice. It took him ages to die. That was a mistake. We needed a much quicker death, not slow agony that confined him to bed, but didn't silence him . . . 'Speak,' Father Ferrando would say, 'talk, denounce the apostates, and the monstrance will be yours. The Viceroy is favorable.' Lie. The Viceroy doesn't want a peep, the Viceroy doesn't want trials or Tribunals, the Viceroy is my partner in the maritime business that has made him rich."

Nobody, however, accused him of Costura's death. Nobody was concerned to know the cause of that stomach-ache that confined him to bed, that the doctor tried to cure with potions. Not even Father Ferrando, who more than anyone needed the informer to live, showed signs of suspecting an unusual reason for that sudden illness. Costura won't be troubling them again. Neither Costura nor the reckless Cap de Trons, the primary cause of the tragedy. They were all buried now and their souls, outside this world, had already been judged by Almighty God. God the Father. God without sons. Only God. How could God the Father leave his son, Christ, abandoned to the sufferings of death? The terrible sufferings of the night of loneliness and desolation. Christ, who forgives, weak and merciful, against Adonai, powerful and just, who demands revenge. "I shan't deny," said the Widow Sampol, "that I'm moved by this image. Alone, praying in the garden of Gethsemane, in the olive grove, deathly pale, abandoned by everybody, knowing as he does what is going to happen to him, knowing there's an informer, a traitor who has handed him over . . ." "OK, but he isn't God, nor is he his son," replied Valls. "Nor is he an impostor, rather a prophet," she said. Her again. Her in the worst moments and the best as well, the sweetest and most hopeful. Blanca lives in Livorno. Isn't this another reason for the joy he felt the day before? The scent of her hair and her smile. The scent João Peres mistakenly pursued, as Pere Onofre told him in a long letter, the last he wrote. Peres is the lucky one, working for the Widow Sampol, who holds him in high esteem. What did Pere Onofre mean in his letter? He may never know, he may never see Blanca again or hear from her, he may stay here until he is sentenced to death. He knows what awaits him. He remembers the trial of that Portuguese boy who was caught fleeing on a ship to lands of freedom. He remembers the difficulty he had climbing on to the stand and his terrible cries when the flames . . . and how he risked gathering his ashes, which Pere Onofre Aguiló took to Bordeaux.

Money, money's what they're after. They don't care about anything else. If they get what they need, maybe they won't skin them alive. Money. He invested a lot in the escape. He and the tailor Valleriola are the ones who paid most, aside from Aguiló and Blanca. The captain gave his word not to keep what isn't his. If he can get away, if he manages to leave the port, they may still be lucky. He'll repay Aguiló and Blanca, who put up a lot of the loan. Deep down he's luckier than the others. Much luckier than Cap de Trons' family, who have nowhere to go, or than Pere Onofre Martí, who still has small children. "Everybody would like to cry with our eyes," he tells his wife when she weeps because her mother's illness tortures her. "Don't complain, woman, you've no reason to complain. You have two strong boys, a good life, good health, and soon you'll be able to praise Adonai freely without pretending."

He can't hear the bells anymore. Or the wind. He's not sure how long he's heard nothing. He may have been so exhausted he fell asleep and woke up again without realizing. Everything hurts, as if he'd been beaten to a pulp. Like a dog. He notices his knees are swollen, his hands still frozen, and his feet are so cold he can't even feel them. He can't stand up. He's thirsty. He rubs his eyes. "Have I gone blind?" He can't see anything. Not a tiny streak of light. He thinks he hears a distant, muffled murmur. He pricks up his ears, listens hard. It's footsteps. Someone's coming. He hears the dull sound of bolts. The door being reclosed. He listens out again. The footsteps disappear down the corridor. He presses his right ear against the wall and tries to catch any sound coming from next door, to know if the prisoner is one of them. Now he's absolutely sure he heard a deep breath and a groan, and thinks he recognizes the Consul. But before shouting his name, he knocks three times against the party wall. Waits and tries again. "Consul," he asks, "is that you? Is that you, Consul? Can you hear me? Consul . . .?"

IV

RAFEL ONOFRE VALLS DE VALLS MAJOR SPENT SUNDAY night and part of Monday morning between the sheets of Limp, who was happy to receive him. The prostitute weighed up both the payment, which, given the risk of failing to observe the sacred precept of rest—it was a holiday and Lent—should have been double, and the young man's finer parts. She was used to training young boys ill-favored by nature and, having been around for a while, particularly skilled at massages to revitalize soft parts, so this tall, robust lad seemed to her a wonderful being, a kind of angel, come down from heaven. She thought maybe the Christ of St Eulalia's had sent him to make up for so much discomfort and requite her extreme devotion at least once in her life. So she just looked at him, observed him, without daring to ask who he was, where he came from, or why he had that bruised look and that tiredness that made him fall asleep as soon as his head touched the pillow and continually wake up in her arms, in a fever, asking where he was, who she was, as she stroked him, and why the bells were ringing in such terrifying fashion. She didn't bother to search his bag or feel his clothes, as she normally did to ascertain the kind of person, working out beforehand the tip she could ask him for if she saw he was satisfied.

For a long time she carried on watching him sleep in the darkness of the room, which fortunately faced inwards and was sheltered from the wind, until, unable to resist the impulse, she went to fetch the candle burning on the sideboard and brought it to the sleeping body. She carefully pulled back the sheet that covered him. Then, shining the light, she looked at him, first slowly, in parts, with scruples, and then all over, as if seeking a mark, a sign to help her understand his origin and what made him different from others, as she had suddenly realized. But all she found was beauty, and this did not seem enough. She caressed him softly, starting with his back and ending with his feet, which she noticed were covered in chilblains, a fact that convinced her this boy was a human being and not a seraph who had lost its wings or a saint come down from glory, because up there they couldn't suffer from the cold. Reassured by her discovery—clearly her sense of touch was much keener than the others—she lay down next to him and tried to get some sleep to keep him company, convinced that she wouldn't be able to stay awake till he woke up.

For about five years, despite a defect from birth in her left leg, Limp had been the most sought after woman in the city, and rumor had it that, since it would have been unacceptable for certain skirts from the Bishop's Palace to frequent the brothel, skirts from the brothel habitually visited the Palace. This secret, proclaimed from the rooftops by the whole Curia, by his Most Reverend Eminence's many enemies, heightened her fame and even her respectability. To associate with the same whore as the Lord Bishop was, if not a guarantee, at least an incentive for lots of artisans, who thought that where they ventured must be a more blessed cranny than that of other whores, who, so it seemed, could not boast such sacred customers. Some even declared that the Bishop, suffering from remorse, something that occurred three or four times a year, pleaded with Limp to become an enclosed nun. His Eminence's motives were not entirely clear. For some this meant wielding greater influence over the wench, albeit with less immediate access; for others it proved the kindness of the cardinal, who wanted her to repent of her evil ways and gain a place in heaven. But the Bishop's unexpected death, one Friday in Lent from a very inconvenient, sacrilegious attack of gout, prevented them finding out where it would all have led. They said Limp wept for him a lot and mourned him, but could not attend any of the funerals that were held or see him for the last time lying in state—not because whores did not line up in front of the coffin like everybody else, but because the Head Bailiff forbade it, informing her through Madò Hugueta, mistress of the brothel, just as she was trying on the widow's weeds in which she planned to accompany the dead man's procession.

She screamed, wept, tore out her hair and for eight days refused to receive anyone, despite the warnings of her companions, who endeavored to point out that such open, undisguised behavior was showing her up. The Bishop's death even affected her mood. She stopped humming graciously as before, when she would encourage birds to take wing. She simply did her job, mechanically and correctly. Despite the lack of merriment, of joy in her work, she was still the most efficient whore in the brothel. Among her merits, spread by sailors around at least a dozen ports, was the claim she had revived a dying man's pillicock in under three minutes. If she had the power to perform such miracles, murmured all those who saw it and later all those who heard about it, it was because she was assisted by some extraordinary force and, since she was no longer under the protection of the Lord Bishop, who had been feeding the worms for half a year, the Holy Tribunal, still underworked, began to suspect that Limp had made a pact with the devil. After all, she could have put the evil eye on his Eminence, who, given the sudden way he died, without receiving the sacrament of penance, might now be feeding the flames of hell.

But she decided she didn't want to put the cart before the horse or give away the fear burrowing inside her chest. She didn't even dare consult any of the authorities who came to her. She waited on events, waited to see the direction the new Inquisitor would take. He had just been appointed and was no doubt unconcerned by the Bishop's death. She waited without ever expecting that the Reverend Félix Cabezón y Céspedes, underworked and oversexed, would feel such an overwhelming desire to meet her that, instead of sending for her to question her, instead of having her imprisoned if he considered there were charges against her, he decided to visit the whore-house as his Most Reverend Eminence had done one day, incognito.

What most surprised the Inquisitor's secretary, who knew that proceedings would soon be opened against Beatriu Mas, known as Limp, lady of easy virtue, was that the Very Reverend Félix Cabezón y Céspedes informed him that he himself in person, unaccompanied by familiars or any other escort, would visit the brothel to catch her unawares.

He entered through the back door used by the boy a few hours previously, the same door where the Lord Bishop appeared one fine day. He was disguised as a gentleman with a showy hat of gleaming feathers, tight pants instead of a cassock, a green tippet and a cloak like that of St Francis. In spite of all this, his priestly air gave him away. There was in the gesture of his hands an excessive number of said Masses. "Is your lordship looking for anyone special?" inquired Madò Hugueta, famous for her extremely courteous whoreship and smelling a rat. "All the girls are at your disposition . . . Though of course they don't all cost the same . . . Would you like to have a look before making up your mind? I'd be only too happy to summon them if you'll wait for a moment . . ."

The selection was easy and quick. He simply twisted his neck and pointed. Limp, lively as a genet, received him as she imagined a lady would, with icy coldness. "Your lordship will say what he requires," she ventured as soon as they entered her workplace, though neither voice nor character suggested impending pleasure. "I'm at your service, sir," she then added with a bow and again waited for the other to indicate what he wanted. But he wouldn't make up his mind. He looked at her scrupulously as if studying her in detail, as if seeking a sign, but not in the way she had watched the boy still sleeping at her side, because she did not believe that a demon would emerge from the folds of his groin as he confessed to her he was expecting, having ordered her to undress. She obeyed, but lingered as much as possible and undressed as chastely as she could, while searching for a glint in those lascivious eyes to tell her what the next order would be. This time he didn't make her wait. "Down on your knees," he commanded as if wishing to spank her with his voice as well. But drawing on a temerity she never would have thought she had, she informed him that she only kneeled before the Host or her confessor, and he was neither of those. "I am the Inquisitor," the impostor declared as she covered herself in a sheet and ran out screaming: "Madò Hugueta, there's a man here says he's the Inquisitor. Who ever heard of such a horrible thing?"

She smiled to remember it, as always when she clung to that daring to feel better. Because that bout of boldness that could have had such terrible consequences for her, cost the hapless Inquisitor his job. This was the excuse used by the Tribunal of Aragon, urged on by his enemy the Viceroy, to give him a pastoral charge in Cartagena de Indias to convert Negro slaves to the true faith.

The boy had entered as suddenly as the impostor one Sunday in March and chosen her. But she suspected nothing harmful in him, nothing that could be dangerous. On the contrary, she thought he had been sent from heaven to make up for that fright. Trying not to disturb him, she occupied the smallest area she could on one side of the bed. She didn't know if she had slept a little or a lot or not at all when the day roused her, its meek light filtering through the cracks in the door. *It must be gone six,* Limp thought, although she hadn't bothered to count the strokes. She had heard lots that night battling with the wind without paying much attention, because the boy's presence comforted her and drove away the fear she normally felt during storms. She wondered whether it wasn't the wind that had made him seek shelter in the brothel, which he had never visited before, she was sure of this, perhaps because he was a sailor—the smell of salt gave him away—and spent more time on board than on land.

The brothel was officially closed, but the normal rhythm of work on a Monday morning continued outside the bedroom door with the din of buckets of water and tow mops on the ceramic tiles. Despite what decent people might think, the whore-house was one of the cleanest places in the city. Dirt was a word that set Madò Hugueta's hair on end. To her virtues as mistress of the brothel, which were many, could be added an obsession for cleanliness.

Rafel Onofre Valls returned with a bump to the land of the living and could not work out where he was. He couldn't understand why he hadn't woken up at home as every day during his nineteen years. It took him a few minutes to realize that the whitewashed walls and the high ceiling with redwood beams were not those of a place he knew. Nor did he recognize the bench where his clothes had been laid out. He felt his body and saw that he had slept without a nightshirt and, on turning to his right, noticed that in his bed there was also a naked woman smiling at him agreeably and murmuring in his ear, "Sweet love, my seraph, heavenly angel," while running her skillful hands over his body and delicately taking control of his manly parts, which were immediately set on fire. The urgency of an unfamiliar desire surprised and embarrassed him. But it was no use putting up resistance. He noticed his vital juices about to overflow as if all of him had turned to liquid. He roared like an animal when he reached orgasm, the humors that filled him with pleasure with an intensity he had never experienced also seemed to come out of his mouth. Still panting, he opened his eyes and could not believe he was mistaken: he had not released his male fluid in his sleep, as normally happened, but awake under the expert guidance of a prostitute. As he became aware of what had taken place—it was his father who told him to seek shelter in the brothel—his face turned sad and the image of Maria Pomar filled his eyes. Limp carried on watching him, seated now on the bed and covered in a sheet. She smiled at him with a maternal, rather than lascivious, expression and did not ask him anything. Rafel Onofre did not say anything either, although at one point the need to lighten the load weighing down his conscience, the same perhaps as provoked the guilt, almost put the words in his mouth. He was afraid. To the feeling of sinfulness for having been with a prostitute, instilled by his father as well, was added a much stronger feeling: that of uncertainty. He didn't know what to do or where to go. He didn't know what had befallen the others. While, exhausted, he rested, who knows in what dark cell his mother and Maria had been imprisoned? He closed his eyes and clenched his teeth to stifle a groan as untimely as the tears that flowed through the stubble that had grown overnight. Limp, however, wasn't at all surprised and didn't give it any importance. If she understood about one thing, it was about naked men before, during and after intercourse, and this melancholic, irritable state after the act was common to many. For this reason she decided that an egg-yolk mixed with sweet wine, kept in the house only for highly distinguished guests, would lift that boy's spirits.

"You must be hungry. You were exhausted yesterday. Don't move. I'll fetch you something nice."

Rafel Onofre Valls did not use Limp's absence to wash in the bowl full of water, which had been prepared in a corner, nor did he get dressed as the prostitute had supposed. On the contrary, he simply waited for her to return, lying down with his eyes closed. He didn't know how long he could stay there without arousing suspicion. He imagined the Holy Tribunal must be looking for him by now, as for the others, unless everyone was already in prison and he was the only one they hadn't caught. Returning home meant handing himself over on a silver plate. The same if he sought refuge in the garden, where perhaps Maria's parents already knew about their misfortune and cursed him twice over: he was the reason for the double loss of their daughter. It would be almost impossible to embark. And not because of the wind, which was calm now, but because the Bailiff would have questioned the captain and seized the xebec. Besides, it was unlikely he could reach Port Pi without being cut off by the Bailiff's men. He couldn't think of any other refuge, at least for the moment, than that room in the brothel.

Limp came in, stirring a glass with a spoon. The egg-yolks—two instead of one—broke, taking on the color of must as they mixed with the wine. With the same smile that for so many hours had accompanied her eyes when she looked at the boy, she brought the glass to his lips. He drank greedily. The fingerprints of both remained on the glass. As she placed the glass on the sideboard in the room, where the bowl of clean water was, Beatriu dared to think, if they were saints, this would be a relic. And again there appeared the figure of Mary Magdalene, whom she had so often invoked in her suffering shared with his Most Reverend Eminence, when, after making love, the cardinal wanted to discipline her. The image of Mary Magdalene, with her long, loose hair, pouring the sacred ointment over Good

Jesus' feet, which she had seen as a girl in a picture in the sacristy where she used to receive alms, was more pleasing to her than that other one she kept among her belongings, where she was penitent and almost naked, staring at a skull she held in her hands. If she liked the first one much more, it was because the boy could represent a St Savior at whose feet, covered in chilblains, she was ready to pour all the scents she had ever used in her life as a whore.

The shouts of Madò Hugueta arguing with the Assistant Bailiff interrupted her reverie. The shouts of Madò Hugueta frightened the boy, who first got quickly dressed and then sat down on the bench where his clothes had been. "No Jew's come in here," Madò Hugueta was heard saying. "Don't you know we're closed in Lent? Don't you know we obey orders? What do you mean, on a boat? Go on, tell us, we don't know what you're talking about . . ."

With lowered eyes, almost trembling, Rafel Onofre tried to listen. But he could only hear Madò Hugueta's angry voice, which sounded much nearer than Ripoll's, possibly because he hadn't even bothered to come in and was questioning her from his horse in the street. Curious to find out what was going on, Limp made as if to leave, but stayed her hand on the key in the door. She didn't turn it.

"No, please don't give me away," asked the boy with a childish sob.

Suddenly Limp understood everything. She understood the reason for the boy's fear, for his strange behavior, for his tiredness the night before, for his feverish state, for his reticence, and she smiled inside, as always when she was right: not in vain had he reminded her of Christ.

"You mean you're one of them?" she spat out. "That's why I didn't know you . . . You never come around here. Apparently you prefer not to mix with Christian women . . . I'm sorry for you, but

I'm not at all Jewish, really I'm not. No joke. But I like you . . . You can have guessed . . . Not so much when you're dressed, but naked you seemed like an angel. Yes, yes, I promise you. So I won't charge you, see? And you haven't even given me a kiss . . ."

Rafel Onofre Valls listened to her with his head in his hands, ashamed, having stopped crying. He had behaved like a child when he thought he was a grown man. He stood up and with all the strength of his nineteen years pressed Limp's body against his own and kissed her, first on the lips, then inside her mouth. With his tongue he traced the features of her face and lingered in the cochlea of her ears. And noticing again how the blood began to boil between his legs, without letting go of her, he laid her down on the bed and took her with a mixture of fury and gratitude, with which he affirmed his young man's disdain. Until he noticed her sighs, deep groans, which Beatriu Mas could put on to perfection, her muffled cries as she sought out his lips, he did not allow his vital juices to overflow again.

Suddenly Madò Hugueta's voice and knocks at the door disentangled their arms and legs. She urgently demanded that Limp come out.

"Wait. Don't move. I'll be back in a minute. Then we'll think what the best thing to do is."

Madò Hugueta was afraid that in effect the man who had insisted on seeing Limp the night before and offered her a handful of money if she called her was one of those they were looking for. This is why she rapped at the door of Beatriu, who was sufficiently reckless to harbor someone who took her fancy. The whore-mistress warned her that to conceal a fugitive, whether or not he was from the Street, much worse if he was, could have disastrous consequences for everybody, but most of all for her. They had confiscated the Street people's goods, boarded up their homes and since yesterday had begun to open proceedings against them. The wench accepted everything Madò Hugueta said and, when she finished, assured her that the boy had nothing to do with the failed escape: he was a bandit's younger brother, an old customer of hers who had decided to spend the night in the brothel to avoid being caught outside by the Bailiff's men after the wall was closed. That same evening he would leave for Muro, where he lived. All he needed was a horse. His own horse was lame and he couldn't use it.

Madò Hugueta did not heed Limp's excuses. She knew her well enough and was aware that her clients often exploited her kindness, especially if she liked them. She warned her before she went back into her room that she wanted to witness the young man's departure.

"What do you know about the others?" asked Rafel Onofre as soon as Beatriu returned.

"Not much, what you heard Madò Hugueta say," she replied, closing the door again and turning the key. "I don't suppose you've anywhere to go. Your houses have been boarded up and your goods confiscated. Apparently you've lots more hidden away, and I can believe it . . . I only have to look at you," she smiled at him ingratiatingly, in case she had offended him. "I'll help you, don't worry, but you have to do me two favors. First, not tell anyone. If you report me, you'll regret it. I'll deny that you've been here. I haven't even confided in Madò Hugueta. It's the first time, as far as I know, I've done it with a Jew . . . Of course, without circumcision, all men are the same. Well, not all, in terms of pricks there's a world of difference, I'm telling you . . . and I know better than anyone. But I liked it, what can I say? May the Lord God forgive me," and she crossed herself and, after making the sign of the cross, kissed her thumb noisily.

"And the second favor?"

"I want to know why you asked for me last night when you decided to take shelter in the brothel . . . Why me, Limp, exactly? Do I have a good reputation in the Street?"

The boy did not hesitate.

"Because a friend of mine told me a couple of months ago that doing it with you was like touching the sky."

"Well, that's nice. Nobody ever said anything like that to me. And do you think the same?"

"I . . . I have a girlfriend and I love her and I thought that I could only touch the sky with her, when we were married . . . at the passing of the moon."

"I have to say I like it, even if you're only saying it. What bad luck!" she added, as if talking to herself. "No Christian ever said such a pretty thing to me!"

And then, changing even the tone of her voice, she ordered him to wash.

"You stink of sea, male and salt. I'll give you other clothes. In these, anyone will report you to the Bailiff, even if they don't know you. I'll be back in a minute," she added with a pleasant smile from the door.

The boy obeyed her. He washed and dried himself with a soft towel that smelled of apples. He had never imagined Limp like this, nor the brothel's customs, although he'd heard lots of talk from friends outside the Street, like that carpenter's apprentice who recommended Beatriu Mas to him, urging him to try that taste of clouds that remains after a visit to glory. She came straight back in with a bundle and untied it.

"Well, it's the best I could find. Believe me, I don't want to make a scandal. God forbid! It's because . . . because it's difficult for Jews to become Christians in the Black House . . ."

And she handed him a friar's habit someone must have left behind in a hurry.

V

AFTER THE STORM THE DAY DAWNED COLD AND CLOUDLESS. The belfries and towers stood out with stark clarity against a sky of brilliant blue damask, slashed from time to time by bands of swifts. If it weren't for the fallen tiles, the piles of leaves, the four uprooted elms and the ruins of a couple of houses, no one would have said that a couple of hours ago all the bells in the city were ringing to ward off the whirlwind that the previous night looked as if it would carry off the whole island. Only by looking at the old sea feeding a numerous flock of lambs unwittingly, unwillingly, could you tell that a storm had just passed over and must have hit hard.

The city regained its composure early on and, now that the danger had passed, the wind been beaten by the deafening din of the bells, its inhabitants emerged on to the street. Many headed for Segell and Argenteria to see the barricades with their own eyes, but the Bailiff's men impeded them. Others went out to estimate the damages. They were still in time to watch how the neighbors removed the felled elms near Carme and quick as a flash happily chopped them into logs to serve as firewood as soon as they were dry. Boys used stones to break up the largest pieces of tiles and pigs hungrily rummaged among the windswept leaves, accompanied by children, whose fear of sharp teeth was assuaged by the desire for fruit.

The effect of the wind was much worse in the orchards. In

a single night the work of months has been lost. Young plants, their leaves scorched and torn, lie listlessly about and trees are without flowers, their tenderest branches mutilated. The fruit, still green, has fallen to the ground and will not now ripen as it should. But despite this, despite the washing the wind swiped, the three dead hens in St Magdalene's Convent, the two ducks the Clares are missing and the number of battered rose bushes in the Palace gardens, a *Te Deum* of thanksgiving is being prepared in the Cathedral because—although, as the day advances, the list of damages lengthens—the storm did not have the terrible consequences everyone had predicted and served as an instrument of the Most High to stop the Jewish heretics who tried to get away. This is why the Bishop, who yesterday urgently convoked the board of theologians to approve the unanimous ringing of bells, has quickly summoned them again to debate a different proposal. Since he found out that, thanks to the storm, the ship carrying Jews could not leave the port, he has been assailed by doubts whether he was right to confront the whirlwind and fight with bells against it.

It now seemed abundantly clear that the wind proceeded directly from the mouth of Jesus Christ, mystic Favonius, the Father's only-begotten Son, to prevent the Jews' journey and, even better, their eternal damnation in hell for being apostates. He wondered, and for this reason wanted the opinion of the board, whether they shouldn't now make amends to our Lord and to that force of nature for having considered it negative, for having mistakenly believed an evil spirit sent it. He wanted to share his scruples with theologians and advisers and summoned them again before the office to see what they thought if after the solemnity he addressed the parish to explain how sometimes the ways of the Lord can appear mistaken, but are not, as yesterday's example proved.

That same morning Canon Llabrés, as Judge of Goods, had met with his Most Reverend Eminence, who had used the opportunity to bring him up-to-date, telling him in advance the reason for the meeting to which he had also been invited at exactly five in the afternoon. This is why, as soon as he arrived at the gathering at Montision, he offered his apologies.

"I can't stay with your lordships longer than half an hour. The board of theologians is meeting at the Palace," he informed them, distressed to see that the tray of iced cakes was not on Father Amengual's desk, the only reason he had attended the gathering that Monday, when he was so busy. He had in fact amused himself on the way working out how many cakes he could scoff, having been hungry since the previous night. With all the goings-on he had fasted more than necessary.

Father Amengual, as host, expressed his sorrow that the Judge of Goods could only stay that time, while thanking him for not missing the gathering that Monday, when *really* he had so many obligations. Father Ferrando went even further and almost embraced the canon to show him how much he valued such a friendly gesture, overjoyed as he was at the mass imprisonment from which he hoped to take a fat slice. *The position of rector is mine,* he seemed to be saying to Father Amengual, looking at him condescendingly, *you can get stuffed. Now they'll have to thank me for everything I've done for the Holy Office, and that cannot be compared with any of your books, that's much more.*

The canon lowered his weight into the easy chair he usually occupied, pleased by the welcome and particularly expectant. He imagined his collocutors would subject him to a rigorous examination regarding yesterday's arrests and today's board of theologians. He imagined Father Ferrando would want to know how the search had gone, while Father Amengual would be more interested in the board. For some time he had been trying to get his Most Reverend Eminence to notice him and value him for once, as his predecessor had done.

"What news is there, Don Jaume? What's being talked about

in the city? Your fatherhood must have been exhausted yesterday. Apparently they almost couldn't cope . . ."

He was wrong. Father Amengual made no reference to the board. He simply remarked the same as everyone else.

"Yes, there was a lot of work. And we've only just begun. We're missing all the inventories of the goods they weren't taking with them . . . Houses, workshops, furniture . . . Everything they left behind, which is a lot."

"You can say that again, Don Jaume," added Ferrando with the assurance of someone who knows what they're talking about and then some. "By the way, I think Puigdorfila acted like a saint, sealing all their houses at once. That will have stopped anybody touching anything. I passed near the Street and the crowd wanted to go in. Most of them were demanding fire and smoke . . . and shouting against the Bailiff's men, who wouldn't let them through."

"Crowds are always dangerous," opined the Judge of Goods. "The vicar of St Eulalia's told me this morning a group wouldn't let Aina Cap de Trons' child be buried. 'Throw him in the sea,' he said they were shouting. The vicar had to assert himself. 'I baptized him,' he told them, 'he's a Christian and he'll be given a Christian burial.'"

"Since the Viceroy put up the price of wheat, everybody's been unhappy. Oh, excuse me, Don Sebastianet, I don't mean anything against your uncle . . . Tell us, Don Jaume, how many prisoners are there exactly? Costura's nephews and niece, Rafel and Isabel Tarongí, for sure . . ."

Father Ferrando did not finish what he was saying, nor did the canon answer the question, because the chronicler Angelat suddenly appeared, the only one missing, and everybody stood up. He nodded and sat down at once. Sure that the conversation under way, which he had interrupted, could only be about one thing, he exclaimed:

"I'm told yesterday was serious. The clerk had to write so much, his hand had to be bandaged . . ."

Captain Sebastià Palou smirked. Still standing next to his easy chair, his sword hanging from his belt, dressed in green velvet, surrounded by dark cassocks, he seemed to be posing for a picture in which the painter had wished to represent in his contrasting figure the vanities of the world as against the austerity of the religious life. Behind him, through the window, the landscape melted in the coolness of March and a gentle light flowed in an almost golden dust. Sebastià Palou dressed with a lot of care. He knew how much ladies, those who were not ladies as well, liked personal attention. Besides, that evening, after leaving the gathering he had to go to the Viceroy's in order to accompany him to the Solemn Office without having time to change his clothes. His uncle had urged him to concentrate the five senses on the conversation that afternoon, which would no doubt deal with the arrests, but without manifesting his interest. Also traveling on that ship were the two well-trained slave-girls who had stayed in his house. He did not want them being questioned by the Inquisition; if they talked, they could land him in an awkward situation. He hadn't asked the Judge of Goods anything and had simply smiled at the chronicler's overstatement, which the canon answered with a quick "It can't have been so bad," as if he insisted on not giving anything away, immediately seizing the mucky rope Father Amengual threw him: to talk about his book again, which had just been published by Guasp of Majorca two weeks ago.

The *Life of the Venerable Eleonor Canals, Who Died in Odor of Sanctity* had been received discreetly. Only the Viceroy's wife had given it the praise it deserved, but unfortunately the Marquise was not considered a reliable authority, in particular regarding the merits of her own family. The Viceroy, on the other hand, although Father Amengual had sent him a specially bound copy to adorn his library, dedicated with various praises, had simply thanked him without adding the smallest eulogy. It was too soon to know what repercussions it would have on the mainland, most of all among leading members of the Society, and whether eventually it would serve as the final recommendation for the post. Since publishing the work, Father Amengual had found nothing to occupy him. Writing fitting poems to head friends' books or taking notes for sermons he had to preach—very successfully, as it happened—on feast-days in various towns was not enough to fill his empty hours, dissatisfied hours because he did not devote them to any noble or lofty cause. He felt almost deserted. Life with the holy nun had been so intense that he missed it. He needed to find another religious theme he could start work on immediately, and did not want to write about another saint, even Sister Tomaseta, "the island's most genuine mystic flower," as the Marquise of Despuig had suggested, no doubt with the intention of competing with the Viceroy's wife. No, what he required was a theme, as the Judge of Goods had advised, that allowed him to display his mystic enthusiasm to the limit. But however much he thought about it—and this is what he was now explaining to his friends—he couldn't put his finger on a suitable enough subject, although he had a title, *Canticles in Praise of the Triumphant Faith*, that danced about his head as almost definitive, but that *really* implied going back to the first martyrs to be able to construct scenes that would touch the reader deeply, inciting him to the defense of dogma . . . And this . . .

"Well, now it'll be easy for you, Father Amengual," said the Judge of Goods, interrupting him. "Write about the acts of faith as a way of exalting it."

"Really?" he asked with interest. "You mean about the coming trials? I'll think about it . . . Yes, I'll think about it . . . Yes, I think you're right, Don Jaume, that this would do . . ."

Obviously he couldn't use the sentence he liked so much for the end of a chapter—*The diligent virgins, dragged by the jaws of warlike lions, perpetuated the faith in the trophy of their palms*—if he began to write about the trials, but nor did he feel very happy when he thought about the hours he would have to spend in terribly dark catacombs, among vicious, pagan Roman emperors. And what most disturbed him was bumping into a whole load of diligent virgins who may well be martyrs, but would inevitably remind him again of Sister Eleonor. Besides, if he focused all his mystic exaltation on the autos-da-fé, he really would compete against Father Ferrando, who these last months had devoted himself exclusively to wearing away the soles of his shoes, toing and froing non-stop from Montision to the Black House and from the Black House to Montision.

Sebastià Palou had still not opened his mouth. But on seeing that the conversation was turning to matters that were not of the slightest interest to him, he decided that the time had come to stick his oar in. They had been together three quarters of an hour—the town-hall bell had just struck half past—and the Judge of Goods did not have long to go. If he wanted to uncover details only the Judge knew about first-hand and his uncle needed to know about as soon as possible, he couldn't carry on playing the fool.

"Father Amengual," said Don Sebastià finally, "the subject suggested by the Judge strikes me as very apt, but before starting you'll have to wait for the verdicts . . . If there are no flames, your work will lose interest. It's no good anticipating events, especially in a matter of . . ."

"A matter of such delicacy," concluded the Judge. "Of course not, Don Sebastià. But if you want my honest opinion, I'm afraid that this time . . ."

"Some of them were reconciled ten years ago, Don Sebastianet, when the Inquisition was less zealous than now. If they've fallen again, we can't let them insult the Lord our God under our very noses . . ."

Sebastià Palou was not at all happy that this idiot, Father Ferrando, who was less tall than a seated dog, should permit himself to use that diminutive when addressing him, since he was twice his size. This may be why he answered him in a harsh tone, unusual for him, since he was normally very polite to anyone in a skirt.

"That has yet to be proven, Father Ferrando. The first thing we have to do is let them defend themselves. We can't judge them while considering them all guilty. I think first we have to consider them innocent."

"Don Sebastià, Don Sebastianet, don't say what you've just said, don't repeat it, for the love of God, or we'll have to think you've reasons . . . that your lordship as well . . ."

Sebastià Palou stood up in a rage, made as if to move towards Father Ferrando, as if he wanted to lay hands on him.

"I will not allow . . . Father Ferrando, I will not have you casting doubt . . . Out of respect for your ministry I can't . . ."

"Don Sebastià," said Father Amengual immediately, wary because as host he could not permit a brawl in his cell, but pleased that the Viceroy's nephew should quarrel with his rival, "Don Sebastià, I'm quite sure Father Ferrando did not wish to offend you . . ."

"That's right, Don Sebastianet. There's no way I . . ."

Fortunately at that precise moment the lay brother appeared with the tray, apologizing for being so late. The Clares had literally just dispatched the lay sister. With all the disturbance last night they forgot to beat the egg-whites in time.

The Judge of Goods stirred uneasily, on the verge of reaching out for the sweets Father Amengual had still not handed round. *Had he been a little later, I couldn't even have tried them. I'd have come in vain,* he said to himself. *What a fool!*

But Father Ferrando, who was desperate not to fall out with the Judge of Goods, although the suggestion he had made to his rival infuriated him, aware of the canon's gluttonous indisposition and to avoid having to continue apologizing for the nonsense with Don Sebastianet, who despite everything was who he was, decided to remind Father Amengual of the need to have tea.

"Your fatherhood remembers that Don Jaume has to leave soon today?" and he glanced at the tray.

Much happier having just tasted the afternoon's first cake and hoping to scoff another three if he was quick about it, the Judge of Goods felt more inclined to come out with some news. The chronicler Angelat, who was not in a hurry and had already worked out the cakes due each person, watched the canon with amusement, his pupils dilated with pleasure and his double chin trembling more than usual.

"You'll be rich now, Judge. You can do all the good works you want without having to borrow money. So tell us how much was confiscated yesterday. I'm told they were taking everything . . ." said Angelat, having licked the last bits of sugar off his lips.

"Yes, everything they could. Hidden in their clothes, jewels and money, title-deeds, references . . ."

"That means they had plans to return," replied Angelat.

"Not to return, to sell some of their goods from abroad, I imagine," remarked the Judge. "Though I don't know how . . . These people are stupid. As soon as we'd seen their folly, we'd have confiscated everything they left behind."

"They must have taken it as security," ventured the chronicler in a derisive tone.

"Some of the captives are the richest people in the Street," said Llabrés with his mouth full. "Valls, the Consul . . . but I'm sure we won't get everything of theirs, they're bound to have someone on the outside looking after it . . ."

"They have protectors who are not from the Street," added

Father Ferrando, looking at Don Sebastià Palou, "and the Tribunal will have to do everything it can to make sure these protectors, if they're looking after money for them, give it back to the Inquisition, to whom it belongs as of this moment."

"Everybody knows, Father Ferrando," affirmed Palou firmly, "because nobody's ever tried to hide it, that certain people from the Street have served the noblest houses . . . Gabriel Valls, for example . . ."

"Absolutely," said the Judge of Goods, "and I'm sure the Lord Viceroy never suspected that Gabriel Valls was still a Jew . . ."

"It's difficult to believe it even now, Don Jaume," interjected Sebastià.

"I understand, I realize . . . The Lord Viceroy is not unscrupulous, I suppose . . ."

"The wind was an instrument of the Lord our God," Father Amengual raised his voice, "to prevent them taking flight. I shall start with the storm. I can write a classical *excursus* on Favonius and Aeolus. What do you think?"

"That were it not for the storm, they'd be off Majorca by now and nothing would have happened," answered Palou, serious and supremely irked.

"How can you say that? How can you say that, Don Sebastianet?" repeated Father Ferrando more condescendingly. "How can you say that nothing would have happened? A lot would have happened! A lot! We'd have burned them in effigy, powerless to stop them burning forever in hell. Now, if they repent, after many years in purgatory, they'll be able to rise to heaven."

"Are we sure they were heading for Livorno?" asked the chronicler.

"It appears so, but the one who knows that best is the captain. He testified this morning before the Viceroy and the Lord Inquisitor. It would seem the fugitives deceived him, assured him they had safe-conducts to leave Majorca and, when he found out they were lying, he made them disembark."

"In that case the wind has nothing to do with it," interjected Angelat now, looking at Sebastià Palou, "it's superfluous . . ."

"Gentlemen, I'm very sorry, but I have to go. I cannot be late," the Judge apologized while standing up in a good mood, because he had managed to scoff all four cakes. "The board is important. The Lord Bishop . . . Until next Monday. I shall see your fatherhood very soon, Father Ferrando. Don Sebastià, my regards to your uncle . . ."

"I shall go too," said Sebastià Palou. "I'm in a hurry and, since your reverence is going towards the Palace and I am going to the Almudaina and it's the same way . . ."

Father Amengual accompanied his two guests to the stairs, which they descended, preceded by the lay brother who had served the tea. In the cell the chronicler Angelat was finishing off the last remaining crumbs on the tray and Father Ferrando was trying silently to gauge to what extent the fact of Father Amengual writing about the Holy Office could damage him. So far each of them had fought with his own weapons, without straying into the other's territory. But now, if his rival crossed the line, he would have no choice but to decide on another course of action that finally put a stop to Father Amengual's aspirations to the position of rector that today, more than any other day, he had seen as close as if it was already his. It was true that thanks to the storm the cursed apostates had not been able to escape and had been captured, but at the root of everything, at the root of the escape, was his religious zeal, his insistence that Costura denounce those who failed to observe God's law and believed in and practiced the redundant Old Law of Moses. The best thing he could do was steer Father Amengual away from that project, persuade him nicely to let it go, because otherwise it would be he, who had much more information, who knew the background to the Inquisition, who knew almost all its secrets and would continue to do so, who would write a book about *The Triumphant Faith* or *The Triumph of the Faith*, he didn't care, with a lot more insight.

For his part, Father Amengual had spent the duration of the gathering thinking about his future work. It would enable him to become famous—the case held interest for everybody—and finally to be taken into account, not like now, when even the Bishop failed to seek his opinion and yet sent for much less learned priests. *They won't be able to say that Father Ferrando renders a more appropriate service to the Church anymore, that his actions are worth more than my meditations . . . Now we'll be busy with the same affairs. Now we'll see who does it more zealously.*

As soon as Father Amengual returned, the chronicler Angelat, as if doubly inspired, struck up a very fitting conversation as a way of provoking them.

"I think your fatherhoods, who rival each other in ardent ecclesiastical zeal," he told them mockingly, "who are both worthy candidates for the position of rector of Montision, should write the book the Judge of Goods was recommending together . . . Father Ferrando could supply exact details, first-hand evidence only he could know about, and your reverence, Father Amengual, the adornment of your pen, the necessary rhetorical flourishes to give light to the truth, which this time will not triumph naked, but discreetly clothed thanks to your ingenuity . . ."

The Jesuits looked at each other in surprise, not knowing whether the chronicler was talking seriously or pulling their legs.

"No, I mean it. I think the Judge of Goods would approve. He had the idea, I'm just giving it a slight nuance. What do you think?"

There was a heavy silence. Neither of them wanted to answer first. Angelat watched them with amusement. He had made that proposal as a joke, but after all why not take it seriously? He was not familiar with any of Father Ferrando's writing and imagined he had little ability for the cultivation of poetics and rhetoric. But this was not an obstacle to writing if even the barber of Pes del Formatge planned to publish a book on sundials.

"I don't think I'd be able to write anything in collaboration," said Father Ferrando deliberately and then, as if he were in the pulpit to preach the sermon on Good Friday, added, "but I shan't deny that I had thought about writing a book on my own. As you say, chronicler, I am well versed in the workings of the Holy Office, at least of the Tribunal acting in Majorca."

Father Amengual, who had remained standing next to his desk, noisily replaced the vacant chairs against the wall and then hawked, rubbing his hands and gazing at the tips of his fingernails. Clearly he was seeking the right words to give his opinion in the most forceful way possible.

"I wish to be sincere and therefore I wish to inform you that a book in common would serve neither the one nor the other. I am *letter-sick*, something Father Ferrando is not. I think I should carry on writing and Father Ferrando acting. And really, let the members of the Society decide which of us possesses greater merits for the post."

"I agree with you, Father Amengual, let each one defend his own territory, as your fatherhood suggested, which is why I think it's unfair for you to write a book about the Inquisition. That is my concern."

"Really! What nonsense! The Inquisition yours, Father Ferrando? Did you hear what he said, Angelat?"

Angelat simply laughed with the derisive shriek that characterized him, but said nothing. It amused him to watch the spectacle like a cock-fight.

"I am opposed. You know this. The chronicler is my witness that I have warned you. Let there be no doubt. If you write about the acts of faith, I assure you that you will regret it, Father

Amengual. And now, if you'll excuse me, Mister Angelat, I also have twice as much work today . . ."

Father Ferrando left the cell, slamming the door, but could still hear his rival: "What do you think, chronicler? Really, how rude!" But Father Amengual's voice, full of furious complaints, was muffled by the sound coming from the street and growing in intensity. The sound of shouts, roars and running.

VI

FOR ALMOST AN HOUR THE BAILIFF'S TROOPS HAD BEEN forcibly preventing that group now filling the old Jewish Quarter from entering the Street. A score of armed men had orders to shoot without hesitation the first person to try to break the chain with which the area had been cordoned off to protect it from assailants. The most daring neighbors who, as every Monday, had opened shops and workshops to show everybody they had nothing to do with the fugitives, had immediately closed them again on hearing the din of that crowd threatening fire and sackings and demanding swift justice to punish those devilish Jews, who had grown rich with money stolen from Christians. It was obvious both from the accent of their cries and from their clothes and the weapons they brandished—weeding hoes, pitchforks and sickles—that these people were not from the city. Those from the city had appeared earlier to see what was going on and, although some had thrown dejected cries, full of insults, at the boarded doors, they had retreated without putting up resistance and had not, as the peasants were just doing, confronted the Bailiff's men.

The group—about fifty of them—came from different places outside the town. Without having reached an agreement, they left at mid-morning as soon as they heard about the arrests. Dissatisfied and hungry, they had the same intention: to travel to the city to see if a chunk of that dead lamb would be for them.

The biggest nucleus had gathered in S'Arenjasa and was commanded by Sen Boiet, a surly peasant who had been around the block. For more than ten years he had alternated sowing with the somewhat more profitable activity of highwayman for whichever group of bandits was best able to engage his services, and had never been caught. He was said to have extremely powerful protectors, who might be Count Mal's stepfather or the Viceroy of the moment. It depended who was recounting his story, but some added that his protection came from even higher up, since during one of his stays outside Majorca Prince Baltasar Carlos entrusted him with a vengeance carried out with chilling precision. True or not, more or less exaggerated, these rumors were sufficiently indicative of his fame and, had he been born a noble, no doubt he would have been one of those chiefs poets feel called upon to praise. His humble origins, however, only meant that everybody openly recognized he had leadership qualities, and his ability to rouse the mob, already roused during a brawl, and to turn its sails in the direction his own wind was blowing was a merit nobody had ever denied him. This is why, when the Head Bailiff confirmed that Sen Boiet was among that rowdy lot, he decided the disturbance could be more difficult to quash than he had supposed when one of his assistants informed him they were approaching St Antony's Gate with not very good intentions. He even rebuked the messenger for having spurred on his horse with unnecessary fury, since he did not plan to take any action until he saw where all this was leading. A quarter of an hour later, Don Gaspar Puigdorfila himself had to assert his authority and order them to go back the way they had come and make haste, to leave the capital immediately without committing misdeeds on pain of death.

"Do not put the cart before the horse, excellency," said Sen Boiet the moment he could make himself heard. "There's no edict forbidding peasants to enter the city as far as we know. We enjoy a good piece of bacon and want to join in the fun like the old Christians we are. We're the first to hate those who killed Good Jesus . . . You should be happy about it."

"I told you to go home. You're not needed here. Go on, off with you! If when the gates close, I find a single one of you still inside, I'll make him pay dear," threatened the Bailiff as the group retreated towards Sala Square, where they gathered around Sen Boiet to discuss what they were going to do.

They didn't take long to decide and were already heading towards Nova Square when they heard shouts coming from the direction of the Black House and saw another group of farmers approaching. There were fewer of them, they were not carrying weapons, nor did they seem to have a leader, at least one of Sen Boiet's stature. They were coming from the direction of Esporles and had entered through the gate of Jesus. Like the others, they wanted to see with their own eyes what they had been told and to vent their anger on the Jews, who were sucking their blood. Sen Boiet persuaded them not to head for the Street because of the Bailiff, who was not bluffing, and invited them to wander round the old Jewish Quarter together and then go to the Almudaina. The price of wheat was abusive in a year when the crop was bad. The Viceroy imported it and had taxed it so high they couldn't afford it. The Viceroy was also after their ruin, like the Jews. Sen Boiet was right: now that they were here, they could protest about both things.

They advanced together towards Nova Square and the Jewish Quarter. They shouted against the Jews and the increase in the price of wheat. They demanded justice, some of them brandishing weapons and others voices. In front of Montision Convent, built on top of the old synagogue, the Viceroy's troops confronted them. It was Ripoll who, blazing with his own merits—since the day before he had felt different, as if he'd swapped the stuff of man for the stuff of a hero—spurred his horse and drove it against the crowd, who screamed out in terror. Some sought refuge in Montision Church, but the Jesuits had already told the sacristan to close the temple doors and secure them with iron bars as in the time of bandits. Seeing they were under attack, the peasants defended themselves with hoes, using their pitchforks and sickles as if cutting the wheat of an impossible harvest. The wounded fell to the ground and were not helped, while the farmers dispersed, seeking shelter, chased by the shots of harquebuses. They no longer complained about the Jews or the price of wheat: now they begged the troops to stop firing, not to punish them with such violence.

This countryside invasion postponed the *Te Deum* by two hours, put the Viceroy in a foul mood, landed a score of peasants in prison, gave the gravediggers of S'Esgleita and Esporles more work, and only Sen Boiet believed he had benefited from the disturbance. Seeing how things turned ugly, he immediately ran towards St Catherine's Chapel, where he received the promised bag of ounces because, in effect, the riot had been pronounced and showed that the disdain for the Jews was as widespread among the real old Christians, the peasants, as the disaffection they felt to the Viceroy.

Rafel Onofre Valls de Valls Major, in a friar's habit, left the premises of the brothel a short while before the bells started ringing to announce the *Te Deum*. Limp had advised him to spend the morning making stations in the surrounding chapels, but he preferred to stay in the whore-house, hidden in the cellar, which was rarely used, than to be forced to pretend he was praying. Besides, although nobody could suspect a friar at prayer, he had never seen one kneeling for more than five minutes inside any church. The boy waited to leave the city by St Antony's Gate, on his way to Alcúdia, where he hoped to embark for Alicante if he could bribe a captain. He preferred to leave at dusk than in daylight, since he was less likely to be recognized in the failing light. The din of the peasants he heard passing nearby helped him up to a point. There weren't many guards behind Olivar because the Bailiff's forces were still concentrated between Montision and the Almudaina, where they were arresting those they considered more suspicious and beating everybody for the sake of it.

He attracted nobody's attention when, mixing with others, most of them farmers escaping the disturbance, he left through St Antony's Gate. To avoid having to walk with them, arousing suspicions he could do without, he told the group already approaching he would go on ahead because he was in a great hurry to confess a dying man, whose family had sent for him urgently. With lowered head, the loose hood covering a large part of his forehead, his hands up the sleeves, he quickly advanced towards the darkness, copying a friar's typical gestures as best he could. This habit, which seemed to have been made to measure—"Oh, what a beautiful monk!" exclaimed Limp as soon as he put it on, looking at him radiantly—was a kind of safe-conduct. None of his pursuers would ever imagine that the rabbi's son might have access to such garments and so nobody would search for him in that outfit if he didn't give them a reason to do so. But the use of such a disguise, which his father no doubt would have censured, made him feel despicable. He was escaping, using the attire of those who hated him most, of those who believed the flames were his only destiny, and he was afraid that a speck, however minute, might enter through the pores of his skin, infecting him with that aversion, making him feel for himself the same contempt they felt.

Although since the age of thirteen he had behaved like a real Jew and only observed Christian rituals for the sake of appearances, as a child Rafel Onofre had believed in Jesus Christ and the Virgin Mary, had confessed and received Communion like one of the faithful, without considering friars and priests as enemies. This is why he did not feel comfortable using such vestments, although he realized this disguise was the safest. However hard he tried not to think about it, he remembered how the Church predicted terrible suffering for sacrilegers like himself who used habits in a fraudulent manner. Pushing aside such thoughts, he walked along the side of the road, focusing on the need to reach Alcúdia. He also rejected the confused images of the xebec and storm, and Limp's adroit hands on his body, which had kept him company all day in the damp of the cellar, stung, however, by the dear faces of his parents and Maria. Not knowing what had happened to them, in what cramped prison they lamented him or where they had managed to hide, filled him with disquiet. He fought to repel the anxiety that sometimes, like a leech sucking his chest, prevented him from breathing normally. He answered in a low voice, mechanically, in a forced, husky voice to disguise his own, much shriller voice, the greetings of the indistinct shapes he passed, almost all of them equipped with a lamp, which he had not thought to ask for and no doubt would need when the clouds covered the moon, to avoid stumbling on stones and scratching himself on bushes. The further he advanced into the darkness, the less he heard "Good night" and wished others "God give you good night," because walkers know that icy March is not a good time to be out on the road.

The boy, who was not used to such wilds, especially in bare feet, noticed how they were being cut under the pressure of the hermit's sandals Limp had also provided him with. He was cold and began to feel his toes swelling. His chilblains hurt like hell and rather than itching, as every night, smarted as if they were stuffed with chili peppers. He soon gave up the idea of reaching Alcúdia, at least until he rested a bit. The sound of sheep-bells nearby, accompanied by the muffled echo of a song, and the sight of a camp-fire on the right-hand side of the road made him stop for a few moments before deciding to head for where no doubt a shepherd was keeping warm. A fresh breeze that bore no relation to the previous night's wind at intervals carried the notes of what struck him as a love-song and immediately reminded him of his songs under Maria's window on much sweeter, gentler nights, summer nights mostly, that now seemed so far away, as if centuries had passed since June instead of months.

He had already taken a dozen steps towards the camp-fire, immersed in the memories of their courtship, when he heard another voice very close, quite different from that young voice singing. Emerging out of the darkness, the voice pleading for help did not seem to belong to a living person, because he could not see any shape or hear anything else in the direction it was coming from. He tried to advance much more quickly towards the fire, suspecting that the voice must be sounding inside his head as a result of the fear he had undergone, a trick of his own imagination. To exorcize the voice demanding his attention, he started singing as heartily as he could:

You who kill with a look
kill me only by looking at me,
who prefer you to kill me than to live
if you do not look at me . . .

but immediately fell quiet, surprised that a friar should be singing that love-song in public with such obvious pleasure. And, on falling quiet, he again heard the voice, now, however, accompanied by a burly frame that moved alongside him.

"What is it, brother?" asked Rafel Onofre.

"I need you to come with me," the apparition answered.

"Come towards that fire, which is where I'm going, and tell

me what you want," decided the boy, whom fear and defenselessness had made arrogant.

Without turning round, out of the corner of his eye, he observed how another man carrying a lamp had suddenly appeared and both were following him. *They've done what I want,* he thought, pleased up to a point and less frightened, and he turned his head to see who was behind him and what their pretensions were. Four hands, like four hooks, fell on him and beat into him. The boy fought, kicked, marked their arms with his teeth, but could not get rid of them.

"I'm not carrying any money," he told them, "besides, what could you want from a poor Franciscan? Let me go, I beg you, I have to confess a dying man. If he goes to hell, you'll be to blame."

"We want you to do what you say," they replied, "to confess someone who's badly injured and, having been a great sinner, will burn for sure if you don't help him. You're coming with us."

As soon as the two thugs let go of him, Rafel Onofre immediately felt his body, thinking, as had happened some hours before with Limp, he was dreaming. Then, on verifying that he was wide awake, he suspected it had something to do with witches and ghosts who, so his poor, mad grandmother claimed, are everywhere and know a man's innermost secrets. Hadn't he said he was going to help a dying man? For that reason the spirits had put this plate of bacon before him . . . He was about to tell them the truth, but decided it wasn't a good idea if they were evil spirits, since they must already have seen through his disguise, whereas if they were flesh-and-blood men who really did want him to confess a dying man, they would find it even harder to believe the excuse that he was a false friar, that all he had of a friar was the habit, if all the same they were prepared to take him at any price.

Guided by the lamp the man leading him held in his right hand, Rafel Onofre hurried to keep up with him. His chilblains had burst and were bleeding. He noticed the iciness of the ground on his feet and the cold climbing up his legs. The sky had filled with stars, and the Great Bear shone ahead with absolute clarity. Rafel Onofre looked for the moon, which appeared from behind some clouds with silver paleness, and again he envisaged Beatriu Mas' smile, after listening to her words. *To touch the sky at the passing of the moon.* He rebuffed the memory and thought about Maria. On nights like this he had played at counting stars: a hundred, a thousand, three thousand, millions of stars above his head, Jehovah's lights to guide men. *We should have embarked today and not last night with the storm. Last night? The night before last?* He had spent last night in the brothel, far from the xebec that was supposed to take them to Livorno, and it seemed to him that everything had happened not in a handful of hours, but in a long time, weeks at least, and he couldn't work out how all this had happened to him, when the only thing that had happened to him in nineteen years was his love for Maria. And Maria could never have imagined him dressed in a friar's habit, borrowed, what's more, from the best-known whore in town, crossing icy fields to go and confess a dying man. Nor would his father have believed it. Only his mad grandmother would have accepted it naturally, because she came and went with witches and ghosts and dealt with spells and evil spirits all day long. What if it was all a trap? And Limp had reported him? She had already informed him she didn't go with Jews. Why did he trust her? Why did he tell her the route he would take? But had Limp wanted him captured, she only had to call for the Assistant Bailiff. No, Limp had nothing to do with all this. He would always be grateful to Limp, though he wouldn't dare explain to his father or to Maria what had taken place between them. Their meeting was a fluke, as that unfortunate storm had been a fluke. He would get out of it with Adonai's help, "If God wills it," he whispered.

"Did you say something?" asked the man guarding him from behind. "Or were you praying?"

"I was praying for my dying man. Is it far to go?"

"Cor, you tire easily! We're almost there," he answered rudely, in a kind of snort, as if he'd borrowed the voice of a donkey.

"It's over there," said the man with the lamp, pointing to some fig-trees the moon picked out, "in that hut."

Through the open door, the flames consuming a couple of logs in the fireplace revealed the body of a badly injured man lying on the ground, on top of a sheepskin, breathing heavily. There was an open wound in the middle of his chest, round and large, like a bloody rose, where death had already laid eggs. Rafel Onofre went up to look at his face. He was not young. Furrowed by the plow of the wind and storms, his skin, like leather, gave away his rustic origins. Fortunately he did not know him. He was clearly departing this life in terrible pain and was finding it increasingly difficult to breathe. Rafel Onofre felt sorry for him. He wasn't exactly the most adequate person to help him go to heaven. Next to him, keeping an eye on him, was another man, who, on seeing the friar come in, stood up and went towards the door. The other two had taken up position there and were waiting.

"You can't complain, Sen Boiet!" said the one with the mule's voice, addressing the dying man. "We're true to our word. You wanted a confessor and we've brought you one. Since you were in such a hurry, he's the first one we could find. We had trouble persuading him. He's left another dying man to attend to you . . ."

The moribund opened his eyes and, in a thin voice that death was already winding, he asked to be left alone with the friar.

Rafel Onofre sat down by the fire, on the only chair there was, and reproduced in tone and gesture the ritual of confession.

"In nomine Patris, et Filii, et Spiritus Sancti," and he made the sign of the cross.

The moribund tried to cross himself, but could only cross the air with a short movement of his right hand, which immediately, without strength, fell alongside his body. Rafel Onofre stood up and went to him.

"I'm sorry, brother, but I can't give you absolution. I'm not a priest or anything of the sort . . ."

But the dying man cannot have understood him because in between breaths he mumbled, "Stolen . . . ounces . . . murderers . . . Viceroy . . . I confess . . . justice . . . I beg . . . sins . . . Inquisitor . . ." while squeezing Rafel Onofre's hand, the hand that with the sign of the cross could have absolved him to prevent him going to hell. The boy tried to detach that hand that carried on gripping him, as if staying among the living depended on this contact. He had seen other people die—his grandfather Rafel, his uncle Josep, neighbors and relatives—but he had never come across such turbid eyes seeking to entrust their life to him or even to infect him with their own death. He had never been alone with a damned soul. *What if Jehovah calls me to account?* he said to himself. *I told him the truth, but he couldn't hear me anymore.* Nervously he closed the other's eyes, crossed his arms over his chest and went to find the men who had forced him to go with them. They were squatting outside, warming themselves at the fire they had lit.

"He's dead. I should like a lamp to return to the road."

"First you must tell us everything he confessed to you. Why do you think we brought you here?"

"You know that we confess in secret. What you're asking is impossible."

"It would be if you were a real monk . . ." said the one with the mule's voice.

"I don't understand," replied Rafel Onofre, horrified.

"Well, it's obvious. Or do you think we didn't see you weren't tonsured when we beat you?"

And, going up to him, he removed the hood.

"He didn't say anything," returned the boy. "He died without a word. I was too late."

"Are you sure?" asked the one who had been guarding the moribund, clenching his fist. "If I were you, I'd try to remember."

And he unleashed the first blow to his stomach with the strength of an ox.

VII

DESPITE THE DISTURBANCE, THE CATHEDRAL ENDED UP being full to the brim. All the candles had been lit and the wax crackled from time to time, joining the murmurings of the crowd, who were waiting for the authorities to arrive so that the service could begin. Praying or talking in a low voice, most of them were wondering what kept them. Many tried to guess the words his Most Reverend Eminence would say and were betting on whether the bells would ring again the whole night, meekly, with humility, as those who claimed to have first-hand knowledge had spread around the city.

Only cripples, moribunds, newborn babies and enclosed nuns had stayed at home because nobody wanted to miss the Bishop's sermon, which would no doubt make reference to the fugitives. Even the prisoners' families had come to the Cathedral and occupied the front pews among the other neighbors from the Street, desperate more than ever to prove their Christian convictions.

Esther Bonnín and Valls' two maids had accompanied the mad mother-in-law, who was gazing at the lights with terrified eyes and no longer shouting or kicking as the day before. She sat with her hands crossed on her stomach, apparently calm, not budging. She seemed finally to have responded to all those infusions of lime mixed with poppy flower that her sister continued to make her drink when she took her into her home, fifty paces from the Valls' boarded front door.

In the next pew Isabel Tarongí's children were holding hands next to their father, who was using the time to make them say the rosary on their knees. Aware of the children, he could only close his eyes from time to time to try and concentrate on the Hail Marys. It was difficult for him that evening to find the necessary recollection to establish contact with the Mother of God, whom he always asked for help in painful moments. Even though, with the force of a hammer, his will had been nailing images of his wife far from the walls of his memory, pictures of Isabel buzzed like a swarm of irate bees inside his head. He fought to repel them, lost track of the rosary, smacked his son, who was fidgeting, but only managed to dress them up in anxiety, regret and self-pity. He cursed the hour when he set eyes on Isabel, the hour he decided to make her his own. As always he blamed her for having deceived him because before marrying she never confessed to him that she was a false Christian. He blamed himself for not having suspected it even, for not having thought that she might be a hypocrite, like so many other inhabitants of the Street. But what was he to know? He came from Sóller and only had fleeting contact with the people of Segell. Had he known, had somebody warned him, he would never have married her, however much that girl resembled the Virgin Mary and giving her up meant death for him. He found out by chance in the fourth year of their marriage, when she refused to try some lobster given to him by some fishermen from Deià, friends of his who occasionally came visiting. Then he realized that she did not refuse bacon because it didn't agree with her, as she claimed, and also she observed Queen Esther's fasts. He tried, first by fair means and later by foul, to make her see the errors of the old religion and the truths of the new. But she would not listen. "All the same," she used to say to him, "I shall die a Jew because all my people lived and died as Jews, which is how you ought to live and die as well." He couldn't understand how that girl, who seemed molded from honey and sugar candy, could have such strong convictions. He suffered like a lamb before the slaughter to think that, if he did not convert her, they would have to spend a whole eternity apart because Jews couldn't enter the home of the Christian God, especially if, like his wife, they were covert apostates, false believers in the religion in which they had been baptized. Because, on the other hand, Isabel always obeyed him and served him willingly and never objected to accompanying her husband to as many Masses as he wanted to hear and not once did she decline to say the rosary or to attend all the novenas he felt like. But at the same time, since she couldn't twist the arm of her faith either, she wanted him to let her secretly practice Jewish rites at home, which couldn't harm him at all, so long as nobody knew about it, so long as he didn't tell anybody. But Martí, who, since changing confessor on moving to the city, did not take a step without consulting Father Ferrando, preferred to discuss this point with him also. The priest, as the penitent had supposed, rejected Isabel's proposal and, on pain of denying him absolution and opening proceedings against him, ordered him to forbid his wife Jewish rituals. If he could not persuade her to recant and repent of everything she had done against the Christian religion, then he would have no choice, if he did not wish to be damned as well, but to report her to the Holy Office. The Jesuit was clear and absolutely emphatic: he could not have marital relations with her again unless she converted. He would not absolve him from the sin of fornicating with a recalcitrant apostate.

He saw Isabel Tarongí—the memories pecked him like starving beaks—with her face covered in tears and that virgin martyr's look that so attracted him, stirring up his masculine desire to the stars, as on the night he told her everything the confessor had ordered and expelled her from the room they had shared for four years. Isabel's weeping did not soften the fury of his cries; on the contrary, it roused their fury and woke the children, who joined in their mother's groans. Following that ill-fated day, everything changed at home. He immediately sent for his mother and entrusted her with domestic matters. Isabel ceased to accompany him in public to his religious practices. She was forced to confess to Father Ferrando, before whom she flatly denied her husband's accusations. This momentarily saved her from proceedings, but, according to Xim Martí, did not make her change her behavior. Despite the vigilance she was subjected to by her husband, mother-in-law and Christian maid, she endeavored to carry on observing the forbidden rituals of her religion much more stealthily than before. She almost did not eat and her state was one of absolute melancholy, broken only by the presence of the children, whom, however, she was not allowed to see alone. Isabel Tarongí only trusted her brother, who became her one carer and consolation.

The escape took Xim Martí by surprise. He also found that situation unbearable, though he suffered from it a lot less, but he never imagined his wife would dare to leave, because she loved the children deliriously and leaving meant giving them up for good. As a Christian he had no choice but to rejoice at the miracle of the wind. Perhaps in this way, in prison, Isabel would come to renounce her errors and they could start a new life together. For his part, he had nothing to fear. His strong Christian convictions had saved his house from the furious sealing zeal of the Bailiff's men, since it was the only one where a fugitive lived not to have been boarded up. Without Isabel he could feel released from the heavy burden of watching her, of constantly warning her. Redeemed from the temptations of the flesh with which that body of jasmine still mortified him and, most of all, free to educate the children as good Christians. He would no longer have to fear the pernicious influence of their mother, who with her sweet resignation wielded over them a magnetic power that turned those two mischievous imps into two authentic lambs who obeyed her in and for everything, as he obeyed her when he fell in love, fascinated by the sweet serenity of her maritime eyes and the iconic features of her face. Despite her far inferior birth, Isabel Tarongí in her youth had rivaled Blanca Maria Pires, the only woman in the entire city who could compete with her, and had come out on top, even though the merchant Sampol's wife used silk and taffeta to dress every day and she only had cheap serge. Even her mother-in-law, who was not at all keen for her son to marry in the city, had to praise his good taste when he made her ask her hand. Caterina Aguiló, who occupied the same pew as her son and grandchildren, beside two women from next door, like everybody turned when she saw the Viceroy come in—*at last!* they'd been waiting over an hour—accompanied by the judges and followed by the noble members of the Great and General Council.

The Cathedral bells, which have been announcing the office for some time, begin to peal more merrily. First Bàrbara and Antònia, then Nova, Prima, Tèrcia, Picarol. Only Eloi is silent. The eleven bell-ringers who sounded the bell the previous night without stopping asked to be paid more to work again today, due to their accumulated tiredness, and the Curia turned them down. *Where would we end up if we accepted today's exaggerated demands?*

The authorities are already in their places in the damasked front pews. The judges on the Epistle side; on the Gospel side, the members of the Great and General Council. In a higher seat, lined with red velvet, his excellency the Viceroy. He took his time, but now it's his turn to wait because the Bishop has not come out. The wax goes down on the torches and candelabra. If the service doesn't start for another hour, some chapels will be plunged into darkness. Nobody foresaw this delay. The most devout, those who were praying, tiredly join those who are talking and the murmur grows. *Was the peasants' disturbance really so serious that the Viceroy had to stay in the Palace?* Some, like Aina Fuster's husband and the tailor Valleriola's brother, yawn from boredom. But nobody moves.

"If the Viceroy made us wait over an hour, the Bishop will want to do the same," says Josep Bonnín to his wife. He is very anxious and afraid that they'll imprison him, following the confessions of his father or sister, Sara de les Olors, who's not very fond of him because he has never taken the visions and ecstasies she has occasionally fallen into seriously.

The Bonníns would like to return home. It's gone seven. It's cold and night has fallen. Last night neither of them slept a wink, terrified by the wind, the bells and the crazy hammer-blows. They live one up from Madò Grossa and her sister. But they know they cannot budge. If they left, they'd attract attention, something they could really do without. They have no choice but to stay put, whatever time it is, whatever happens, like everybody in their circle, frightened and expectant, and to ask Jehovah with all their might for that stain not to spread even further, for that boiling oil not to splash on them as well, even if they're not so compromised as those who took the decision to embark.

Esther Bonnín thinks that, if the Bishop doesn't put in an appearance soon, she'll have to go out with her sister, who's growing impatient and stands, sits and kneels mechanically, all the time.

"If she shouts, we'll have to take her out," says Esther to the maid. "Quickly too."

But the Bishop is about to enter. He is preceded by a throng of acolytes, sacristans, priests and canons. "He only made the Viceroy wait half an hour," some say, while others think it's longer. The bells drown out the ringing of Figuera. As they supposed, he is in pontifical dress, but because of Lent the color of his cope is not the white and golden he usually wears at the most important solemnities. Nor does he use black, but purple, with which he disguises the sorrow of the season in the joy of the arrests. Before starting the office, which will consist of the previously announced exposition of the Host, he addresses his parishioners with his fiery speech, which usually provokes tears of repentance when he alludes to the eternal torments with coals that never go out, slugs that leave a fiery slime on the bodies of the damned, turned into toads or putrid leeches, according to the level of offence to the Lord God. But today he says nothing about the eternal torments, today he only talks about joy, joy because the wind, God's instrument, saved the fugitives from certain death on the high sea and, by bringing them back to land, afforded them the possibility of going to heaven. "Not only have the false Christians been preserved by divine providence, which watches over everybody and knows everything," he exclaims with all the might of his voice, "but also some of our brothers with sinful interests in the xebec that would never have allowed them to gain eternal life. Brothers in Christ," his Eminence continues after a pause to calculate the effect of his words, "who should have known better given the important posts they hold."

Captain Sebastià Palou, who occupies one of the front pews behind those reserved for the authorities, looks towards the Viceroy, but cannot see his face. *Who is the Bishop railing against? Who is he referring to? Who does he think he's accusing from his throne? And why is he doing it in front of everybody, in the middle of the service? To deepen the crisis? The cur says nothing about the peasants who shouted against the Viceroy a couple of hours ago. What's this open conviction for? What's he up to? Uncle will be furious,* Sebastià Palou is sure about this as he seeks a response to the questions he has just asked. The Bishop descends from his throne and heads towards the altar. His Most

Reverend Eminence, surrounded by canons, priests and sacristans swinging the censer, exceeds in dignity and pomp the figure made by the Viceroy in his seat of honor, even though to attend the service he's wearing a new, velvet doublet with silk-lined sleeves and a green, damasked cloak reaching down to his feet. This time he is not accompanied by his wife, who's lying in her cambric-infested bed owing to one of her frequent headaches, which make her feel nobler: not in vain does she share them with the Queen Mother. What's more, relations between the Marquise and the Bishop are strained at the moment. According to the Marquise, his Eminence is not doing everything he should to accelerate the cause of beatification of Sister Eleonor, which is taking an inexplicably long time, nor did he want to send for Chiapini on her recommendation to continue with the frescos in the Bishop's Palace, which he has just entrusted to a friar who has yet to prove to anybody that he can paint. So the headache was extremely convenient. It was sent by the Lord God to mortify her, but its mortification favored her. Besides, she didn't know what dress to wear. She didn't have a new one, and the solemnity called for one. Everybody would have clapped eyes on her as she entered the Cathedral.

The bells begin to make amends to the wind as soon as the service is over. The Bishop leaves the temple through the sea door, which is better placed for the Palace, while the Viceroy leaves through the main entrance, closer to the Almudaina, accompanied by his entourage. The crowd, having followed his Most Reverend Eminence's speech attentively, tries to work out from the faces of both authorities the direction future relations will take, because, if one thing was obvious, it's that the most pointed part of the sermon was aimed at this brother in Christ who should have known better. The Viceroy is the highest authority. But nobody notices even the slightest gesture of bitterness or sees him twitch a single alert muscle or blink nervously, despite the fact he's taken a good hiding this evening. Outside the temple he responds to the aristocracy's greetings and courtesies and with a placid mien returns the smiles of ladies and the farewells of gentlemen and citizens. He gives the respectful bows of the merchants and artisans he meets a benevolent wave of his right hand.

Despite the time, after eight in the evening, he ambles homewards. The Cathedral's proximity to the Almudaina meant he refused the carriage as always, even though he's been advised to take it today. Now that the disturbance seems to be under control, he's pleased not to have heeded the advice calling for greater caution and almost demanding cowardice as a security measure. He lingers with the Count of Santa Maria de Formiguera at the front gate. He disguises the hurry he's in to get home, the anxiety that eats away at him to hear the news he's sent for. He appears to be the least busy, the calmest man in the world. Only when he crosses the Palace courtyard does his discomfort show: he breaks into a run and his heart thumps as he enters the hall, having negotiated the steps two at a time.

"Is anybody waiting for me?" he asks the butler, who immediately came to open the door when he heard him and gives way with a bow that makes him lean so low as if he were suddenly to start walking using his hands as well, having turned into a four-legged animal.

"No, excellency. Only the Marquise asked for your lordship and bid me ask you to go and see her at once. Her headache has worsened with the sound of the bells."

"Blast!" exclaims the Viceroy, who has never known why he finds his wife's migraines so irritating. "Tell her ladyship I'm not in the mood for her headaches, I have much worse headaches to deal with."

"As your lordship requires. I'll tell her you hope she feels better, excellency. I mean I'll tell her chambermaid at once that you'll visit her ladyship as soon as you can."

"Tell her what you like, Tomeu. I do not wish to be disturbed. I'm expecting two urgent visits. If anyone asks for me, show them in. Whatever time it is."

Followed by the butler, who accompanies him with a candelabrum and goes ahead to open the doors, the Viceroy crosses the five rooms separating him from the library, where he is accustomed to work.

"Does your lordship wish to divest himself?" asks Tomeu, seeing the heavy cloak he is wearing.

The Viceroy turns down the offer. Only a short while ago he wanted to throw off these clothes stifling and oppressing him, especially the pants that are too tight, but then he decides not to. He doesn't want to waste a second. He is consumed by impatience to see his emissaries as soon as they arrive. Were they to come in while he was changing his clothes, it would take him a few moments longer to know his future and in particular the strategy he must follow in his ever-complicated relations with the Church, especially now, after hearing the Bishop's open attack on his person. He can't devise a counter-attack until he has all the information he's sent for. His nephew has not been much help this time. Notwithstanding all his willingness to attend the gathering and question the Judge of Goods on the way to the Palace, he didn't tell him anything he didn't know.

As soon as the servant who was poking the fire left the room, the Viceroy drew his armchair up to the flames and flopped down. He no longer had to carry on pretending and could show the look of concern and pensive mien of a man who has been cornered, overtaken by events. With one hand supporting his left cheek and the other draped over his protuberant belly, as if he were posing for a picture with a gesture that was not meant to be studied, he stared at the flames that were quickly devouring the cherry logs, his favorite firewood, because it has a clean and lively way of burning. The image of fire, unlike other mortals, who for him do not amount to two dozen, does not induce him to weigh up the torments of hell, but makes him think of the passage of time and life, a flame that passes from spark to ash in the brevity of a moment. But despite this unhappy image, especially in low moments like now, fire fascinates him. He may well owe this, like many other pleasures he has, to the wet-nurse who told him stories next to the vast hearth that presided over the kitchen in Boradilla del Monte Castle, where he was born fifty-six years ago.

It was a meditation next to the fire, next to this very fireplace, before similar flames—at times like now a brilliant blue almost—a meditation on the transience of life and the short duration of the few pleasures it affords us, that urged him only a fortnight ago to see if those Moorish girls he had been given, whom he only made dance for him or for a group of select friends, could fan his own embers. He also had the right—as people were doing in the street, despite the ban he himself had signed, because it had been a hard year owing to the lack of wheat—to celebrate his own private carnival as he pleased. *I'll dress my soul up,* he thought. *The confessor will absolve me anyhow. I'll do double penance if he wants.*

Outside he could hear the cries of masqueraders, a hullabaloo that would no doubt disturb the Marquise, who would have liked to celebrate carnival properly, with a ball in the Palace. But he refused. He had no choice but to set an example in a year of famine. No merriment. What he now had in mind could not be understood as such. Didn't he own the slave-girls? Weren't they from a harem? There was nothing to fear. He sent Tomeu to fetch them and ordered him to withdraw. It was after eleven. "Time to sleep," he told him. Nor did he want any other servant hanging around to help him undress. "Thank you, I'm in good company," he added when the butler took his leave, closing the door and bowing as usual.

"Dance how I like," he ordered the slave-girls, settling into his armchair next to the fire, "naked," he warned with a smile that was meant to be obscene, but turned out to be grotesque: an off-white tongue sticking out through gapped teeth.

The girls danced as they always had done, but this time were aware of a different gaze on their bodies. The master was not trying to enjoy the view, purely for the pleasure of contemplating those young, lithe limbs abandoned to the rhythm, dancing in his honor. Now each look seemed to conceal the threat of a poker about to prod them. Aixa was the first to observe how right in the middle of the Lord Viceroy's groin his trousers could not disguise a growing protuberance she had never noticed. *We've excited him,* thought the girl, *it had to happen some day. We'll see what he wants us to do in a moment.* But the moment never came because everything happened right away, as if his excellency had realized what the slave-girl was thinking. He shoved her on to her knees and, having freed the viceregal lump from the clothes that held it prisoner, he forced her to take his semi-erect penis in her mouth.

"Now you," he said suddenly, a little later, calling for Laila, who was watching, rooted to the spot. "Let's see if you can do any better." But despite their disciplined efforts, neither of them could fan those embers into a flaming stick.

"You two don't know a thing about making birdies fly," said his excellency irritably. "I should pack you off to Limp's for a while. She'd soon teach you . . ."

The slave-girls did not dare to reply. Laila, frightened, grabbed her clothes to get dressed, but the Viceroy would not let her.

"I prefer you to be naked. Don't tell me you're cold. It's boiling in here. Now let's have a bit of fun."

And he stood up to fetch a bottle of malmsey and some honeyed sweets he had hidden for the occasion in a box. They turned down the wine and ate the sweets; he fasted, but drank greedily.

"Wouldn't you like to play for a bit before going to sleep?" he asked them in a thick voice. "So that you can see that I like you, I'll entertain you now."

And he got down on all fours and began to bark and gambol on the floor, as if he'd turned into a playful dog, despite having a moustache that was too long to suggest a pup's elasticity. To start with, the girls laughed at that grotesque spectacle that no doubt everybody in the city, from the nobles down to the last artisan, would have paid to watch. The dog attempted to turn somersaults and offered its right paw for the girls to take between laughs. The dog lolled out its tongue and passed it over their legs, reaching up to their thighs, drooling. Up to this point the Viceroy remembers it perfectly, he only wanted to relive the times in his childhood when, to make his wet-nurse angry, he barked and licked her legs, thighs and breasts till she, laughing, told him to stop. What was wrong with recalling those games if it was carnival and he had two slaves who belonged to him? It was after this, perhaps because of all the glasses of malmsey, that things turned ugly. The dog between drools, spasms and barks, tried to stick its tongue in the girls' fannies, but suddenly, without knowing how, found itself digging its two remaining canines into Laila's clitoris, which started to bleed, while she cried out in pain and asked for help, even though she knew no one would come to her aid. But the tragedy arrived minutes later when Aixa, to defend herself against one such assault to her right nipple, the dog having risen on its hind legs, grabbed the fire-tongs and tried to hit the ribs of the furious beast, which, seeing it was under attack, ground its teeth and ripped off the nipple of the slave-girl, who fell down, bleeding and in pain.

Madò Grossa entered the Viceroy's house early in the morning, through the door to the stables used by servants, to see how she could patch together that breast ruined by the barbaric assault of a Moorish slave-boy the Lord Marquis had already imprisoned.

Days later the slave-boy was found guilty, condemned to row in a galley and not hanged, because his excellency mercifully issued the pardon in time. "Carnival and malmsey can cloud anybody's judgement," he resolved in order not to send him to the gallows. But since Moors are born liars and traitors and who knows what falsehoods those two shameless slave-girls might spread around, once they were on the road to recovery, the Viceroy thought it better to dispose of them and furtively used the fact Captain Willis' ship had anchored in Port Pi to check them out. Given the direction things had taken, it could be said his decision was mistaken because the Bishop would like nothing more than for the slave-girls to relate in detail everything that had happened on being interrogated by the familiars who had boarded the ship. This is why, that same afternoon, he had ordered a band of loyal men to go to the xebec and abduct them.

From the Bishop's words, from that allusion to sinful interests, he could deduce that the slave-girls had spilled the beans, but, if everything went well, as he hoped, they could not keep on accusing him without more convincing proof. His Most Reverend Eminence was on a hiding to nothing. How could anyone believe the word of two wretched Moorish slaves bearing false witness against a Viceroy no less? That is why God was punishing them, he wasn't. He was only acting as God's instrument, sending his two most loyal followers, to whom he entrusted the most delicate missions, rewarding them liberally afterwards, to take them off the boat and make them disappear from Majorca in the way they considered most efficient. Any other interests he could have in the xebec were far from secret. Nobody forbade doing business with converts and, besides, he wasn't. He was only looking after the affairs of his wife, she was the rich one, something he always did indirectly. They wouldn't catch him out, even if everybody squealed. He wasn't glad about the arrests because Valls most of all was an excellent mediator between Pere Onofre Aguiló and him; but since Costura's demise he had been expecting the Inquisition to act and had already taken steps to do without both partners.

The Holy Office could say Mass and more. If he managed to prove that the previous day's shenanigans had been organized by the Church, as he was almost sure they had been, he could confront the Curia with newly sharpened weapons. Not for nothing had he made everybody wait this evening, while he saw to affairs of government on account of the disturbance that kept him longer than he would have liked: to arrange for Sen Boiet's capture was more complicated than he had supposed and it wasn't easy to find reliable, willing men, especially if, as he wanted, they had to make him confess, before killing him, whether he was being paid by the Inquisitor or the Bishop or both.

Part Three

I

NEWS CONFIRMING THE FAILED ESCAPE REACHED Livorno forty days after the arrest of the false converts. Spring was already sweetening the air with garden scents and the summer promise of tasty fruits.

Pere Onofre Aguiló, who had been watching the mouth the xebec would have to come through day and night for a month, had run to the quay on recognizing the green hull of *The Aeolus* entering the new harbor. He could feel his stirred blood quickening his pulse as a knot of breathlessness squeezed his chest. He was afraid he would burst with joy before he had a chance to embrace the friends he had at times given up for dead. A dream, recurring for weeks, plowed by ships that sank after a useless combat, frequently filled him with gloomy forebodings. He was hard pushed to repel them, but his hope in Adonai was strong and helped him to hold out faith that they might still arrive safe and sound at any moment.

Over the last few days his hope had increased and, whenever he could, he went down to the port. He would walk nervously for a time in front of the monument to Fernando I, from where he could look out to sea. *If they arrived now,* he would say to himself, *I'd fling my arms around them and whizz them off to the houses waiting to take them in.* He would pace up and down among the Moors sculpted by Giovanni de l'Opera on the quayside, as if by dint of his activity he could hasten their arrival, which seemed more imminent from there than from anywhere else in the city. He soon became obsessed with these figures, which were commissioned to celebrate the founding of Livorno only one hundred and twenty years before, and already it was so rich thanks in large part to the Jews. In their tormented faces he recalled those of the Consul and Valls and also his own, turned into bronze, immobilized for ever, condemned to gaze in vain at an impossible sea. Fortunately he could laugh now at all those terrible omens. *The Aeolus* was approaching. He lifted his arms to greet his brothers and sisters and waved them joyfully like the sails of a mill driven by a fair wind. He started to shout out the names that were dear to him. "O Consul, Valls, Rabbi, Valleriola, Rafel Onofre . . ." Soon people, seeing him so happy, crowded round him. He explained to them all what was happening. They also welcomed the fugitives. The city was prosperous, money flowed freely and nobody distrusted those who wanted to settle there. All the better if they were Jews. They would soon contribute to Livorno's growth by opening businesses, building houses, for the benefit of all.

Aguiló suddenly fell silent and stopped waving when he realized he had confused his people with the sailors working on deck, when he saw that none of them resembled the Consul and his sons or Valls and his family. None of them looked like the tailor Valleriola. Not one was anything like the brethren who had fled Majorca. But he retained a glint of expectation, a glimmer of hope. The xebec had reached the Medicean port and was preparing to drop anchor. It would at least bring news. Not everything was lost.

A few words from the captain were enough to cover the horizon in clouds of smoke and fiery reds. The Majorcan merchant could not believe it. Now, with tears in his eyes, he was afraid he would die from the shock. He still felt breathless. The disastrous imprisonment was the worst news he could have received. Nothing more bitter could have befallen his brethren from the Street. Pere Onofre blamed the captain for everything. His excuses were worthless, although he cited the wind and the storm that arose quite unexpectedly. The Majorcan merchant insisted they had paid him a lot of money up front and the sum was more than enough to confront whatever risk. Even though Willis assured him that to weigh anchor in such conditions was impossible without the loss of life, Aguiló still would not believe him. He accused the captain of having broken his promise to transport them to Livorno at all events. He threatened him with shouts full of insults. He was about to lay into him, to channel his rage into blows. But the captain was twice his size and younger. There was no point fighting. He could only hurl words at him. He pressed him with captious arguments like fists to see if he was telling the truth. He had known Willis for some time, they had done business together, and he had never given him cause to complain, but now he suspected that, to keep the money without accomplishing the set task, he might have informed the Inquisition about the passengers Aguiló had so dearly entrusted to him on closing the deal only two months before.

Realizing how excited Pere Onofre was, Willis did his best not to take offence at his suspicions and answered calmly, always the same, blaming bad luck, the unfortunate coincidence of the wind and storm. Having regained his composure, Aguiló asked the captain to accompany him to the Widow Sampol's house so that he could give her the news himself. He didn't feel strong enough to inform her of the disaster on his own.

A thick, warm, smooth blue sky, without a hint of cloud, presaging fair weather, welcomed Willis, who, even though he was stepping on dry land, jolted along as if he were still being pushed by the sea's blows. He liked Livorno. And not only because in its free port there was good work and better profits to be had than in any other. There was a completely mysterious reason he could not fathom. No, it wasn't just the order, the cleanliness of the streets, which Aguiló had urged him to emphasize to the fugitives during the journey, explaining all the good they would find when they arrived. It was true that in Livorno he had never seen groups of pigs wandering about as in Marseilles, Genoa or Majorca City, or goats or hens either. Dogs and sparrows at the very most . . . But he didn't mind about that. It must have had something to do with the character of the local populace, a very mixed populace, since lots of foreigners lived in Livorno, all of whom obeyed the laws and observed pacts—something they would no doubt make him do, despite the huge losses—and tolerated the customs and even religions of others.

As soon as they entered Blanca Maria Pires' garden, it suddenly occurred to the captain that the Flemish doctor who the previous year traveled on *The Aeolus* from Antwerp to Barcelona was absolutely right when he claimed the year had to begin in mid-March and not on the first of January. Spring was the start of life, and not the cold, a prelude to death. That's why the calendars were wrong. Christ, he ventured, was born not in December, but in April. In December shepherds don't spend the night out in the open. Christ, promise of life, could never have come into the world in winter. Now he could touch it with his hands: the scent of quince and lemon trees pervaded all. New life coursed down every branch, sprouted splendidly wherever he looked, also in the Widow Sampol's rosy cheeks, her dewy, almost maritime eyes, and the curves concealed by the silk and pale taffeta of her dress.

The Widow Sampol was with Jacob Moashé, who as every afternoon after instructing her son was keeping her company. The lady introduced the captain to the rabbi and invited him to sit opposite her, gesturing to Pere Onofre to come to her side. A shiver must have run down her spine, because both men noticed how her flesh trembled. The air in Livorno at that time was warm and only occasionally offered a gust of salty humidity, like a garment left from the previous winter.

Contrary to what the captain thought, Blanca received the news with greater equanimity than Aguiló, without making the slightest fuss. Used to controlling her emotions as a child, she would not have allowed that stranger to see her cry. She simply looked at the rabbi as if seeking the necessary help to withstand that cruel blow. Moashé placed his small, short-sighted eyes in hers and said nothing. His presence disturbed Pere Onofre. This little man who seemed to have emerged from a Gothic miniature and believed he possessed the truth, directly inspired by the breath of God, made him nervous. Perhaps he was influenced by his wife, who had ended up hating him, but he found it difficult to understand how the lady could heed his advice even in business. And he realized that it was partly down to him that she continued helping the others in Majorca.

Blanca Maria Pires had asked Willis again to relate in detail everything that had happened. She fell silent and listened, without interrupting, to the captain's booming voice as he went over the rosary of that fateful night, constantly reiterating his willingness to go through with the escape. He pointed to the fact that on the morning of that inauspicious seventh of March—eighth, he corrected himself—he had decided to notify the Jews again as soon as he felt the wind abating and thought it possible to leave the port. He had already ordered a trustworthy sailor to prepare the boat when to his amazement he saw armed men approaching, gesturing to them to surrender and not to try to defend themselves. It was a troop sent by the Bailiff. It was useless telling them he was from a foreign nation, had the necessary safe-conducts to enter and leave the port, had paid the requisite ounces to unload and load. They accused him of having sheltered the fugitives, who had been caught on their way home, had their goods confiscated and now faced proceedings. He was handcuffed, forced to abandon the xebec and escorted ashore.

He spent five days in the cramped prison of the so-called Angel Tower. He was given virtually nothing to eat—water and a little bran, as if he were a chicken—and had to undergo a series of interrogations by followers of the Viceroy, thanks to whose intervention he was not taken to the Black House, where they wanted to open proceedings against him. The firmness of his replies may have stopped them and saved him greater hardship. He always answered the same, using the same words: he made the passengers disembark when he saw they didn't have the safe-conducts they needed to abandon the island. He had lied, it was true, because the converts would never get them, especially at a time of crisis, as Pere Onofre himself had told him on closing the deal two months before, right here, in Livorno. He had lied, he confessed, but thanks to this lie he had saved his own skin, protected the crew and not lost the cargo. He did, however, have to pay a large sum of money to be allowed to walk free, without awaiting trial. A fistful of the money he had received for the trip had gone to greasing the palms of jailers and making donations to the Holy Office. Another had been stolen by the wretches who boarded the xebec on the first night after his arrest and took everything of value they found, including two Moorish slave-girls a servant of the Viceroy asked him to remove from Majorca. "This is why I can only give you back a bag of ounces," concluded the captain, rounding off his tale, which did not differ in the slightest from the one he had told Aguiló.

The Widow Sampol, who had listened to Willis without wanting to look at him, training her tearful eyes on the rings she wore on the fingers of her left hand, suddenly raised her head, but did not confront the captain, as he expected. Nor did she look at Moashé. She tried to seek refuge in the gaze of Pere

Onofre, who, with his face in his hands, did not realize. On his adobe forehead, the only part of his face he left uncovered, the Widow Sampol proceeded to contemplate the cracks of his wrinkles and the numerous folds that led to those furrows and suddenly it seemed to her that Aguiló had aged a hundred years. She waited for him to speak, but the merchant remained silent, without stirring for a long while. The silence became heavy, almost magmatic. A peacock's cry broke it suddenly and the lady came to and, as if taking it for a long-awaited signal, sent to rouse her, decided to confront the captain on her own.

"Willis, your arguments do not entirely convince me. You have blamed the wind, you have said it was Valls' deranged mother-in-law who unwittingly gave them away, and I find it hard to believe. Would it not be easier to suspect you, captain?"

"Madam, I cannot allow you to doubt my honor even for a second. Do you think if I'd given them away, I would have suffered prison?"

"Who's to say it's true? But we'll soon find out. We have loyal friends in Majorca, Willis."

"It would be better if you told the truth," interposed Aguiló, having come out of his depression, "because if what you say does not hold water, you'll face the same fate as Captain Harts. I suppose you heard the story . . ."

"Ships are full of such stories. Nights on board are long. I never entirely believed it . . ."

"You did well, captain," remarked Blanca, who had been surprised at Aguiló's intervention, "Harts lied. What's more, he broke his promise. He received money and jewels to take on board a group of fugitives, a lot less money than you . . . You received three times as much and you didn't complete the voyage either. The terms catered for this. You have to give back the money paid in advance. You signed it, captain. I have the agreement. You're a man of honor, are you not?"

"I am, madam. Do not compare me to Harts."

"Then you'll give us back all the money," said Aguiló.

"I can't give it all. It's only fair I should discount what I had to pay to get out of prison and what was stolen . . . This visit is proof of my goodwill. I ask your . . ."

"That's going too far, captain!" Pere Onofre got worked up again. "I was the one who went looking for you, who made you come . . . Do you know how many days I spent watching for your arrival? Do you know the pain you have caused me? I forced you to come here. Or do you think you came here because you wanted to?"

"You work for us," added the widow. "It's not a question of goodwill."

"I could simply have not returned to Livorno."

"You know that's impossible!" replied Blanca firmly. "You'd have had to abandon your trade and find another job, change your name, go to the Indies . . . Not returning would be like signing your own death sentence."

"He tried too," added Pere Onofre. "Of course he did! Why else was he late? The journey from Majorca to here takes a week at most. You left Port Pi more than a month ago. Your obligation was to come back immediately, at least to tell us what had happened."

"I had no choice but to alter my course. I was afraid that the Majorcan corsairs, knowing my route, would attack me. I went first to Algiers and then to Marseilles. I swear it. I'm a man of honor."

"That is what we hope, captain."

Blanca Maria Pires lifted the swirl of her dress with her left hand and stood up, announcing the end of the interview.

"Tomorrow, eleven o'clock sharp, before notary, we will settle accounts," she said in farewell. A maid accompanied Willis to the street. The rabbi and Pere Onofre simply stood up, but Blanca did not invite them to sit down again. Her eyes had filmed over and she wanted to be alone. She did not want them to see her cry.

"What if Adonai were testing us by abandoning us?" asked the widow. The question seemed to be addressed to the rabbi, but he did not answer, Pere Onofre got ahead of him:

"Jehovah has never ceased to protect his people. If anything, we're the ones who've abandoned him."

The rabbi smiled enigmatically. His small, oblique eyes had just vanished behind his eyelids, looking like two slits full of aqueous humor. He added:

"God's justice is infinite and our sins innumerable."

He stopped smiling on finishing his sentence and fixed his pupils on those of Pere Onofre as if he knew his faults and thought they were the cause of all the misfortune. Aguiló met his gaze for a few moments, then lowered his. He parted his lips a couple of times, but said nothing. He remained standing in front of the rabbi, in front of Blanca, who also watched him, realizing his discomfort. Pere Onofre took his leave. He felt excluded by the presence of Jacob Moashé, who, on looking into his eyes, seemed to have looked into the depth of his heart or conscience, stirring the extinct embers of his past sins, which, in the form of repentance, resurfaced to make him feel responsible for the disastrous expedition.

"As soon as I can, I will return to Majorca," Aguiló blurted out, as if talking to himself. "I do not want to think about the flames."

"We'll prepare everything calmly, Pere Onofre, don't worry. I need you tomorrow at eleven with me," she said in that seductive way of hers, emphasizing the fact her friend was essential to her, and now, looking at the rabbi, "a woman on her own can hardly stand up to a rogue like Willis. With you at my side, it's quite another thing."

Aguiló walked mechanically down the streets of Livorno, without noticing anything or greeting anyone. He would have to inform the Council, go to the synagogue, explain the disaster to all who had helped with money, and he didn't feel strong enough. But if he didn't do it, Moashé would be sure to take the initiative and they'd think he was a coward. At all events he had to accept the cruel blow because he, even more than the widow, persuaded the Jews of Livorno to contribute to the charter, assuring them that Adonai would safely direct the ship to the Medicean port. He even dreaded telling his wife that the expedition had failed. He was afraid of her tears. She had prepared the guests' rooms and made their beds herself. She had changed the flowers in the vases lots of times for them to feel welcome on their arrival. And she had not skimped on provisions for the welcome dinner.

"Where are you going, looking so low?" he heard someone ask from behind. He recognized the voice and turned around. João Peres bowed politely and smiled at him fondly. Thanks to his help, he had been able to settle in Livorno and enter the Widow Sampol's service.

"Our Majorcan brethren have been imprisoned. Go home at once. The lady will need you."

II

FORTY DAYS AFTER THE FAILED ESCAPE NOBODY, EXCEPT for the inhabitants of the Street, the prisoners themselves and the members of the Holy Office who had started judging them, gave it a thought.

Conversations that shortly before were still full of "Jews who killed Good Jesus, blasted Jews sucking our blood" suddenly changed their appearance. Words of malignant hatred—because nobody could resist the idea of the future spectacle of fire and smoke and charred flesh—were swapped for much softer, gooey tones full of music, festivity and gallantry. The Viceroy had secretly informed the one person he knew couldn't keep a secret that the Queen Mother was interested in visiting Majorca that same summer, hoping the news would spread quickly and widely around the city. Everybody immediately believed it. Some claimed they had heard it directly from the lips of town-criers who never got to proclaim it. Others with not such a wild imagination waited to read or to be read the edict that would be published at any moment with the good news. Everybody thought they simply had to receive the Queen as she deserved and help with the preparations. The carpenters, blacksmiths and stonemasons reckoned they would finally have a bit of work building the necessary structures, the stages and platforms that would be erected in at least three places around the city: next to the wall, where her Majesty's ship would berth so that she could disembark in

Portella and not Port Pi, much more conveniently; in front of the town hall and in Born, where games and jousts would be held in her honor. The tailors, hatters and drapers, who this year had suffered due to the cancellation of carnival, took courage, imagining their customers would not waste an opportunity like this to wear new clothes. The bakers and confectioners totted up the amount of flour, eggs, sugar, lard and quince they would need to prepare enough cakes and sweets. The Viceroy, who enjoyed her Majesty the old Queen's favor, would do his bit and tax the wheat on which their work depended. Everybody, rope-makers, cellarers, porters, harness-makers, thought they simply had to be there. But those who were sure their profits would increase were the chandlers. "There has never," they kept on saying, "never, since the world is the world and Majorca, Majorca, been a party without lots of lights!"

The artisans' joy was contagious. The religious orders and the Curia also felt satisfied. Since the visit of the Emperor on his way to Algiers more than a hundred years ago, no king had deigned to call at the island, and this couldn't be good. Viceroys did not always perform their functions as they should. Now the Queen would see her subjects face to face and everybody would help to show the representative of God on earth their filial affection with *Te Deums*, High Masses and benedictions. The Inquisitor had even suggested to the members of the Holy Office bringing forward proceedings for the auto-da-fé to coincide with the stay of her Majesty, whom he would do the honor of asking to light the torch of purificatory fire.

The nobles were the only ones who, although they had no confirmation of the royal visit, feared it. The Queen's stay would prove very expensive. They would have no choice but to loosen the purse-strings and contribute to the cost of the festivities. The odd perk they might obtain from Lady Mariana of Austria would be nothing compared to the losses her visit would suppose. What's more, many of them were involved in privateering and did business with the Jews, all of which was now at risk, following the confiscations, substantially lowering their income.

But fifty days after the arrest of the Jews another event abruptly halted the flow of words on the royal advent and redirected conversations to the Inquisition's prisons, where Beatriu Mas, nicknamed Limp, had just been admitted. The news traveled from mouth to mouth, ear to ear, that at dawn on April 27, in the year of our Lord 1688, the Bailiff's men, commanded by Ripoll, had torn her from the arms of a client she was about to take down the road to hell or glory—this point differed according to the source—forced her with blows to cover her privates and quickly shut her up in the Black House by order of the Holy Tribunal. But there was another version that changed and added details and may have been right because, knowing Limp, nobody could be surprised that things had happened in this way: Beatriu Mas, seeing how they banged at the door of her workplace and hearing the cries of Ripoll, whose hoarse voice she knew well, stopped them short. Opening, but blocking the way with the spectacle of her nakedness, she told them to be so kind as to wait while she finished the job in hand, the man she was with had paid up front and had nothing to do with the disturbance. They agreed. Limp was not long. It took her a quarter of an hour to emerge and give herself up.

Not everybody believed this version of events, and not because anybody doubted Limp's professionalism. What they doubted was such a courteous gesture from Ripoll, whom they all considered to be a four-legged animal. Whatever happened, the news of her arrest had again unsettled the city. Some even thought it more important than the imprisonment of the Jews, maybe because it affected them more closely: not only did it deprive them, for a good while at least, of her agreeable services, to which they were so accustomed, but, if she was made to speak, she had some pretty compromising things to say. They were already placing bets on the time she would spend in prison, the charges that would be brought against her and whether this would lead to other arrests. Contrary to what had occurred with the Jews, there were many who defended her, but nobody was as fierce as Madò Hugueta, who took it out on the Bailiff's men, spitting and scratching, and called them bullies and bastards, seeds of Satan and worse things, except sons of whores. Madò Hugueta never used this insult. She was still young when she decided to delete these words from her vocabulary, which, intended to offend others, offended her. Mother-in-law of a whore was as far as she went when she was really angry.

"What are you taking her for?" she exclaimed in a rage. "Why my dear, sweet daughter? What's she done wrong?" she shouted and wept while tearing her hair and dashing madly about the brothel, asking the other whores to come out and help Beatriu.

"I thank you, Madò Hugueta, but I don't need protectors. I can look after myself," it is reported she said while leaving with her head held high, as if she were a princess surrounded by that troop.

"Well, would you believe it?" murmured the other women at St Antony's Gate on seeing her cross the market. "Why it's Limp in handcuffs! I knew she would get her come-uppance some day. They don't even respect Lent! The brothel was closed, but both her and Madò Hugueta stayed on . . . And do you know why? Just in case, oh look out, here's a sinner in need or a heretic who can't wait . . ."

Many stop to watch the procession. She walks alongside Ripoll, who today is on foot, dressed in her Sunday best. She looks at those who look at her, smiles at those who smile at her and insults those who insult her. "She's like a queen," says a boy, whose mother, hearing him, slaps him across the face. "What's that you're saying? She's a prostitute. And don't you forget it!"

In the Dark House nobody awaits her, nobody addresses her. As if she'd come for a visit, she is shown into a narrow room with closed windows in lukewarm shade. Limp looks at everything closely. She doesn't want to think about what's happening to her. She's asked Ripoll a thousand times what she is accused of, but he replied that he doesn't know and cynically added that it couldn't be good. She cast her eyes over the redwood beams on the ceiling. *They're in need of a lick of oil and the walls could do with a coat of whitewash.* A layer of dust like a film of silk covers the shutters. *The brothel's much more impressive than this palace, however holy it might be . . . Where've you ended up? Men are no good at cleaning, because it's obvious no women ever come in here, unless they're prisoners like me.* She amuses herself by examining the few pieces of furniture: a desk with lamp, writing materials and two chairs. *This must be the reception room, you see, Limp, what an honor? I should tidy up my hair, but I can't with my hands tied. I need a mirror . . . I thought about that and about a comb too. With a mirror beside me, I'm another woman.* She slipped the mirror and comb down her cleavage. That's all she brought. Why? She knows that any jewels, any money, will be confiscated. Madò Hugueta will take care of everything else. She knows her well and she's the mistress of the city brothel, one of the best-known brothels among sailors, except for Venice of course, where the girls are covered in diamonds. What Limp really wants is to amuse herself, not to think about the torture the Holy Office applies. But what can they do to her? What's she done? Everyone knows she's a prostitute. That can't surprise them, but she's not a witch. She's never believed in such things. She's Catholic, Apostolic and Roman. A heretic? Not a bit! She believes in God and in Christ and the Virgin and her patron Mary Magdalene. She'll deny the accusations. The brothel open during Lent? *Never!* Her, the Bishop's tart? *That was an invention by the other Inquisitor, a lie fed by the worms of envy, but you, reverence, cannot believe it.* Wagging tongues had accused her of being his concubine. She knew about this. False, cursed tongues, may they fall to the ground in pieces! May they rot in their open mouths! The Lord Bishop, God rest his soul, was a holy man. She wouldn't let them defame this shepherd who was dead and could no longer defend himself. *My conscience is clear, reverence. I'm a sinner, everybody knows it. Who doesn't sin in this world? But aside from my sins, may God forgive them, I've nothing to be accused of. In the brothel it's me who prays most. I commend myself to the Lord when work is difficult. I say the rosary whenever I can and always give thanks to God for my health and many clients. I'm a whore because my mother was, and my grandmother too, I think. And I'm good at what I do, clean and decent. I know others are jealous of me because of that and would like to swap places with me. Without us, nothing would work, the world would stop. Where would the ox go without a plough? Where would they deposit all their seed? A whore, yes, Most Reverend Lord Inquisitor, at your service. A whore, yes, but that's all. I've never used other tools than my body, I've never turned to potions or remedies made from a ram's testes, an adder's tongue, a quail's head, a hedgehog's spines or another's hair. The only cream I know I make myself for smoothing my skin, the only concoctions I know are scents for avoiding the smell of sweat or overstrong privates. Preparations of rose, carnation, nutmeg, the leaves of quince, medlar and service, boiled in rainwater. Everything else . . .*

She'll adopt the tone she thinks most convincing, a little mellifluous, but not so much as to crouch, kneel, take it lying down . . . *Whoever heard of the Inquisition taking an interest in prostitutes, reverence? They really don't have much to do! They really have stooped low!* Because she's not a Jew, she's an old Christian on all four sides, on all four, she's not entirely sure she knows who her father was, but she knew her mother . . . and her mother would never have gone with a Jew. As she would never . . . has never gone to bed with someone who's circumcised, is not aware of any Jew ever having set foot inside the brothel . . . *You're lying, Beatriu Mas, daughter of Beatriu Mas and a hundred anonymous sailors! You're lying! Or don't you remember your angel? You didn't want to fall there, did you? And now you see: in the end you've fallen flat on your face . . . What will you say when you're accused of aiding and abetting? I'll deny it . . . You'll deny you gave him the habit? Who else could have accused you if not him? Fool! Didn't you think, silly girl, he would tell the truth? Why did you trust him so much? Thanks to you he hid in the brothel, in the brothel that was closed during Lent. Thanks to you he escaped, dressed as a friar . . . Do you realize what you're playing at, Limp, when you lend someone clothes? He possessed you . . . Oh, silly tart, how delicate you've become, now you remember! He possessed you, you say, he didn't fuck you . . . He touched the sky at the passing of the moon. You were afraid the first, the second and the third nights, once you found out he'd been arrested, half dead, beaten to a pulp, but after time, after a week, it wasn't so hard to go to sleep as in the beginning and your sleep got heavier. The first few days, it was so light, so sensitive to rumors, you started hearing the woodworm you've been sharing your bedstead with for years and years. Little by little your confidence came back. He's brave, you said to yourself, brave and good, and he won't mention my name, he won't want to hurt me however much he's hurt. And if he reports me, if he says I gave him the habit, I'll deny it. Is a whore-house anything like a convent? Of course, when you think about it, it is . . . Madò Hugueta like the Mother Superior? And wouldn't I make a good novice-sister with my looks and experience? Oh, Limp, don't talk nonsense! Walls have ears and, even if you don't shout such things aloud, God hears you and he won't like . . . God and walls recording everything in their grainy skin. I must be brave. I'm a good Christian, everybody knows it, not a bit like a heretic or false convert. I observe the feasts. I confess and receive Communion at Easter. I do penance, a lot. What greater penance than handling birdies all the blessed day! For every one that flies, eh, your lordships, there are three hundred . . . Limp, don't say that, you be careful not to fall into the fiery pit, not to fall into the boiling oil! St Mary, St Mary Magdalene, my patron, who art in heaven, pray for me, my dear.*

"I want to know what I'm accused of," cries Limp on seeing the familiars come in, neither of whom she knows. Like all familiars, they're dressed in talaric robes, long as cloaks, like the threadbare frocks of friars. Their faces appear to have been steeped in vinegar and lemon. They're revolting to look at. *They've never been around our place, because if I knew them, if I could say to them, "Good day, Llorenç," or "How's it hanging, Bernat?" I'd be angrier still. It's better like this, that we've never set eyes on one another.*

"I want to see the Inquisitor," she says resolutely. "Didn't you hear? I want to know what I've done to deserve such rough treatment. To know what I'm accused of . . . You hear? Hello? Were you born deaf?"

"We won't answer you," they both say almost in unison. "The Inquisitor will receive you when he feels like it. Come with us, please."

"What is this nonsense? Where am I supposed to go with you? I hope you don't think . . ."

"Really, Limp," says the scarecrow who's just opened the door, "you are stupid! You'll come with us, please. First we'll search you, then we'll take you to your cell. In silence, Limp, we don't want to hear you."

"Will you untie my hands? I'd like to comb myself."

"As soon as we've searched you. We want to see what you're hiding in your clothes."

She now enters another room, which is big and fresh; even though there is sunlight, it's cold. Beatriu Mas shivers. "Wait," she is told, "we have to inform the Judge of Goods."

"I don't know why I like this wood so much!" Limp says aloud. "But it could do with a lick of oil. Of course, I'm not the most suited . . . but give me a good ladder and I'd turn it around in a couple of days. I have a knack for such things . . ."

"Really, Limp, don't tell us you want to decorate, we all know what job you do."

"And what does that have to do with it? I'd like to know. There's nothing I hate more than dirt, and sometimes I have to go through some pretty narrow places . . ."

The Judge of Goods appears, short of breath as usual. The work of the last fifty days has aged him. He can't keep up.

"Untie her," he says without looking at anybody. "So, Beatriu Mas, how old are you?"

"Thirty-two."

"Oh, come on, another ten at least; but the prosecutor will decide that. I'm in a hurry. Strip."

"Strip, sir? In front of . . .? Oh no, sir, I mean reverence, I can't. I couldn't."

"What's that, Limp? Anyone would think you're a lady . . ."

"Of course I am, your lordship."

"I mean an honorable lady, you tart. Strip or I'll have them strip you."

The Judge of Goods and the two familiars, who had never visited the brothel, but had been furnished with intimate details concerning Limp's body—the mole near her navel or the bush of pubic hair—felt excited at the spectacle the whore would soon provide for nothing. She drew on all her modesty and began to strip as she imagined female saints would in front of their torturers. She took off everything except for her pants and bodice.

"Continue," said the Judge of Goods in a voice that implied an excess of blood in some part of his body.

"No, your lordship, that's enough."

"OK, Toni, finish her off. Let's see what she's hiding underneath."

Limp resisted. She shouted and screamed for everybody to hear. "Brutes, pigs, wretches," she exclaimed, "get your hands off me!" As the last garment fell to the ground, so did the mirror. This and the comb were the only two things she had confiscated. The mirror cracked, but fortunately did not break. Limp would have struggled even more. A broken mirror was worse than prison: it meant death.

The clerk took her statement, noted down everything she said, even her age, which she insisted on not correcting. Then Limp, still shouting, still agitating the nerves of those holy men, was led to her cell. She went through a couple of rooms, a large courtyard, two corridors, descended some stairs and finally reached her destination. The assistant jailer leading her mockingly showed her in with a bow.

"You'll be very comfortable," he said to her, "with a girl and a madwoman for company."

Limp's eyes took a while to get used to the lack of light, wounded as they were by the brightness outside. But her nose immediately registered the stench of fug, damp and excrement, and she felt like vomiting. She groped inside and, while attempting to work out the dimensions of the cell and the furniture it contained, asked who the other inmates were.

"I'm Maria Pomar and that's Sara," she heard a delicate, almost childlike voice answer her.

"I get you. You were caught trying to escape. Oh, little Jews, dear, sweet sisters, you're the ones from the boat . . . The jailer was right. This is a fine mess I've gotten myself into!"

"And who are you?" the same voice asked.

"I'm Beatriu Mas, but people call me Limp. Now do you know who I am?"

"Oh yes!" replied the voice whose body Beatriu was beginning to make out in the half-light. "The shameless hussy from the brothel."

"Who do you think you are? Blasted Jew! What are you saying, when you should be in hell?" she gabbled, as if she'd been bitten by a snake.

"I'm not saying anything," said the girl, "only that first you take Rafel Onofre and then, pretending to help him, you give him away . . ."

"No," said Limp, lowering her voice and sitting next to Maria on a stinking mattress on the ground. "No, you're wrong to accuse me. I never gave anyone away, believe me. Besides, I don't know who this Rafel Onofre is. I've never met him."

"Yes you have, Limp, though I wish you hadn't. I'm his girlfriend."

"I can back her up on that," said the woman who had yet to speak and was standing against the wall, watching hazily. "I can read people's hearts. It's a gift the Virgin gave me."

"What's she on about?" asked Limp.

"Things of hers," answered Maria. "Poor Sara! Nothing to do with you."

"Our Lady of St Roser! Where've they put me?" exclaimed Beatriu Mas, who was beginning to appreciate the cell's exact size and grow used to its stink.

III

DURING THE FIRST WEEKS, THE MEMBERS OF THE HOLY Tribunal only took statements from the children. The four children—Pere and Miquel, Quitèria's sons, and Aina Segura's orphaned grandchildren, Josep and Joan—were immediately shut up in a cell on the second floor, not very welcoming, but reasonably well lit, as far away as possible from their families.

They first sent for Miquelet, who had involuntarily helped Ripoll confirm the suspicion that this group returning home one Sunday evening had been up to no good. The child declared they did not eat bacon or pork at home and had even refused to try lobster the day they were invited round to Xim Martí's.

Pere, who was three years older, contradicted his brother, arguing that if they didn't eat pork, it was because they didn't like it. Their mother, Quitèria, loathed these animals that wandered freely and rummaged all day in the city streets, and that is why she endeavored to do without lard, ham, sausages . . . But even Pere ended up confessing, while they bent his arm back till the bones cracked, that they didn't eat pork because Jews weren't allowed to.

Josep and Joan Tarongí, Aina Segura's orphaned grandchildren, aged twelve and nine, gave details about the escape and the prayers they said on board the ship, led by the rabbi, Gabriel Valls, and they were quite explicit about the preparations made in the home of their great-aunt, the healer Madò Grossa. Josep, who had been promised freedom if he confessed everything he knew, also confessed everything he didn't know and he thought might satisfy these men in black. The child's only wish was to get out of there soon, because he wanted to go back to playing in the streets with his old friends, who were under his orders, since he was the most adept at smiting small birds with a sling. Away from his grandmother's vigilance, he reckoned he could wander at large all day long and, now that summer was coming, he didn't mind about sleeping wherever and accepting a bowl of soup from some neighbor. Joan, on the other hand, was so petrified of these scarecrows they had to force him to speak. He wept and sobbed and from time to time affirmed he was Catholic, believed in Good Jesus, Jesus Christ and the Blessed Virgin, to whom he said three Hail Marys every night.

After the first round the Inquisitor gave the order to interrogate the women, who had been imprisoned in twos. Although they thought that such women's testimony was often unreliable, since their reasoning lacked intelligence, the members of the Holy Office knew that from what they might say they could draw enough threads to knit a fabric that might cover the other prisoners in disgrace. From the way they declared they cooked or spent Saturday, the inquisitors easily worked out whether their customs were Jewish or not. Furthermore, even if those hypocrites lied, they had statements from neighbors and maids they planned to cite in each case.

They preferred to leave the men to last, except for Rafel Onofre Valls de Valls Major, who was questioned the same day he was transferred from the Angel Tower to the Dark House.

Rafel Onofre's case had pitted the Curia against his excellency the Viceroy and wrecked already rocky relations. The Marquis accused the Church of having caused the disturbance against him led by Sen Boiet the day after the converts' arrest. The Church, more specifically the Lord Inquisitor, accused the Viceroy of not wanting to hand over that prisoner who was theirs by right. Not for nothing had he taken part in the failed escape and then made off in a friar's habit. But the Viceroy insisted on keeping him in the Angel Tower because he believed his testimony might prove useful. The boy, even though he preferred to stay with the Viceroy, who had, after all, done business with his father, than to end up with the Tribunal, which packed a weightier punch, was unable to invent a confession by Sen Boiet that would satisfy the Viceroy, helping him to escape from the Inquisitor. With the same determination with which he was unable to say what the Viceroy wanted—that Sen Boiet had told him before dying he was being paid by the Bishop—Rafel Onofre declared in front of the Tribunal that nobody had given him the habit, he had stolen it from a friar who was begging in the city streets the same night those two strangers forced him to confess a dying man. But the statement of a woman who lived opposite the brothel spoiled things: she declared she had seen the boy—and she had noticed because she had little work to do—entering the cellar of the brothel early in the morning, already dressed as a friar. To the testimony of this fine, underworked lady, who saw everything that went on outside her window and faithfully kept God's commandments, was added that of Ripoll, who visited the brothel an hour earlier, suspecting that Limp might have hidden someone.

The Inquisitor Rodríguez Fermosino, thanks to Rafel Onofre Valls de Valls Major, now had the imminent possibility of imprisoning Beatriu Mas, whose case he had carried around among his documents since his predecessor in the post left it open, without deciding to act.

Three words were enough for Rafel Onofre, finally transferred to the premises of the Holy Office, to crumble and confess the truth, three words that felled him at one swoop, three words that in no time at all achieved what two hours of torture had not: "Limp reported you."

After these statements, Valls' younger son was taken to his cell and was not questioned again until the morning prior to Limp's arrest. For more than thirty days the Inquisitor mulled over the best way to catch Beatriu Mas unawares. He decided to take his time and lull her into a false sense of security.

Maria Pomar was summoned for the second time immediately after Rafel Onofre testified. The girl, who knew nothing about the fate of her beloved, wept when she heard the news of his arrest. But the tears froze in her eyes when the prosecutor pointed out that Rafel Onofre did not deserve any of her sufferings, since he had cheated on her with Beatriu Mas, nicknamed Limp, prostitute in the brothel. Despite being knocked by this news, Maria Pomar put on a brave face and replied that she didn't believe that pack of lies, no doubt invented by one of their enemies to deal them a blow.

"It must be Beatriu Mas, reverence, who for some unknown reason, since we never did anything to her, falsely accuses Rafel Onofre."

"Never did anything?" asked the prosecutor mockingly. "Never did anything, you say? From killing Good Jesus to trying to flee Majorca!"

"I wasn't there when they nailed him!" exclaimed the girl in tears. "I assure you I would never have let them hurt him so much."

The Inquisitor let the other members of the Holy Office take care of the defendant, who without speaking, biting her lips so as not to cry out in pain, resisted the turns with which they crushed her arms. Rodríguez Fermosino, shut up in his office, read his breviary, trying to concentrate on his prayers in order to forget that sweet child's face plowed by tears. Maria Pomar started to scream, the pain became so unbearable, and ended up accepting that Costura was right: Rafel Onofre had taught her that Jewish prayer they used to recite together before saying farewell on warm nights in the garden, but she was certain he didn't know it was Jewish. It was a prayer addressed to the Almighty Father, a prayer that united them and gave them strength, a prayer they also said when they were apart, so that they could be praying to God at the exact point the city bells struck six in the evening.

Maria Pomar, half dead, was dragged in a blanket back to her cell. For ten days her companion, Sara de les Olors, thought she would give up the ghost at any moment and informed the jailer, asking for a doctor, but was only sent Father Ferrando, who tried to confess her without being able to, since Maria was delirious. Her arms hurt so much she didn't know how to lay them down. All the colors of the rainbow appeared in her poor, maltreated flesh and the jailer, alarmed, informed the Warder, who allowed Madò Grossa to go and wash her wounds and try to patch together the bones with her bandages.

With a burning forehead and restless because of the fever, despite the persistent pain, Maria Pomar gradually recovered. She sometimes thought she wouldn't get over it, death would come soon and she would die without knowing what truth there was in everything the prosecutor had said, whether Rafel Onofre had really cheated on her, and she accused him of having been unfaithful, of having landed her in that prison, in misery because of the failed escape. When she was so happy in the garden with her parents and sister before he arrived, before he poured unease into her blood, which had stopped flowing in the same way through her veins since he told her he loved her. From that point, her whole body was a furnace that only went out when she was next to him. Her only wish was to be his wife soon, to be his wife forever. She sometimes accused, cursed, blamed Rafel Onofre's name and immediately repeated it, lovingly sweetening it, and praised it after forgiving it. He didn't make her embark. He wasn't the cause of her misfortune. She was the one who asked him a thousand times to take her with him, who resolved to follow him wherever he might go. She was the one who begged her parents to let her embark, because Gabriel Valls and his wife, seeing the love their son had for her, decided to ask her hand.

Livorno for her was like honey. There they would be married as soon as they got off the boat. She didn't care if she didn't have a sorry adornment embroidered by her mother, a sad sheet. She didn't mind being the poorest of brides, if Rafel Onofre loved her. To be his wife was everything she wanted in this world, to live at his side till death parted them, hoping to meet again in the heaven of God the Father or Adonai, of whom her fiancé had spoken to her with such unction. No, Rafel Onofre had not cheated on her, that was impossible. He was as happy as a pair of castanets when he saw how resolved she was to escape. She only had to recall how he looked at her and said, "Everything will be fine, my love, joy of my heart." She only had to close her eyes to see his eyes seeking out her pupils to sink in them, to communicate pain and desire. Nobody had ever looked at her like Rafel Onofre, in that way, searching for her soul to merge with it. During those days, Maria Pomar was unable to touch even a crust of bread. But she drank all her ration of water and was always thirsty. She was lucky to have Sara de les Olors, who took pity on her and not only brought the bowl to her lips, but also renounced her share of water so that she could drink a little more. Sara, who the first few days didn't even look at her, she was so focused on her prayers and the coming of the visions God, the Virgin and a host of angels gave her, changed her attitude as soon as she saw she was needed. She then focused all her attention on that poor, defenseless girl and did everything she could to make her better. She fed her as if she were a bird that had fallen prematurely from its nest, with the same care her mother had shown her. She crumbled the bread, mashed it in the wooden spoon and gave it to her as a pulp, so that it would go down more easily. It was not at all difficult for Sara de les Olors to attend to that girl who responded to every gesture with a smile and willingly acquiesced to her treatment because she wanted to get well to see if there was some way she could bribe the jailer to arrange a meeting with Rafel Onofre. Much more than by Maria's sky-blue eyes or childlike face, Sara was captivated, right from the start, by her long corn tresses, which when loose reached down to her waist and which she used to tie in a thick plait. During her recovery, Sara managed to persuade her to let her comb them. The lack of a comb meant she used her fingers, which skillfully sank in that dense forest and did their best to disentangle the knots and searched to see if the lice had already laid their eggs.

Sara gradually stopped waiting for the visions she had received since she was young, which she considered a gift from the Most High, to devote herself to looking after Maria, who even at times reminded her of that sweet, melancholic Virgin she had seen also with long, saffron-colored hair over the top of a lemon tree. "You're a mini Mother of God, my daughter," Sara would tell her in a thin voice, softened by emotion, before stroking her so that sleep would not delay and she could at least rest.

Sara was questioned before Maria, one Friday in March. She confessed herself Catholic, Apostolic and Roman, a devout believer. If she accompanied her father on the expedition, it was because he told her to and she couldn't let him leave on his own, old as he was. She declared that her father often reproached her for cooking with lard when he only wanted food cooked in oil, because he said the others didn't agree with him. She only half accused her father. She knew there were other aspects of his behavior that could interest them a lot more, but decided to keep quiet. Even though he had never taken the benefits God afforded her seriously and had terribly maltreated her, she still owed him her life. Besides, if things got worse, she would tell them. It was enough for now. The inquisitors agreed and did not torture her. But Sara was not at all sure that, when they sent for her again, they would do the same, especially after seeing what they did to Maria. She only had to think about it to be seized by mortal pains and worse palpitations than those she experienced after fainting as a result of the ecstasies. Pain turned her into a coward. Maria's bruised arms were a frightening mirror in which she saw the reflection of her own. Many nights, after she had gotten the child to go to sleep, lying on her damp and stinking mattress, she tried to find the words that would help her defend herself without accusing anybody. She knew that if she was subjected to torture, she would say everything the inquisitors wanted and would be able to tell even on Maria, whom she had begun to love in an unfamiliar way, as she did not recall ever having loved anyone. "Help me, Blessed Virgin," Sara repeated, "you who have always taken pity on me, you who are my real mother, the mother I never had on earth . . ."

Sara de les Olors was orphaned at birth and her father, who only had two children, decided a maid and a wet-nurse were enough to help him raise them and refused to remarry. She grew up among men, watered down only by the Christian wet-nurse, who passed on her beliefs and filled her head with prayers. She had the first apparition, aged four: she saw a Virgin just like the one on the altar of Our Lady of Sorrow in St Eulalia's Church, her heart transfixed by arrows and knives, blood trickling from her breast, approach and make her put her little hand on that wound. The wet-nurse assured her she had dreamed it, such things only happened to saints and there weren't many of those or, at least, she wasn't one: she didn't do what she was told, she fought with her brother and told lies. But the visions continued.

The more she was reprimanded, the more heavenly angels accompanied the Virgin's train, the more seraphim appeared, different because of their small, bodiless heads, with wings coming out of their cheeks. Angels and seraphim, flitting their wings, like trained turtledoves, were at the feet of the Virgin Mary, who never touched the ground and remained levitating the time the vision lasted.

Minutes before the apparition, Sara realized it was coming because, wherever she might be, in her room or right in the middle of the street or inside church, she was warned by an abundance of unsuspected smells, often quite varied, but always extremely pleasant. What's more, Sara would comment aloud on that faculty God gave her, because none of those who were with her could smell the scent of orange blossom, the aroma of incense, the flood of marjoram and mint, the fresh perfume of basil or the sweet waft of lilies, which she named while claiming to smell them as if they'd just come into bud. The smells were a prelude to a kind of ecstasy. She rolled her eyes and waited for the vision to become reality. It wasn't long before they nicknamed her Sara de les Olors or Sarah of the Fragrances, which she didn't mind at all. On the contrary, she liked it, she thought this name gave her a nobility and dignity different from that of other local women, who had family nicknames that came from long ago. She, however, had earned hers, if not through her own merits, then through the merits God chose to grant her with the gift of those apparitions that soon sallied forth and reached the ears of the members of the Holy Office, who sent for her. But since the Inquisitor she met realized this girl was a little dotty, he preferred to ignore the apparitions and let her go, though he did warn her, in case they should give rise to scandal, unlike Cabezón y Céspedes, who opened proceedings against her. Sara de les Olors was lucky that the tenure was short of this Inquisitor who was unseasonably attracted by proceedings involving women and that Fermosino was not particularly interested in the folder containing her report, concerned as he was with other affairs of greater significance. But now that she was in prison, her case took on a new importance and added to the mass of documents for cases opened against the fugitive Jews.

IV

During the first few weeks, Gabriel Valls desperately tried to remember a conversation he had with Josep Valleriola in front of the Consul when they were preparing the escape, in which Valleriola explained to them how, in the time they called of complicity, time past, ten years before, in these very prisons they had worked out a secret code that kept them together and in contact, without the inquisitors knowing. Three knocks on the wall meant that they were still true to the faith of Adonai without confessing it, the three knocks matching the points of the triangle that is sometimes used to represent the ineffable. Three knocks plus one, that they had declared they were Christians in front of the Tribunal, three knocks meaning God and one, the only-begotten Son, the Messiah, according to the religion of their enemies. Three plus two, that they had stated they observed Christian rituals, went to Mass and said the rosary, these two referring to the Church or the mother of Joan Peroni. But however hard he tried, he couldn't remember anything else. He cursed himself for not having agreed with the others on a secret language, in case that terrible outcome should happen, but he had so much confidence that everything would go well and the immediate embarkation caught them so unawares, he preferred not to think about it. Now he regretted it strongly.

He tries with a clenched fist to knock on the wall three

times in order to identify himself, at least as an inhabitant of the Street, in case on the other side there is somebody who was imprisoned before or happens to know the code. What's more, he has the intuition they have shut the Consul in the cell next to his and for that reason he insists, because, if it's him, at some point he'll have to remember the conversation with Valleriola. At times he thinks someone is shouting also on the other side of the wall, but, when he answers, they pretend to be deaf or do not hear him. He spends many hours listening to the slightest murmur coming from outside: the sound of other doors giving on to the corridor, footsteps that come and go, groans and weeping when the guards drag somebody towards their cell. Even though the constant shade in which he lives encourages only slumber, Gabriel Valls barely sleeps and, when he does, the ugliest scarecrows fill his dreams. He sees his younger son, Rafel Onofre, surrounded by corpses brandishing pitchforks, just as if he were witnessing a performance of the Dance of Death his grandfather used to describe to him when he was a child. The corpses dressed in pale tunics twist and turn somersaults around the boy and mock him with jeers and taunts. In the end they drag him off with his hands tied, encrusted with blood. The dream makes him fear the worst.

But sometimes, especially after praying for a long time, he was sure that he had been able to save himself, that he'd even managed to embark from Alcúdia for Alicante. If Adonai had shown him this grace, if Adonai had been willing to protect his son, he would consider prison and all his future calamities worthwhile. But if his son had been arrested, the same as his wife, he would find this captivity a bitter pill to swallow. He thought about Pere Onofre more than anyone. He was old when he had him and he loved him most. God showed him abundant grace with such a pleasant son, who had only been a source of happiness and who willingly accepted his people's religion. He thought little about Maria, not because he didn't consider her the best wife he could find and warmly respect her, but because in the long, empty hours the Widow Sampol rose above the image of any other woman, however hard he struggled to avoid it. Was she already aware of the disastrous outcome of the expedition? Could she help them from Livorno?

He replied to these constant questions with the same answer—with the cheery eyes of Maria Aguiló watching him in the quiet of the garden—and rejected the bitter sneer of her mouth, bitten by time. He then forced his memory to come up with the best moments in their life together: their secret wedding, when his father, who had to consult ancient records, improvised the Jewish wedding ceremony in front of their closest friends, after they were married at St Eulalia's; the birth of their children—God had given them five, but only two had survived; her willing disposition to do all the housework—she was the best in all Segell at preserving quinces and everybody praised the cloth embroidered by her hands that she spread over the table on a Friday evening. She killed poultry in accordance with the Old Law, without making a fuss like many women; she always had something ready to give the poor and had willingly accepted the gardeners' daughter as her own, wishing to make her the daughter Adonai had not allowed her to raise.

He recalled everything good about Maria, but he had to force himself. She also forced herself to follow him on the expedition, leaving her mother, her aunts, nephews, nieces and cousins with tears. Maria would happily have stayed at home or in the garden, where she felt so comfortable. He was the one who impelled her to that unfortunate adventure she never approved of, even though she didn't let on, she was always very clear about who was in charge. The Widow Sampol, on the other hand, would have opposed him if she had judged the escape premature. Blanca did not mind fighting for what she thought best.

Maria bowed her head because this is what she had been taught to do, what all women did. *Oh, Jehovah, help me, don't torture my heart any longer!* Jehovah was always the best refuge. *If I didn't have faith,* he told himself, *if Adonai abandoned me, I'd go mad like my mother-in-law and be unable to stand this darkness, the disturbing noises in the night, the prattle of Father Ferrando, the fear of long mornings broken only by the scurry of rats and the distant squabbling of sparrows.*

He asked the Jesuit, who is instructing him in the faith of Christ, whether he knows when they plan to send for him so that he can finally confront the Tribunal, because the waiting seems to him even more painful than the possible torture. He begged him to give him news about the others, but the Jesuit revealed nothing of importance.

Often, when the jailer deposits his sad food—almost always crusts, the occasional Sunday a piece of bacon he doesn't touch, a jug of water—Valls tries to detain him, to ask him if he has any news of his son, whether he's been imprisoned with the other boat people, and if he's any idea when they'll call for him. The jailer, who never replies with kicks and insults, as he does with the other prisoners, whom he considers beneath him, still refuses to give him any kind of information, although Valls insists that if he helps him, he'll know how to reward him.

One day at the end of April, it's the Warder himself who brings his food and pleasantly asks him if there's anything he needs. "To know what has happened to my son," Valls replies, "to know who's been questioned and why they haven't sent for me yet." The Warder informs him that he doesn't know what plans the Tribunal has concerning the interrogations, so far they've only summoned the children and women, and one man: his son, Rafel Onofre.

Valls took the blow, but thought a mountain had fallen on top of him. He asked what else he knew about his son, how and where he was. He begged to be allowed to see him, even for a split second, and was surprised when, contrary to his expectation, the Warder agreed to accompany him to Rafel Onofre's cell.

The failed escape paled before his son's wounds and feverish eyes. The Warder required them to be brief, so Rafel Onofre hurriedly explained everything that had happened since the moment they separated. Rage lodged in Gabriel Valls' pulse and at every beat threatened to explode. He would have taken it out by punching the walls; but he simply stroked his son's burning forehead, as he used to when he was a boy. He did his best to console him. He told him they might not torture him again, he'd done well to confess. Why keep covering for someone who'd betrayed him? In front of him, he tried hard not to appear defeated and encouraged him with the confidence that everything would work out. When he returned to his cell, even though he struggled to recall the holy patriarch Abraham, to cite a biblical example that might serve as a model, he found it very difficult to accept that Adonai might also be asking for the sacrifice of his son.

He didn't sleep a wink all that night. At no point had Rafel Onofre blamed him for what had happened, but he felt guilty on two accounts: first, for having involved him in the escape, and second, for having told him to hide in the brothel, somewhere he never should have thought of, convinced they wouldn't search for him there . . . God hadn't inspired him in this either. Perhaps he wanted to test him. *I'm not like Job, Lord.* Adonai unleashed his fury and, although he had every right, he wasn't sure he could resist it. Rafel Onofre had asked him what he knew about his mother and Maria and, on saying this last name, had broken down. "I got her into this mess," he sobbed. He was wrong. There was only one person responsible for the premature escape, and that was him. Could he have done things differently? Putting it off, taking time to prepare it, was very risky. Anybody could unwittingly betray them or slip up and betray themselves. Putting it off meant passing up the opportunity handed them by Pere Onofre Aguiló and the Widow Sampol. No, they couldn't let the xebec leave empty, after the agreement their friends in Livorno had come to with the captain. No, there was no way. A series of unfavorable circumstances had brought about the failure. Adonai had allowed it. Why? Why? They were escaping in order better to observe his law, to stop trying to please all the people all the time, to leave hypocrisy behind once and for all. Others just because of fear . . . The Lord had punished them. But who was he to judge? Who was he but a poor Jewish-born merchant who accepted the law of Moses as the true law, because it was, above all, the law of his parents and that of his parents' parents, perhaps with the same stubbornness with which those who had tortured Rafel Onofre accepted their own? Whoever is not with me is against me and must be cast out. Like a dry stock he'll be thrown on the fire and burn, insisted the Jesuit. And what if it was true that Adonai only existed in the stubbornness of his people and God the Father in the selfsame stubbornness of their enemies? If they were men before being Christians or Jews, if they felt like such, they'd respect one another before destroying each other and live in peace. But is he prepared to renounce the beliefs that till now have given his life meaning and have made him to be respected in the community, the most respected of all, the rabbi? No, or perhaps only for his son, only to save his son from the wrath of God the Father and the wrath of the Lord . . .

The milky light of dawn covers the city. The Bailiff's men prepare to open the gates of the wall. Carts full of produce line up to come in. Outside, the sunlight gives life meaning. Here, life dissipates in the dark . . . "The worst bit were the mornings," Valleriola told them, "when the day starts for everybody except for the prisoners, because inside the cell it doesn't matter whether it's light or dark." And he's right. Valls misses the light. He never thought it so pleasant and never understood the terrible fate of the blind so well as now. "In the mornings," Valleriola explained to them, "the jailer's footsteps resound in a different way. Is he coming for me perhaps? For me? He passes by . . . What rest to carry on pining away in the flood of darkness!" Valls prefers to be sent for. He can't stand it any longer. The sooner it's over, the better, they can clean him out, so long as they let him go. And let his son go . . . They'll start up in business from scratch. *I'll keep as much as I can quiet. I'll only accuse myself. Will I keep quiet under torture? What if the pain doesn't let me? How will I stop them torturing the others? Will I be strong? Will I manage to resist? What if this time, instead of settling for the confiscations, instead of making us destitute, they consign us to the flames?*

He tries to put it out of his mind. He doesn't want to think about that. He's never been one for anticipating events, however much he suspects the rigor is greater this time than ten years ago, when the prisoners went out into the courtyard each morning and were allowed to amuse themselves by reading comedies or playing the guitar. Now the discipline is much stricter. No going out. No books of comedies or musical instruments. The days never end inside the cell. Eight paces by twenty. A thousand times he has counted the steps he can take in a morning, since he prefers to walk than to sit on the straw, to walk than to lie on the bed, looking at the cracks and damp patches covering the ceiling, a high ceiling, too high for the space he's cooped up in. He knows when it's daytime, when the sun has taken complete control of the horizon, towards midday, because before that the light is so diffuse, so weak, nobody would say the night is over. He's sick of the stagnant air that is never renewed because the door only opens when the jailer comes with the water and meager rations twice a day or when Father Ferrando visits. Today he has the intuition he'll stop by his cell again; today, when he really doesn't feel like listening to his accusatory prattle. He doesn't know why he keeps coming. "You're a lost cause," he told him the last time. "Stones would soften more easily than you. You've a snake in your heart." Father Ferrando's insults don't bother him, he finds them normal. They slip off him. He listens as if he's listening to rain. Their conversation, the only one he's allowed to have, is not a relief, but an irritation. Father Ferrando is responsible for the failed escape, niggling Costura till he turned informer, wringing out his last days to see if, between one spasm and the next, Costura might raise one more testimony.

Valls hears footsteps approaching, the iron jangle of keys. Here they are, they're coming. He'll opt as always for silence. He'll accept the sermon, he'll accept the insults without a word. That little man, the Jesuit, gets on his nerves. But it isn't Father Ferrando who appears, at least it's not his voice. It's a darker, softer voice, although it also seems priestly. Talking to the jailer. He can't understand what they're saying. They must have decided to give someone else a go, who might have more luck or more inspiration than Ferrando. He's used to the captious arguments by now. He's sick of them, of hearing he's hateful just because he's a Jew and the Jews killed Christ. That makes him guilty for ever. As if Christ himself and the apostles of the Catholic Church weren't Jewish, as if they'd been born out of nowhere. "To deny the virtues of the Jewish people," he told Father Ferrando the last time, "is to deny the Christian virtues. Where do Christians come from if not from the Jews? Where does the new law come from if not from the old?"

Father Ferrando is driven to distraction by the serenity of that man who seems to be very clear about everything, who speaks little, who always waits a few seconds before opening his mouth, and who the last time he visited justified his reserve, pointing out he'd never regretted being silent, but he'd often regretted saying words. "Before speaking," he added, "I am master of my words, after it's my words that become my lord."

Father Ferrando informs the Inquisitor he prefers to leave Valls and devote himself to the Consul, whose soul seems more responsive to divine grace, to Valleriola and Martí . . . That man exasperates him, but he doesn't realize this renunciation goes against him and will immediately be exploited by his rival, Father Amengual, who, as soon as the news reaches his ears, does not hesitate to offer his assistance. And the Inquisitor, to get rid of him, tells him to try, why not. The two priests on duty are overwhelmed, most of all since the arrest of other inhabitants from the Street, who, despite not taking part in the expedition, appeared suspicious. The prison is bursting at the seams. They can't cope, especially if they want to resolve cases quickly. The royal visit must coincide with the first auto-da-fé, that much is clear. "Surely you're aware, reverence, I'm writing a book, really, the triumph of the faith over heresy, and I'd like to research it closely . . . To assist Valls would be perfect. I count on God's help to be able to convert him."

Ferrando is furious when he finds out the Inquisitor gave his *placet*. In the convent, word has it he's breathing smoke through his teeth and even blaspheming. His threats were to no avail. Amengual has stepped right into his territory! His and his alone, however much he might think it's nobody's territory and add, the imp, whoever has clay can make pots . . . Nobody has ever seen the Jesuit so happy, especially since he's been looking sorry for himself lately. Ferrando seemed to have been born with a silver spoon in his mouth, while his had been buried in the ground. He'd even heard rumors that the Viceroy, his nephew and the High Judge had split their sides, reading some paragraphs from his book about Sister Eleonor, in particular one of those he considered most inspired: *Sacramental Jesus from the shrine threw her some oranges, as lovers do on earth, and she caught them in her lap with blessed unction. Then the holy angels, captained by her Guardian, appeared to her and gave her blackberry jam, which, because it had been made by heavenly hands, tasted different from the one we all know. Said jam was like manna in the wilderness, seraphic food for Sister Eleonor, sweet, angelic compensation for her fasts and penances.*

Fortunately the Monday gathering has been postponed until after the summer, because otherwise he doesn't know with what expression he would have to receive Don Sebastià, whether with sour grapes, acknowledging what had happened, or with the usual pleasantries, ignoring it. He has been saved all this by the Judge's workload, which doesn't allow him to spare a minute, and the growing hostility between him and Ferrando, who have stopped talking to each other. The chronicler Angelat also prefers to let the heat pass, immersed as he is in the *Memory* he has to write on the city's behalf to present to her Majesty the Queen on her forthcoming visit. He is, however, sorry about the Clares' iced cakes, because, however hard he tries, he'll never taste any like theirs. Only Sebastià Palou did not object to continuing to meet on a Monday, so long as there was somebody other than that idiot Father Amengual, whose conversation he relished like a rotten acorn. The Jesuit was not too bothered about the adjournment either: *I'll have more time to write. This has to be my masterpiece. There's no way I can waste this stroke of luck, really . . .*

They've been talking. About him? Now they're right in front of the door. He hears the jailer put the key in the lock and turn. When it opens with a grating noise, Gabriel Valls, whose eyes are used to that semi-darkness, observes the stranger. No, he doesn't recognize the bony face with sunken eyes and fleshy lips. From the cassock, the same as Father Ferrando's, he knows he's also a Jesuit. He is surprised to see he's holding an inkpot and pen in his right hand and, under his arm, a small folder. Accustomed to keeping quiet, he waits in silence for the newcomer to be the first to speak. But the latter says nothing. He simply gives him a half-smile and is unable to avoid a gesture of distaste. In the end it is the jailer who introduces them—"Father Amengual will keep you company for a while"—and turns to leave and close.

"Couldn't you keep the door open?" asks the priest. "It stinks in here!" he adds, half covering his nose with his left hand.

"It's forbidden, reverence. I'll only be round the corner. When you wish to leave, shout and I'll open up."

Valls takes an instant dislike to this man who cannot, even for a moment, bear the unfortunate smell of that hole, which stinks like all the other cells. The straw mattress was already soaked in urine and sweat and blood when he arrived and, needless to say, nobody's changed it. In a corner he keeps the pot full of excrement he's only allowed to empty once a week. The stench is thick and bitter. The jailer has brought a chair so that Father Amengual can sit down.

"Please forgive me, reverence," says Valls finally, exuding irony. "I would have received you somewhat better at home. As you can see, the Holy Office's prisons are anything but holy, at least as far as the stink . . ."

"Really?" inquires the Jesuit, who doesn't know how to take the defendant's sarcastic remark.

There is another silence. The prisoner paces up and down, and Father Amengual observes him, not knowing where to begin his sermon, even though he's done nothing else since yesterday but prepare it. He is forced to look at the notes he's carrying inside the folder. His nerves give him away and, when this happens, his memory fizzles out, *really* . . . He carefully undoes the ties. He finds it difficult to read his own handwriting because he can't see it in that dark. Gabriel Valls does not stop watching him expectantly, while Father Amengual uneasily turns pages, using the tip of his thumb, moistened with saliva, taking care not to upset the inkpot and pen he's finally balanced on his knees.

"I've chosen some excerpts from the Holy Fathers that talk about the Jews to discuss together," he tells him. "I'm writing a book on *The Triumph of the Faith*. It's up to you whether you appear in it as a well-converted Christian or a heretic. Listen, listen to this text by St Gregory of Nyssa: *The Jews killed our Lord, murdered the prophets, rebelled against God and showed him their hatred, abused his law, resisted grace, renounced the faith of their fathers. Followers of the devil, brood of vipers, traitors, slanderers, blinded, Pharisaic yeast, Sanhedrin of demons, execrable, cursed, stoners, enemies of all that is good* . . . Well, what do you think?"

"What can I say, Father Amengual? Isn't it written by St Gregory of Nyssa? I don't think anyone can object to his authority."

"Now you'll hear another by Origen," resumed Father Amengual, satisfied by Valls' docility. "*The Jews will never return to their former state, for they have committed the most abominable of crimes by killing our Savior. Therefore, it was necessary for Jerusalem to be destroyed and the Jewish people scattered* . . ."

Father Amengual falls silent. He waits for Valls to say something without having to prompt him, but Gabriel has chosen to speak as little as possible and prefers to hide the disgust he feels for those texts, whose arguments he can refute perfectly. Amengual insists:

"Really, what do you think?"

"It forms part of the diatribes that since the second century have justified the Jewish people's misfortunes as a divine punishment."

"Yes, yes . . . But what do *you* think?"

"What can I say, Father Amengual? If Origen says so, what's a poor fellow like me to think?"

Smashing, thinks Amengual, *I've convinced him, I'm sure. That's enough stench for today. When I come back, I'll bring some sprigs of basil with me.*

The priest dipped the pen in the inkpot, scrawled a couple of lines on a blank sheet he pulled from the folder, waited for the ink to dry and collected his things. Without telling Valls he was concluding their first interview, he stood up, clapped his hands behind the door and called out for the jailer, who took a while to appear.

"I was on my round," he said in apology. "I thought you'd be a little longer, Father Amengual."

As he left, the Jesuit offered the prisoner his hand, overcoming the nausea this caused him. With his own, dirty hand, Gabriel Valls shook it, but did not kiss it, he only made the gesture.

Amengual's method took Gabriel Valls by surprise. He did not imagine the priest would simply read out some texts, however offensive and recriminatory they might be. He supposed his attendance would be based, like Father Ferrando's, on a string of direct insults in the form of questions, which he always refused to answer. It suddenly dawned on him that Father Amengual was the author of that book devoted to the Marquise's relative, who died in odor of sanctity. And he burst out laughing: someone had told him how the Jesuit explained that a nailed Christ had appeared to the Venerable when she was still in her mother's womb. *If he has to lead me from darkness to light,* he said to himself, *I'm done for.* And, thinking this, he approached the door again on hearing the key turn in the lock.

"I've brought you some good news," said the Warder, whom he hadn't seen for some time. "I have it on very good authority that the Viceroy and the President of the Great and General Council have addressed a petition to the King, complaining about your imprisonment and the confiscations, which could be the ruin of Majorca."

"And their own," inserted Valls, "but I'm glad and I'll know how to thank you. I'm pleased you've brought me the news right away."

V

THE COMPLAINTS OF THE VICEROY AND THE GREAT AND General Council, which Gabriel Valls had received with so much hope that midday in April 1688, were in fact counter-productive: they turned the Curia even more against the civil authorities and irritated the members of the Tribunal, who considered them totally unacceptable. The Judge of Goods ceased to greet Sebastià Palou and did so on the third Sunday in April, as he was leaving Mass in the Cathedral, in front of everybody. Days before, they had disagreed about the confiscations. But it was the Holy Office's prosecutor rather than Canon Llabrés who most encouraged the Inquisitor to press ahead, not to delay proceedings, but to speed them up, in this way showing he stopped at nothing and felt no fear for the kingdom's authorities. No doubt to assert himself and prove his determination, the Inquisitor not only followed this advice, but continued to imprison every inhabitant of Segell he thought suspicious, confiscating their goods.

To demonstrate to what extent the Holy Tribunal underestimated the Great and General Council and the Viceroy in person, Rodríguez Fermosino, with the Bishop's support, threatened the nobility, stating he didn't care what kind of tree he had to tear down, he did not intend to let any green fruit become dried if he considered it suspicious, however many crowns might protect it. On the contrary, he would knock it off and let it rot on the ground till the worms had feasted on it. The Inquisitor's message was not at all difficult to understand. Rodríguez Fermosino had a predilection for parables when he wanted to be particularly forceful. He felt that similes enabled him to express himself with far greater clarity. Not for nothing had he been born in Galicia and studied with the Roman Curia.

Alarmed by events, the Viceroy decided to go to Madrid and solicit the old Queen, the only one who could help him in such disastrous circumstances. Don Antonio Nepomuceno preferred the Marquis of the Bastida, the President of the Great and General Council, who had offered to accompany him, to remain in the city. "Two of us will be stronger than one," Nicolau Montis said to him, but the Viceroy tried to persuade him to stay behind, arguing that if the kingdom's two most important authorities took to their heels, all hell would be let loose. Besides, the Curia would understand it as a desertion or, worse still, a victory. The Viceroy was less concerned about this than the fact that if the President of the Great and General Council accompanied him, sooner rather than later he would find out that the Queen's journey was a lie he had invented; and the Marquis of the Bastida would certainly not forgive him his deceit. He went weak at the knees every time he thought about the money he would have to pay for the Sovereign's visit, which, when it came to it, would not resolve much, however much the Viceroy might suppose the opposite. To make her come at any price, whatever it might cost, was Boradilla's prime intention: he gave it priority over the petition's requests.

In the same threadbare nun's habit she put on half an hour after Felipe IV died and would never now put aside, looking worse for wear and old before her time, her Catholic Majesty the Queen Mother received the Lord Viceroy of Majorca one afternoon at the end of May, in the Palace's private audience chamber. Boradilla, who in terms of manners could have defied the most gallant courtier in the whole of France, bowed so solemnly and heavily his nose almost touched the floor. The bones in his right knee cracked and he noticed he had a cricked neck. Since living in Majorca, where he didn't need to employ such risky greetings, he was out of practice. *All I need now is to have broken something,* and he tried to ward off that evil, while remaining with his head down, waiting for the Sovereign to invite him to rise. *It looks as if her nose has grown with the years. What a snuffer! Anyone in Majorca would say it's from the Street,* the Marquis mused. *It must be all those novenas and visiting convents . . .*

The Queen was accompanied by a priest instead of her chambermaid. The Marquis did not like this detail at all, but decided to ignore it and, despite finding her uglier than ever, allowed himself to compliment her respectfully, before asking her anything, indirectly, albeit hyperbolically, praising her matchless beauty, which he carried engraved in the purest corner of his soul, as if it were a most holy relic. *This is going swimmingly,* Antonio Nepomuceno said to himself on spotting Lady Mariana's smile. Although she was no longer wearing the ring with the health-giving stone he had given her, the Viceroy did not take offence. *She must be better,* he thought, *and doesn't need it anymore.* But he still inquired about her health before explaining the reason for his visit. She was frank:

"The Lord our God favors me with attacks of mortification. What is it, Boradilla?"

And her Most Serene Catholic Majesty smiled to the priest, who, although he was standing next to her, seemed to be running the conversation.

Antonio Nepomuceno took the bait her ladyship offered

him and repeated the lesson he had rehearsed over and over again during the days of his journey.

"I have come, madam, to request from your Majesty the favor of your royal visit. Your Majorcan subjects anxiously demand your royal presence . . ." It was the most convincing and yet discreet tone he could manage.

"Wouldn't they rather her Majesty my daughter-in-law?"

"Madam, in purity you are the Queen. Her Majesty the Queen, Lady Marie Louise of Orleans, God preserve her, has yet to give an infante to the King our Lord."

How could she, the Marquis wondered, *if she must still be a virgin?* The road was the right one. Mariana of Austria openly smiled from her throne and did not conclude the interview or even invite him to say the rosary—as she was rumored to do to other visitors—even though she had one in her hands. But, despite the good reception, Antonio Nepomuceno Sotomayor y Ampuero, seventh Marquis of Boradilla del Monte, Grandee of Spain and Marquis Consort of Llubí, left without the Queen accepting his request. It would seem Mariana of Austria had no interest in accentuating her terrible headaches with a long, tiresome journey and said no. But she did so with such ingenuity—of course she would think about it, she would leave it for later, she would see after discussing it with her confessor—that the Viceroy thought this *no* could be understood as a *yes*, which relieved him of the burden of deceit and, even if the trip never actually happened, nobody could now claim he had pulled it out of his sleeve. "The Queen will come," he would say when he got back to Majorca, "what we don't know is when: the Court will inform us at the last moment. It depends on the Sovereign's many engagements and, above all, on her health, which the weight of summer and the lurching of carriages make much worse."

As for the other matters, the cases opened against the Jews

and, above all, the exaggerated confiscations of goods, the Queen was unable to comment because she was not familiar with the details. But, to be honest, she approved of whatever the Church did or undid. The priest acknowledged her words with a nod and the Viceroy felt defenseless. Mariana of Austria must have noticed because, after a pause, she added that she was still directing him to her son, his Majesty Carlos II, to whom the petition was addressed.

The King received the Marquis one week after he had craved an audience. This was an extremely good sign. But, as he suspected, the interview was useless. Carlos II was not accompanied by any of his influential advisers, but by two nobles in his service whom the Viceroy had never taken into account, thinking them idiots, though now he regretted it. They would certainly not help him by urging the King to act in favor of the petition his Majesty knew nothing about. And what did that matter? It wouldn't have made any difference if it had reached his hands since he almost couldn't read and had to make a Herculean effort to join up. This proved how matters stood for the Republic. Boradilla ended up feeling sorry for that squalid boy with a toad's complexion and hanging lips, through which he seemed about to dribble. No, the poor lad had not improved at all. His face, elongated like a horse's, still expressed the amazement that had worried everyone when he was a child, in case it was congenital. His Catholic Majesty seemed not to understand anything about affairs of State or anywhere else. He asked the Marquis if it was long since he had arrived from the Indies, if the lands the Viceroy was from belonged to New Spain and if the native islanders felt proud to be Spanish . . .

The Marquis left that interview, very disappointed. Don Carlos struck him as much more than a poor, sickly boy raised with a great deal of effort. He was much worse than all that: he was a nidget from top to toe. Not only must his private parts be constipated, as was said at Court, which is why he couldn't beget princes to continue the line, but also, and more so, his brains. "My God!" exclaimed Boradilla as soon as he left the vast hall, dark despite the good weather, its walls lined with gloomy paintings. "My God!" he exclaimed again, not caring much whether the major-domo took him for a madman or at least a first-rate boor. "Now I understand why the clergy eats us alive!" The Viceroy spoke in Majorcan, which nobody at Court understood, when he flew into a rage and, to avoid laying into the first person he met, let off steam by talking to himself.

Although he was advised to consult the Prime Minister, the Marquis could only try. The secretary informed him that his excellency had so much work he could see him in two or three months at the earliest. Sick with nausea, his tail between his legs because of the failure, but putting on a brave face, the Viceroy returned to Majorca one Monday at the end of June.

Of Court, which he liked so much before, he now had the worst memories. Madrid, which for so long had been his favorite city, sweetly missed, had struck him as poorer and sadder than Palma, which at least boasted a reasonable Cathedral, something the capital didn't even have, and a market worth looking at. In the streets of Majorca City, even though there had been more poverty of late, he did not recall ever having seen that horde of cripples, blind people, professional beggars, that rushed at the carriages to ask for charity, rudely, threatening to open the doors and take it . . . As for the government he represented . . . Court had given him only one joy: to see that his two bastard sons continued to increase prestige and fortune with two highly advantageous weddings to be celebrated soon. But as always, in front of everybody, he praised the capital's beauty and extolled the monarchs with blatant lies: Don Carlos had recovered his health and governed well and sanely, with discernment. Queen Marie Louise would soon grant them an heir . . . From the audience with his Majesty the King it might be deduced that the monarch sided with the Great and General Council.

"But didn't he give you a document, a letter to back it up?" complained the Marquis of the Bastida, who suspected the Viceroy was spinning a yarn.

"He'll send one soon, don't worry," affirmed the Viceroy with all the conviction he could muster to stop the President of the Great and General Council dizzying him with more questions.

He only admitted the failure of his journey in front of his nephew and recounted at length his true impressions of Court.

"We're getting old, uncle, and the years fill our eyes with soot. We see everything blacker than it is. I wish everybody could cry with our eyes! Look at those unfortunates from the Street . . . That's what I call having a bad time."

"With worse to come . . . Here only the Church is in charge. There's nothing we can do."

"I'm getting married, uncle," said Sebastià Palou suddenly, changing subject.

"So you should. I'm happy. Now I understand why you say you're older: you've seen sense. Lluïsa must be very pleased."

"I'm not marrying Lluïsa. The Orlandis are ruined. They've been more affected by the confiscations than anyone else. Aunt's losses are nothing compared to theirs. Besides, I've never liked Lluïsa very much, as you know . . ."

"But you've given her hope, it's not the done thing," remarked the Viceroy, as if he'd suddenly suffered an attack of strict morality.

"You're right and I'm sorry. The fact everybody considered her my future wife deprived her of opportunities. She'll be difficult to marry."

"Not just because you've led her on . . . What's more important is that she isn't rich and she's ugly, I mean she isn't pretty.

By the way, you still haven't told me who you're marrying. I suppose you've chosen well."

"Bàrbara Bellpuig. We'll be in-laws as well as uncle and nephew . . ."

The Viceroy was flabbergasted. He could never have imagined his wife's younger sister might interest Sebastià in the slightest, not even for money. Bàrbara had been widowed a year before by one of the richest men in Majorca. She had a solid fortune, built on maritime business, like so many others, but for some time it had not depended on privateering or relied on the availability of people from the Street. But his sister-in-law was even uglier than Lluïsa Orlandis, than the Marquise, and so devout the Marquis knew he had visited her house an hour later just by the stink of wax and holy water coming off his clothes. What's more, Bàrbara was full-grown. She must be at least ten years older than his nephew. The Viceroy couldn't get over it. So much so, that Sebastià had to ask him what he thought and if he gave his consent. Although he was only the son of a cousin, he considered the Viceroy to be the head of his family. Besides, he was still the most distinguished of his relatives.

"I approve, if it's what you want. My sister-in-law's fortune is large," said the Viceroy. "But isn't she a bit past it for you?"

"I've always liked mature women. My favorite, the Widow Sampol, was older than me."

"The Widow Sampol was a beauty and only a couple of years older."

"Well, I suppose I've never gone for girls, uncle," Sebastià Palou remarked in order to say something and immediately realized he had unwittingly aimed a direct hit at the Viceroy.

"Nephew, your supposition is in bad taste. These moments of weakness have been expensive enough. The Moor girls were taken to Algiers, or at least that's what Captain Cent Cames told me, where they were released. What more do you want?"

"That's not why I said it, uncle, I assure you. With the light out, you yourself have said all women are the same: young and old, ugly and fair, offer the same service. Bàrbara is pleasant . . ."

"Yes, and stuffed with ounces."

"That's my point. I can't deceive you. I need them now more than ever. I have it on good authority those in the Black House are after me and, according to the Judge of Goods, that big, lousy traitor, since I've almost nothing to confiscate, the Tribunal would appreciate a donation, a generous gift . . . Can you believe it? Llabrés confided in the chronicler Angelat, who naturally sent for me at once and told me. A gift full of ounces to make them forget the rotten fruit on the crowned tree. As for you, uncle . . ."

"They wouldn't dare touch me. It's one thing to wage war, another to put a price on my head. Besides, the Curia thinks I have weight at Court, that they respect me."

"I'm afraid they don't even think that, uncle."

The Viceroy, seated in the easy chair he usually occupied in his office, sprang to his feet and confronted his nephew, who was pacing up and down the room. Staring into his eyes, as if questioning his soul, he timorously asked him:

"Tell me everything you know. You're hiding something."

"I was trying to save you the embarrassment, but I'll tell you. Besides, I'd have had to tell you sooner or later. You've always treated me like a son."

"Stop beating about the bush, Sebastià. What's happened?"

"Three days after you left for Court, the Vicar-General went and came back a week before you with some news that didn't take long to spread: the imminent appointment of a new Viceroy."

Antonio Nepomuceno Sotomayor y Ampuero thought he would faint. He slowly sat down and, without saying a word, put his head in his hands. For almost eight years he had been in the post of Viceroy, a post he had sought obsessively, especially after marrying his second wife. He knew it wasn't a post for life, it was normal to switch Viceroys from time to time so that they didn't become too entrenched in the places where they represented his Catholic Majesty, but he never expected it would be his turn so soon, what's more, in such circumstances, without anyone at Court letting him know. He felt betrayed on two accounts: for the King to say nothing, well . . . What could he know about who governed the viceroyalties if he thought he'd just come back from New Spain! But she did, his former protectress; she should have warned him.

"It's a stinking lie spread by those rogues of the cloth with devil's horns to sink me! Those devilish bastards!" he said a few moments later, while banging his fist on the arm of the chair. "If it were true, I'd have known before anyone. It can't be true. I was received at Palace. The Queen was agreeable."

"The Queen did not like your complaint against the Holy Office, nor did the priest who was with her. Didn't she say she approved of everything the Church did and undid?"

"Yes, I told you."

"But not in those words, uncle. That's exactly what she said. And the priest who was at the audience, the Reverend Ignacio García Zaragüelles, informed the Vicar-General, his friend, and finally got the Queen to persuade the Prime Minister to appoint a new Viceroy."

"I can't believe it, it's beyond me. Damned believer! I hope you burst."

"Uncle, it's the Queen! I also find it hard to swallow, but I fear the worst . . . And forgive me, it was very painful for me to have to tell you. But it's better to be forewarned . . ."

"Does my wife know?"

"I'm not sure. I didn't dare ask her and she hasn't said anything to me. In your absence, Father Amengual almost hasn't come here and, since taking on Valls' conversion, he's been very busy. What's more, I think someone told him we were laughing about the *Life of Sister Eleonor*. According to Angelat, he's already halfway through the work that will immortalize him. Which reminds me, the chronicler was furious when he found out the Queen never intended to visit. The Vicar-General let that be known as well. Angelat had been working like crazy on the *Memory* . . ."

On her husband's return, the Marquise was not in the city. She had moved a few days earlier with her maids and Joanet to Son Gualba to spend the summer there. The child, whom she had promised to look after, benefited from the mountain air. Besides, the city was stifling. And why should she endure the heat if she could avoid it? When the Marquis dispatched Bernat, the coachman, with the carriage to bring her back to Majorca, the Marquise decided she didn't want to leave. Pleading one of her bad headaches, she sent the servant back with a message for the Viceroy to go and see her. It was completely impossible for her to move in those conditions. The Marquis, who was infuriated by the mere mention of feminine headaches, lost his rag. His wife wasn't just a weed, she was a narcissus the size of a belfry. She had never done him the smallest favor, not even now that he was beaten and felt all alone. But he bowed his head, entered the carriage and let himself be driven to Son Gualba to hint to the Marquise that she might have to get used to the idea of no longer being the Viceroy of Majorca's wife.

Onofrina Bellpuig went so far as to insult him, blaming him for the dismissal, which she already knew about. She told him he thoroughly deserved it on account of the terrible relations with the Church, which he had been unable to maintain, and gave him examples that angered him even more.

"Do you think Father Amengual has any time for your banter and jesting? Don't you think he heard everything you and

Sebastià said unfairly about his book on my aunt? What about the Bishop? One thing is to make him wait a while, another to keep him an hour, however many urgent meetings you might have, as happened the day of the *Te Deum* of thanksgiving for the fugitives' arrest . . ."

"What! But you weren't even there!" remarked the Viceroy to protest against that cart thundering down on top of him.

"I was in bed with one of my headaches, which is not the same. If you can't take the dust, don't enter the threshing floor," continued the Marquise with unusual talkativeness.

And it's not that she hadn't warned him to be more careful with the Curia, as she had been with the Bishop, though she didn't like him. But he was as stubborn as an Aragonese mule. It was only her headaches that made her change house in the middle of June, July almost, when it was so hot! And this worried her. She didn't want anyone finding the chest she kept hidden in her dressing-table, where she stored her private treasures: Gaetano's letters, a piece of Sister Eleonor's habit, a lock of Joanet's hair and the first copy of Father Amengual's book.

"But you've yet to receive official confirmation, Antonio," she said finally. "We can wait. Here Joanet's recovered his appetite. What can I say? I don't mind if you're not Viceroy anymore, I don't care. For all the good it did me . . ."

VI

DURING THE MONTH AND A HALF THE VICEROY REMAINED at Court, things got much worse in the Holy Office's prisons. Many inhabitants of the Street who had appeared as witnesses, intending to accuse the prisoners, incriminated themselves. They were not helped by their willing disposition to cooperate, which the Tribunal affirmed it would bear in mind, because they almost all succumbed to the prosecutor's captious arguments. They only had to accept that at some point in their lives they had changed shirt on a Saturday or turned down fish without scales to be considered Jewish heretics. The increase in arrests had meant putting prisoners in the same cells, except for Gabriel Valls, who was always on his own. Life together, instead of giving them courage and preparing them to respond to questions better, knowing what they had declared and what they were going to keep quiet, led to serious confrontations with insults and scraps, which obliged the jailers to handcuff those who had come to blows.

Among the women, perhaps because they were imprisoned together from the start, this didn't happen. Not even Limp, who had immediately sharpened her tongue against Maria Pomar, promising to give it to her, went so far as to ruffle her feathers. Beatriu Mas, who was used to living with other women, settled down more easily than anyone could have imagined to sharing that tiny space, and soon persuaded the jailer to slip her a comb and shard of mirror like the ones they had confiscated. She also managed to borrow a scourer, some lye and a couple of buckets of water to clean on a Saturday.

The smell of lye, which every week, for a short time at least, replaced the stink of sweat and excrement, made Limp feel she hadn't completely left the brothel. What she used to call men's white blood, something she had often seen dripping, gave the lye—to her nose—a special meaning neither of her companions could understand.

"Oh, you're virgins, Jewish nuns," she joked the first Saturday, aware that they weren't at all impressed by that smell and saw no likeness in the whitish color either.

"Really, do you not think lye makes a good male scent?"

But neither Maria Pomar nor Sara had any idea what she was talking about. Neither of them had known a man. There was nothing strange in this. Maria had just turned fifteen, three days after being imprisoned, and Sara, who was already in her thirties, had never had a lover. She once almost married a mattress maker, like her father, but this was so long ago she didn't even remember the face of this man who had dallied under her window a dozen times and her father finally refused. The future son-in-law wanted a dowry the mattress maker was certainly not inclined to pay. Deep down, although he didn't get on with his daughter, old Bonnín preferred her to remain single than to have to live with a stranger—the suitor was from Muro and from a lower caste than theirs, since with a name like Miró he couldn't descend from the tribe of Levi as they did—and possible children or else to move in with his son, who had a wife he found impolite and a bit dim-witted. Sara didn't mind when her father broke off the engagement, since she preferred not to have to marry. Men frightened her really. She supposed that men away from home would be like her father and brother, who had a short temper and were always threatening her, when they weren't laying into her, without her knowing very well why. At night, while she prayed, watching for apparitions, she heard them snoring soundly. She made an effort to reject the conviction that a witch had turned them into hogs. The wet-nurse, who some summers took her to Sant Llorenç des Cardassar, where she was from, explained the trouble she had from her husband, who was permanently drunk, and even hinted that her poor mother was happier single than married. When she left home, after the wedding, to go and live with the mattress maker, she burst into tears and was never consoled again. She went from being the happiest girl in the world, always laughing with her friends, to being somber and crestfallen.

"I think rather than dying of a fever when you were born, the poor thing died of sorrow. Your father didn't beat her, I don't think, but he was more jealous than a Moor, almost never let her out and wouldn't allow the friends your mother spent evenings with when she was single, outside in the open or next to the fire, to come and visit. But the Lord our God punished him: sweet Sara, you're nothing like your father. You're just like Margalida Bibiloni, who was very close to your mother, may she rest in peace . . ."

"And Margalida Bibiloni, what happened to her?" asked the girl with curiosity.

"An enclosed nun," replied the wet-nurse. "A nun at St Magdalene's. She wasn't stupid! She chose a husband who never leaves."

Limp listened quietly and seriously one wakeful night, with Maria seemingly asleep, to everything Sara de les Olors dropped like remnants of a dress.

"Well, I like men, Sara. Not all of them, of course. Maybe it's because I didn't know my father or any brother and so they couldn't bother me as they did you . . . I couldn't know if my father was good or bad, a noble, an artisan, a priest or a friar. My mother never wanted to tell me. The poor woman can't have known . . . But a real man gives joy to life, take it from me. A good man like Rafel Onofre, a boy like Maria's . . ."

"So it's true what happened and you denied, you bitch!" exclaimed Sara in a rage. "And I had started to believe you. You witch! Shame on you! I hope you die!"

Sara, full of insults, jumped up from the bed to lay hands on Limp, but Maria stopped her.

"Thank you, Sara, but I don't want you fighting for me. Lie down again. And leave her to me. Now you'll tell us everything, Limp. Now it's your turn to do the talking."

"OK, but I want one thing to be clear. I didn't give him away. Unless you accept this oath," she said, crossing her thumb and forefinger and kissing them noisily, "I won't say anything."

"Believe her," said Sara. "It's me asking, darling, and I know. She's telling the truth."

Limp proceeded to unwind the skein of her meeting with Rafel Onofre, almost without hesitating. She omitted details that might be offensive to Maria and highlighted those she knew would please her, like the boy's regret after making love, his sorrow at having cheated on her even though he wasn't principally to blame. She was the one who accosted him in his sleep, who aroused him.

"He could have held back, all the same," the girl lamented and added on the verge of tears, "I think he must have enjoyed it."

"I wouldn't be so sure. Men, Maria, have a piece of quaking meat hanging under their bellies, which almost doesn't belong to them. Believe me, I've touched it with my own hands."

"By all that's holy, Limp! A piece of quaking meat hanging under their bellies! Do you mean a tail?"

"Oh, come on, Sara, you can't be serious! Are you really so naive? And you, Maria, don't cry, we don't need more crying. If you want to know, when I asked him why he was sad, he talked about you. He told me you'd be very hurt by what had happened, you wouldn't forgive him and he couldn't bear that, he loved you and could only touch the sky with you."

"Do you mean it, Beatriu? Do you think I should forgive him?"

"Of course you should, woman, of course. I wish all men were like your Rafel Onofre and not the mincing little bastards out there in the world! I've some stories! If this body told you everything they've done to it, you'd be amazed! I've come across some who aren't satisfied till they draw blood with blows and punches . . . Others who hire two prostitutes to see what . . ."

Limp falls silent because she realizes nobody is listening to her. Maria sobs, hiding her face in her hands, seated on the mattress, and Sara, standing, watches her.

"Limp," says Sara, "why don't you lend me your comb? Can't you see the knots the girl has!"

Limp gets off the bed. Under the mattress she stores her only treasures: the mirror and comb. Maria gradually calms down as Sara combs her.

Limp was sent for three days after this conversation, early in the morning. Sara started praying as soon as she left and carried on praying for two hours, until they brought her back. She prayed to Our Blessed Lady of Sorrow that they wouldn't torture her. And they didn't. Contrary to what the three women supposed when they came for her, Beatriu wasn't questioned. She was solicited to exercise her profession and shut in a secret room upstairs with someone who, given their appearance and the clothes they were wearing, can't have been a prisoner. The prostitute did what was expected of her, accomplished the task in hand with care and precise technique, even more willingly than if she had been working in the brothel. And not because she liked this man, advanced in years, whom she didn't know, but because, being smart, she suspected she could take a fat slice of that rounded bread. For now it was a favor, a big favor, the Warder owed her, since he was the one who requested the service, offering whatever was in his power in return. Beatriu Mas wanted nothing for now, but asserted herself and gave to understand that if he let on, he would regret it, even if that reverend or familiar or whatever he was—she didn't ask, since she was sure the Warder wouldn't want to reveal his identity—was a factotum in the Tribunal. Limp kept the change for later. To have the Warder in her hands was one of the best things that could happen to her.

From that day, none of them had to eat rye bread and water again, which, except for Sundays, had been the standard fare. The Warder would divert to their cell some of the delicacies his assistants swiped from the kitchen where food was prepared for the members of the Holy Office, whose palate was not at all coarse. But this was a bonus he sent them out of courtesy, because Limp still hadn't asked for anything. The cleaning materials, the comb and mirror, really could not be expected to balance the scales. She had gotten these without giving anything in return.

Beatriu Mas was solicited by the Warder at least seven or eight times and quickly led to the secret room. It was between the fourth and fifth visits she decided that if the Warder could run the risk of taking her upstairs to do her business, he could also risk bringing Rafel Onofre to the cell she was in. And she explained this to him one evening they were hurrying down the corridor leading to that remote room. He raised a whole series of objections. It wasn't the same to help someone who was in charge as someone like Rafel Onofre, who was a prisoner and virtually condemned. "Condemned? Why?" asked Limp in confusion. "It's not my fault? If it is, all the more reason to see him."

When three days later the Warder again asked Beatriu to go with him, Limp refused to leave. Clinging to Sara's arm, she backed against the wall and from there told him he first had to bring Rafel Onofre and a proper lamp. She was sick and tired of being in the dark and wanted to be able to see him.

Maria Pomar was furious. Weeping, she waited for the jailer to leave to have it out with Beatriu, but the whore immediately silenced her:

"You fool, if I wanted him for myself, do you think I'd bring him to the cell? I wanted him for you. When he comes, Sara and I won't look."

"I will," said Sara. "I'll watch in case Maria needs me."

"Why would she need you, woman? Don't be so naive!"

Maria Pomar didn't know what was happening. Sometimes she felt so happy she flung her arms around Beatriu and Sara's necks and was about to sing and dance up and down. Other times she almost wept because the emotion of seeing Rafel Onofre again made her eyes film over. It seemed impossible that what she most desired could happen to her, that she might finally see her Rafel again. Oh, and how she would take him in her arms, how she would want to make him her own! At his side she would forget the wrong he had done her, she would forgive him . . . Beatriu Mas advised Maria not to scold Rafel Onofre, not to reproach him for what had happened in the whore-house. She told her not to deny herself or him anything when they were together. And, with all the tact she could summon, she warned her that the embrace she so desired and was still prepared to give him, without waiting for Livorno, without waiting to get out of prison, the embrace that before God would make her his wife for ever, might hurt her a little bit.

"Hurt her? No way!" Sara again interrupted in alarm. "Holy Mary, Mother of God! I won't allow it!"

Then Limp offered Maria her mirror so that she could do

her make-up as much as possible, and told her to save a little water from the ration the jailer would bring to wash a bit.

"I'll make you a nice, straight plait," offered Sara at once. "Lend me your comb, Limp, first I'll get the knots out."

The Warder only took twelve hours to appear with everything Beatriu had asked for: Rafel Onofre and a lamp. Maria thought she would faint when she saw him. He was thinner and much paler. But his eyes shone intensely. Rafel Onofre glanced at Limp briefly before embracing Maria.

"She didn't betray you," the girl whispered in his ear.

With envy, Sara stared at the couple shamelessly.

"Come on, you and I will wait in that corner," said Limp, pushing her, "and pray. Let these two confess everything . . ."

Opposite where the lovers kissed, just under the barred window, Sara, on her knees, asked the Virgin for the miracle of an apparition. Since she had been imprisoned, the Virgin hadn't granted her this boon. "I need you more than ever, my Mother of God, today more than ever. Come through the bars, Holy Virgin, and you won't have to cross any walls, which are thick . . . You only have to pass in front of the window, and I'll see you at once and know that you haven't abandoned me . . ." Sara prayed aloud because she preferred to hear her petitions and not the lovers' deep breathing, and she continued in her prayer in order to forget that Rafel Onofre's strong arms, and not her weak arms, were squeezing the delicate, turtledove's body of that child she considered her own. Facing the wall like Sara, Beatriu struggled to forget what was happening behind her, through her intervention. Often, in the brothel, she had shared the same space as colleagues engaged in the labor of love, without getting at all excited. But now she noticed desire like a puff and trembled all over, as if a shiver had run down her spine. *He's not yours, Limp,* she said to herself, *and since you've been as lavish as a princess, don't spoil it. Don't go near. Don't touch him. Maria would never forgive you, nor would he, nor would he, if you want him to remember you till death. Aren't you satisfied with what you've achieved? Haven't you said all your life that, after yours, a bawd's profession is the best in the world, that when you retire you wouldn't want any other?*

"Limp," Sara interrupted her, "Limp, she's coming, she's here!" And, as she said this, she stood up, but immediately fell back on her knees. "Jasmine," she said, "I smell jasmine and orange blossom."

She felt her head begin to spin. The bars disappeared and the window grew larger, wide open to the sky. Clouds of incense rose in front of her eyes, as if to greet the Holy Sacrament, merging with other, soft, white clouds of starlight. Ecstasy was not far off. She felt the breathlessness in her chest, her muscles tense, her mouth ajar. The intense breathing, more and more intense, suddenly burst in a spasm of glory: the Virgin was there, in front of her. She hadn't forgotten her. But this time she wasn't covered with a blue mantle or surrounded by angels. Nor was her heart bleeding, full of terrible arrows that opened awful wounds. The Virgin appeared in the form of a butterfly, a butterfly with iridescent wings, glittering with an array of colors, which came in through the window for a moment and, after alighting on Sara's forehead, disappeared again, moving away, up into the sky. Sara shouted out and fell to the ground in a daze. She rolled her eyes and saliva trickled from her mouth. Her body was a pure spasm. Limp started slapping her so that she would come to.

When the attack passed, she found herself lying on her bed, watched over by her companions. But she only paid attention to Maria and, embracing her, said:

"This time, my darling, the Blessed Virgin did me the honor of dressing up as a butterfly. The most charming butterfly you could ever have imagined."

And, as she said this, she endeavored to hide her face, still contorted and a little slimy, in Maria's bosom.

Seeing that Sara was better, Beatriu went to bed. For a long time she was accompanied by the rhythmical weeping of those women, who were surely not crying for the same causes, though deep down they shared the same reason. Beatriu fell asleep, thinking they were much luckier than her. She had never loved anyone and no one had loved her as it seemed Sara loved Maria and Maria loved Rafel Onofre.

VII

IN THE FIRST, MILKY LIGHT OF DAWN, ONE TUESDAY IN THE month of June, Pere Onofre Aguiló left Livorno for Marseilles. From there he had arranged to board a small galley heading for Barcelona. For the journey, the Widow Sampol had offered him her favorite mare, Llamp, nervous and quick as a flash, which he agreed to ride to the first stage, where he had ordered fresh horses. He took the minimum baggage and turned down any company. Next to his skin, hidden under his shirt, he carried the bags of money, partly returned by Captain Willis and partly borrowed again from the Jewish community of Livorno, which could only be used to help the poor prisoners.

All of his friends had advised against the journey. The way things stood, he wasn't exactly the most suitable person to go to Majorca with the mission of bribing the members of the Tribunal in exchange, if not for the prisoners' freedom, at least for their lives. The Holy Office must know by now that the charter had been organized from the Medicean port and who was responsible. But Aguiló, who after receiving the terrible news decided to return to Majorca, refused to listen. Neither the weeping of his wife, who accused him of suicide, nor the pleading of Blanca Maria Pires, who thought he was mad for putting his life in flagrant danger, persuaded him to change his mind. The Council, which included two of Pere Onofre's brothers-in-law, argued that, since the expenses of the expedition had been met by many members of the community they represented, they also had to make sure that the money safely reached its destination, and Aguiló was too easy prey. The three auditors appointed every two years, whose job it was to oversee public expenditure, were similarly opposed. Some of the money earmarked for charity, and therefore taken out of the citizens' taxes, had gone towards paying for the charter of *The Aeolus* and, now that with difficulty and hard work they had finally managed to get almost half back, they really did not want to risk it again. The Majorcan merchant had no alternative but to bow his head and reach an agreement. He would be given the money to take to Barcelona and from there a person of confidence, who also happened to be related to the Villarreals, one of the most important Marrano families in Livorno, would embark for Majorca to do everything he could for their imprisoned brethren. But the journey of Pere Onofre, who only partly managed to assuage the feeling of guilt, having barely eased his remorse-stricken conscience, was a failure. He didn't even make it to the first stage. The widow's mare, used to being mounted by another rider, nervous and possibly too quick for Pere Onofre's poor horsemanship, played a dirty trick on him. At a bend in the road, perhaps frightened by the approach of a carriage they came across, it bolted. The Majorcan merchant was unable to control it. The mare went on a mad dash cross-country. Aguiló fell so unfortunately that Llamp dragged him along at a gallop. Bruised all over, with a broken leg and two dislocated ribs, Pere Onofre returned to Livorno two weeks later, when the doctor looking after him considered he was up to the journey. His own carriage went to collect him. The Council only had to lament the misfortune and subsequent delay to the mission, because Aguiló gave back all the money to the last coin. He met the expenses of the accident out of his pocket.

Such bad luck put Pere Onofre in a foul mood. He felt he was dogged by a wretched destiny. Chance had thought up every kind of impediment to his ever managing to buck the burden of the guilt that prevented him finding peace. If he had insisted on personally carrying the money, despite his unwillingness to undertake such an exhausting journey, it was because he believed that only through sacrifice could he obtain Jehovah's forgiveness, which would have to redound to mercy for the Jewish prisoners. The Majorcan merchant thought that Alonso López's ashes, secretly buried in a field of wheat, had turned against him, demanding revenge, since he failed to deliver them to the community in Bordeaux. He broke his promise and lied. Now his sins would affect his relatives and friends in prison and none of his efforts to overcome the obstacles that prevented him traveling could help to redeem them. He believed his decision to endure the heat he hated so much in the time it took to cross half of Tuscany and a large part of France had not been valued by Jehovah, who also refused to accept the sacrifice involved in riding for days on end, from dawn to dusk, to arrive as soon as possible or in having to sleep out in the open or in a barn if he didn't find a hostel to stay in. He felt rejected by God and this sensation, linked to the remorse he thought he would never now be without, much more than any broken bones, kept him for many days in a state of absolute depression. Not even the fact of knowing that finally a post would leave soon for Barcelona, charged with fulfilling the mission he had been unable to complete, lifted his spirits. He left all business in the hands of his assistants and let his partners decide about future imports of grain, oil and silk, and their distribution, without caring at all which captains would make the charters, something he had always arranged himself. Shut up at home, he spent the empty hours in bed, in a virtually catatonic state; his eyes fixed on the wall opposite, it seemed as if he wasn't there, as if his spirit had abandoned that stricken body. The doctors didn't know what medicine they could cure him with. They had tried more than a dozen. His condition didn't improve at all. It was very clear that Pere Onofre was suffering from an illness worse than the spells of melancholy that the Widow Sampol also endured from time to time and he had often criticized, considering them ailments peculiar to women.

The widow, on the other hand, became almost frenetic in her activity, perhaps because she thought that, with Pere Onofre being ill, she was the one who had to take charge and decide how to help their brethren in Majorca, who included some of the friends she loved most, like Gabriel Valls. Blanca Maria Pires was very fond of the city's rabbi. Thanks to him she had persevered in her religion in moments of utter weakness, when the Catholic rituals she observed seemed to her sufficient for salvation and she had almost made up her mind to abandon the secret worship of Adonai for ever. Furthermore, in the early stages of her widowhood, when she still felt unable to assume control of the maritime business left by her husband, Valls took care of everything, watching over her and her son as if he were a close relative, a brother or a father, and never wanted to accept any payment or compensation. Thanks to Gabriel Valls, she and the child managed to leave Majorca before the Inquisitor Cabezón opened proceedings against them, based on the rumors spread by Captain Andrew Harts about the planned escape of Jewish fugitives, because the rabbi put the widow's houses and possessions in his name and borrowed money to pay her for them generously, in advance. Later he calmly sold them and, instead of taking the profit, sent it to Blanca, who had already settled in Livorno and didn't need it. Valls, who had never asked for anything and had never even hinted at the difficulties and headaches looking after that property had caused him, therefore deserved that any returns now should be absolutely generous.

Blanca Maria Pires convinced the rabbi Jacob Moashé to join her cause and from the synagogue to ask for the faithful's support. The widow believed that the money allocated by the Council and returned by Willis after tricky, tedious negotiations was not enough. For her part, she decided to part with her jewels. She could have given money because business was going extremely well and with the money made from exports she had recently opened some textile factories—the first in Livorno, which were already receiving numerous orders, even from customers in Venice—but she wanted to forgo her jewels. In this way, because they were irrecoverable, Blanca Maria Pires made a double sacrifice. Money didn't bother her, it was easily come by. The jewels did, and that's why she offered them. Gabriel Valls had often told her that Jehovah appreciates much more what is truly difficult for us than what is easy or even superfluous. Many of her gems, like a giant emerald, had belonged to her mother, whose memory evoked a whirl of contradictory sentiments, which went from love and the sweetest tenderness to a violent hatred that appalled her. Some of the precious stones, a real fortune, had been bought by Gracia Nasi, called Hannah and also Beatrice de Luna and known everywhere as the Lady, from whom her mother, on her deathbed, confessed she descended; among other secrets that would upset her much more. Perhaps this is why Blanca Maria Pires never wanted to look into that possible genealogy, but during those days the memory of the Portuguese woman seemed too close for her to try to reject it, as she had done so often. She was increasingly convinced they were joined, if not by blood, at least by a similar destiny. Like Lady Gracia, she married a rich merchant who was twice her age and was widowed very young. She took charge of her husband's business interests and administered them skillfully, increasing profits. Like Lady Gracia, she left Portugal and lived in Antwerp, Ferrara and Livorno. In her travels she never forgot to lend a hand to the needy. Like Lady Gracia, she had a horde of suitors. It's true that Captain Sebastià Palou could not be compared to the English prince they say wanted to marry the Widow Mendes, but he was a Viceroy's nephew and belonged to one of Majorca's oldest families. Rabbis also fought to direct her soul. And couldn't João Peres, whose real Jewish name was Joseph, who had dreamed of her long before they met, be considered, in part, a kind of Joseph Nasi or João Miques, the Lady's nephew, who was also in love with her?

But there were other similarities, and these might have something to do with heredity. Her mother insisted a lot on the resemblance: "A mirror, my daughter," she kept saying in her agony, "a kind of reincarnation. You've her skin and eyes, her aura." But this held little interest for her, although she liked to know she was beautiful and to notice how much men were unnerved by her looks. What worried her most were the spells of melancholy she had been told beset the Lady, as happened to her. From time to time she would fall into a kind of dark well, into thick, putrid waters that held her down. Her anxiety on occasion was so great she desired death. She consulted doctors and rabbis. The former prescribed cures that achieved nothing. The latter sought out the hidden guilt that Blanca Maria Pires was not prepared to confess, had buried precisely under those waters, it had hurt her so much, caused her to shed so many tears. She promised her mother on her deathbed she would keep it secret, resolved as she was that she would leave this life in peace and not after an agony full of terrors, and granted her the forgiveness she craved, even though that revelation was the worst disgrace she could have passed on to her.

For a long time, the knowledge of the mystery of her birth prevented her regaining the necessary serenity to face the future, accepting the past. Shut up in her room in the old, empty, rambling house in Lisbon, cut off from the world, she did penance and fasted, partly to save the soul of someone she had until recently considered an adoptive mother and partly to expiate the sin of her conception, which was so abominable in the eyes of Jehovah and God the Father, punishable on all sides. She had plenty of hours in the day to go through the whole of her childhood as an orphan taken in by the munificence of Lady Gracia Pires, who, when she turned fifteen, gave her what she had most desired without daring to ask for it: her family name. From that moment, the newborn baby, who had been deposited at the door of the lady's house one freezing morning in December, albeit enfolded in the finest linen, was adopted by one of the richest women in Lisbon. During long, sleepless nights, tiring early mornings, she lingered over the memory of the time when Lady Gracia's eldest son turned up after a prolonged stay in Antwerp and moved into the house. She understood many things that had previously seemed incomprehensible to her, like the way her adoptive mother tried everything to keep her from the son she had fallen in love with, believing the lady would bless their union, since she always declared she loved her like her own daughter. Lady Gracia first tried to talk her out of the idea, then put a stop to the relationship. She claimed she was thinking about her, doing it for her own good. She loved her so much she couldn't allow her to marry a man who, despite being her son, she had to admit it, had led a totally dissolute life and filled half the orphanages in Europe with bastards. With bastards like João-Joseph Peres, whose origin she refused now to investigate so as not to discover again that the revelation of a mystery incurred a terrible prohibition. The boy attracted her. At his side she felt protected, as if only by his presence João could deliver her from all danger. But, contrary to when she was young, she was not now prepared to let any dangerous or uneasy feeling make her change her character or sway the firmness of her decision. She appointed Peres as her secretary, put all her trust in him, to the extent of sending him on such complicated missions as taking revenge on the shameless

Captain Andrew Harts. She was seventeen years older than João. A big enough gap to serve as an obstacle. Besides, Lady Gracia Nasi, who was only five years older than her nephew, never requited his love, despite all the tokens he gave of it. But if João Peres was, as she believed, her brother's son, he was more than just her nephew. She did not want to take the necessary steps to find out. She forbade the boy any mention of his father, with whom he had rarely come into contact, in case a terrible chance should bring them together, guided perhaps by the pull of blood. In doing this, Blanca Maria Pires was only keeping the other oath her mother asked of her: not to have dealings with Joseph, to disappear from his life for ever, without sharing with him the secret that could have spurred his desire with the lure of transgression.

Like Gracia Nasi, whom she took as a role model, she chose Deborah, Judith and Esther as mentors and with great drive, full of courage, she went from house to house, from palace to palace, to ask for charity in support of the Majorcan Jews' cause. She collected a substantial sum. Nobody felt able to resist the pleading tones of her smoky voice. By this act, which some considered unsuitable for a lady of her standing, Blanca Maria Pires wanted to appear humble and, with humility, to be more pleasing in Jehovah's eyes. She then wrote to Sebastià Palou, sent the letter with a post leaving for Valencia, since from there it wasn't difficult to find someone trustworthy to take it to Majorca. To know the prisoners' situation was absolutely essential for the help to reach its destination. The captain answered soon, using a xebec heading for the Medicean port. The prisoners were in danger, unless things quickly took a turn for the better, which seemed unlikely. He feared the worst: the flames.

It was by means of the captain's letter that the Widow Sampol learned that the relative of the Villarreals' mission had failed, long before he informed the Council. Villarreal hadn't even secured an interview with Rodríguez Fermosino. He had only had dealings with Jaume Mas, the Warder of the Holy Office's prisons, whom he had liberally bribed. And the Warder, to familiarize him with the prison, had only had the idea—readily accepted by the emissary—of arranging a liaison with Beatriu Mas. Villarreal, who was unable to seek the Viceroy's help since he remained at Court, did have long conversations with his nephew. Sebastià Palou talked him out of using force. An assault on the Holy Office's prisons entrusted to a gang of ex-bandits, the only ones who would consider such a dangerous undertaking, was guaranteed to fail. The rogues and bandits Livorno money could buy would not be reliable. Besides, hatred of the Jews, widespread among such people, made it likely someone would betray them before the assault. No, they had to choose a different path that had nothing to do with armed force and a lot to do with deals and commercial transactions.

Blanca Maria Pires showed the captain's letter to her friend Aguiló. She first weighed how much the bad news would serve to worsen his condition or might jolt him into action. But Pere Onofre simply burst into tears like a child and, still crying, sank back into his world of darkness. Once again the Widow Sampol had to take the place of a man. She requested an audience with the authorities to inform them of the failure of Villarreal's mission. With determination she galvanized the Council into taking a decision. She discussed with the auditors what the new strategy should be to help the Majorcans. She considered the various options, examined the pros and cons and finally, seeing how slowly everything was moving, resolved not to wait another day and to go it alone. As on other occasions throughout her life, when faced by difficult situations, she was sorry she hadn't been born a man, though she immediately repented, since she felt proud of her femininity. Rather what she would have liked is to be able momentarily to turn into a man, so she could settle that affair with greater ease. She sometimes imagined herself dressed up as a gentleman, like those daring women who defended their honor in many of the novels she read as a girl, and dealing firmly with the Inquisitor until she succeeded in liberating her friends. But she was too well known in Majorca to attempt such a hazardous approach. She ran the same risk as Pere Onofre, or even greater, because nothing could have pleased the Holy Office more than to catch also those who prepared the expedition from free lands. Besides this, she had fled Majorca quickly and without the necessary safe-conduct, albeit under the protection of the Viceroy's family; but that was no guarantee at the moment, quite the opposite in fact. The Viceroy, as Sebastià explained, had fallen into disgrace as a result of the intrigues of the Curia and Holy Tribunal. No, it really wasn't a good idea for her to go to Majorca. Even the hope of returning there one day seemed now more distant than ever. She needed a person of confidence, someone who wasn't suspicious, who *from matins to lauds* couldn't be imprisoned, and who would be willing to put their life in danger for a noble cause and clear-sighted enough to know where the inquisitors' weak points were and to negotiate with flair. She thought of Salomó Abrahim, the Tabarkan merchant, Pere Onofre's benefactor, with whom she had done business, as the most suitable person. He was a Jew, not a convert because he had not been baptized, and this safeguarded his life. He couldn't be imprisoned because the Tribunal only pursued false Christians or heretics, not Jews. He had called at Port Pi, was familiar with the city and knew the character of its people. And Sebastià Palou would help him. But Abrahim was afraid. He didn't think he had the strength to undertake such a long journey for a cause he considered utterly lost. He was old and tired. He hated to disappoint the widow, he had great affection for Aguiló and felt sorry for him. He was also flattered that the lady had proposed that mission to him first, to him and not to any of those black rabbis who stuck to her all day long like flies to sugar candy, to milk her for money with the excuse of comforting her soul.

It was then that Blanca Maria Pires resolved to send for João Peres, who had gone to Venice in her name, to ask him if he would embark for Majorca, despite the potential risks, on the first ship leaving port.

VIII

FATHER FERRANDO WAITED FOR FATHER AMENGUAL TO cross the courtyard in the opposite direction so that he wouldn't have to meet him. He didn't want, in front of outsiders, to turn his face the other way, as they both did in the convent to avoid greeting one another. The Jesuits' mutual dislike had increased in recent months. Even the Vicar-General had warned them about the bad example they were setting, which was totally counter-productive for the post they disputed so rancorously. Father Ferrando was the angrier of the two because he couldn't bear the fact that it was precisely his enemy looking after Valls, even though he himself had asked to be relieved of that mission he considered virtually impossible to carry out, so he could devote his time to much more profitable causes, many of which had already borne their fruit. Obviously most of them were women, who were always easier to ply, given the shallowness of their brains. To have persuaded Polònia Miró, Aina Fuster, Aina Segura, her sister Madò Grossa and Aina Cap de Trons to see the error of their ways and accept Christianity as the only religion, thanks to him, who convinced them, struck him as a merit that everyone would have to recognize and that fool, Father Amengual, could only envy. But that wasn't all, three of the men entrusted to him had also professed the Catholic faith: Joaquim and Baltasar Cap de Trons and Pere Onofre Martí, Moixina. Among all the priests and friars the Holy Office had assigned to convert defendants, he was possibly the one who had scored most highly, which filled him with holy pride. What's more, his rival hadn't gotten any yet. Valls was a hard bone to gnaw and Father Amengual had hardly any teeth.

But Amengual wasn't unhappy. It's true that Valls was not especially forthcoming, but the book, though initially he had trouble finding a style that was solemn, ardent and at the same time easy to understand, was coming along nicely. Contrary to what he had done with the *Life of Sister Eleonor*, he would fill *The Triumph of the Faith in Three Cantos* with Latin quotes, almost all drawn from the irrefutable authority of the Holy Fathers. Ah, how his work would be lifted by such illustrious company! Often, when visiting Valls, he couldn't resist the temptation of reading him paragraphs written the night before. The prisoner listened like someone listening to rain, but the Jesuit was sure his soul could not fail to be moved by that inflamed word. Valls' conversion thanks to *The Triumph* was the best present the Lord God could ever give him, except for the position of rector. But, unfortunately for Father Amengual, it wasn't a passage from his book that shook his ward, causing the first tears, but the news he himself gave him that the Consul had asked the inquisitors for an audience to retract everything he had said two days before, because finally our Lord Jesus Christ had been gracious enough to send him his light and he was prepared to confess everything he knew about everyone.

Valls' tears were not, as Amengual wished to understand—and informed the Inquisitor—tears of repentance, but of rage, impotence, shame and also pity for the poor Consul, scared and wrinkled, dominated by the weak little man he had always carried hidden inside him, which, despite having been beaten many other times, was now taking control, daunting him, as if by magic a giant had fallen under the sway of a dwarf.

"O Consul, Consul, what did they do to you?" said the rabbi

in a barely audible voice, between sobs, while thinking that to make him talk they must have tortured him, no doubt promising him death in the flames if he didn't turn informer. *But what if it wasn't true? And that shameless Amengual told me this to make me suffer? And it was all a lie?* Gabriel Valls made an effort to recover hope and, drying his tears with his fists, asked the Jesuit how many prisoners besides the Consul had asked for pardon.

"Forty of the eighty-seven prisoners have been questioned, and only seven have stood their ground . . ."

"What about my family, my wife and Rafel Onofre?"

"I can't tell you that. Each case is secret. But the high number of converts will give you an idea of which is the triumphant faith."

"It gives me an idea of human weakness in the face of death. Pain is inhuman, Father Amengual."

"Really, such heresy! Oh no, I can't allow that. The Lord our God died on the cross and you're saying pain is inhuman? The man of sorrows is Jesus Christ and you believe suffering is not for men? Really, I can understand women being frightened. Their lack of intelligence, their poor attitude of mind, the innate sluggishness of this sex inferior in everything to our own, allows them to be weak, but not us . . . No way! You only have to think of the saints who carried off the palm of martyrdom with such gusto . . ."

Amengual paused, not to observe the effect this highly accomplished passage had on the defendant, but to open the folder, dip the pen in the inkpot and write it all down, word for word. *Really*, he couldn't afford to waste such rampant stuff! The Lord God might not allow him to convert Valls, but at least he was showing him abundant favor while he tried. Much more than his rival, Ferrando, confessing women who were much more pliable.

As Father Amengual left the cell to go and unwind the

thread of his lofty inspiration in Montision, Gabriel Valls decided he had to speak to the Consul, whatever the cost, to find out what truth there was in everything the priest had told him. *If the Consul's talked, if it's true the Consul's said what he knows, if he's given us away, everybody will confess. They won't have enough with all the money they've taken from us. They won't stop until they consign us all to the flames. And I, not Costura, will have been the cause, I, not Costura, the reason for the misfortune. I invited Costura to the garden to probe his plans, I poisoned Costura to stop him informing. I exacted justice in your name, Adonai, Lord of Justice, to save your body of believers; but now you, Lord of Justice, dash your fist on my head, wring my neck with your mighty hands because I'm to blame for the failed expedition . . .*

Gabriel Valls listens out behind the door for the jailer's footsteps. He won't even wait for him to bring the water and bread, as every night. As soon as he perceives his footsteps, as soon as he hears him, he'll shout to him to come near and ask for the Warder and ask him for an interview with the Consul, whatever the cost. The Warder can name his price, he doesn't care. He'll promise him everything he wants, if the money that's made him so agreeable isn't enough. Money that some friend has paid on the outside. Not everybody seeks his ruin. He'll sign a document to pay him when he gets out. He'll pay him if he gets out, if the Lord does not abandon him and he doesn't end up in the all-consuming flames that turn bones to ashes after impossible sufferings. He still remembers Alonso's cry, the deafening cry of that poor Jew from Madrid, the appalling cry he'd never heard before when the flames reached his stomach and he fell sideways on the stake . . . No, he doesn't want the image that till now hadn't appeared, he doesn't want to see the boy's face, a face swollen with suffering, a face full of horror.

He'll wait to hear the Warder's footsteps. In the dark, his sight has worsened, but, in compensation, his sense of hearing has sharpened. Sometimes, at night, he wakes up, aware of the tiniest noise that before he would never have noticed. The Warder does his round several times a day; as soon as he hears him, he'll shout out.

"Hey, Warder," he says on hearing his footsteps right in front of his door. "Open up, for the love of God!"

Love of God, he says, like Christians. He also says other things he learned as a child, things he confuses with those he addresses to Adonai, his God.

"What is it, Valls?"

"I'm begging you, I need to talk to the Consul as soon as possible. Name your price."

The Warder raises objections. Now that there are so many prisoners, although you might not think so, the vigilance has increased. He's taking a big risk by doing this favor. The price will have to be in accordance.

"Whatever you say, I've already told you. I'll sign whatever document you like. I'm a man of my word, you know this."

He seems to be convinced. He'll try for tomorrow. He'll bring him news in a short while . . . He'll talk to the Consul.

Valls doesn't have to wait long. He already hears him approaching. Drawing back the bolt. He already makes him out in the doorway.

"I'm sorry, but the Consul doesn't want to see you. He told me to let you know. He's confessed he regrets having been a Jew, he regrets having followed you to the garden, which has now been sown with salt."

He doesn't say anything else and closes. Valls doesn't ask anything. The garden sown with salt? The garden sown with salt! The garden that gives beauty with its freshness, its shade and the music of water in its ditches. The garden with such good seedlings and branches with such sweet scents. The garden where they invited their friends on those Sundays now gone for ever . . . Oh yes, it was Costura, Costura who lied, Costura who must have called their pleasant conversation a Jewish conclave. It wasn't even necessary for Costura to say anything . . . For some time it was rumored he taught the Old Law under its amorous vines. Did Maria know? O Adonai, how awful! Did Rafel Onofre know, poor thing, and Maria Pomar? Poor, wretched child! And what about their wedding! O Maria, she loved its rose bushes, how she must have cried!

Gabriel Valls cannot sleep, there's no way he can begin to doze. He feels drenched in sweat. Bad all over . . . The garden wasn't Paradise or the promised land, but at times it seemed it, at times he thought the green of its vegetation, the freshness of its trees, could be likened to it. A corner of the world to feel at ease, a haven that protected them like the shadow of the promised land. His eyes would never see any seed grow there. Never again would he be able to walk there. Never again set foot there. *O Maria, have you seen what they've done to us? Have they told you, my wife? It's better for you not to know, not to find out. You'd die of unhappiness, I'm sure. You'd die if you saw the barren land, the dead plants, the sawn trees . . . And what for? Why this disaster? What does the land have to do with my beliefs? As if the land could be considered guilty or innocent. Why do you allow it, Lord? Why do you punish us so? Why do you blot out what I love most?*

Exhausted, Gabriel Valls still took a long time to fall asleep. He woke up a moment later, hearing his own voice as if it were another's, shouting to be led before the Inquisitor. To this other, sleeping voice is added his waking voice, which again shouts for the Warder to inform the Tribunal. Since they refuse to question him, he wishes to crave an audience. He has every right. He wishes to tell them to stop seeking culprits, to stop poisoning the land, torturing more people, imprisoning innocents. If they want a culprit, there he is. If they don't want to receive him, he'll stop eating, he'll stop drinking water, he'll let himself die and then they won't be able to get anything out of him.

The Warder falls over himself to tell him. He really doesn't need Valls dead. He needs him to live and be pardoned. The Inquisitor is pleased at the news. He was of the opinion that it was better to delay the audiences as long as possible, until Valls cried out to be judged, as had just happened. This gives them the advantage. But they still make him wait another week. They want it to be very clear that the Holy Tribunal is not pushed about by anyone, and much less by vermin like him.

The Warder opened Valls' cell early one sultry morning. Valls, who had taken off his clothes because of the oppressive heat, got dressed in a jiffy, wiped the sleep from his eyes with his fists and followed the Warder. In front of the closed door of the audience chamber, he waited for a long while on his feet for the members of the Tribunal to decide that the moment had come to assemble. Finally, when it was after eight, they called him in. From behind the table, which was covered in red damask and presided over by a silver St Savior, five pairs of eyes watched him. Only one, the Inquisitor's, was protected by glasses, the others looked at him directly: bulging, the Judge of Goods'; sunken and red, the Notary of the Secret's; piercing and alert, the prosecutor's; sleepy, the defending counsel's.

The room is large and well furnished. Tapestries hang on the walls, embroidered with gold thread with the Inquisition's shield and the Spanish coat of arms. And pictures of large dimensions: St Dominic on the right and, on the left, Faith triumphing over error, falsehood and heresy, symbolized by three bleeding heads fallen to the ground, humbled by a brave woman riding a kind of winged horse. The inquisitors sit in chairs with backs lined with red damask and arms of wood dark as their talaric robes. The full light of day and the cries of swifts, messengers from distant lands, enter through the open window.

Life, thinks Valls, *goes on outside without worrying about us prisoners. Only here everything happens at night and time passes in the dark.* Instead of looking at the inquisitors, Valls stares at the patch of sky he sees through the window. *Nature is much more just than men. It's true the rain or shine is not to everyone's taste, but the rain and shine are for everyone, from King to pauper, for Christian and for Jew.*

"Name?" he hears the prosecutor ask. Then comes the whole list: age, status, profession, parents and grandparents, whether they were all Jews . . . And the first audience is over, having lasted a couple of minutes.

The Inquisitor rings a silver bell and a familiar comes in, accompanied by a servant. They take him out.

Fortunately the recess is short. Once again the defendant appears. And the prosecutor continues:

"Do you know why you have been imprisoned?"

"I'm not sure, but I have an idea, reverence, because your lordships think I'm to blame for the failed expedition, and I am. Nobody except me planned it and put it into action. I decided who should go and who should not. I paid the captain out of my savings."

"That's not true," intervenes the prosecutor. "Try not to be arrogant. Others took part in the crime. It wasn't just you. But I want you to tell us, why were you escaping?"

"We hoped to lead a better life in Livorno, a life without so many hardships. Also, a lot of us have business there. We import worsted and silk, even wheat. Those with less money, because of the confiscations of ten years ago, wanted to settle there and open shops that would help them make headway. Livorno is a free port."

"Is that the only reason, Gabriel Valls?" intervenes the prosecutor with a carping voice and knowing smile addressed to the other Tribunal members, a smile that still doesn't manage to wipe the sneer off his face. "Surely that's not the only reason. We know your race would do anything for money, but in this case money is not everything . . ."

"For the others, I can't say, reverence. Ask them yourself. But for me, of course not."

"Do you accept that money is not everything for you?" inquires the prosecutor joyously, as if he'd dealt the prey a fatal blow. "Why is that?"

"Because I want to be able to express my beliefs without fear, freely to observe the precepts of my religion."

"Do you accept, therefore, that you're a Jew?"

Gabriel Valls does not answer. He looks back at the window. At the bright blue sky, festooned with a flock of birds.

"Do you accept that you're a Jew?" he insists.

The defendant turns to the prosecutor. He holds his gaze, which is meant to be a cheetah's, though it only manages to be a genet's.

"Yes, reverence. I do."

The Tribunal members stir their bones in their chairs and shuffle uneasily. Valls' declaration seems to have roused them from the slumber they had fallen into after the recess. All their faces are suffused with religious zeal. They watch Valls pitilessly. More than one would like to lay right into this natural enemy who confesses his crime without turning a hair, with the same tranquillity he would use to talk about the current good weather and recent heat wave.

"But like all inhabitants of the Street you were baptized, is that not so? And if you have received baptism, you have no alternative but to live in accordance with Christian laws."

"My ancestors' baptism was forced on them."

The Judge of Goods smirks. He bet that Valls would use this argument.

"Nobody can feel obliged to receive such a wonderful favor as baptism," intervened the Inquisitor, who normally didn't speak, since it was the prosecutor's job to question the defendant. "They could have chosen to leave Christian lands, to go or let themselves be killed like the Maccabees."

"You're referring to the converts of 1435, reverence," exclaimed Valls angrily. "As for us, we never had this option, which I consider unjust by the way. You have to be very strong to choose death, reverence. Baptism on the one hand and death on the other are not equivalent, do not weigh the same in the scales . . ."

"Would you like to continue, reverence?" the prosecutor asks the Inquisitor, who declines, leaving the questioning to him.

"Do you accept, therefore, that you're an apostate? Do you know that apostasy is the most terrible of crimes? Do you know that, by being a practicing Jew, you're much worse than the most impious Lutheran, worse than any heretic? Heretics disagree on one point with the Christian religion, whereas practicing Jews renounce the lot."

Valls does not reply. He again stares at the window. The Judge of Goods seizes this opportunity to drink water, but chokes on the second mouthful and noisily puts the glass back on the plate. The Inquisitor gives him a withering look. Valls still doesn't speak.

"Do you accept that you're an apostate?" insists the prosecutor.

"I accept that I'm a Jew."

"And do you not repent? Do you refuse to accept that your religion is old and has been superseded by the new, which leads us towards salvation? Christ is the true Messiah, who died on the cross to save us . . ."

The Judge of Goods is still coughing and clearing his throat. Valls waits for him to finish.

"I can't see how it is possible for the creator of heaven to emerge from the womb of a Jewish woman, to come into the world as a newborn child, then to be abandoned in the hands of enemies who nail him to a cross and finally buried like everyone else . . . It seems contrary to reason, or at least difficult to believe . . ."

"It is horrible to listen to you," intervenes the Inquisitor.

"Christ rose on the third day," proclaims the prosecutor with solemnity. "Nobody can dispute that: it's proven."

"Proven for those who believe it, but not for those who don't. We Jews do not persecute Christians. We respect those who embrace the new law. That doesn't mean we don't suspect they're wrong, but we don't think they have to be burned alive for it . . . Would it not be easier, reverence, to believe that everyone will go to Jehovah or your God's heaven who has done good and freely observed the commandments? I understand some Christian kings forbade attacking synagogues because they're houses where God's name is praised."

"We do not persecute Jews, Gabriel Valls, make no mistake: we persecute lapsed Christians. Had you left these lands during the expulsion, you could continue to practice your false rites without fear of punishment. Only by word and example could we convert you . . ."

"I do not consider myself a Christian, reverence."

"We don't like your arrogance, Valls. It'll only lead you to the flames and eternal fire after that. There is no other God than God the Father, three distinct Persons. There is no salvation outside the Catholic, Apostolic and Roman Mother Church," says the Inquisitor firmly.

"No one, reverence, can have more interest than me in being saved and going to heaven."

"There is no worse blind man than the one who does not wish to see, Valls. Notwithstanding your interest, only the Catholic, Apostolic and Roman Church can take you there. Outside the Church, no salvation is possible."

"Outside the law of Moses."

"We will have to torture you to make you see sense. Perhaps this will appease your arrogance and humble your pride in being a Jew. Do you not think your God would help you if he were powerful? Or didn't you know that after the coming of Christ the normal condition of Jews is captivity?"

Valls is unfazed. Torture, now, doesn't frighten him. He feels courage. Adonai is guiding him.

"It is Jehovah's plan. The seed is in the soil, invisible to the eyes of men, and seems to merge with the earth and water, but, in the end, the seed with its substance transforms the earth and also the water and fructifies. So God's people pave the way towards the Messiah, the true fruit."

"I don't like what you're saying, Valls. I find it stinks of rabbis and Talmudic books. Is that what you taught in the garden?"

"No, reverence. I never taught the Old Law in the garden."

"We have evidence to the contrary, Valls. You cannot deny you instructed your guests in the Old Law."

"No, reverence. I can swear it."

"Do not use God's name in vain, do not swear. Do not profane it. Your son, Rafel Onofre, confessed. You can't deny it."

For the first time his lips tremble. He swallows saliva.

"It must have been under torture, reverences. My poor son would never say such a thing."

"Your arrogance stems from the devil, Valls. Don't deny what we all know. The escape was planned long ago in the garden. With flying machines even!"

"Flying machines?"

"Flying machines the mattress maker Bonnín was putting together in his attic."

Valls appears to recall. *They know. You may as well talk. Costura is the informer, Costura must have explained that conversation last summer, one diaphanous Sunday . . .*

"Reverence, I know what you're referring to: a conversation held in the garden between Pere Onofre Aguiló, the Consul, the saddler Pons, the merchant Serra and Costura. A conversation without taint of sin. Aguiló spoke of events happening in the world, stories of flying men, inventions of fanciful people . . . All of them outside Majorca."

"Do you remember any of these inventions?"

"Yes, we talked about sponges soaking up water in the port of Antwerp and a machine for soaking up bad thoughts . . ."

"And don't you think they're inspired by the devil?"

"No, reverence, I don't think that. Your lordships operate the machine of forgiveness in God's name."

"Tell us, what else did you talk about?"

"The Selenites, who live on the moon."

"What witchcraft did you practice in the garden?"

"None, reverence, none. I give you my word."

"Word of a pig, of a Jew. You won't eat pork because you're a sow's children . . . You fornicated with her."

"That's the doctrine of Luther, reverence, the heretic of Worms."

"That's right," remarks the Inquisitor. "I'm impressed by your knowledge, Valls. Where did you get it from?"

Valls does not reply. He wonders what the next attack will be. He's tired. He wishes they would at least let him sit down. The Inquisitor continues:

"Jews descend from Hagar, the slave-girl . . . Christians from Sarah . . ."

"Then we're all children of Abraham, reverence."

"Jews were born slaves and must die slaves."

"Reverence, your Christianity would be nothing without our Judaism."

"Enough, I don't want to hear any more blasphemies. Retract what you've said. Ask for forgiveness at once!"

"I didn't wish to offend you."

"Accept that you're mistaken. Abhor the Old Law right now."

"You can't just stop being Jewish, reverence."

The Inquisitor rings a bell on the table. The clerk drops the pen and wipes his forehead. As the sun rises, the heat becomes more intense. A familiar requests permission to come in. The Inquisitor bids the torture chamber be made ready. The clerk reads as he writes:

Gabriel Valls Major being under suspicion, we have to and do condemn him to be placed under torture, where we require he be and remain for as long as we see fit, that he may tell the truth concerning the accusations . . . And if under said torture he should die or be crippled, with the outpouring of blood or mutilation of some limb, it shall all be his fault and to his charge, not ours, for having chosen to continue renouncing and not accepting our holy religion.

Bloody and unconscious, Valls was dragged back to his cell two hours later.

IX

Don Antonio Nepomuceno Sotomayor y Ampuero was not officially removed from his post for another three months. During this time, despite continuing to give orders, he did so with distaste and problems. The President of the Great and General Council confronted him in the name of all its members, nobles, artisans, citizens and merchants, accusing him of having deceived them with the Queen's supposed visit. The Bishop organized solemn rogations to ask again for the rain that refused to fall, without consulting him, as had been his custom, and, worse still, when he complained about the snub, threatened him with excommunication. Those he thought were his friends, with the excuse that it was summer and they were on their estates, outside the city, acted as if they knew nothing about his misfortunes, and none of them, except Sebastià Palou, gave him their support. "In this Calvary," the Marquis would comment gratefully, "you're my Cyrenian."

Although during the summers there was little social life because the nobles played at leading the lives of peasants, someone would usually throw a party to break the monotony of protracted days, with evenings difficult to fill. But this year neither the Orlandis, possibly offended by the rebuff to their daughter Lluïsa, nor the Montis, short of cash, nor the Suredas, ruined by the confiscations, arranged anything. The Viceroy was distrustful and imagined that to these reasons was added above all the fact they didn't want to invite him. The only ceremony he attended in all that time was his nephew's wedding. Although it was celebrated in private, with Lady Bàrbara's confessor officiating—the Marquis persuaded Sebastià not to ask the Bishop, to avoid a further insult when he turned it down—the Viceroy put on full dress. He wore a new cloak despite the heat, not wanting to miss the opportunity, since it was his right as the kingdom's highest authority. As a present he gave his nephew a choice of the gold-embroidered Flemish tapestries he had brought from Madrid to decorate one of the Palace rooms, which everybody admired for their incalculable worth. Sebastià Palou favored one that showed the abduction of Europa, but the nymph's excessive opulence would not have pleased his future wife. Although they had never discussed such matters, the bridegroom was sure that, being so devout, she would not be partial to female nudes and what's more, given her anatomical constitution—thin and with less flesh than a sardine—she would probably reject all women, alive or painted, who did not look like her. So he chose a Vulcan breathing fire, surrounded by helpers at the forge, which anyone would have ascribed to Old Nick, since there was nothing compromising about it. Those blacksmiths' naked torsos could hardly arouse Barbareta, and the whole was valuable enough to hang in any of the many reception rooms in the house his wife inherited from her first husband, where they would live after the wedding.

The first showers in October—the rogations had finally worked, though with some delay—postponed for a couple of days the end of the viceregal move, which was being directed by the Marquise in person, with all the care and meticulousness she could summon, especially with regard to her own possessions. The paintings full of sad ancestors, who seemed to have been portrayed in state and not in life, given their air of extreme unction, were transferred to the Marquise's town house, since they almost all came from her family. The tapestries and furniture were sent to Son Gualba in a row of carts, for storage, while the Marquis decided whether to share them out among his children or leave them on the country estate, waiting to renovate so he could open a couple more rooms and give them the solemn setting they deserved. The Marquise could not allow the frescos painted by Chiapini to remain in the Palace. She thought it a crime to have to do without that contemplation that evoked such sweet memories, and pestered her husband to find a way to move that ceiling, albeit through the needle's eye. But the Viceroy paid no attention.

The rain in October, so eagerly awaited and necessary for all Majorcans, slightly spoiled the festivities for the arrival of the new Viceroy, the Lord Marquis of the Casta, for which, to calm the excited spirits of the artisans, who had been looking forward to the royal visit so that they could breathe a little, the Great and General Council almost ran into debt. Water sports were held in Born, but this didn't stop the nobles dressed in blue, green, red and white showing off both their natural gallantry and the skill of Majorcan tailors in cutting and sewing the clothes they wore. The Marquis of the Bastida put on a well-attended gala ball that enabled the ladies to show off their taffeta and silk. The authorities waited for it to stop raining before ordering the city streets to be lit up with torches and lamps. The budget for illuminations had been spent and there was no point saving them. "For two nights," wrote the chronicler Angelat, "the sun did not set in the Majorcan capital."

The new Viceroy, who was much more devout than Boradilla, pleased the Curia, whose intrigues till now had been so successful, bringing about the latter's dismissal and the appointment of a like-minded person. The Marquis of the Casta immediately met with the highest ecclesiastical authorities. He first called on the Bishop to thank him for the *Te Deum* held in his honor. And the same day, to avoid suspicions, received the Inquisitor. He also had to give him thanks for the offer he had made, in the name of the Holy Tribunal members, to light the purificatory torch at the first auto-da-fé, which was almost ready. The Inquisitor had been forced to move it forward—although, he assured him, this had in no way hindered the course of justice and the detailed examination of each and every one of the cases that had been closed—to help calm the spirits of good Christians, taken in by Boradilla's deceit, which now would not let them improve their wretched situation with a royal visit.

"Thanks to the preparations for the autos-da-fé," remarked the Inquisitor, "the tailors have work again, the painters have been contracted to paint the defendants' portraits, as well as the flames on the sanbenitos, the woodmen are hurrying to cut down trees, the chandlers have run out of supplies and the bakers . . ."

"My assistants have brought me up to date," the Marquis cut in, "and I know what you want to say, reverence. We'll find wheat under the stones if necessary so that, as well as helping the bakers, your reverence can distribute white bread to the people in attendance . . ."

"We planned to give them a roll and dried figs. The Holy Tribunal will put on a lunch for your lordships," smiled the Inquisitor smugly.

Although he was sure the inquisitors were acting in good faith and would not have hesitated to report their own father if they considered him guilty, the new Viceroy was appalled at the idea of dining between sentences, in view of the condemned, who would sometimes cry, kick or defecate with no respect for their audience. He knew that the banquet offered in Born ten years before had brought together the cream of Majorcan nobility, who had sampled four courses, not counting the hors d'oeuvres and desserts, albeit in an extremely pious way . . . Now he would do his utmost to prevent it.

"I think, reverence," he said, "the cost of a banquet could be avoided. The list of paupers on the island is long enough. They also should derive some benefit from the autos-da-fé. They're poor, but Christian . . . Besides, I would say St Dominic's Convent is a better venue than Born and a meal inside the church is not perhaps . . ."

The Inquisitor had already sensed he would come to a quick understanding with the new Viceroy. Canceling the banquet would save a fistful of ounces. Alms would work out much cheaper.

During that conversation held in the Almudaina palace, with a cup of chocolate, in an austere room—Boradilla had always received him in the large salons, their walls covered in mythological scenes he detested—the date was fixed for the first auto-da-fé. If everything was ready, what point was there in waiting any longer?

In the thick darkness of the prisons, the days continued to go by without cracks or fissures, in a dark, overwhelming monotony broken only by audiences and torture. Till now, during those eight long months of captivity, two of the prisoners had died: Rafel Tarongí, on the rack itself, because he didn't want to retract or give anybody away; and the tailor Valleriola's wife, possibly because of the hardships, too much for someone of her advanced age. The others, many wounded as a result of torture, some with broken bones, resisted because the survival instinct was stronger than any of them could have imagined, in the hope that they would soon be judged. They trusted that the Tribunal, having confiscated their goods, as happened the last time, would have little interest in holding them in prison and would prefer to let them go, while at the same time keeping a close eye on them, condemning them every Sunday to go to Mass in the Cathedral, wearing a sanbenito, as a lesson to all. They clung to this hope because they certainly didn't want to die, especially in the open square, being watched and mocked by everyone.

They used the long periods of inactivity carefully to go over their existences. In the sooty muddle of memory there arose small details that had not previously been considered, but now served almost as crutches in the frail, limp, crippled life they were forced to lead. Were it not for this, were it not for these trifles that identified them, singled them out, were it not for favorite colors, the preference for one or another meal, the skill at training pigeons or making jam, it would have been difficult to distinguish one existence from another, they were so similar, except for the family of Valls or Sara de les Olors. The other prisoners, both those from the boat and those arrested later, had too many features in common to provide a separate profile. They were Jews by tradition, though they could be considered Christians because they had been baptized and outwardly observed the rituals. This contradiction often tortured their consciences and in prison acquired even greater strength. To many it was obvious that Adonai had abandoned them and so they prayed to him with less fervor than to God the Father, to whom they had transferred almost all their pleas. Many, comforted by the idea that Christ would never turn his back on them, as Elohim had done, held on, in the hope that they would soon be freed owing to his mercy.

Among the women, Sara de les Olors was the most convinced that she would be saved. Even if she was sentenced to death, the Blessed Virgin would come for her in the form of an eagle and carry her off in front of everyone, up, up, piercing the clouds with its beak. Sara's ravings were influenced by the obsession of her father, the mattress maker, who in the attic at home tried secretly to build some wings, using hens' feathers, so that he could escape through the sky to lands of freedom. Bonnín, who had been imprisoned the last time, wanted nothing more than to leave Majorca. Although few knew about his invention, he frequently claimed the day would come when the island's sky would be covered in flying people and nobody would find it strange. Sara believed him. This may be why she now consoled herself with the hope of the Messianic eagle she sometimes had make a second journey to free Maria as well and a third to carry off Beatriu. Other times she claimed they would ride together on the back of the animal, which was strong enough to lift that burden.

Sara sighed when Maria insisted with a sad smile that she didn't like this form of salvation at all. She didn't want to fly into the sky, but to stay here on earth and die old next to Rafel Onofre. After the day they saw each other in the cell, after such brief glory, all she wanted was to live, to live and stay in his arms forever and feel again that intoxication that almost made her faint. Maria was convinced that something similar was happening to Rafel Onofre. And she wasn't mistaken. He also wanted to live at any price, even by admitting that Jesus Christ was God's only-begotten Son and not a prophet, but the Messiah who had already come. Love gave him wings to imagine that his father would understand, his father would not feel betrayed if he accepted before the inquisitors that the law of Moses was the Old Law and no longer valid before the new law of God the Father Almighty. Saving himself from death was the only thing that mattered, the only thing he was prepared to fight for with all his strength. Living for him was more important than being damned or going to heaven. He never would have thought he would cling so furiously to the possibility of not dying. He dreamed useless plans of escape and trusted in a general pardon at the last moment. And already he was free and happy again at Maria's side.

His mother, Maria Aguiló, had offered Adonai her life if Rafel Onofre was not arrested and could manage to get off

Majorca, leaving danger behind. Later, when they told her during the third audience that he had been imprisoned, she entrusted him to the Christ of St Eulalia's and made the same offer: *My life in exchange for his, Lord. If you save him for me, I will die a Christian.* Maria Aguiló, although she refused in the first audiences, succumbed before being tied to the rack: the shame of appearing naked in front of the torturers was stronger than the conviction that her husband would never forgive her for this weakness.

Only Isabel Tarongí, among the women taken prisoner on the night of the expedition, had suffered torture without retracting her heresies. Her husband and mother-in-law had testified against her. Xim Martí, persuaded by Father Ferrando, believed he was contributing to his wife's eternal salvation and in this way demonstrating his love. Isabel did not reply to any of the accusations the prosecutor brought against her. She never wanted to accept that the only true religion was Catholic, Apostolic and Roman. Without opposing any arguments, she just kept quiet with her eyes lowered, kept quiet and listened with her eyes full of tears. Her brother's death under torture, which the inquisitors mentioned to demoralize her, instead of weakening her gave her strength. Her Madonna's beauty moved the Inquisitor, who in the fourth audience prevented her being put on the rack again. He declared that this woman was mentally deranged, since it was impossible not to bow before the evidence and to insist on following the customs of the Old Law just because, for the simple reason she came from a Jewish family. *Only if they hurt the children,* Isabel said to herself, *only if they torture them in front of me, only then, Adonai, will I renounce you and everything inherent in the law of Moses.* The children were too small and the Tribunal didn't even allow them to testify. Isabel Tarongí praised God inside her heart. Death didn't frighten her, she thought it worse to be left forever in that dark cell, unable to see the children, who could easily end up cursing her. Death was no more than a bitter pill to swallow, a few moments of agony and then Paradise forever. Perhaps Adonai would let her contemplate the children from on high, see how they grew and reached adulthood . . . She could continue to watch over them from on high. Quitèria didn't agree with her: "I'm just sorry I ever embarked, I should never have done it. They didn't bother me the last time and I'd have been saved. Whereas now . . . I should never have believed in Valls, not on my life. He was our undoing." Isabel Tarongí was annoyed by her cell-mate, especially when at night she started shouting and blasphemed against Adonai for having betrayed them. She would sometimes bang her head against the door. "Let me out of here," she would cry, "I want to go. I can't take any more."

There were times Valls couldn't take any more. For two months he had convalesced, helped by the Holy Office's doctor, because the torturer, despite being advised not to go too far, had been overzealous in applying torture. The inquisitors were keen for the ringleader to make it to the auto-da-fé on his own two feet, and they did not want to have to burn him in effigy. As soon as he was able, the audiences continued, in which the Inquisitor rather than the prosecutor had the chief say. This man with kind eyes, who had been fat and glowing when he entered prison and was now just a bag of bones, seemed to him the only opponent worthy of consideration among all the prisoners. Someone—unlike that coward, the Consul, he despised, however much he might profess Christianity—who knew how to rise to his own destiny, however bitter it might be. The Inquisitor soon realized that, if Valls ever abhorred the old faith, it wouldn't be because he'd persuaded him, but because in the loneliness of his cell he'd finally been convinced. But, though Valls did spend many hours meditating on the figure of the Messiah—and in this he accepted a recommendation from the Inquisitor, whom he also respected more than Father Ferrando or Father Amengual—this Christ had little to say to him. Had he accepted the new law, he would never have inclined to the orthodox proposal offered by the Holy Tribunal, but to one many years before, almost forty, offered to him by Joan de Santamaria, whom he had met by chance. Sometimes, when he immersed himself in the past to derive some benefit and made as if he were living back then, far from the unhappy present, Gabriel Valls again heard his voice, slightly muffled, almost hoarse from so much talking, from so much trying to transmit his message wherever they would listen.

As he evokes him, the presence of that little man becomes familiar and diverts him from the hardships, allowing him to settle in Ferrara again, in the home of his powerful friends the Álvares Dos Santos, exiled Portuguese Jews who show him hospitality and welcome him like a son when, sick, he seeks their assistance. The long conversations with Santamaria help him a lot and serve to clarify many obscure points, to shed more light on those he already understands. They often debate, but they never quarrel, they always respect the other's opinions, weigh them up and sometimes, although they do not share them, even admit that the other may be right.

"Christ cannot be the Messiah," rejoins Valls with the impetuosity of youth, "as you maintain, because he solved nothing. Is the world better off since his coming? What's more, the Most High would not have sent his son to suffer terrible torments to no avail. Adonai is infinite wisdom, obviously he would not have let him be crucified."

"You're only partially right, my Jewish brother," replies this squalid little man who, to be seen and heard, uses a stool or climbs on to the first chair he is offered. "The Christ of Rome, the Christ of concubinary, corrupt priests, has served only to fill the coffers of convents. Ours, however, serves for a lot. The true Messiah implies salvation because he is the source of all hope.

He makes us big and just and noble. He affords us in faith the opportunity to be good, better than we are, more pure. Through him we help others as if they were our brethren, our children, our parents . . ."

He had fled from Valencia, where he was born into a family of Jewish converts, closely related to the Lluís Vives, but he declared himself to be Christian, not Catholic or Lutheran either. He belonged to a sect that gathered the fruit of the illuminati wiped out more than a century before by the Edict of Toledo, also followers of the doctrines of the great Erasmus of Rotterdam, whose books he knew and read with the same unction as he did the Bible and New Testament. They became friends and, while he recovered from those fevers that kept him bedridden for two long weeks, Joan de Santamaria expounded the fundamentals of his religion, which only obliged him to obey his own conscience.

"Christ came to waken men's consciences," he would say. "Christ and conscience are one and the same. Christ is the Savior because, by opening all doors to us, he has saved us from ourselves, offering us the mirror of our brother who watches us."

But he made it clear he had no intention of converting him, he would gain nothing by proselytizing because in this new Church each member communicated directly with the divinity, without intermediaries of any kind, among other reasons because the divinity was each man and each woman in a state of purity. Neither he nor any member of the new sect ever chased anybody to convert them, except by the example of love, because this was the only commandment they believed in and this had been the new Messiah's great discovery. Love exalts people, makes them different from all the other creatures inhabiting Earth, and that is why it's understandable that all governments, all republics, are strongly opposed to it. Love is humankind's greatest revulsive, the best force it has to change things.

"Love gives us wings, makes us bigger, makes us like God. Love does not judge or blame or condemn."

Joan de Santamaria's eyes colored his words with bright sparks. Women, above all, felt drawn by that force that came from inside him and, when he talked of his religion, made him seem blessed. The whole of him shone and this shining reached those who listened to him. Many would have liked to hear the words he addressed to the congregation in their ear, at night, on the same pillow. But although when citing Maria de Cazalla, whom he called a saint, he would say that couples in the act of marriage were in contact with God, just as if they received Communion, and the divinity entered bodies that gave each other love, he was chaste. Rumor had it he was impotent. But, while Valls admired him, he didn't make him waver in his Jewish faith, which is what happened to the Álvares Dos Santos' eldest son, who abandoned his parents to follow Joan de Santamaria on his world pilgrimage.

What had become of him? Valls never heard, though throughout his life he often wondered. But never till now had his words touched his memory as if he'd just listened to them. "There's salvation for everybody. Everyone finds the heaven they deserve. Everyone is master of their own life." It was a shame he had wanted to command the lives of others, influencing those who were unsure about the escape, to enlist them in the failed expedition. Now, however much he repents, it's too late. There's no going back. Even if he obtains their pardon, something he doubts, he won't manage to throw off this agony. Besides, a pardon can only soothe the poor in spirit, because a pardon does not alter or redress the past. What's done is done. He can't change anything in this life. In the other . . . He's also had time, a lot of time, to reflect on this, time to imagine what the heaven of the blessed will be like, where they'll all meet again: his sons and wife, the Widow Sampol and Pere Onofre Aguiló, who helped them so much in vain. But what if it was all a sham, there was no heaven or hell, everything finished with this life? What if the beyond was only an illusion of men clinging to futile hopes? The beyond was only dust and ashes? Dust and ashes . . . Could there being or not being eternal life depend on his beliefs? On the need for his faith? But the fact of believing in Paradise does not guarantee its existence. No deceased ever resurrected to show how souls live after leaving the body, the spirit after abandoning matter. And what if he had quickened Costura's end to send him to nothingness, instead of to Jehovah's judgement, as, against his will, he was about to send those wretches he persuaded to escape? What would be the point of such misery?

The Tribunal members were responsible for going down to the prisons and reading the defendants their sentences. As of Saturday, they had seventy-two hours to repent and seek the forgiveness of the Lord God, whom they had so deeply offended. Otherwise those sentenced to death would be burned alive. If they recanted, made a good confession, the secular arm would take pity on them and garrote them before they were consumed by the flames.

With the solemnity the occasion demanded, the retinue left the Chamber of the Secret. It was made up of familiars preceding the Holy Tribunal members and the jailers' assistants carrying the door keys. They were followed by the priests whose task it was in those days to ensure the prisoners had a good death. This meant they had to convert the heretics into fervent Christians. Father Ferrando and Father Amengual, separated by a Franciscan and two Mercedarians, were still ignoring each other as they had done almost all that laborious summer. Both had just found out that their rivalry had been for nothing, the new rector of Montision Convent had already been appointed and the position had not fallen to either of them. Amengual consoled himself with the thought that Father Ferrando was worse off than him, since he was about to finish his book *The Triumph of the Faith in Three Autos*. He was only missing the scenes that would unfold in three days' time. The rest had already been written out and learned by heart from so much rereading it: *To please much more than the stalk tends the flower, but to owe the stalk the triumphs of its beauty tends the flower, which could hardly stay beautiful without the stalk. Thus the most florid piety of the kindness of God man wished for the flower to stand out from the clemency of its being, but also for it to be understood that its sovereign softness depended on the hardness of the stalk: Egredietur virga de radice Jesse, flos de radice eius ascendet.* If it sounded good to the ears, how could it not sound even better once printed in the eyes of pious readers?

The procession had already entered the corridor leading to the cells occupied by the women. Everything was ready for each of the defendants arrested on the night of the expedition to hear from the lips of the Holy Tribunal members the sentence they still didn't know. Maria Pomar fainted in Beatriu's arms when the prosecutor informed her she had been given the maximum penalty for being a Jewish heretic. Sara de les Olors, for being possessed and a visionary, would also go to the flames. Limp was not sentenced, her case was not yet closed. She wept and shouted, pleading for mercy for her companions. Nobody paid her any attention.

Maria Aguiló went through the same narrow place as her future daughter-in-law. Like her, repentance could save her from dying in the flames, first she would be garroted. Aina Cap de Trons was reconciled, sentenced to life imprisonment and to wearing a sanbenito. The Tribunal had taken into account her spirit of collaboration and hatred towards Valls, who she said had forced her with threats to embark. She exuded the same poison against her father, whom she blamed for the family misfortunes. The Holy Tribunal included Cap de Trons among the dead who would be disinterred and burned in the first auto. Cap de Trons would be accompanied by the remains of Rafel Tarongí, wayward and perverse, who died under torture. Isabel Tarongí, his sister, condemned as a Jewish apostate, convicted and confessed, would be handed over to the secular arm to burn alive if she did not abhor her errors, something that by merciful tradition would allow her to be flung on the flames, having been garroted. Quitèria was luckier than Isabel because, like Aina Segura, Madò Grossa's sister, she was only punished with fifteen years in prison: her repentance had made the Tribunal reduce the penalty. Polònia, Costura's former maid, Aina Fuster and Madò Grossa, although they had also abhorred their mistakes and shown signs of being well converted, received the death penalty, given that their previous heresies had been particularly offensive to the Lord God, first and supreme Inquisitor of human sins. They would burn after dying.

The procession reached the prison occupied by the men half an hour later, with the same ceremonial and without some of the priests and familiars, who had already been ordered to begin at once admonishing and supervising those wretched women. The first cell they entered was occupied by Rafel Onofre Valls, who shouted on receiving the death sentence. The jailer had to handcuff him because he pushed the Notary of the Secret and shoved a familiar. They were much less severe with the Cap de Trons brothers. They had also criticized their father, who they explained had wanted to circumcise them, although he had only given them cuts because they defended themselves, since they did not agree with his faith. The Cap de Trons would be made to row in a galley. Josep Valleriola, condemned for reoffending, was sent to the flames, while his cousin, the tailor Xim Valleriola, was punished with twenty years in prison. The charges against him were reduced because of his hatred towards the rabbi, whom he blamed for everybody's misfortunes, his own in particular, maintaining that he had asked him for money to import wheat, with the promise of a healthy profit, and invested it without his knowing in the charter of that ill-fated boat. Pere Onofre Martí, Moixina, even though he appeared before the judges, saying he recognized Christ's new law to be true, and made confession of his errors without being asked, was, like the Consul and his two sons, sent to the flames. The same thing happened to Miquel Bonnín.

The Inquisitor in person reserved the right to read his sentence to Gabriel Valls, who occupied not only the worst of the cells, but the most uncomfortable and remote. Having seen and conferred his case with learned doctors of grave letters and sciences, his crimes being so great and pernicious, they had decided that next Tuesday he would be handed over to the secular arm to die in the flames. Valls received the sentence without flinching.

Only the children, who had not reached the statutory age to remain in prison, were freed. They emerged poor and orphaned, to learn from their families' example. From now on they would do well to consider themselves bastards, as if they'd just been born.

X

HE'S JUST DISEMBARKED IN PORT PI. HE MAKES HASTE along the ring-road to St Catherine's Gate. On passing near Bellver Wood, he watches with curiosity how large numbers of woodcutters sweep up the fallen leaves, while others stack heaps of recently hewn branches. They look lively, as if it's a job, driven on by a foreman barking out orders. He doesn't understand what he says very well, but he seems to be urging them on. Were he not in such a hurry, he'd go over and ask what all the fuss is about. From the gunwale, on turning into dock, he's already noticed that yellow spot among the pines going down the side of Bellver to the road that connects the city with the port. But he prefers not to waste a second. He wants to arrive as soon as possible. If he finds a cart or carriage that isn't full, he'll stop it and ask to be given a lift to the wall. He trembles to think that he hasn't arrived in time, the trip has been useless, he won't now be able to fulfill the mission the lady gave him, his risks are in vain. He gestures with his hand, but no carter man says *whoa!* to his beast. Perhaps they distrust his appearance, his clothes, which indicate he's a foreigner, or perhaps his speed. *Anyone in a hurry is up to no good. God knows if he isn't running from some misdeed!* he imagines must be in the mind of these people who are used always to traveling slowly, to doing everything as if time for them were overflowing. He strides along among the groups of peasants also heading towards the city.

They walk in clusters, accompanied by children and elders, chatter loudly and seem at leisure. On passing through the gate, he bumps into even more people. The bustle strikes him as unusual for a Monday, when there isn't normally a fair or big market as far as he knows, nor is it an observable feast. He didn't come across this commotion a year and four months ago, the first time he visited Majorca. *No, this isn't a good sign,* he says to himself. Rather it suggests misfortune is near and, in effect, it's too late. But he doesn't dare ask anyone. All these farmers may have come to the city for the festivities to celebrate the appointment of a new Viceroy, who has only just arrived, he was told in Barcelona. He hopes so. In a short while, when he is received by Captain Sebastià Palou, all his forebodings will vanish and he'll finally know whether it's still possible to do something and not everything is lost. Before reaching the Church of the Holy Cross, he is met by the fishwives hawking their wares: "Exquisite sardines, lively rockfish, first-rate mullet! Come on, girls, buy! Come and buy!" No, he doesn't want to ask any of them if this is the right way to St Magdalene's Convent. Nor will he ask the host of unruly children playing at flying kites. He carries on walking among a horde of cats that have heeded the call and are pursuing the fishwives, who've now stopped as if their way was blocked, to attend a customer leaning out of the window. The foreigner is sorry that the persistent odor they give off has stuck in his nose, because he doesn't like it at all. He much prefers the perfumed scent of the pines and resin, of the recently hewn branches of the castle wood he planned till now to conserve.

He's already by Holy Cross and suddenly the bell seems to unleash the first toll in his ear. As he moves away, it's followed by eight more. *Not a good time for unexpected visits,* he says to himself. But he imagines the captain will be able to forgive him. The mission he's been given does not allow him to put off the meeting at all. The captain will understand. He's almost sure about that. He has to hurry and not to get lost. Each moment could be precious. He hesitates which way to turn and, on seeing an old priest with a kindly expression, asks him if he could tell him if this is the right way to St Magdalene's Convent, which is situated next to the great Sebastià Palou's home. "Straight on," he answers, "after you go past the Montcadas' chapel, turn by the Tagamanents' house, then left again. You're a foreigner, I see. Captain Palou and I were neighbors, I've known him since he was a boy . . ."

This is like Livorno, thinks the young man, *everybody knows each other. Knows what's going on. You can't keep the tiniest secret hidden. In no time at all, everybody will know I'm looking for Don Sebastià Palou. But I've nothing to be afraid of. Nobody will recognize me. Not even the Bailiff. With this moustache my face is different and my hair has grown a lot. I don't look anything like the poor sailor they put in prison. Now I'm a gentleman, as is obvious from my Tuscan-style clothes.*

"His lordship is not here," says the maid who opens the door and bows politely. "He doesn't live here anymore."

But immediately, noticing the displeasure reflected in the face of the foreigner, who is almost as young as her and so good-looking, she smiles and assures him she'll explain how to find him: "At Dalmau's, after you pass the inn called S'Estornell." And she describes the quickest way to get there.

The foreigner quickens his pace, barging down narrow streets, past people who are in no hurry. He doesn't want to run so as not to attract attention, but he has fire in his shoes. He turns down those who offer to put him up with dignity in a decent hotel, the water-sellers who approach him on seeing how sweaty he is. In Nova Square he stops short. He recognizes the place, even though today it's occupied by the farmers displaying their produce on improvised stalls. He can't resist poking his nose in Segell Street: he sees barricaded homes with the green cross painted on doors and also people standing about. He again makes haste. Now he recognizes the street he paced up and down all night, waiting to enter through the secret gate that never opened, and thinks he sees in the wall enclosing the garden the same cracks and fissures, damp patches in some areas, he must have dreamed because it was too dark to remember it all with such precision. But the gate, yes. He's sure it was this one . . . "After the garden," the maid said. But just in case he's taken the wrong road and an unsatisfied desire is what has brought him back to this place, he asks a housewife carrying a basket of vegetables and a loaf like a millstone under her arm. "Dalmau's? Right here. Very close. The main entrance is on the other street, just around the corner."

Sebastià Palou and his wife are still having breakfast, having attended the first Mass of the day. The mouthful of biscuit crunches in their mouths with matrimonial unanimity and the cups of chocolate wait in front of them. The biscuits are a present from the Clares. *Lady Bàrbara's charitable disposition towards convents has to do some good,* thinks the captain, who's only been married for two months. Sixty-one days of prayers, novenas and pious works, desperately boring. If only Beatriu Mas weren't still in jail! . . . The butler asks permission to interrupt the couple's breakfast:

"A foreign gentleman wishes to see your lordship. He says his name is Loureiro and the message he's carrying for your lordship is urgent."

"It must have something to do with Uncle," remarks Sebastià to his wife. "Excuse me, Bàrbara, I'll be back in a moment."

And he places the napkin on the table, having used it to wipe his lips, and kisses his wife's hand with gallant resignation.

The room he has been shown into is one of the most luxurious he has ever seen. The high walls are covered in tapestries from top to bottom. More than three dozen chairs of crimson velvet with golden studs, embellished with a fringe of gold thread, surround him in a row. A huge brass pome hangs from the ceiling. Directly underneath is a well-turned walnut sideboard with a large oil lamp. The young man doesn't dare sit down because he doesn't know which chair to choose. He prefers to walk about, but is unsure whether to turn to the left or right, because on both sides there is a door. The captain might enter through either of them and he wants to see his face at once. Besides, it's not polite to show his back to him.

"I'm here," he says, "on behalf of Lady Blanca Maria Pires, whom I serve and who sends you her greetings. A more hazardous journey than I would have liked delayed me two weeks, since the lady sent for me almost as soon as she received your letter. I go by the name of Loureiro, but I can tell you my real name is João Peres."

"In that case I can ask you for proof that what you're saying is true. You'll understand, in such times . . ."

"Of course. Just as you said in your letter. The lady told me on seeing this you'd have no doubt . . ."

The foreigner approaches the captain while removing the ring that shines on the little finger of his right hand and offers it to him.

"I wore it because it seemed the best way to protect it. To take it, they'd have had to cut my hand."

"Thank you," answers Palou, surprised, while playing with the ring. "You must be tired and hungry."

"Very tired, sir. But that doesn't matter so long as I've arrived in time. I saw lots of people in the streets, as if they were waiting for some extremely important event. The new Viceroy?"

"The new Viceroy was received last week. They haven't

come for the Viceroy, but for the cremation. The first auto-da-fé begins tomorrow. As far as I know, almost all those from the boat have been judged . . ."

Sebastià Palou talks in a low voice, observing the effect his words have on the young man.

"The lady . . . I don't know how I can tell her I didn't arrive soon enough."

"To be honest, it wouldn't have done any good this time. Things have been very different from ten years ago. Thanks to my wife's generosity, I tried to buy the lives of Valls, the Consul, and their families, after Villarreal left without managing it. I did this, thinking about Lady Blanca and Pere Onofre Aguiló. How is my friend?"

"He's still not walking and feels very depressed. He blames himself for the misfortune."

"It's not his fault, poor Pere. If there's one good person in the world, it's him."

Captain Palou approaches the sideboard and shakes a silver handbell. Immediately a servant appears, bowing.

"Tell the kitchen to make a good breakfast and serve it in the library once it's ready."

Sebastià Palou, followed by the foreigner, crosses four more rooms with high ceilings, crowned with redwood beams, lined with square and rectangular paintings, some of them enormous. A black chest inlaid with ivory reminds the boy that a similar piece presides over a room in the Widow Sampol's house in Livorno. A shepherd dog comes running up and sniffs at him just as he goes through the door of the library. Books replace paintings on one wall. Portraits of priests and courtiers hang on the others. The captain shows his guest to an easy chair lined with green damask, like the hangings over the windows and doors. He, however, remains standing and begins to walk about the room.

"While you're in Majorca, you'll stay in this house. I've been living here for two months, since I was married."

"I appreciate it, but I've a place on the galley. My lady sends you her congratulations on your wedding and thanks you for letting her know."

"Do you not have a letter from her for me?"

"No, sir. She wrote to you, but then tore it up. She thought it was dangerous in case I then didn't arrive, in case there was a mishap and I was arrested. She gave me this money to help the prisoners . . ."

The boy took two full bags, hidden in his clothes, which Sebastià Palou declined.

"It's not needed now. Give it back. Tell her to use it to do charitable works. And give her the ring as well."

"The lady told me it's yours, that SP are your initials."

"But it was a present. We agreed she would accept it and use it for a just cause, a good work, because otherwise she wouldn't have wanted it."

"She did that."

"Yes, and Harts committed the folly of having it valued by Costura, and he must have gone straight to his confessor . . ."

"I was luckier than Gabriel Valls and the Consul. I recovered the ring just eight months ago. The lady asked me to give it back to you if it couldn't be of use to the captives. Take it as a wedding gift."

"Tell her I did everything I could, before and after Villarreal came. Everything," said Palou, looking at the ring. "I bribed familiars, made substantial donations to the Holy Tribunal, as I was advised, thanks to which I've been left alone, but those aimed at easing the prisoners' hardships were rejected. I only managed in the first months to bribe the Warder to help Valls. After that, nothing. The Inquisitor, who I met with to plead for clemency, wouldn't budge. He wasn't interested in money like other members of the Holy Office and, hard as I tried, I couldn't find a weak point to open a breach and launch an attack. He struck me as a strongly fortified place of defense, impossible to break down. And he didn't want to hear about Christian charity, only justice."

Sebastià Palou paused. He stopped walking about and sat down opposite his guest, looking at him searchingly, and then continued in a low voice:

"Tell your lady, if it's any consolation, nobody could have done anything; not even her, had she been a man, as she sometimes would have liked, so she said. She can be calm."

"Don't worry, sir. I'll tell her everything, without missing a word."

Palou appears not to hear the boy, at least he doesn't thank him for his courtesy, although he immediately asks if he can confide in him. His loyalty to the lady he serves acts as a guarantee.

"Lady Blanca," he begins, "tired of so many verses, so many love letters, worn out, I suppose, by my insistence, one day demanded proof, asked me what I was prepared to do for her, and I answered anything she liked, she only had to say it. She thought for a moment and then grinned before exclaiming, 'I want you to do what I couldn't and yet would like . . .' Many years have gone by, ten if I'm not mistaken, but I've finally done it . . . without achieving anything . . ."

"My lady owes you some compensation . . ."

"None. It wasn't a bet. That would not have been gentlemanly."

Sebastià Palou is interrupted by some knocks at the door. The servant places a silver tray on the desk, with the foreigner's breakfast. Palou gestures to him to eat.

"One question, sir," says Peres between mouthfuls of crystallized fruit. "Did the lady live near here? A year and four months ago, I myself spent a night pacing up and down the street between the house and the garden, thinking she lived here."

"Yes, this was her house. When she left Majorca, my wife's first husband bought it before marrying to enlarge his own, which was next door. She did well to escape; the Inquisition would not have passed up this substantial property. Such is the way of things, you and I have just walked through the rooms where she must have received Harts."

"But Harts only had words with her . . ." the boy cuts in firmly.

"She took Queen Esther as her example. I don't know how far her sacrifice or obstinacy went . . . Judith seduced Holofernes . . ."

"It can't be true," says the boy. "I'm sure."

"Why?" asks Palou with curiosity, unable to remain seated and walking about again, toying with the ring.

"Because I was responsible for punishing Captain Harts, who admitted the story he had spread was a lie."

"In a house as big as this one," remarks Palou, "servants sometimes assume functions that don't belong to them. For a couple of months, the lady had a very beautiful and bold chambermaid, capable of latching on to Lady Blanca's suitors, pretending to be her. Harts was summoned to close a deal, to transport Jews . . ."

"You baffle me, sir. First you talked of a sacrifice, now of an impersonation."

"Do you know your lady? Do you know her well? Have you suffered her coldness, her severity, her fatal attraction? Ask her what exactly happened with Harts. Ask her while looking in her eyes, that is if you don't burn in her pupils."

Sebastià Palou speaks excitedly. His face is flushed, his voice almost trembling with rage. The boy lets him calm down.

"Tell her from me that I'm very well and very in love with my wife. She won't believe it. Who cares! Don't tell her anything . . . As for the ring, it's hers. Give it back to her, please."

The foreigner replaces the ring on the little finger of his right hand. He stands up.

"With your permission, sir. Is there anything else for your friends in Livorno? We set sail the day after tomorrow and we may not see each other again. Pere Onofre Aguiló asked me to visit his mother."

"You won't be able, she's in prison. But, if the information I've received is correct, she hasn't been sentenced. In tomorrow's auto, only those from the boat have been condemned. It's all bad news for my friends in Livorno . . ."

"Not all, sir. You're well and newly wed . . ." he adds with ironic complicity the captain doesn't like in the least. "May I leave through the garden?"

"Leave whichever way you like," and he rings another handbell for the servant to appear.

The boy now isn't in any hurry. So he walks slowly between the sweet-smelling oranges, listening to the rhythmical gurgle of the water, which pours from a spout into the fountain's basin and then runs along a ditch. Flower-beds are laid out on both sides of the path, full of zinnias, rose bushes, mystic roses, jasmine and basil with a deadening scent. The plants have blossomed, weaving garlands of various colors, yellow, red, white, pink. Honeysuckle climbs the walls and ivy spreads its tentacles to reach way up high.

A maid, no more than a girl, leads the foreigner. She has on country clothes with a scarf protecting her hair and a coarse apron covering part of her serge skirt. She's not wearing a veil in the Moorish tradition, like the girl in Harts' story, though in her manner of dressing she does resemble Aina Cap de Trons, whom he picked up on that ill-fated day.

The boy cannot believe that he's finally reached the place he so insistently desired to set foot in, nor can he believe everything that's happened since he disembarked from *The Minerva* in Port Pi and an accident led him to prison and then to Pere Onofre's cabin and Livorno. His story is much more worth listening to than Andrew Harts' fantastical tale. He didn't manage to find here the woman of his dreams, but from here he was conducted to her side, because his wish to look for her was stronger than anything. To search for her, he abandoned everything. They're now passing under the vines that filter the light and refresh the heavy hours of sun. Blanca had vines planted in her garden in Livorno in memory of these, palms and cypresses as well. Often of an evening, after Jacob Moashé's visit, he keeps her company in their shade. He's been in her service for a year and three months now. In this time he's seen how the image of the lady evoked by Harts in his story, which coincided exactly with his dreams when, as a seminarian mortified by the flesh, he would wake up in a fever, desperate to make her his own, has changed to match the true image of Blanca, fickle, unpredictable, as Sebastià Palou just said. Does he know Blanca well? Does he really believe she had nothing to do with Harts? And Queen Esther's sacrifices, which the captain referred to . . . the courage of Judith and Deborah, aren't these her favorite heroines she is always mentioning? What if Harts had gone to bed with the beautiful and lustful chambermaid, with Blanca's complicity? Or if Blanca herself had pretended to be her maid? He's been in her service for a year and three months and has never managed to be admitted to the lady's private rooms, even though he's her secretary. But he doesn't want to lose hope that one day Blanca herself will call for him. He knows her secret, he discovered it by chance in Antwerp, when he returned there to avenge her. He knows that Blanca Maria Gracia Beatriu, Portuguese like him, who married the Majorcan merchant Andreu Sampol, was both the daughter and the granddaughter of a rich Jewess in love with her first-born. But for him, also a bastard, this stain in her ancestry is nothing hideous. On the contrary, it likens Blanca to the goddesses of Greek mythology, who have always attracted his attention and from time to time allow themselves to be loved by a lucky mortal.

Captain Sebastià Palou orders all the windows to be closed because he doesn't want to hear the uproar. As the day wears on, the disturbance increases. Nobody wants to miss the event. Many farmers have come from the country with their families to occupy the front rows in the streets through which the procession is due to pass the following morning, going from the Dark House to St Dominic's Convent. Many will sleep in the open. They've brought blankets to wrap themselves in and baskets with a few provisions. They trust that, after the religious ceremony, as the town-criers have proclaimed, bread and dried figs will be distributed among those who've traveled a long way to watch how, by means of the Holy Office, God wreaks his vengeance on the cursed Jews who killed his Son and now bring about the ruin of good Christians. Others prefer to rise early. They'll get up when it's still dark and set out for the city, riding on their carts. Some won't even go in. They'll head directly for Bellver, because what they want to watch is not the procession, but the spectacle of the cremation. Elders will admonish youngers, and youngers the children, always to bear in mind what they're about to see, never to forget it. Ever.

Only the nobles, the civil authorities, the inquisitors and familiars of the Holy Office, have the right to witness the ceremony. Honorable citizens and some artisans, who have so zealously raised platforms on both sides of the main nave, fitted chapels with lattices to enable ladies to watch the spectacle at ease, will only be able to get in if there's spare room. Two knights, like angels guarding Christ's tomb, keep an eye on the door to decide who is trustworthy and who isn't; which people they consider worthy to wait outside while this act of sovereign justice is accomplished.

In the church, almost everything is ready. The foreigner, who left the garden a while ago, follows the inquisitive crowd as it approaches the convent. The Head Bailiff commanding the troops keeps them at bay. There'll be no poking noses in the church with the excuse of making a station. "The Holy Sacrament has tabernacles in lots of other chapels," he tells them to ward them off. There are still men working inside. They hear hammer-blows, the sound of planks being dragged along. A band of apprentices enters through the main door with a brand-new canopy of red damask, which provokes cries of admiration from the women watching. "That must be for covering the seats of the inquisitors," hazards a man who claims to remember perfectly the old canopy, which was a less fiery red than this one, from the auto-da-fé of ten years ago. Another group of artisans pushes past the onlookers. "Clear the way," they tell them, "come on, get back, we've a cart to get through." The wheels spatter the crowd's clothes with mud. "Bloody . . . Now look what you've gone and done!" They've put on their Sunday best to come and see the festival. Lucky it's not raining. Last week was enough. It was like a quagmire round there. "Whoa!" says the cartman to the four mules pulling the two carts to which a kind of platform has been tied to carry the huge cage. The cage is a real work of art. Seven highly renowned carpenters and four blacksmiths have been working on it for a month, copying the model used at the auto-da-fé in Madrid in 1630, but improving it a lot. From here, from this humiliating place that appears to be for enclosing lions and cheetahs, wild beasts, and not persons, the Jews will hear from sacred lips their final sentences, which are not subject to appeal. In the crosses of its bars, the cage reveals the image of Christ's Passion in the martyrdom caused by the prisoners who killed him, while at the same time deterring demons from their usual misdeeds and driving them to hell. The boy gazes at everything without saying a word. He doesn't even answer the questions of those around him about where he's from and where he's going. He prefers to make out he doesn't understand. He carefully takes everything in, because he'll have to relate it carefully in Livorno, as soon as he arrives, to the lady and Pere Onofre Aguiló if he can listen.

The day concludes with a night full of dark terrors. The foreigner has gone back on board and is trying to sleep. He finds it difficult to doze, despite being tired, because he can't stop thinking about the prisoners and the futility of his voyage. Sebastià Palou doesn't sleep either. The prisoners are also awake, accompanied by priests who subject them to prayers and admonitions. Thanks to these prayers and admonitions, all but two have repented, abhorred their errors, and, although tomorrow they'll die, although tomorrow their time is up, they will gain the other life, they will gain Eternity forever. Some still trust in a miracle. Sara again tells Maria not to worry, the eagle is ready. But Maria clings to the hope of a last-minute reprieve much more than to a poor madwoman's visions. Bonnín also, like his daughter, thinks about saving wings . . . Ah, if only he'd been able to finish his mechanical device in time! They'd never have caught him! Rafel Onofre pleads with the confessor to ask for clemency. He offers his life for that of his fiancée, he got her into this mess. Isabel Tarongí again tells them there's nothing she can do, she was born a Jew and will die a Jew. They can pray if they like, but Adonai sustains her in her faith. Madò Grossa, like her sister Aina and Quitèria, at times accompanies the priest's Hail Marys, at others can't concentrate. Aina and Quitèria think about the children's vulnerability, their poverty. What most frightens Madò Grossa is the walk to the stake, being mocked by everybody, she's sure, by the wretches she often helped cure of ugly illnesses, foul wounds no doctor would touch. Madò Grossa is more afraid of the chorus of cries from that mob than of the skill of the executioner working the garrote. She feels more sorry for the young ones than for her own life. She's old now. She can't last . . . Maria Aguiló, however, is desperate. She's losing everything she has: husband, son, future daughter-in-law.

Gabriel Valls has asked Father Amengual to pray in silence, not to disturb him with the string of rosaries he adorns mechanically, to let him rest for a while. The Jesuit lowers his voice. Valls lies on the bed and closes his eyes not to sleep, because he can't, but to compose himself. He has spent the last almost three days in a terrible state of excitation. His body has collapsed. He could never have imagined his terrified bowels would play on him the dirty trick of making him throw up all the time, filling the pot for excrement with a foul stench.

"You're rotten, Valls," said Father Amengual, looking at him in disgust, "rotten inside and out."

"It's the fear of a body in rebellion," he answered, trying to control the trembling that overcame him as soon as the Inquisitor left, having read the sentence.

Luckily he remained stoical in front of him, as if he were above the fear of death. But it's not true. He is afraid. He is no better than the others, who no doubt in their cells, like him, have vomited and defecated without stopping, their heart beating, with terrible fits and faints. The others may be pardoned, their errors excused, if they convert. A good thing if they do! A good thing if they abhor Adonai and decide to follow the doctrines of Christ, whom they also abhor or will later abhor, because nothing that is forced, imposed by sword or fire, can ever result in anything but rejection! A good thing if they save themselves! Life is the most precious gift. There is no other. He's sure, and everybody must order their own. Not he order the lives of others as Rabbi, so he's called. Oh, and how he repents! But that is why he can't avoid death in the flames. He can't be pardoned. He must be consistent in death as he wanted to be in life. He is responsible for the failure and so he must pay the price, demonstrating that he's a man, a real man, before he's a Jew or a Christian.

In the last days he's thought a lot about the moment he'd finally be left alone, the moment Father Amengual dozed and fell asleep until snoring. He's seen how fragile the earthenware jug for the water is, how one blow would be enough to break it and keep a sharp enough fragment, because he's never been left a knife, a carver or even a razor. The veins on his wrists are fairly pronounced. It wouldn't be difficult to make a cut. Alonso López circumcised himself with a shard of pottery in these very prisons to present himself before the Most High as he considered necessary. He died in the flames. His foreskin reduced to ashes . . . To avoid the fire's torment! To decide for himself, before he is made to leave here in the sanbenito and cardboard miter and forced, having had the sentence read out in front of everyone in St Dominic's Convent, to cross the city on the back of a donkey, on the way to the stake, being mocked, spat and jeered at by the crowd. *I'll suffer as little as possible. They say those who cut their veins have a very sweet death. My pride will be preserved before Father Amengual, before the Inquisitor. But before my people?* Before those driven to the flames through his fault . . . No, he can't abandon them. He's afraid his voice will rebel, like his bowels, and make him ask for clemency. But that can't happen. Absolutely not. Better not to think about it. Better to believe the fire will quickly devour him up. His fate was decided the day he planned the expedition, there's no way he can change it now. With Jehovah's help, or without, abandoned by God, he has no choice but to become a martyr for his faith, the faith he's now lacking because he's reached the only possible certainty: that of the man who, to show he is a man, walks, overcoming life, serenely towards death.

Sebastià Palou dresses slowly, helped by the servant. It's a good thing he doesn't have to share the bedroom with Bàrbara, as he imagined would happen at the beginning of their marriage, at least he can sleep alone. Because he's spent the night walking up and down, restless, wide awake. Yesterday he talked too much in front of Blanca's secretary. And he's sorry. He has a splitting headache and is not best pleased. He is annoyed at having to attend the auto, but has no alternative but to accompany his wife, whose devotion is running high before the cremation. Luckily Valls won't be able to see them in the chapel they've been assigned, behind the lattice. He won't have to confront his eyes. His uncle did well to leave before they light the flames, saving himself the spectacle, and Angelat, with the excuse of a sudden illness, to avoid having to chronicle this event that horrifies him and has destroyed his appetite.

The foreigner has left the galley. The road from Port Pi to the city is swarming with carts and people arriving on foot. Everyone's in a hurry. Everyone wants to be on time to show their blood is clean and not tainted by Jewish blood. They're happy because they also feel they're taking part in that festival of faith triumphing over perverse heresy. They'll shout with all the strength in their lungs against the foul heretics when they see them come out in procession behind the white banner with the green cross, like bedeviled, fallen souls, which not even the Lord God wanted to accept in his infinite mercy, but refused, consigning them to darkness. "Thank God," the preachers told them from the pulpits during Sunday Mass, "thank God you will be able to see with your own eyes the punishment that will be laid on this race of dogs, unbelievers, heretics. Lift up your voices and give thanks for this grace . . ."

The night has already broken waters and the milky light of dawn covers the sky. The walled city opens its gates. All the bells ring out together. A layer of bells covers everything and curtails the flight of birds that have woken in alarm at the deafening din. The procession has started. In front, carrying candles, walk all the old kingdom's male religious orders, drawn up in perfect lines, like worker ants. Then the Lord Viceroy, the President of the Great and General Council, the High Judge and other authorities, escorting the Inquisition's sacred banner. Behind, the defendants in miters and yellow sanbenitos, some with two crosses, others printed with inverted flames, and only two covered in demons, their own faces painted on the degrading tunics. A tow rope around the neck and a candle in their right hand. With lowered eyes, they tread barefoot on the stones and shards of glass the boys have strewn about to mock them even more, proving they're good Christians. Alongside, the priests and friars attending and constantly admonishing them. Then, with their usual reserve, the dark cassocks of the Holy Tribunal, familiars and advisers, and another host of burning candles to the profit of the kingdom's chandlers and praise of the Lord our God.

The foreigner turns back. They won't let him in the church. He'll wait near the stake, with the crowd that's gathered. There are more than twenty thousand scattered over the hillside. They chatter and laugh, some dance and others tell jokes. Today is a great feast. They'll get a free lunch. The sun is still high, but now thick clouds seem to be coming from the east. "It would be a shame if the rain spoiled everything," say some, "we could do without that." What they want is a fine sun to show off the spectacle in all its splendor. The executioners are ready. They had to send for two from Mahon not to go short. The procession approaches. The crowd lets out a whoop at the convicts riding on the backs of donkeys, their hands tied behind them. The disinterred remains of Rafel Tarongí, the tailor Valleriola's wife and Cap de Trons follow in three coffins. On seeing the heaps of firewood, Rafel Onofre Valls throws himself off the mount and breaks into a run until he finds Maria. But he can't even embrace her. The soldiers sent by the Viceroy to protect the despicable Jews from the people's assaults immediately drag him off without another thought. "Maria!" the boy still shouts, and to his shout is joined Sara's, "Maria, Maria!" Maria answers with a groan: "Rafel, I don't want to die!" Gabriel Valls would like to rip off his ears. His son's cry is like a knife emptying his heart. He is the first to climb on to the stake. Father Amengual asks the crowd to join in his prayers for that heretic to die in repentance. In unison they say a couple of Hail Marys. There are lots of voices. *With their sound I shall round off the book,* decides the Jesuit. *Oh, how beautiful is the spectacle of the Majorcans' faith triumphing over perverse heresy! What a solemn and edifying end!* Amengual warns Valls to repent for the last time. The defendant shakes his head. He almost smiles. He appears calm. More than forty thousand eyes are on him, watching his every move. Father Amengual withdraws irritably. Father Ferrando looks on with satisfaction: he also has failed to convert this vermin, who will burn for ever.

The foreigner is in the second row next to the platform. He is taller than the people around him. All he wants is for Valls to notice him. To understand that somebody at least is looking at him not with hatred, but with piety and admiration for his courage. But Valls doesn't see anybody. His head turned a little, he seems to be gazing at the sea, which starts very near here, on the other side of Bellver. It was the inquisitors' wish that the cremation should be next to the place the convicts chose for their escape, to teach them a twofold lesson. What's more, this way, the smoke and stench of charred flesh will not invade the city. The executioners check the tightness of the knots with which they've just tied the defendant to the post sticking out from the piled branches, as if it wanted to pierce the sky. The soldiers make way for the Lord Viceroy. The crowd roars again in expectation. The clergy shout to make their prayers heard over the hubbub: "God of Justice, we have exacted justice in your name. God of Justice, may your justice . . ." The time has come, there is a thick silence. The Viceroy lights the torch of purificatory fire. Valls squirms. His face suddenly assumes all the world's suffering. He opens his mouth, but does not ask for mercy, he groans. A few moments and these flames that make his stomach pop will be embers. Ashes. Then nothing. Nothing at all. His body bends to the left, bursts and falls like a spent brand. The sparks almost singe the crowd lined up in the front rows. The foreigner, like everybody, takes a step backwards, then is pressed forwards again by the mob . . . He chokes on the smoke. Sweats. Wants to escape. Doesn't want to see how Isabel Tarongí is tied and how the flames will again take possession of her body, burning it up. As best he can, pushing and shoving, he tries to leave his place. More than anything, he wants to escape. To go far, far away, for the galley to weigh anchor at once and disappear quickly, hopefully, out, far out in the last blue.

Deià, 1978
Barcelona, Majorca City, Sitges, 1989-1993

Author's Note

THE HISTORICAL EVENTS *IN THE LAST BLUE* IS BASED ON TOOK place in Majorca City in 1688 and 1691. On March 7, 1688, a group of Majorcan Jewish converts, fearful that proceedings would be opened against them as a result of an informer's accusations, decided to embark for lands of freedom on the boat of Captain Vuillis (Willis?). The bad weather, however, made it impossible for the ship to set sail; the fugitives had to disembark and, on their way home, were captured. The arrest, it seems, was a matter of chance. The shouts of a poor madwoman, whose family had left, disturbed the Street and attracted the patrol's attention. Unintentionally she was the one who spread the net all those who had taken part in the expedition got caught in. That same night, the Head Bailiff had them taken to the prisons of the Inquisition's palace, known by Majorcans as the Black House, where all their goods were confiscated.

The cases opened in March, 1688, were not closed until 1691. Four autos-da-fé were held in that year (March 7, May 1, May 6 and July 2). Thirty-seven people were sentenced to the stake. Three of them, Rafel Valls and the siblings Caterina and Rafel Benet Tarongí, since they refused to abjure their religion, were burned alive.

Taking these events and recreating them, I have written this book. I have condensed the action (shortening the stay in prison and bringing forward the cremation) to make it more compact and more intense in the second and third parts. In the first part, however, I have sought to prolong it so that the reader can enter the conflict gradually. I don't think I need mention that João Peres' appearance is made up and his arrival in Majorca triggers what follows. Similarly I invented various characters who never existed, like Blanca Maria Pires, the Portuguese lady, who derives from fairly obvious literary sources it's not worth going into. Some critic will do this and I hope the work is polished. Nor did Pere Onofre Aguiló, the Majorcan merchant who settled in Livorno, ever exist, or Don Antonio Nepomuceno Sotomayor y Ampuero, the Viceroy, or his nephew Captain Sebastià Palou. For Beatriu Mas, known as Limp, prostitute in the brothel, I had reserved a minor, functional role, but, as often happens, the character acquired such strength I had no choice but to devote lots of pages to her, viewing her with the sympathy she deserved from the first moment.

Other main characters are inspired by historical figures who took part in or endured the terrible events, such as Rafel Valls, known as Gabriel in the novel, Rafel Cortès d'Alfonso, turned into Rafel Cortès, Costura, and Pere Onofre Cortès de Guillermo, changed into Rafel Cortès, Cap de Trons. The Jesuit Father Sabater gives rise to Father Ferrando, and the author of the abominable *Triumphant Faith*, Francisco Garau, inspires the character of Father Amengual.

I have deliberately altered names, surnames and nicknames to make it clear that my book is not historical, but fictional. In the realms of history, no material should be manipulated; in that of the novel, albeit historical, so long as verisimilitude, the truth of cohesion, is maintained, everything is valid and, therefore, legitimate.

While avoiding anachronisms, I have endeavored to give the reader sufficient guidelines to understand how Majorcan cryp-